BLACK STARS

The Life of Queen Hatshepsut of Egypt

Linda Barnett

VANTAGE PRESS
New York

This is a work of fiction. Any similarity between the characters appearing herein and any real persons, living or dead, is purely coincidental.

Cover art courtesy of *National Geographic*

FIRST EDITION

Published by Vantage Press, Inc.
419 Park Ave. South, New York, NY 10016

Manufactured in the United States of America
ISBN: 0-533-15305-0

Library of Congress Catalog Card No.: 2005907051

0 9 8 7 6 5 4 3 2 1

BLACK STARS

1

Heart-rending moans, scarcely louder than the mewing of a lion cub, seemed to fill the room as wave after wave of pain wracked the slender body of the beautiful, young princess. She was exhausted, so weak from the agonizing hours spent in the throes of childbirth that she was barely conscious.

"Physician! Attend my daughter. This baby must be born, and it must issue from her womb healthy and well formed."

The court physician, old Senmet, was wise not only in the art of medicine but also in the art of reading the hearts of men. He understood that the unborn babe was of great importance to the Pharaoh. And so, he trembled with fear as he prostrated himself at his ruler's feet.

"Oh, mighty Pharaoh, beloved son of the great god Ra, ruler of all Egypt . . ."

"Enough," Thothmes I roared. "Why is not the babe born after all these hours? You must bring about this birth!"

"Mighty one, I tell you the truth. The child is large and healthy and most willing to be born, but the hips of Princess Meritamon are narrow, and the babe cannot make the passage from womb to this world."

Thothmes moved away from the couch where Meritamon lay. "Do whatever you must to bring about the birth. The babe was conceived from the coupling of the gods Horus and Isis, using my daughter and myself as their earthly counterparts. See that no harm comes to the child. If such occurs, you forfeit your life." As he turned away, Pharaoh felt great sadness at the thought that his lovely, young daughter must be sacrificed in order for the child to survive. But the child of such gods must live. All Egypt was awaiting the birth.

Even with their substantial knowledge, doctors of ancient Egypt knew nothing of cutting open the belly of a woman, removing the baby, and then stitching the mother back together. Senmet did as had always been done. “Hand me the opium,” he ordered the maid who was assisting him. “She will fall into a stupor and will feel little.”

He mixed the opium with wine and held the goblet to the lips of the princess. “Swallow, my child. And now a little more. There, there. You will feel much better soon,” he said, even as his hands trembled at the thought of what he must next do.

As the opium performed its magic and Meritamon fell into unconsciousness, Senmet carefully cut through skin and muscles, exposing the uterus. After making a small incision near the top of the womb, he laid aside the knife. No risk must come to the baby. Inserting his fingers in the opening and gritting his teeth, he ripped apart Meritamon's uterus with his bare hands and lifted out the struggling infant. The cord was tied and cut as the unconscious thirteen-year-old mother bled to death.

All attention focused on the child. A girl child. “Give me the bowl of water and wine,” the physician ordered the maid. The mixture made a mild, antiseptic solution, and the tiny body was cleansed with it. Fine oil was then rubbed into her pale skin, and she was bound in white linen.

Senmet placed the baby in Thothmes' arms. He gazed at her a moment and then cried out in wonder, “This is truly the child of Horus and Isis. Look, all of you upon her eyes; they carry the stars of the sky within them.” The nobles of the court had been present to witness the birth, and all gazed at the child in awe. The color of her eyes was green, and the center of each was a black star, irregular in shape, but a star nonetheless. Truly, she was a daughter of the gods.

The baby's name had been selected long before its birth, a name chosen by the priests and priestesses who served Horus and Isis; a name that could be given to either a male or female child, even though in literal translation it meant “Chieftainess of noble women.”

All began to chant: “Hatshepsut, Hatshepsut.” She would receive many noble titles and names later in life and after ascending the throne of Egypt, but, for now, she would be celebrated throughout the country as the child born Hatshepsut, Chieftainess of noble women.

Queen Ahmose, Great Royal Wife of Pharaoh, mother of Meritamon and grandmother of Hatshepsut, stood near the bed, seemingly overcome with grief. Ahmose was a beautiful woman with a loving and gentle countenance. Her body was soft and round, her manner idyllic, and her smile, tender. However, she was not as she appeared. Inwardly, there was complete disregard for anyone other than herself and the great god, Pharaoh. She tolerated her daughters only because they pleased her husband.

Even as her daughter lay dying, she considered only herself. *How great I am. There is none other so clever or so beautiful. And now I shall retain my rightful place beside the mighty Thothmes as he rules. Power and wealth will remain mine.* And she reflected on how this had been brought about.

Since she had failed to give birth to a son who lived, Queen Ahmose had begun to fear that Pharaoh might cast her aside in favor of one who was younger and more fruitful, as Great Royal Wife. Except for Meritamon and one younger daughter, no living child had come from their union. After a small boy child, Sitamon, was born only to die within a short time, all succeeding pregnancies had ended tragically, months before fulfillment. Both the court physician and her necromancer, or physician of magic, had then told her she was barren.

Desiring to rule at Thothmes' side and retain all the power such a position afforded her, she devised a scheme to preserve her standing in the royal court. And so, last year, long before this day of tragedy, Queen Ahmose embarked upon the course she hoped would bring her plans to fruition and insure her rightful place as Great Royal Wife and Queen of Egypt.

Ahmose clapped her hands and called, "Nefur. Come at once!" Her elderly maidservant, an expert in the art of applying decoration to the body, glided silently into the room. "Fetch your paints and brushes. Get out my most appealing, diaphanous linens. I must look especially desirable tonight." The old woman backed from the room, only to return quickly to the royal chamber with the pots and brushes she used to wield her magical skills.

The previous evening, Ahmose and Euripides had talked long into the night. He was a Hittite, dark-skinned with long, curly black hair, which he oiled and perfumed. He served Queen Ahmose well, and she kept his thin fingers and arms covered with gold and precious stones. This day, when the sun was at its highest, he had brought her two vials. "I leave one with you for Thothmes I; the other I will administer to Meritamon."

"Apply first the scented oils to my body," commanded the queen. "Then, the paints."

Nefur complied. After anointing the queen's exquisite body, she drew the line of black kohl long beyond the outer corners of Ahmose's eyes. Next she crushed brilliant blue stones to powder, which she applied to the upper lids. A peach and red wax was rubbed into her cheeks; and as a final touch, a sable brush from Punt was dipped into gold dust and touched upon her eyelids, chin, and the rouged nipples of her breasts. Ahmose wore no jewels other than a small diadem, which encircled her head, holding down the wiry, brown hair that fell to her shoulders. Her head was clean-shaven, as was the custom, and this was but one of her ornate wigs. Tonight all must seem simple, innocent. Nefur wrapped the gossamer white linen around the queen's body and fastened it just below her breasts. There she placed a single, pink lotus bud, which concealed a small vial of white liquid.

While Nefur was plying her skills, Ahmose reviewed her plans. She knew that Meritamon had already drunk watered wine laced with the drug and lay as a small, beautiful goddess in a seldom-used room prepared especially for this night. Erotic hangings adorned the walls, and soft cushions were spread about the marble floor. Her body was painted and oiled, golden dust sprinkled over her nakedness. Euripides would be there, kneeling at her side, telling her that the Great God Horus would come from the heavens to bestow much honor upon her.

Ahmose turned to her mirror of polished gold and smiled at her reflection. Pharaoh would think her a child again instead of a mature woman of thirty years. Following her instincts, she slipped off her golden sandals, walked through the doorway, and went barefoot down the long hall. Wicks, burning in bowls of oil, lighted her way, as her smooth feet drifted over the fish, lotus-flower, and water patterns marked perfectly onto the colorful stone tiles polished to a lustrous shine. She seemed a pure maiden floating over water to meet her love.

None of this was lost upon Thothmes. He stood by a pillar at the entrance to his apartments, watching her. He had partaken of but one small jar of wine this evening—just enough to arouse the passion within him. *Lovely, soft Ahmose. Even after a night spent enjoying the beauties in the harem, it is you of whom I think. How will I bear to replace you with another so that I am assured of an heir?*

But this was now, and he loved her. He would not speak of such things tonight. "Come, my love," said the Pharaoh Thothmes, a giant of a man, covered with battle scars but gentle with the woman he loved. Tenderly, he enfolded her in his arms and led her to his couch. His arousal was evident; and looking upon it, Ahmose feared he would waste it upon her before the night could bear its fruit; and so she asked for wine.

"Please drink with me to our love, great one, and I will pour the wine for you with hands always mindful of the fullness of your heart." It was a pretty thing she said, and he was pleased. Taking down their special, matching, gold wedding goblets, Ahmose poured wine in each; and turning, she placed them upon the nearby ebony and ivory gaming table. Like a child, she playfully detached the lotus bud, holding the small vial behind it with her thumb. "My Thothmes will taste of the flower of love with his wine, for he is my love." So saying, she dipped the pink lotus slowly into the goblet and adroitly poured in the contents of the vial. He smiled, contemplating the lovemaking soon to follow. They both drained their cups and laughed, for the wine was strong.

Thothmes sat upon his bed, made soft with feathers from ducks' breasts, and leaned back to await her. *Truly, this is a magic evening. I feel as though I have all wisdom and as though I am floating freely upon the water.*

Euripides had warned Ahmose that the potion would take

effect quickly and last but a few hours. And, although she had planned all she wished to say and do, fear overcame her, and she was momentarily frozen. But quickly—she must begin . . .

"Dearest love, I have come with a wonderful message from the Great God Horus. Do you understand?" Thothmes smiled in contentment and nodded that he did. "Oh, Pharaoh, this night you will be as one with the Great God Horus, mighty god of all Egypt. And Isis, the Goddess of Love, will come to you. Her gift of love will be yours tonight."

He stirred slightly in anticipation. "The goddess Isis will come to my couch tonight? Truly, I am honored, for she has never before come to a pharaoh. This is a night of nights."

His speech was slurred; his movements slowed. The potion was weaving its spell. Ahmose felt a surge of power. The great one was hers to command. Tonight she would secure her place forever and ever.

With soft, gentle hands, she stroked Pharaoh's manhood more and more rapidly, until he was hugely aroused. All the while she whispered over and over that Isis, Goddess of Love, eagerly awaited him in a secret place; one to which she, Ahmose, would guide him.

"Oh, mighty Pharaoh, great in war and intellect, beloved of all the gods, arise now and follow me to the golden goddess Isis who yearns for you."

Thothmes I glowed with happiness. Although his smile was soft, his desire was great. He arose, as would a sleepwalker. *Great honor will come to me tonight if I but go with my beloved Ahmose. The moon and the stars will look down upon the honor no pharaoh before me has received. For I am Horus, the living god, and this night I will couple with Isis. Goddess of Love.* He caught up the tiny hand of Ahmose with his large and calloused fingers. *How wrong I have been to think of casting her aside. No one has ever loved me, as does she.* Thothmes' face was complaisant as he followed her toward a nearby chamber filled with soft lights and shadows.

As Euripides knelt beside Meritamon's couch, he reassured himself that tonight was the perfect night to carry out the deception. Certain thoughts ran through his mind. *The time is exactly right. Her monthly flow is not long past, and she could conceive this night. If not, we will manage other nights.* He was using an ostrich feather to lightly stroke the pink nipples of her breasts and her soft inner thighs. That, combined with the potent drug she had been given and his crooning voice, aroused her desire, until it seemed she would be consumed by it. She writhed slowly, gleaming with gold and oil, upon her soft cushions. Her arousal had produced lubricating fluids from her womanhood. Her body pulsated, and her small nipples stood out hard, begging to be kissed. *Oh, will the Great God Horus never come? I shall die if he does not.*

Ahmose stepped aside as Pharaoh entered the room to which she had led him. When he beheld the small princess lying upon the bed, he knew she was indeed the Goddess of Love. All was misty, beautiful. Never had there been a pharaoh so fortunate. He walked slowly toward her, a golden emblem of love; and she called out with fervor, stretching her small arms up to him in rapture.

As Euripides and Ahmose watched from behind a fall of gauze, Thothmes, with wanton abandon, mounted the child and drove deeply into her body. Meritamon whimpered with pain but soon succumbed to the ecstasy of fulfillment. They copulated again and again, each release seemingly as electrifying as the one preceding it. But in less than an hour's time, the drug took full effect, and the couple fell asleep, arms and legs entwined.

It was done. The face of the Great Royal Wife was wreathed in a cruel smile, and she looked with hard, dark eyes into those of Euripides. "If this union produces an heir, your talents of gold will be many. But beware if it comes to naught, or if mighty Pharaoh learns of our complicity. Now, let us retire, and let them awaken in each other's arms."

"Great queen, the potions were such that neither Pharaoh nor Meritamon will recall our part in the work of this night. I shall await the rising of the sun and observe their actions. If any one thing is amiss, I will know; and we will deal with it as occasion demands. Sleep well, and may you remain Great Royal Wife forever and ever."

Queen Ahmose stole quietly back to her apartments, well pleased with herself. All had happened exactly as she and Euripides had planned. When Thothmes awoke, he would be distressed at what had occurred. It was not unusual for a Pharaoh to bed his daughters, thus preserving the dynasty, but this pharaoh was a man of dignity and of principle and honor. Even though it was his prerogative, he would not think well of himself when he realized what he had done.

Ahmose smiled. *I will comfort him. I will be his most understanding confidante. My power and treasure shall become boundless. I will be Great Royal Wife forever and ever.*

As Nefur bathed her with cool water and wrapped bed clothing about her, a brief laugh escaped her lips. She need only wait for the fruit of this night's magic.

2

All the battle-drums of Egypt were pounding in the head of Thothmes as he awakened. *What place was this? Surely, I must have partaken of many jars of strong wine.* His father, Pharaoh Amonhotep I, had often warned him against drinking too much wine. The Pharaoh of Egypt must always be on his guard, must always be in control of all things, lest he come to harm. Even in his own palace.

Committed to these concepts, it was the practice of the anointed ruler to slay his siblings. Otherwise, he lived in fear of those with great ambition. Thothmes had arranged the accidents that took the lives of his younger brothers. They lay now in magnificent tombs in the Necropolis of Thebes. Down through the dynasties, others had tried, and sometimes succeeded, to depose the ruling pharaoh, thus enabling the perpetrator to wear the double crown through the use of force. But, since Amonhotep I had avenged his father's death at the hands of the Hyksos and founded the eighteenth dynasty, the richest and most powerful in the history of Egypt, strife had been absent from the land.

Has someone tried to poison me? Are there traitors in my palace? Confused thoughts rambled through Thothmes' brain as he struggled weakly to his feet and looked about the chamber. He was stricken with great remorse in an instant. The scene told him what had happened—there could be no mistake. Lying on the crumpled cushions was the listless and spent body of Meritamon. She lay naked, sleeping, looking like a crushed flower—the bruises of the uncontrolled coupling beginning to darken, and darker still, the blood smeared and caked between her thighs.

"Amon, protect and forgive me!" cried Thothmes. "I have coupled with my sweet daughter, and yet I remember naught of the night just past. What have I done?"

He walked slowly to his chambers and clapped loudly for servants. He needed to be cleansed in a heated bath and brought food. He hungered as though he had not eaten in days, and his limbs remained weak. He, Thothmes, the mighty warrior, weak! It was incredible that he had committed this act. He seemed to remember a jar of wine and the sweet smile of Ahmose. Had she been present? Surely not. She would not have allowed what had transpired. *She must come to me now. We will bathe together, and she will lighten my burden and ease my mind.*

"Guards, inform the Great Royal Wife that I ask her to bathe and breakfast with me. And have the servants bring food and sweet morning wine and beer."

In moments, Ahmose entered his chamber, eyes filled with love and a sweet smile upon her lips. Bejeweled and perfumed, she directed the laying of small stands that were set with dishes made of the gold so plentiful in Egypt and of alabaster, polished to a smooth thinness, and also of glass blown into lovely shapes. These were filled with condiments: dates, cakes of date flour called "shat cakes," and honey in which to dip them. The meal was simple, as the ruling classes of this time were temperate in their morning and noonday meals in order to remain lithe and graceful. The more lavish meals were served only in the evening.

Servants divested them of their garments and wigs; and, hand-in-hand, Ahmose and Thothmes stepped down to an alabaster pool. Nefur had accompanied Ashmose, and she lifted one vial from among many on a marble step and poured perfume into the water as the two gods (for that was how she viewed them) sank gratefully into the warm bath. Ahmose gently massaged the shoulders and arms of her Lord Pharaoh s he reclined in the scented water.

"My love," said Thothmes, "you need not perform this task for me. You are my queen and my love forever."

Ahmose smiled and kissed his hands though her heart quaked with fear. *Is he toying with me? Does he remember? If he remembers, what will he do?* When she spoke, her voice was calm and quiet. "My only love, what I do for you gives purpose to my life. My one desire is to please you. But I feel great concern for you this day, as you seem anxious and overtired. What causes my beloved's brow to crease so deeply?"

Thothmes, Pharaoh and living god of Egypt, sighed heavily with remorse. He decided to confide in this woman who insisted that her life was lived only to please him. Surely she, in her calm wisdom, would ease his troubled conscience and advise him well.

Pharaoh closed his eyes as the warm, scented water caressed his body. Embraced by Ahmose's arms, he responded, "Beloved, I am torn in my heart. I have committed a grievous sin against Isis, Goddess of Love. I awakened with the dawn to find myself beside the sleeping Meritamon. I coupled with my daughter in the night but remember little of it. I must have imbibed too much wine last evening, and I cannot recall all that passed. Surely, all the gods will despise me for this act; and you, in spite of your love for me, will think me vile. I am desolate and do not know how to set things aright."

Behind her composed features, Ahmose was exultant. *He does not remember my part in this. He turns to me for help. My rewards will be immeasurable, and I shall be Great Royal Wife forever! But carefully now . . .*

"Oh, great Thothmes, cast aside your despair. Isis, Goddess of Love, demanded this of you. And, it is your right, nay, your duty, to plant your seed in the vessels that carry the pure blood of the Thothmesid dynasty. You who are descended from the sun itself, son of Ra and Horus, can do no wrong. You have only followed the wills of Ra and Isis. Come husband, rise up and let yourself be anointed; and we will go together to offer sacrifice on this day of days. Be happy for you have done as the gods wished."

He arose and smiled with great joy at Ahmose, his wonderful Ahmose. She was right, of course; he was but an instrument of his father Ra. For although Thothmes was fierce in battle and wise in government, he was easily used by those he trusted. And since he, himself, deceived no one, he looked not for deceit in others.

Radiant with success, Ahmose helped him from the pool. Servants dried and dressed them, and they walked together to share their morning meal. Everything had come about as Euripides had foretold. Euripides! He must be rewarded and well. She gave no thought to Meritamon, for Ahmose's thoughts concerned only herself.

And so, they spent much of this day being anointed with oils and unguents. Then riding in procession to the house of the god Ra, they prostrated themselves upon his altar and gave him praise.

That evening there was a great feast.

The Egyptians had made fine food and its preparation into an art. The legions of cooks in the great cookhouses were separated according to their specialties. Some prepared the many kinds of meat, while others prepared only fowl. These were stuffed, roasted, and basted, each kind with its particular seasonings and from recipes passed down from one generation to another. Others prepared vegetables, roots, nuts, and dates. These foods were carefully simmered, then placed upon gold or glass dishes and arranged in forms representing scenes of the Nile, with crocodiles and birds—all done with an eye to color and presentation.

In the great hall of the palace in Thebes, large bowls of flowers scented the air. Some contained roses of all colors; others, the lotus. The lotus was the favorite flower, and its scent was sweet and pervading. Many times a pharaoh would select a lady from his harem as his companion for the night by touching her body with a long-stemmed lotus. Guests at court were given a lotus to carry during the evening hours so the bearer would be enfolded within the sweet, cool aroma. And lotuses were the only flowers depicted in scenes of happiness and honor on the painted walls of tombs.

Bearers in short, pleated linen skirts glided among the guests, serving the meat of lamb, beef, wild game, and fishes. Dates, eggs, and onions accompanied the meats. All diners, both rich and poor, ate onions. They were considered an aid to health when eaten raw like an apple, and a delicacy when roasted within a fowl.

Thothmes and Ahmose sat upon golden thrones high above

the feasting nobles, as black Nubian slaves, brought from the upper Nile, manipulated large, ostrich plume fans.

At a gesture from Thothmes, the royal goldsmith, Khenem, came forward. Khenem carried a small casket made of fragrant cedar. He knelt and held up the case before Pharaoh. Thothmes looked warmly at Ahmose and opened the lid. There, upon folds of linen, lay a wide, gold necklace, solid and stiff in parts, but linked in places to allow it to fall evenly upon the chest and back of its wearer.

As Thothmes removed the necklace and placed it around the neck and shoulders of Ahmose, its beauty transfixed all. The heavy gold was worked in beads of precise sizes, joined to squares of gold inlaid with lapis lazuli and amber. This necklace had lain in Thothmes' treasure room for many years, and he had intended it to be part of his tomb treasure. But Queen Ahmose, the Great Royal Wife, had brought him release from guilt, and this would reward her well.

The queen gasped with pleasure. She possessed a treasury of gold and jewels but nothing so fine as this necklace. She was triumphant; more than that, she was safe. Earlier this night, Pharaoh had told her he would take no other to wife. He had said that one of their daughters, Meritamon of Neberudhet, would reign as queen when he crossed the River Styx to live in his royal tomb forever and ever. The daughter would choose a half-royal son from his issue in the harem to wed and share the throne. All was as it should be.

In another part of the palace of one hundred rooms, her old nurse and her handmaidens tended the child-woman Meritamon. Drafts of fresh air, wafted from the tall roof through tiled airways, cooled the chamber where she lay in a daze upon sheets of white linen. Her lower body was wrapped tightly, for she had been badly torn by Pharaoh's huge, thrusting power. She whispered to her nurse, Beka, that Horus had come to her in the night and that he was wonderful. Beka nodded and spoke soothing words to the girl. She had been in the palace many years and knew much of the intrigue that was carried out. She had seen Euripides enter Meritamon's chamber, cup in hand. As in all such places, there were walls within walls and doors within doors. From one of these secret sites, she had watched all that had transpired last evening and knew by the timing of the child's last flow that she could well carry the offspring of Pharaoh.

After the birth of Meritamon, Ahmose's breasts had been bound. No consideration was given to nursing the babe as nursing caused unsightly sagging. Thus, Beka had nursed Meritamon at her own breast. She loved the girl as if she were her child, and she ached with the hope that there was indeed a pharaoh to be born to the girl. For Meritamon had been set aside, as had her younger sister. Neberudhet, so that the star of Ahmose could shine more brightly. *Ah, selfish woman. Do you believe that a child conceived of Pharaoh and his daughter will save your position? Foolish queen!* She, Beka, would see that the child would steal Pharaoh's heart. Ahmose was upon the brink of middle age. As she withered, the young one would grow. The living god, Pharaoh, son of Ra, roamed this earth in the form of man. Of men, Beka knew much.

Meritamon missed one monthly flow and then another. A glowing Ahmose told Pharaoh that he would be given this child of Isis and Horus, gods of love and power. Each day he visited the sickly Meritamon. As she grew large with child, he ordered apartments near his own to be prepared for her. Amusements of all sorts were devised for her pleasure.

The priestesses of Isis came to chant incantations and strew flowers about the rooms of the honored one. The priests of Horus came, bearing charms and gifts of gold, linens, precious oils, and unguents of myrrh. Priests of other gods, not to be outdone, came also. All bore blessings and gifts.

As the months passed, Ahmose's triumphant glow turned into an indignant glare. This daughter of theirs was the center of far too much attention. Pharaoh still sent for her but spent much time talking of the sweet Meritamon and the babe in her womb. And all along the Nile, nobles and peasants alike spoke of the wonder of wonders soon to be born.

Seething with jealousy, she called for her necromancer. Euripides appeared beside her as if swept in by an invisible force. He had entered her bedchamber through the sandstone panel that composed the niche for the statue of Isis. It was cleverly set upon spheres of metal and swung completely around soundlessly. The inner walls and hidden passageways of the palace were not known to many. Euripides was one of the few who knew where all were to be found. Ahmose often wondered what this foreign man had seen and heard during his years at court. She had chosen him and protected him, and he was hers to command. Hers, no doubt, until she was powerless. And then, hers no longer. But that day must never come. This, Euripides must prevent.

During his ten years in her service, Ahmose had seen to it that he prospered with each successful deed. And all that she had asked of him had met with success. He had been rewarded lavishly with wide, gold bracelets and a larger house with extensive fields and more slaves for his part in the plot to deceive Pharaoh and bring about the pregnancy of Meritamon. Now, she would ask him to perform an action easily done if one had certain knowledge. In deceiving Pharaoh, he had risked his life. This request would simply be to take one.

Ahmose bade Euripides to rest upon a cushion and ordered her handmaidens to serve him and to wash his hands and feet, an act of great courtesy. She smiled the smile usually reserved for Thothmes and spoke to him softly. "You are kind to visit me. I wish to make use of your vast knowledge. And have you brought me more of the wonderful ointment that bids each wrinkle to depart?"

"Yes, my queen, this I have done," he said. Nodding her head, Ahmose sent her servants from the room so that the two of them could consult in privacy.

As the chatter of the girls faded away, she looked upon her necromancer. He was grand, indeed, with a lush head of black hair and a black beard ringlets, all oiled to a shine. Gold hung from his ears and his neck and decorated his sandaled feet. His lean body was brown and soft from oil massages and lack of physical labor. His mouth was upturned and red, but his large, hooked nose gave a look of cruelty to his countenance. It was his eyes, however, that Ahmose watched with caution. They were like the eyes of the cobras she had seen in the desert—small, glittering eyes that held malevolence. She thought they must be the mirrors of his soul.

As always, Ahmose was most careful in her dealings with Euripides. So far, he had remained faithful to her and thus he must remain. Were he to tell all he knew, she would be food for jackals. On the other hand, was he not the most fortunate of necromancers? Who could provide for him and reward him with such valuable gifts other than she, Ahmose, Great Royal Wife, beloved of Pharaoh Thothmes I? Having successfully banished all disturbing thoughts, she reclined contentedly upon her narrow, gold bed, propped up by pillows in order to face her friend and helper.

"Euripides, you know all that happens within the walls of this palace of one hundred rooms. Therefore, you must be aware of the honors and affections bestowed upon my daughter, Meritamon. Is that not so?"

"Yes, oh mighty queen, this I have observed." As he answered, his snakelike eyes became hooded with caution.

"My daughter has become much too beloved of Pharaoh. If I am to remain in total favor, she must cease to live in this world and go to join her ancestors in the great Necropolis, there to live again in royal splendor forever and ever.

"But the unborn child must be spared, for truly Pharaoh's heart would break with the loss of a babe sired by Horus and born of Isis. Indeed, I would fear for all our lives should that occur. Is it within your great powers to accomplish that which I ask? If you do so, your lands will be doubled and perhaps more."

Euripides appeared to be sitting in thought, seeking a solution, but such was not the case. Poisons were numerous, and many of them tasted of honey and smelled of perfume. Some were instantly deadly; some, less well known, made the victim linger and wither—a wasting-away death that usually confused and confounded court physicians.

The queen's necromancer would give much thought to the

manner in which he would fool the physicians, for the matter of the poison itself was simple. As he raised his eyes to look upon those of Queen Ahmose, he smiled the smallest of smiles and intoned deeply, "It shall be as you wish, but you must convince Pharaoh Thothmes to procure a wet nurse at once for the babe, or it, too, may die if it drinks its mother's milk."

Ahmose, rejoiced at the thought of the coming death of her daughter. Once again, she would reign supreme at the Great Royal Wife, the only beloved of Thothmes.

The baby was born. Despite the death of the princess, the palace overflowed with joy. Runners were sent to all outposts with the news, and fires were lit along the banks of the Nile in anticipation of the passage of barges of the priests of the great gods. They would come to bless and pay homage to the child.

And so, upon this day, plans were set in motion to celebrate the birth. Before any honors could be bestowed upon Hatshepsut, however, Pharaoh decreed that the country would remain in mourning until her mother, the Princess Meritamon, had spent twenty-eight days in mummification and had been placed in the tomb he, Pharaoh, would provide.

Poor unloved Meritamon! Used by her mother and discarded in death by her father, was carried into the night to hastily erected tents outside the gates of the city. The tents were well guarded, and the workers and priests were there assembling the necessary implements needed to carry out their assigned tasks. Each hastened to complete his particular function, for Thothmes was allowing them but twenty-eight days, half the usual time allotted to the process.

Statues of the God of Death, Anubis, stood at each corner of the main tent. His was the body of a man with the head of a jackal. He would protect Meritamon on her journey through the underworld and oversee the weighing of her heart, so that she might live again in her tomb with all she had enjoyed in life.

The body was placed on a wooden platform surrounded by the items needed by morticians and priests. There were mounds of salt, jars of oil, perfumes, spices, and tools for removing the organs. Four large Canopic urns, purchased hastily from a nearby merchant, stood to one side of the tent. Workers were busily preparing the cartouche of Meritamon to be placed on the sides of the jars.

A cartouche was a simple enough thing—an oval piece of clay with hieroglyphics carved upon it. In the case of Meritamon, the cartouche bore her name and cited that she was the daughter of Pharaoh Thothmes I and Queen Ahmose.

As Meritamon lay upon the platform, a hooded priest, carrying a curved knife, entered the tent and made a rapid but precise incision in her left side. Although the mutilation of her body made this rite difficult to perform, it was somehow deftly accomplished. "Ai-ye, ai-ye," he screamed, as he ran from the tent to escape the "ka" or soul of the dead princess.

Her chest and abdomen were emptied of all organs except the kidneys and the heart. She must keep her heart so that Anubis could weigh it upon the scales of righteousness after she entered the underworld. It is not known why the kidneys were left, but many scholars have suggested that, since the kidneys held odious excrements, they might have befouled the body if cut away. Wire hooks, inserted into the nostrils, reached up into the brain and brought forth the tissue, piece by piece. The removed organs and the cavities from whence they came were washed with wine, palm oil, and the most pungent of spices. Rags and rough matting that had been soaked in resin and salt were stuffed into the abdomen, chest, and head.

The final stage of this part of the mummification process was the removal of the stuffing materials. The body was then covered with mounds of salt, and one end of the table was raised to allow remaining fluids to drain into jars placed at its foot. "You will live again forever," chanted the embalmers over and over, as they performed their sacred work upon the body.

After half of the usual time, Meritamon's body was washed free of all salt and anointed with oil; then restuffed with linens that had been dipped in resin. The body openings were then sealed with liquid resin. Again, the body was anointed, this time with precious myrrh, and hot resin was poured over her from head to toe.

Finely woven strips of linen of a prescribed three-inch width were wound about her body. A few golden images of the gods were tucked between the wrappings, but all was done in haste, and little treasure was used. All entrails, body fluids, and rags used in mummification were placed in the Canopic urns, which were then sealed. Pharaoh pushed impatiently for completion. The preparations for the feast honoring Hatshepsut were going forward, and all Egypt looked forward to the celebration.

Exactly thirty-one days after her death, the body of Meritamon in its wooden coffin covered with layers of pounded gold was taken in procession from Thebes to the City of the Dead, or Necropolis, on the outskirts of western Thebes. Professional mourners wailed and threw dirt upon their heads as they walked behind the bier. They were followed by the nobles of the court and then by her father, mother, and sister. All were dressed in white, denoting both grief and respect; all carried wreaths of flowers. At the rear were servants bearing the foods prepared for the ensuing banquet.

A burial site had been excavated in the rock beside the monument of an ancestor. The coffin was placed deep within the tomb, surrounded by the Canopic urns, childhood toys, hair trimmings, and such furniture and foods as would be needed when the god Osiris allowed Meritamon to live again in the underworld. Also placed within the tomb were the jewels she had possessed and the mummified remains of her cats and her monkey, there for amusement in her afterlife. The tomb was sealed with her cartouche and covered with sand.

And now the celebration. Accomplished musicians played drums, lutes, lyres, and harps. Food was spread out beneath tents, and all joined in the feast. It was a time to rejoice. The proper ceremonies had been performed. One last meal to be shared with the soon-to-be-forgotten princess.

Ahmose rode in her gold chair behind that of Thothmes. She rejoiced in the day's events. *I shall be the one who guides the mind and hands of Pharaoh. I am the Great Royal Wife and my power and beauty will be forever!* The hot, late afternoon sun burned down upon them as they retraced their path to the palace. The oiled, black skin of the bearers dripped with sweat that did not evaporate in the early evening air.

Guards at the forefront of the party blew trumpets and were answered by trumpets from the palace as the procession moved through the city of Thebes. All people bowed low to the ground as the living god, gleaming in gold and wearing the double crown, passed by to be carried into the palace grounds and to his chambers.

As Thothmes and Ahmose stepped from their chairs, he pulled her into his arms in a loving embrace and bade her bathe with him. Later they would share love in his golden bed, and he would be greatly pleased and would please her greatly. His world was complete. Had any man ever been more at peace?

From a hiding spot in the walls, Euripides observed all that had just occurred. He quickly slithered through the passageways to his own apartments. He had meant to place himself at the disposal of the queen, had planned to take credit for the princess's death in anticipation of receiving yet more gold. But as he reclined upon his couch in imposing finery, he rethought his strategy. Capable hands removed his jewels and clothes as other slaves filled the alabaster tub. Sinking into the perfumed water, he had a change of mind. It would far better to efface himself before Queen Ahmose and tell her what she already knew. He had no hand in the death. Far better to appear honest and trustworthy at this time. Later, other opportunities would arise. He would be of service again, and his rewards would be much larger.

When he finished bathing, he ordered a servant to send the young male slaves to anoint his body. As they worked oils into his dark skin, he chose one to take to his couch. After all, a man must take pleasure wherever it could be found. Although this practice was frowned upon in the Egypt of that day, no one dared defy the necromancer of the queen.

Slaves and servants by the score had been hard at work preparing the great hall for the sumptuous feast—a feast in honor of Hatshepsut, daughter of the gods. Wax candles and charcoal braziers were aglow. Incense drifted across the vast room with its massive stone pillars. The banquet was about to begin.

As Thothmes I and Ahmose stepped to their thrones, cymbals crashed and a primitive oboe wailed woefully. These were the sounds that preceded all great state occasions.

Pharaoh wore his double crown of red and white with the spread cobra on his brow. His shoulders were covered with a gold collar. This collar was not so delicately fashioned as were many of his others, nor did it contain precious stones. To him, however, it was far more valuable, for it had been worn in battle by his father, Amonhotep I, when he wrenched Egyptian lands from the Hittites and in so doing returned Egypt to its majesty. Thothmes had fought many battles wearing this collar, and he revered it greatly. His arms were encircled with gold bands and gold was at his belt and his feet.

Gold was everywhere—glittering on the nobles, decorating the walls, and even shining from the dishes set about. It seemed that there was no end to Egyptian gold. This, of course, was the reason the pharaohs of this land must be powerful and ready to do battle. Always, others came to wrest their gold from them.

Beside him, Queen Ahmose glowed with inner satisfaction. She was sure there had never been a woman cleverer or lovelier than she. With cosmetics skillfully applied and clothed in beautiful garments, she was the epitome of a queen worthy of reigning beside the mighty Pharaoh.

A young female servant had been found to aid Beka in nursing and caring for the motherless child. Both were already enslaved by the tiny princess and would be bound to her for life. This night Muta placed the one-month-old infant in a crib at the feet of Pharaoh, and all present began the chant—"Hatshepsut! Hatshepsut!"—over and over. The child with black stars in the green of her eyes looked solemnly about her. As candlelight wavered upon the glitter of the chamber, Thothmes stepped down and raised the child in his arms. Silence fell upon all, and his voice was heard—the voice of their god.

"This is Hatshepsut, living daughter of Isis and Horus. She is most royal and most holy. I do name her my heir as ruler of

Egypt. Do all of you rejoice in her! She is the chosen of the Sun God and of all other gods to bring honor and glory to our land."

All day, the barges of temple priests had floated down the Nile. Each carried an image of a god placed beneath a canopy as priests chanted their blessings upon the farmers and villagers living on the banks.

There was Hopi, God of the Nile, who was represented by a crocodile.

Osiris, represented as a sun disk, was gold as was the figure of Amon. Amon was a gold idol that was fed and bathed in his temple in Thebes—an idol who spoke mysteriously from his open, hollow mouth.

Min, the Goddess of Sensuality, was the figure of a woman that had been carved with lettuce leaves at her feet—a food identified with romantic emotions.

Thothmes sat upon his throne with the baby in his arms as each god was carried forward followed by its priests, who gave presents to the child. The child reached out with her hands and grasped the crook held by her father. His roar of laughter fazed her not a bit.

The guests assembled in the chamber believed completely in the importance of this child. Child of the gods, "Hatshepsut, Chieftainess of noble women," she had been named. They would have been astounded could they have seen ahead into the coming years. This infant was to become mighty Hatshepsut, one of the greatest female rulers in history.

3

The tiny princess toddled through the halls and gardens of the palace, with Beka or Muta always by her side. Never was Hati alone. Although there was no reason to fear for her safety—all about her adored her—she was Hatshepsut, the daughter of the gods; and Pharaoh had ordered her attendants to practice a ceaseless vigilance.

"If aught befalls the child, the wrath of the gods will rain down upon you. Ra, himself, will determine your punishment. And I, the living god, will carry it out. Beware!"

"Oh, mighty Pharaoh, I beg you, worry not. She is as my own child, as was her mother before her," replied Beka in a voice barely above a whisper. Thothmes had always treated her kindly, but she was well aware that when angered, he dealt harshly with those who displeased him.

Momentarily annoyed that the old woman spoke in such a familiar manner about this child of the gods, Thothmes glared down at her as she knelt at his feet. Then thinking better of it, he let the moment pass. After all, would her care not be that much more diligent if she loved the child as deeply as she said?

As she grew into young womanhood, Hati became more and more lovely. Her limbs grew long and lithe; she was graceful in every movement. Her hair, golden as a babe, had darkened to a warm brown and fell in deep waves. Black brows took wing upon a high forehead and long lashes outlined her startling eyes. High cheekbones curved above rounded cheeks flushed pink with health. A full and sensitive mouth seemed always to be curved in a sweet smile. And, her eyes—eyes that held black stars as prisoners. All who looked upon these flashing eyes regarded them with awe. Hati, the goddess.

Hati patiently endured hours of bodily care. The bathing

rooms in the palace contained large marble and granite pools, each with water of a different temperature. Charcoal fires of varying sizes in pits beneath the pools heated the water.

Near the pools were large tables upon which she was to lie. Each morning as she lay upon one, handmaidens lathered her with foam made from pounded cactus roots. Then she was led to the pool with the hottest water. When she submerged herself in the water, the foam washed away; and Hati became languid from the heat. Usually, she next chose a pool with much cooler water. The shock brought about when she lowered herself into this pool sent blood pulsing so that she tingled all over with renewed energy.

When the bathing was completed. Hati moved to a marble table where servants carefully dried her. Next came the anointing of her body with oils and perfumes and finally a massage. Beka oversaw all. She selected the oils and perfumes, explaining to the princess why each choice was made.

"See, little one" (Hati was still young enough that Beka could address her in this familiar manner), "oils from almonds are used to prepare you for the early morning, and they are followed by the juices and oils from crushed citrus peels and blossoms. This combination of cedar oils" (she held up a second vial) "will prepare you for sleep. For an important procession or the evening meal, you will be anointed with essence of myrrh. But of that, we do not use so much. It comes from far away, from the land of Punt. Pharaoh sends for it even though the danger is great and the cost, high." True as all this was, it was the oil and wax from the rare gardenia blossoms that Hati preferred and which she coaxed Beka into using as frequently as possible.

It was the custom to shave the heads of young nobles, both male and female, except for a side lock. Hati, however, adamantly refused to undergo this ritual and kept her long, wavy hair. She was, after all, the child of the gods and would do as she wanted. Even so, as hair appeared elsewhere upon her body, it was plucked away, hair by hair, and this would always be done, until the follicles were so damaged the hair grew no more.

Hati was not only beautiful. In early childhood, there were signs that she was unusually intelligent, due no doubt in part to her Greek bloodline. Courtesy and obedience to parents and elders were cornerstones of family life; and when lessons commenced at a younger age, she offered no resistance. Mathematics became a game to her. Languages were another; eventually she mastered six—all spoken in her world. Lessons in refined table manners and other intricacies of court life rounded out her education.

At the age of ten, Hatshepsut became obsessed with horses and chariots. At a time when a young princess' interests were expected to center around selecting materials for her many gowns or flowers to decorate her chambers, Hati was in the royal stables. She adored the horses that were hot blooded and powerful. She demanded to be taught how to drive a chariot. The stable hands were dismayed; Beka was aghast—Meritamon had not acted in this manner. Again, Hati would have her way. Not even her father, mighty Pharaoh, could deny her.

Hatshepsut's fascination with horses increased as she grew older. By the time she reached young womanhood at the age of fourteen, it delighted the self-willed princess to race her chariot madly through the palace gates, through Thebes, out into the surrounding plains, and up the low cliffs. Attendants tried valiantly to keep up with her as she lashed the Arabian steeds into headlong dashes, then suddenly whirled on one wheel, charging toward her followers with a man-sized spear cocked over one shoulder. Her deep laughter echoed from the sandstone cliffs as the riders stopped short as if in great fear. She was a wild thing, possessed with limitless energy. But there was no evil in her—only the joy of sand and space. Desert winds pressed the pleated linen of her dress back upon a young woman's body. Small breasts appeared, silhouetted against the linen. Shapely legs supported her and broad shoulders gave her the added strength necessary to clutch the spear. The princess was maturing into a creature of rare beauty, all the more so because of her unquenchable spirit.

When court appearances were required, Hatshepsut, her liveliness subdued, walked with stately grace. Linen folds, held in place with the gold circlet of royalty, covered her hair. As heiress to the throne of Egypt, she walked immediately behind her parents.

Pharaoh Thothmes had aged gracefully and was still a man strong of body and full of vigor. He visited his harem more often than before, leaving Ahmose to bewail her loneliness in her sumptuous apartments.

For Ahmose, supposed mother of the princess, found that her beauty was fading. Wrinkles appeared in fine rivulets on arms and face. Until a year ago, Euripides had forestalled the appearance of age with mud baths, massages, and aromatic oils. However, even the magic of a sorcerer must succumb to the devastation caused by time, and he could no longer disguise its effect.

She could have taken lovers, as had many other queens forsaken by their husbands. But power, not love, was what Ahmose craved; and to retain this, she must have Thothmes by her side. She determined to regain his attention at any cost. With venom burning in her heart, she sent for Euripides. *He must show me how to regain my beauty or he will no longer be necromancer to the Queen of Egypt or to any queen. I shall see him put to death!*

Euripides was far from being a fool. He was well aware of Ahmose's deep despondency and of its cause. He knew that Thothmes visited the harem with great frequency; and he realized also that Pharaoh was showing more and more interest in Hatshepsut. All of Ahmose and Pharaoh's children were dead: Meritamon, from childbirth; the younger daughter, in a boating "accident" conceived by Queen Ahmose and carried out with the assistance of Euripides; and Sitamon, the boy-child, shortly after birth. Ahmose had believed that the deaths of her children would place her in control of Thothmes and, therefore, of Egypt.

In his smoky chambers, Euripides waxed deep in thought. *Foolish woman. Did she really think she would be beautiful forever, that age would never stalk her? I have given her every treatment possible, so what does she require of me now? I have grown rich from here coffers, but I would have more—gifts that only a supreme ruler can bestow. Young Hati will one day have that power. I have made myself agreeable to her. I have healed her pets and whiled away hours in her company, telling amusing stories, playing games, and teaching lessons about other peoples and their cultures. She trusts me, and I can become her dearest and most useful confidant. But first, I must deal with Ahmose and do so with great care. The court has many physicians, and they must suspect nothing. Well, I shall carry out my plan and give her the final gift.*

Euripides had foreseen that the time would arrive when Queen Ahmose would become a danger to him, but he had no intention of allowing her to imperil his life. Thus, a few days earlier a young servant boy, who had no tongue, had been sent to cut the branches of a certain flowering shrub, one that contained deadly poison in all its parts.

While Ohm was on his errand, Euripides took a vial of perfume and another of clear oil from his chest and emptied them into an alabaster bowl. The boy was soon back with a sack full of oleander. Euripides filled the bowl with leaves stripped from the branches. Using a mortar, he patiently ground the leaves into a thick, milky-green paste. He sniffed it cautiously and added more perfume of citrus. Next, he placed the mass of paste and scent in a muslin bag and twisted it tightly over a clean bowl. An opaque, sweet-smelling liquid drained from the bag. The citrus would make the skin of the queen tighten and shrink as her body absorbed the fluid.

Euripides smiled as he stepped through the secret entrance into Ahmose's bedchamber. He bowed before here and said, "Old Nefur tells me that you have a request, great Queen."

Queen Ahmose lay nude upon her couch. Her once full-bosomed and lush body was shrunken and wrinkled. Still, bright eyes looked with hope upon her necromancer. *Good Euripides. He has never failed me. How wise I have been to keep him by my side all these years.*

"Euripides, I must have youth and strength. I find it is time to deal with Hatshepsut, as Pharaoh looks too fondly upon her. Come; give me your magic remedies, for I would be a young girl again for my pharaoh. Do this, and you will be richer still."

He bowed again and said, "Mighty Ahmose, I have recently come by new knowledge. I have learned of potions that will make you lovelier than ever, and I have them with me. I live only to serve you."

"Well, then, apply these ointments. Let me regain my beauty."

"As you wish, my Queen. I will need an empty bowl and another filled with water."

"Nefur! Do as my necromancer directs. Quickly now."

Nefur moved as rapidly as her aging joints allowed. Queen Ahmose had little patience these days, and it would not do to upset her.

Euripides had Nefur place the bowls on a table near the bed where the Queen could not see them. He poured the contents of a flask into the empty bowl. With one hand, he lifted out a small amount of the thick fluid and smoothed it upon her face, especially her eyelids and lips, and then upon all parts of her body, concentrating upon areas where blood was closest to the surface. Each time that he turned to obtain more liquid, he surreptitiously rinsed his hands in the basin of water. It would not do to poison himself as well. Nor could another to do this for him. A handmaiden might well sicken and die from handling the mixture. If such a death coincided with the death of Ahmose, the duplicity of Euripides might be revealed. No, he dare not take that chance.

"Rest now, my Queen. Lie still for a few minutes while the lotion restores your youth. Soon you will feel and see its effects."

When the mixture had dried completely, Euripides guided Ahmose down the steps to a reflecting pool. She was pleased with what she saw on the water. She came up, brushing by the draperies, to stand in front of her electrum mirror and was pleased again. It was as though hands had pulled the skin of her face backward and upward, giving her a smooth complexion once more.

She turned to Euripides with a triumphant smile. "You are clever and I am pleased. Come again tomorrow and repeat this treatment. I will not reward you today; but if I recapture the attention of Pharaoh, you shall receive much gold. Go now to your quarters."

After sending Euripides away, she summoned Nefur. "Bring me a new gown—one I've not worn before; one that will catch the attention of all who see me." Nefur came forward and enfolded her in a new material obtained from trade with countries to the east. It was sheer with strands of purest silver entwined in the fabric so that it shimmered as the wearer moved about. Silver sandals completed her costume.

"No gold now, is it?" Euripides murmured to himself as he made his way through the passages. "Selfish woman! You may be surprised at how well you shall gift me. I have started you upon a glorious journey to sleep with your gods." His demeanor was not grim but rather one of satisfaction. After all, death was a business in Egypt, especially a royal death. Now, he must turn immediately to Hatshepsut. His groundwork had been laid carefully, and he must move with speed.

Princess Hatshepsut was at the stables when Euripides found her. As she watched, a horseman worked with a young Arabian mare, having her drag the traces of a chariot. Euripides sidled up to the princess and begged permission to speak.

Hatshepsut considered him indifferently. He seemed always to be scurrying around her mother, and besides that, he was hairy and overly perfumed. She had heard rumors of his preference for young boys and was puzzled by such behavior. Still, he was a member of the court and she must treat him with courtesy.

"Speak, Euripides, but please be quick. As you can see, I am occupied at the moment. What think you of my new mare? Will she run like the wind?"

"She is spectacular, my princess, and she will pull the loveliest lady in Egypt if she is harnessed to your chariot. You will race more swiftly than eye can follow," said Euripides. "But I have come to you with a concerned heart. You know I am devoted to your family, and I fear your mother, our beloved queen, does not appear to be as well as could be. Perhaps you can have a physician more worthy than I to observe her, as I fear she needs attention. Only, please do not reveal my concern to Queen Ahmose, as she will become angry with me if she learns that I say she does not appear to be well."

Hatshepsut turned and stared at Euripides. She took in his dark face framed by curls, his gleaming skin, and his many ornaments of gold. As always, his face seemed to her empty of emotion. He had been a good tutor and always flattering in his remarks. *But why is he coming to me with this observation about my mother? Why did he not go to Pharaoh? Perhaps he is only exactly as he seems to be, a trusted retainer concerned with the welfare of my family.* She softened her countenance with a smile. "I will see that Queen Ahmose is examined by a court physician, and she shall have no knowledge of your report. I thank you for your concern." She dismissed him with another smile and determined to be kinder to him in future. All rulers needed loyal followers surrounding them.

As Euripides moved toward the palace gardens, Hati turned her attention back to the now quiet white mare. The intelligence she had noted in the horse's large eyes was showing itself in the tractability she displayed.

Horem, captain of the palace guard, came forward from the training ring and bowed low to the princess. "I believe your mare is ready to pull your chariot. May I have the honor of the first trial? No harm must come to you, my lady."

Hatshepsut's gay laugh rang out. "Lash her to my winged chariot, Horem. We will fly to the monuments of my ancestress. I go to the temple at Karnak to admire her carved praises and wish myself into her great image."

"But princess, she is untried . . ."

"Say no more, Horem. She is my mare and I alone, shall drive."

Although Hatshepsut wore by choice the short, pleated skirt of a prince or young boy, she could not resist the beautiful, jeweled sandals worn by women. She was an enticing vision as she climbed into the chariot. The mare stood perfect still as Horem adjusted the harness. And when Hatshepsut urged her forward, she moved as though she had been born knowing it would one day be her duty to safely transport the princess.

Once beyond the confines of the city, Hatshepsut soon had her flying at top speed into the desert. Queen Tetisheri had built the monument at Karnak as a mortuary temple. Hatshepsut would stand in awe in the vast edifice and look up beyond the giant pillars of stone to read the hieroglyphics declaring the glory of a king's wife, and mother of a king, who had wielded enormous power. Hatshepsut visited Karnak often. She wished to be as worthy of this ancestress, and she also wished to be remembered with such a building. As she wandered through the pillars and into the temple, she daydreamed about the monuments she would create. *Perhaps I should start building soon. First, I think, I shall have obelisks hewn from red granite, my favorite stone. And they shall be topped with electrum. The gold and silver melted together will catch the warmth of the sun, Amon, in its first and last gleams of the day. They will be splendid.* And so she dreamed away the remainder of the day, pausing now and then to nibble upon her favorite shat cakes and drink sweet wine. To the horse, she gave nothing. She wanted to train the animal to do without food for long periods of time, for Hatshepsut imagined that one day she would ride the horse in triumphal procession or even into war—if such occurred.

"What can I name her?" she asked herself. "What name is befitting this wonderful animal?" And then she thought of the strength the horse would develop and of the color of her eyes. "I shall name her Lazuli—she will be as hard as the stone and her eyes mach its color."

After leaving the princess at the stables, Euripides slipped into the lush greenery surrounding Queen Ahmose's private lake. He crept close to the edge of the water and saw that she was being helped down the stone steps and into her reed and gold boat. As she was being rowed to the small, covered pavilion floating on the lake, he heard whimpers of pain.

Ahmose was seeking relief from the worries that beset her. She would rest in this private refuge, caressed by gentle breezes and attended only by two handmaidens. She felt strange, oddly weak. *I must regain my strength. When Thothmes sees me to-*

night, he will notice my beauty and take me to his couch again, and all will be as it should be.

A handmaiden dared to speak. "Oh mistress, you appear flushed. May I bathe you with the cool water?"

Ahmose nodded her consent. As her maid placed a wet cloth on her face, the cream Euripides had placed there diffused and loosened its hold upon her skin; and Ahmose could feel it falling into the sag of age. She was furious, and despite her weakness, slapped the woman. "Fool! See what you have done to me," she cried. "Send for my necromancer at once! I must have him here immediately!"

Euripides observed all that had taken place. He smiled slightly. *The poison has made her ill, but too ill this soon. If I am to conceal my actions,* he reasoned, *I must take a palace physician with me, and let him see me prepare a harmless skin preparation.* He slipped away to wait in his rooms for the summons. Then, he would seek Knum, third physician to Pharaoh.

Knum was with Pharaoh, applying hot stones and healing leaves to his right shoulder. Thothmes was nearly fifty, and old battle wounds had healed badly. The heat from the wet stones, wrapped in aromatic leaves, soothed his pain and his senses as well.

Euripides entered the room with a worried expression on his face. As always, he waited for permission to speak. He was careful to observe all the courtesies demanded by royalty when in the presence of Pharaoh.

"Well, necromancer, what have you to ask of me?"

"Oh, Great King, your Great Royal Wife is in distress, and I beg you to allow the royal physician to aid me in her cure. I fear that my own learning is inadequate and seek the greater knowledge of Knum, if she is to be comforted."

All in the palace were aware of Euripide's legendary prowess with cures of all kinds and also of his understanding of all black arts. For him to make a request of this type was most unusual.

"You seek aid from another? Is the Great Royal Wife more ill than you imply?" Despite his recent sexual indifference toward her, Thothmes still cared for Amose and was suddenly anxious for her well-being.

"Mighty Pharaoh, I am uncertain. That is why I ask the assistance of the honored physician Knum."

Pharaoh nodded his consent. "Attend the queen at once. And make me aware of your findings."

Now, Knum was full of personal pride and ambition, and it was with a supremely superior attitude that he led the way to Ahmose's chambers.

Ahmose was lying on her bed, listless and moaning in distress. Although her face and arms had been washed to cool them, the slow-acting poison remained on her neck and torso, and its evil work was progressing.

When Knum saw Ahmose, he did what all good doctors of ancient times did: he took a deep breath. Many illnesses have a distinct odor; and from this, physicians could often ascertain the cause of an ailment. But not this time. Knum smelled only citrus, the odor of the combination of oranges and lemons. Next he asked old Nefur to obtain a bowl of the queen's urine. Holding it up, he fanned the aroma toward his nose. It seemed normal; there was the odor of wine and that of citrus and something else, an elusive odor much like that of the leaves he had been using on Thothmes. Perhaps the smell was still clinging to his hands, though he had washed them well. That must be it.

Knum asked Euripides for a sample of the ointment with which he had been treating the queen, for all in the palace knew of her desperate search for renewed youth. Euripides brought forth a container of citrus crushed with herbal oils. He tasted of it to show Knum that it was harmless.

Further examination revealed no reason for Ahmose's distress, so Knum decided to give her a draught of opium to ease the pain and help her sleep, hoping that when she awakened, her discomfort would be gone. She resisted at first, demanding that Euripides make her young again; but he begged her to follow Knum's suggestions. He told her he would return in the morning to "treat" her. Thus reassured, Ahmose drank the wine laced with opium and sank into a stupor. The physician dismissed her servants, and they left, grateful for the opportunity to bathe and rest.

Euripides generously offered to have his boy sit with Ahmose; the same boy who had gathered the deadly leaves. As he followed Knum from the room, an understanding glance passed between Euripides and his servant. Thus far, all was well.

Once alone, Ohm did as he had ben instructed. He took a braided circlet adorned with a beautifully carved tortoise-shaped clip from the folds of his skirt and used it to attach the linen headdress around Ahmose's shaven head. Nefur observed this action as she reentered the chamber but saw it only as a thoughtful gesture. *The boy is sweet to care. I wonder where Queen Ahmose got that clip; I don't think I've seen it before.* Nefur was old and simple, and she accepted what had passed. She felt no trepidation as she settled down with Ohm to await the passage of the opium.

The apartments of the queen abounded with luxury. The chamber in which she lay had silk hangings on the walls and furniture of exotic woods adorned with gold. Close by her bed was a large cedar chest containing her treasury of gold and jewels. The chair in front of her cosmetic case was covered with glass tiles; ivory wings flew backward from her gold bed. Against one wall was an enormous, polished bronze mirror and against another, one of electrum. The sandstone floor was crossed in patterns with smooth marble. Stairs led from the room to the Nile-fed lake in her private garden. The draperies had been lowered now to keep out the chill of the desert night, and a small charcoal brazier heated the room. Through the carved double doors that led to the next room could be seen a sea of soft cushions where her ladies slept, their musical instruments leaning against a wall. Chests containing her childhood toys and her shorn hair were stacked against another wall, for royal Egyptians threw nothing away. All was saved to be placed in their tombs to be enjoyed in the afterlife. The third room was packed with the necessities to maintain her station: soaps, oils, perfumes, linens, and silks.

As dawn approached, Nefur's chin fell upon her chest and she began to snore. Ohm had remained awake; and, once certain that the old woman was sound asleep, he stood up and soundlessly moved to the revolving altar of Isis and pushed just a little. Long fingers grasped the small opening, and the lean shape of the necromancer slid into the room and moved directly to Ahmose's side. All was silent except for Nefur's snores.

Removing a small vial of pure, liquid opium from his tunic, Euripides poured it into the open mouth of Ahmose. She stirred slightly in her sleep, swallowed, and became instantly still, but as yet, not dead. He slipped the beautiful clasp from the band on her head and, with his knife, cut the tiniest tip from one end. Secreted in the clasp was venom that he had milked from a deadly asp. He poured this into her open mouth also and quickly replaced the clasp on the circlet. No one would know what had transpired. All was accomplished in a few minutes and in complete silence. Euripides slipped from the room, and the boy sat as before, only now he pretended to sleep.

Nefur roused with the rising of the sun and stepped toward the draperies to open them and greet the great sun god, Ra. As the golden rays fell upon her mistress, she realized something was amiss. She hurried over to the bed and drew down the coverings. Ahmose's body had turned dark in death; but because of the opium, there were no signs of pain and struggle.

Nefur screamed and screamed again at the sight. She turned and ran through the doors and down the hall to Pharaoh's chambers, never ceasing her loud wailing. All thoughts of court etiquette were erased from her mind. She fell at the feet of the man guarding the entrance to Pharaoh's chambers and gasped her terrible news. The guard passed the message to the king's chief retainer. With great apprehension, he awakened Thothmes and informed him of Ahmose's death.

"What say you?" demanded the king as he arose from his bed. "How can this be? She was but overly tired. The draught that Knum gave to her was no different than those he has given me many times. Who told you this thing?"

As he helped Pharaoh into his clothes, the quaking servant could only repeat the message Nefur had given the guard. "I shall see to this immediately. Send for all the court physicians:

mine, the queen's, and every other one in the palace. They are to attend me in her chambers at once."

Thothmes was first to arrive at the queen's apartments. It was obvious that Nefur had been correct in her story. The queen was dead. Soon all the physicians were assembled. None could discern the reason for Ahmose's sudden passing to dwell with her ancestors. Kneeling at the foot of her bed, Euripides was beset with grief. None doubted his loyalty; none placed blame upon him. After all, had he not acted in concert with Knum, one of Pharaoh's most trusted physicians? Had not the treatment been mild? Surely, she must have suffered a mysterious malady of the heart. It was simply the time for her to go to her ancestors. There was no blame to place.

Thothmes accepted the death of his queen with little remorse. He had loved her passionately in their youth, but youth was gone and she had become old and faded. More and more, his thoughts were turning toward the blooming Hatshepsut. She was, after all, the child of Isis and Horus, powerful gods. He did not consider her his daughter. His part in her creation was full of hazy half memories; and years of accepting the belief held by all Egyptians that Hatshepsut was a goddess had inured his mind.

Hatshepsut walked into the chamber followed by Beka. Ahmose had treated the girl pleasantly enough in her lifetime but never with real love. That had come from Beka and Pharaoh. Despite this, Hatshepsut was truly sorry that Ahmose was dead. She placed lotus flowers on the breast of the queen and stepped to her earthly father's side.

Thothmes placed an arm around her to comfort her, but his heart beat hard in his chest as he held the lovely princess. Her youth held the aroma of warm milk, and the feel of her was round and soft. As she gazed up at the tall king, her eyes, holding dark stars hostage, locked with his; and she felt a shock of awareness. In that moment, she knew what he was planning for her. Others also noted Pharaoh's flushed face and intense stare.

This cannot be so. Hati trembled in apprehension. Surely her gods would save her from a loveless marriage.

Beka's thoughts differed from those of the child she had

cared for from birth and guarded with diligence. She had great hopes for a marriage between Hatshepsut and Thothmes. Such was the custom in Egypt in order for the blood to pass in purity for the succession of the crown. If Hatshepsut became the great royal wife, she would hold the crook and flail of a ruler. Hatshepsut would be a very young queen of Egypt and would rule long after Thothmes was in his tomb.

The thoughts of Euripides were a mixture of elation and apprehension. No one placed any blame on him for the death of the queen. However, would Hatshepsut accept him as had her "mother," Ahmose? He must go to his rooms and make many plans. It was the time to think deeply of many things.

Pharaoh broke from his entrancement to give a fearful order. The elderly maid, Nefur, and the servant boy of Euripides would accompany the queen across the river of death to wait upon her in the afterlife. They, too, would be mummified and would lie at her feet for all eternity.

Nefur was old and devoted to her mistress. She believed, as all Egyptians did, that the afterlife was a wonderful world. As a lowly maid, she had never dreamed of so fine a mummification or that she would lie in a tomb so rich, there to awaken and enjoy with her queen all the beautiful goods and foods contained therein. She followed gladly behind the soldiers who were carrying Ahmose away on a litter.

But the boy, Ohm, had been captured in the upper cataract of the Nile in Nigere, and he feared death with great horror. He was dragged away struggling, his mute mouth open in silent screams.

Now to complete the task at hand. Thothmes summoned priests and issued orders for mortuary tents to be set up outside the gates of northern Thebes. There, the three bodies would be mummified. He would allow the full sixty days of preparation. Ahmose had been a queen for many years; as accepted mother of Hatshepsut, her treasures in the afterworld would be great.

The will of Pharaoh was done.

4

Ahmose was the last Great Royal Wife to lie in the mortuary city at Thebes. As her body fluids dripped into Canopic funeral jars in the mortuary tents, preparations were made for a procession befitting a Great Royal Wife. There were also other preparations. These were in the palace. The huge apartments of the dead queen were swept and washed. Incense burned in each room to clear the air of death.

Thothmes had ordered all of Ahmose's possessions: her bed, chairs, clothes, mirrors, cosmetics—everything—moved to the tomb he had begun for her on their wedding day. Even her small reed and gold boat and her cedar float in the lake were taken to her tomb. Her priceless gold collars were laid out and one was chosen for the mummy itself, along with a crown and earrings and bracelets. All remaining jewelry was placed in a casket of ebony to lie at her feet.

At the same time, Pharaoh Thothmes sent many bolts of exquisite materials to Hatshepsut with instructions that she was to choose what pleased her most to decorate her new chambers. Because she was a loyal princess of this land, she would do all that was expected of her even though sick at heart. She chose materials of fine linen and silk. All were white.

With the cleansing of the apartments completed. Thothmes ordered that Hatshepsut's possessions be moved there. Her golden bed and chairs, her cedar and ebony chests, her cosmetic chests with fine alabaster pots and fur brushes, her games—all were placed in the rooms close to his. When Pharaoh saw how perfectly the shades and textures of white suited her, he made one contribution of his own. He sent hunters in haste to bring back fine leopard skins that were to be tanned to soft perfection and strewn over her bedroom floor.

At the foot of the steps leading to the lake, a new, small boat was moored—one almost as fine as the one in his tomb. It glittered with electrum and gold. In the lake floated a strange, new pavilion. It was built in the eastern fashion with many carved peaks to its roof and thousands of tiny silver bells that whispered, instead of ringing, in the breeze. All of this to give Hatshepsut pleasure.

In her new surroundings, diverted by unaccustomed delights, Hatshepsut sometimes forgot to think about what lay ahead for her. She was just fourteen years of age. Still, so wise was she, so well learned and tutored, that her budding body seemed to belong to one much older. She was pale yet sultry, sensuous and seemingly wise in the ways of her world, yet innocent. Everything, in fact, that could captivate the Pharaoh of the most prosperous dynasty in Egyptian history.

Gods were consulted and given rich gifts. Soon the news was called up and down the Nile. "The Great Pharaoh Thothmes I goes to bury Queen Ahmose, and upon his return, he will make the Princess Hatshepsut his Great Royal Wife."

The proclamation was a joyous one for all Egyptians. Hatshepsut had been revered as a goddess from birth; and now she would be co-ruler of Egypt. All crops would be abundant after the annual flooding of the Nile. Many sons would be born and fortunes would flourish. Taxes would easily be paid, as farmers would have extra bushels of wheat and more cattle, sheep, and geese. The Nile would teem with fishes and ducks. *Long live Hatshepsut, more beautiful than anyone.*

On the sixtieth day, the mummy of Queen Ahmose was placed upon a bier to be carried to the Necropolis. Her bier was followed by those of Nefur and the servant boy, Ohm. After them came trained musicians—female slaves, dancing to the beat of hand drums held face high. Young girls added to the rhythm with hand clappers. Mourners trailed behind, throwing dirt upon themselves and wailing.

Following at a distance were Thothmes and Hatshepsut. For the first time, she rode at his side in the gold chair of a queen. Upon her brow was a figure of the hooded serpent, a cobra spread wide in anger. She wore a long dress of pleated linen, and her hair was concealed under a woolen wig threaded with gold hoops and jewels. White ostrich feathers were held above the heads of the pharaoh and the princess as the litters were rapidly carried to the outer walls of the Necropolis.

Ahmose was laid in her painted, wooden coffin inside a granite sarcophagus. The nurse and boy were placed on the floor at the foot of the sarcophagus. Many dishes of food were laid out in the coolness of the tomb.

Hatshepsut and Thothmes ate a last meal with the dead queen, as others feasted outside. He seemed to consume the slender girl with his fervid gaze. Color was high in his cheeks. When he had but barely slaked his thirst with wine and tasted bread and salt, he reached down to help Hatshepsut rise. “Come, sweet new wife. We go now to be joined as rulers of our land.”

Hati’s breath came with difficulty. She longed to find a way to postpone this but she did not know how. He was the supreme ruler and she must obey him in all things. Faltering steps carried her to her chair. The procession returned to Thebes, with all except Hati infused with new gaiety.

The pillared great hall of the palace would sound with music this night. The servants arrayed flowers and gifts, and cones of scented wax were on tables by the door. These perfumed cones were placed atop the wigs of nobles and representatives from foreign lands. As the heat from braziers and food combined with the heat of closely assembled humanity, the wax melted and ran down upon the bodies of the wearers, adding new fragrances to the air.

King and princess descended from gold litters to the marble steps of the palace. They turned as one to wave to the populace of Thebes, all there to receive free beer, bread, and beef in celebration of the wedding taking place that night.

Oboes blew mournful joy, and drums beat in excitement. The golden pair ascended the high dais and sat upon an even level, thus signifying to all that Hatshepsut ruled equally with Thothmes.

The chief priest of Amon-Ra stepped toward them, holding out the white cone-shaped crown for the queen. Its golden cobra glittered in the candlelight.

Suddenly, Thothmes stood and reached for her crown. He, himself, would proclaim her as supreme royalty. As he stepped up to place the crown upon her head, Hatshepsut looked into his eyes. Set in folds of wrinkles, Pharaoh's eyes were filled with lust. His lips were dry, and he moistened them with his tongue.

Thinking himself to be invincible, he performed an unusual act. He bowed, and then knelt on both knees before the Great Royal Wife. A hushed awe fell upon those of the audience who were watching. The priests of Amon, Isis, and Horus whispered among themselves, "Does Pharaoh know what he has done? Does he realize that he has placed himself as secondary ruler by this act?"

Thothmes stood and faced the revelers, most of whom were unaware of what had transpired. "Gifts!" he cried. "Gifts for the Great Royal Wife, Hatshepsut."

Bearers trotted into the hall with large boxes suspended from poles. Four bearers were required to carry each box; and there were three boxes in all—one for each season of the year. The first contained gold pieces, newly struck, with the likeness of Hatshepsut on one side and that of Thothmes I on the other. The second contained layers of silk bolts in many colors and run through with gold and silver threads. The third held an array of gold and jewels. There were cups, plates, bowls, and various pots. Some where encrusted with lapis lazuli; some ringed with precious amber drops. There were pearls and small bags containing rubies and turquoises. A fabulous fortune, enough for many queens.

Before Hatshepsut had time to examine all that was placed before her, Thothmes clapped his hands to summon Khenem, the goldsmith. He entered, followed by an additional four bearers bowed down under the weight of a most beautifully carved casket. Khenem prostrated himself at the feet of the royal pair. Thothmes nodded his head, indicating that Khenem might speak. "Mighty Pharaoh, may these specimens of my poor talent please you and bring pleasure to the Great Royal Wife."

Thothmes stepped over to the fourth casket and opened it. He reached inside and lifted out a collar of gold and lapis lazuli, so delicate in its proportions and manner of formation as to bring joy to the eyes of any woman. Knowing of Hatshepsut's delight in the blue marsh birds, he had had this collar overlaid with birds in blue turquoise. Each bird had an ebony star for an eye. The necklace, when placed around Hatshepsut's slender, ivory-white neck, was an exaggeration of the eyes that gazed above it. She was so beautiful. His heart raced with desire.

From the same casket, he lifted a wide belt made of woven strands of gold that moved easily. Large teardrop-shaped pearls were fastened irregularly along the bottom edge. He placed it around her waist, but it was too large and slipped to her hips where the pearls swayed in a charming fashion.

The last thing, at the very bottom of the box, was a heavy ring in the shape of a large gold beetle. It was the humble scarab, or dung beetle, a god symbolizing the endurance of Egypt. He placed this powerful symbol on her middle finger. It made clear to all that she was the holiest of goddesses.

"Now," cried Thothmes, "we feast in honor of this marriage. You will all pay homage to my holy presence and to my Great Royal Wife. We will bring new life to Egypt, a new succession to our dynasty—the most successful and bountiful of all the ones who have come before us and of all who will follow after. Play the music; drink the wine; bring the food."

Feasting began anew. Great platters of peacocks, baked with onions and salt and stuffed again in their feathers, were offered to waiting guests. Beef joints, roasted over charcoal and sliced into pieces, were served with cheeses and fruits. Loaves of bread, some dark and rich, others light and sweet, were carried in on gleaming platters. And always there were bowls of honey in which to dip all food.

In her desperation, Hatshepsut could scarcely pick at the foods set upon a small table beside her throne. Her hands trembled so that she was forced to hold her wine goblet tightly lest someone observe her nervousness. A goddess must not show weakness—ever.

Thothmes drank deeply, and his cup was filled many times.

He was light-headed and paid little attention as the priests came, one after another, to pledge their loyalty and obedience to Hatshepsut. They approached her first, a clear indication of her superiority. Had she not been born of two gods? Did not Pharaoh himself bend his knee to her?

Hatshepsut looked closely at her father and now, husband. He was full of wine; perhaps she could delay the inevitable for a time. Leaning against his throne, she thanked him for his lavish gifts and asked a favor. "My husband, can we not go for a ride in your chariot? The palace is so warm, and the night air will be cooling to our skins. I have seen you race your chariot across the sand, and I would ride in it with you beside the Nile."

Thothmes was both pleased and flattered and willingly assented to her request. The child of this morning had become a lovely queen by nightfall. Her crown made her seem taller and she glittered in the flickering light of many candles.

Hatshepsut called for her nurse and serving ladies. They removed her crown and placed a small gold circlet around her head to hold in place the wavy brown hair that fell to her waist. She took Thothmes' hand, and they walked together to the palace steps where he called loudly for his chariot and finest stallions.

His chariot was magnificent. Made light for battle, its delicate spokes and bed were formed from tough, close-grained bentwood. Meshed leather straps made a resilient floor. The curved front was the height of his waist, and leaves of gold covered carved wings that curved around the housing of the wheels. It was pulled by a matched pair of Arabian horses, dark in color. The breastplates on the horses bore his cartouche.

Pharaoh stepped up into the wings of his chariot and extended his arm to Hatshepsut. She stepped in beside him, and he clasped her to his side with his right arm. He held twin reins in his left hand and flipped the long leathers around his upper arm. His muscles were still strong, and the avenging conqueror of the Hittites, Hyksos, and Nubians maintained total control over the horses.

At a shout, the soldiers drew back from the horses' heads, and they were away, racing under the dark sky. Some Egyptian nights are death black, but others are sprinkled with stars and a moon that gives the desert a luminescent glow. This night the stars seemed close enough to reach out and touch.

There were two black stars in the chariot, centered in the green of Hatshepsut's eyes—eyes now wild with excitement. Her blood was racing hot in her veins. "Oh let us go faster, faster still," she cried. Foam from the fine horses flew back upon them; and, as she laughed loudly in her pleasure, Thothmes drew her tightly to him.

"Enough! Back to the palace, my love. Tonight we will entwine our bodies, one god with another, and bring glory and greatness to the two lands of Egypt." Pharaoh spoke these words into her ear, and she realized she must accept her fate. It had always been so in this land, and Hatshepsut was obedient to the land. Egypt over all, Egypt above all.

Dashing back along the sandy banks of the Nile, he crushed her even closer and whispered of his love for her, his Hati. She gripped the chariot with small hands turned white in the starlight. Nothing, no one, could change her destiny. It was Maat, the order of things.

Throwing the horses' reins to a palace guard, Thothmes turned and lifted his queen from the chariot and carried her up the palace steps with hurried gait. Modesty decreed that she be left with her handmaidens to bathe and prepare herself for their union, but he was Pharaoh. He would have her now!

Slaves sped ahead to open chamber after chamber, until, at last, he held her in his innermost room. One wall overlooked the river and opened unto a balcony with hanging plants. The other walls were covered with electrum, and the floor was of rose quartz.

Suddenly gentle, he stood his lovely queen upon her small feet and slowly removed her long, white dress. He placed her gold and pearl belt, her diadem, and her sandals on cushions by his down-filled bed. Laying her tenderly on the silk cover, he removed his finery, being careful to place his sword close at hand. He lowered his naked body beside that of his lovely Great Royal Wife. His urgency returned and was such that he took no time to arouse this young girl but knelt and spread her legs apart with hard, brown hands; then, falling upon her, plunged over and over again until the final shudder of release gave respite to Hatshepsut. She lay torn and bleeding beneath him. Thothmes rolled off her still form and in seconds began to snore.

Hatshepsut had not cried out; had not whimpered. But now, in a slight voice, she called, "Beka. Beka, come to me and help me. I cannot move."

Beka was concealed behind the curtains in the king's chamber. She dried the tears she had shed at the sight of Hatshepsut's ordeal. Leaving her hiding place, she moved to the bedside and helped her Hati to stand. Gently, she placed her arms around her and led her through the doorway into the hall with the mosaic floor of fishes and water lilies. Four Nubian eunuchs were there, standing by a large carpet.

Once she lay, still bleeding, upon the carpet, Hatshepsut was carried into her own apartments and down the circular stair to her bathing room, where she was placed in a bath filled with warm, medicated water. Beka had called upon Euripides when she realized what was to occur. He had placed soothing herbs and belladonna in the bath. Belladonna, when applied on the skin, relieved pain. When taken orally, in a large amount, it caused death; but he had no wish to harm Hatshepsut. He felt that if he came to her aid at this time, she would come to reply upon him as had Queen Ahmose. This he believed. He had no reason to know of Hatshepsut's strengths. He thought her simply another rich and spoiled queen. He would learn later how wrong he was.

Beka accepted all that had happened, as did Hatshepsut. Egypt over all, Egypt above all.

Beka was not a foolish woman. She knew there would be no child, as Hati's flow had ceased just two days previously. Hati would heal; and with the aid of Euripides, would not soon conceive. She would not be ripped asunder in childbirth as had Beka's long ago darling. Meritamon, Hati's mother.

Euripides prepared a goblet of wine, adding a few drops of laudanum to ease Hatshepsut into restful slumber. He lifted the queen's head upon his arm and her eyes fluttered open. Her eyes!

Euripides was drawn into their depths. He who practices what he believes to be magic oft believes in its power himself. At that moment he felt the unmistakable presence of a mysterious being and was awed.

Despite her unsettled state, Hatshepsut maintained her regal manners. "My thanks to you, gentle Euripides, for my pain is much relieved, and I shall remember your kindness. Would you have me drink this potion?"

"It is but a mild drug I have put in the wine to help you sleep a long while so that you might heal more easily. Have no fear of me, Royal One. Beka called me here, and she loves you well. I also love you well and am honored to serve you when you need me. Drink now, and then you shall be carried to your cool bed."

Hati smiled an innocent smile, underscored with the wisdom of a much older woman. She suspected that Euripides was not as he would have her believe, but he had helped her now, and she was certain she could make further use of him—up to a point. To Hatshepsut, it was logical: The more loyal followers in the palace, the fewer enemies about which to be concerned.

Beka lifted the goblet to Hati's lips and she drank. The Nubians removed her from the herbal bath and placed her on a clean carpet. She was almost unaware of being wrapped in sweet-smelling linens and placed in her own bed before she fell asleep.

Thothmes awakened at sunrise as was his habit and lay bemused for a moment. Then the events of the night returned. *How beautiful and sweet my Queen. But I? I was as a beast. I must awaken her and declare my love!* He turned to speak to her, but all that he saw was blood on the linens. Poor child; no, not a child. She was a woman now—his wife. He would go to her in remorse and show her his love in a more tranquil manner. Even so, his sexual desire was greatly aroused. By all the gods, he felt as a young warrior again.

He was bathed and anointed by servants. Then, a short, pleated skirt was wrapped around his waist. He sat impatiently as leather sandals were placed upon his feet and a blue and white linen kerchief was knotted around his shaved head to hang low on both shoulders. Two golden armlets and a belt with jeweled daggers completed his attire. While being dressed, he breakfasted upon watered wine and a small fish. But the curse of Ptah! He must sit still yet again for the removal of any hairs upon his face and arms.

Now! Now he would visit Hatshepsut. He strode purposefully down the hallway. As he brushed past the guards at the entrance to her apartments, he saw both Beka and Euripides in her bedchamber. Immediately, they prostrated themselves before him. Looking across the large room, he beheld a small, still form lying motionless, with long hair cascading to the floor.

He moved to the side of her bed and bent to kiss her mouth. Her breath was sweet, and over all was the pervading scent of gardenia. He softly called her name, but the lashes curling upon her smooth cheeks did not flutter. He called more loudly but she remained motionless. Alarmed, and remembering the blood in his own bed, he spoke sharply, "Beka! Euripides! Come here and tell me why my queen sleeps so deeply."

Trembling at Pharaoh's sudden anger, the two rose, crossed the room, and knelt at his feet. It was Beka who spoke. "Great Pharaoh, your queen did cry out in pain. We have but done our best to remedy her discomfort. She was torn and bleeding, and Euripides treated her with herbs. She needs time to regain her health. Fear not, as you know her never to be ill. It is but the pleasures of the night and her youth that leaves her thus."

Pharaoh felt much relief at Beka's words. Mixed with the relief, though, was guilt. He had been coarse with this beautiful child. Not so again. He would be gentle; and in time, she would learn the ways of love. There must be a babe from their union, but time enough for that. What now? What to do about the desires he felt? Perhaps a visit to the harem in a short while. For now, exercise—that would be his answer. He turned to Beka and Euripides. "Rise now. Stay with the Great Royal Wife, physician and nurse. See that her every wish is granted; and Euripides, use all the learning you possess to heal her quickly. I go to test my horses."

Thothmes walked from the queen's apartments and through the palace. Slaves had labored through the night, and the great throne room was cleared of the remnants of the lavish celebration. Sweet incense wafted through the room. On the roof of the palace, other slaves pulled ropes that caused long, leather strips to sway moving the still air back and forth and down the tiled pipes and tunnels to the lower rooms. As the air descended, it cooled; and the lower apartments and ceremonial chambers were pleasant even on the hottest days.

Of the one hundred rooms and chambers, the topmost housed the personal slaves and bodyguards of the royal family. They spent little time there during the heat of the day but enjoyed the rooftop during the evening and night, as did all Egyptians in their homes. The members of the royal family and honored officials had airy balconies and gardens of their own adjoining their apartments. Other persons of the court lived in beautiful villas situated just far enough above the banks of the Nile to escape damage during the spring floods.

Egyptians who could afford to do so owned varying sizes of tri-sailed reed boats called "feluccas." Aboard were delicacies to be consumed and jars of wine to be drunk. In the cool of the evening, they sailed up and down the Nile like butterflies of the night with sails of bright colors.

Pharaoh arrived at the stables and watched as slaves exercised the horses and then groomed them. He ordered two horses harnessed to his chariot, thinking to drive out into the desert. On the way, he came to the palm-lined drive leading to the royal harem and abruptly changed his course. His disappointment at Hatshepsut's condition could be easily remedied. He had no favorite in the harem, but one of the many women there could provide novelty to slake his amorous thirst. The harem was vast; with so many women housed there, a young girl of tender age could arrive and live out her life without ever having contact with the Pharaoh.

The guards saw him approaching and quickly opened the thick gates set in the high walls of a compound the size of a small city. It was so large because rulers of both conquered and friendly lands were forever sending their daughters to Egypt in appeasement and in the hope that they would bear a royal son. It had been the practice to wed Egyptian princesses of pure blood to the half-royal sons of these foreign princesses. Thus was gold gained from Pharaoh for their fathers.

The women, some only young girls, were of every size and hue, from fair-haired, white-skinned beauties to exotic black Nubians who possessed unusual talents for pleasing a man. When male children were born here, they remained with their mothers until they were eight. Then they were sent to live in the monasteries of the priests who served the various gods, there to be superbly educated and groomed. For, when the time arose, a princess must have intelligent, well-mannered young men from whom to choose. Those not selected for a royal marriage became priests. Because of this practice, many of the priests of Egypt were of royal blood. This accounted not only for their courtly behavior but also for the power they held as individuals and as followers of the gods they served.

Altogether, the harem was a delightful place to live. Lovely villas were situated around a large lake kept fresh with water carried through canals from the Nile. Date palms swayed in gentle breezes. There was a bakery, a kitchen, and a large storehouse for beautiful cloth and for oils and perfumes. Other provisions were brought in daily. Far from the center of the harem, against an inner wall, were the hovels of the many serving girls and eunuchs. In this same area, but in a much grander house, lived the physician who tended the women.

Still, the harem was a prison. No one was ever allowed to leave, under threat of agonizing death. Hard by the steps leading down to the Nile was kept a pen of crocodiles. Any woman devising an escape was always caught. At such a time, the other women in the harem watched as the gates opposite the entrance were thrown open, and the screaming girl was led down the steps to be fed to the reptiles. First, her feet were slashed and lowered into the water. As the crocodiles chewed and swallowed and pulled, eunuchs held her in a tug-of war, so that she was slowly eaten alive, to die only when the beasts reached her heart. This greatly discouraged any other attempts to escape.

And so, the hundreds of women in the harem spent hours in

caring for their bodies and applying imaginative make-up. They learned exotic dances and to play harps and flutes and they formed small groups for games. The greatest game of all was ambition. As had happened in the past, a young man chosen to marry a princess could rescue his mother, if he loved her, and ensconce her in a luxurious dwelling, from which she could wield great power. Thus the women lived, and thus they schemed.

The gates were opened for Thothmes, and the chief eunuch greeted him formally, prostrating himself at Pharaoh's feet, never daring to raise his eyes to the god of Egypt. "Will Pharaoh allow me the honor of arranging a selection of the most delectable beauties from which to choose? Have you, sire, a desire of a special kind? Shall food and music be prepared? Only speak what you wish, God of Amon and Ra, and it will be done."

Thothmes felt a natural dislike for this creature whom he viewed as less than a man. However, Montu could be trusted in all things pertaining to the royal harem and performed his particular duties well. To dismiss him would be folly; besides, Thothmes' urgency and desire for pleasure was great.

"Montu, I leave all things to your good judgment. Before you proceed further, however, send a soldier of my guard to the palace for a chest of jewelry from which I may select a gift for the woman if she pleases me greatly. In my haste, I have overlooked my manners."

Montu rubbed his ample belly and grinned as he sent the soldier on his way. Surely, some of the baubles would fall into his hands. He would make certain of that.

And now, to work. Montu escorted Thothmes to an intricately carved pavilion and helped him settle upon soft pillows. Musicians played pleasing melodies—music that was off key, yet melodious and deep, of an eastern origin. Robust red wine from a freshly opened jar was poured into a delicate glass and faience bowl. Thothmes put aside his impatience. He intended to spend the day here, and he decided to savor every pleasure.

The women were wild with excitement, frenziedly donning their finest gauzes and silks. Slaves had whispered that Pharaoh was visiting the harem, and each woman wanted to appear before him dressed as beautifully as possible. Those whom Pharaoh had favored previously wore the golden armbands, bracelets, or rings he had bestowed upon them. These experienced women had come from all parts of the known world. As daughters of kings and emperors, they had been educated in the ways of love and tantalization. They were supremely confident and haughty. The others—the newer, inexperienced arrivals—trembled with fear. What would Pharaoh think of them? Each woman possessed two slaves, more if they had given birth to sons; and these servants tried to outdo each other in making their mistresses appealing.

And then there were the aged women. Some had never shared Pharaoh's couch and had spent their lives in frustration. Some had been favored once or twice long ago but had since been passed over, even though among them were those who had born sons now living in monasteries. The old ones would attend the choosing out of mere curiosity. After all, gossip was important to those who would never again see the world.

Montu sensed Pharaoh's urgency and thought first to send only the ones he deemed to be most beautiful and entertaining; but let there be one misjudgment and Pharaoh might have him fill the stomachs of the reptiles in the pit. Better and safer to have a general gathering. After Thothmes made his choices, Montu planned to present erotic entertainment to afford the sovereign further enjoyment. All the women were gathered in the garden of roses, either preening or quivering, and Montu led Thothmes to them.

As the broad-shouldered Pharaoh appeared at the oval gate, silence fell. This was Horus, son of Ra, Pharaoh Thothmes I of upper and lower Egypt. Battle scars crossed his chest and arms, and he stood rock solid and powerful. *Oh to be chosen to lie in his arms, and, perhaps bear his son!* There were many stories handed down of long-past harem women who had captured their king's heart. Today, all were thinking, "Oh please, Isis, Goddess of Love, let it be me. Let it be me!"

At a nod from Thothmes, Montu directed row upon row of

women to pass before Pharaoh. If the girl were new, he told from whence she came and of her accomplishments in music and dance. If a woman had been in the Pharaoh's bed before, he need say nothing. All passed in review; and as one who appealed to him approached, Thothmes tapped her shoulder and she passed into the silken-hung pavilion. None of the newest and youngest girls were chosen. Thothmes remembered what had transpired with Hatshepsut. Today, he would have women with experience, women who knew many ways to give great pleasure and suffer no harm. He would cause no hurt to a young girl this day.

When he tired of choosing, five women awaited him. He returned and walked into the pavilion, following the musky scent that trailed behind. He settled himself among the pillows and bade the ladies with him. Musicians somewhere beyond the walls were playing harps accompanied by the throb of deep drums. Yes, today he would enjoy himself.

The women, nestling close to Pharaoh, used every means, of which they knew many, to entice him. They offered cups of fine wine and bites of fruit, making certain he caught provocative glimpses of their bodies. All was done decorously; Thothmes was known to have distaste for common behavior.

The youngest, most lush of the new girls, were chosen to entertain with dance and song. All had been well trained by their royal families. Pharaoh would understand the words of their odd songs, as he spoke many languages. No one need interpret the swaying, spinning dances.

They came one by one. The number of musicians had increased, and the tunes they played were seductive. The first girl who stepped onto the fine carpet was unique among the newcomers. She had arrived in a long boat with a great dragon carved on its prow. Those who brought her were hairy, brutish men, intending to raid and pillage as they sailed up the Nile toward Thebes. They had been overconfident and killed many farmers before being slain themselves by Thothmes' army. A girl child of eight years, with thick gold braids, had been found in the vessel and placed in the harem. She was now fifteen, and this was her first appearance before her ruler.

Her yellow hair hung below her wide hips, and her breasts

were overlarge. She was a true oddity. Although beautiful and artfully made up in the Egyptian manner, she moved heavily. She would have been a rare prize to a Hittite, but Thothmes thought her ungainly and asked Montu to write upon a wax tablet that Pharaoh be reminded to use her as a gift when one was needed.

Next to enter was a pair of Oriental twins. The girls were gymnasts and Thothmes laughed at their antics. Although pleased with the entertainment, he had not forgotten the women surrounding him. He began to fondle a beauty on his right. She was a Hyksos with dark skin and a pungent aroma. A girl behind him began to rub her body against his back. Most delightful!

By the time the last girl began a teasing, weaving dance, swaying on small feet with bells on her ankles, Thothmes could no longer contain his ardor. He ordered that all lamps but one be removed. His lust was boundless. All five women were favored by him, and with great shouting and laughter, they pleasured each other. As they fondled the man before them, many breasts were bared and rubbed. Thothmes watched two women locked together in lustful embrace as he, at the same time rode the others, one after another. Much later, as he lay sprawled among his love mates, he felt sated and happy. And hungry!

Meanwhile, Montu had been busy indeed. He was not the chief eunuch without reason. Directions had been given, and the kitchen slaves were preparing many delicacies. Knowing Pharaoh's habits, Montu caused great platters of food to be brought to the pavilion.

Before eating, Thothmes insisted that they all plunge into the cool lake to wash away the residue of the afternoon's romp. Much splashing and giggling accompanied the refreshing swim. Pharaoh had honored all the women, and each felt she was surely to become the mother of a royal son.

Small tables set with dainty dishes of fine foods and jars of sweet wine were scattered around the pavilion. The food had been prepared just as Pharaoh liked it, and he ate and drank his fill. The women he had chosen had pleased him greatly, and now was the moment to bestow the gifts he had sent for.

"Montu, I am greatly pleased. Get the box my soldier has brought. I would reward the lovely ladies who have given me much pleasure." Montu came quickly. He was certain he had done well and was looking forward to a reward of his own.

Thothmes was careful to be equally generous to each woman. He had no desire for discord in his harem, and it could be said he was always fair. He presented each woman with a wide gold ring holding a small but precious stone. The women were delighted with his generosity, and each had a new jewel to flash before the ones not chosen.

To the reliable Montu, he presented a long, thick chain necklace, made the more valuable because its clasp bore the cartouche of Thothmes I. Montu was vastly pleased.

As Thothmes drove his chariot to the Thothmes' palace in the late night hours, his mind darted back to the night before and the remembrance of Hati this morning. Surely there could never be another so sweet, so beautiful. With bodily desires sated and peaceful mind, he would sleep deeply this night. Tomorrow he would speak gently to his new bride, and they would adjust to their life together in Maat, the order and peace of life. Always, it seemed, his heart would draw his mind back to the Great Royal Wife.

5

Hatshepsut lay with closed eyes, body still, and breath shallow. She heard Thothmes' guards as they came to attention far down the hallway. Pharaoh's steps grew nearer, and he paused at her doorway and then passed on to his apartments.

When all was quiet, large green eyes opened wide. Hatshepsut, Queen of all Egypt, rose and wrapped a woven sheep's-wool cape about herself. Beka heard her stirring and rose also. As she neared Hati, she stopped and drew back in awe. This was no longer her little one. Beka felt as had Euripides when he looked upon Hatshepsut's face the night before. A queen stood tall and straight before her. Fire burned in her eyes. The moonlight that fell upon her through the open wall made a glow around her. Her long hair was electrified from her linens and stood away from her in luminescence. By all the gods of Egypt above and below the world, here was a real queen of mystery.

"Send my handmaidens to bring food and wine. But first, Beka, send to me the captain of all the guards. He is Kamare. Tell him the supreme ruler of Egypt, Queen Hatshepsut, demands that he attend her now," Hatshepsut ordered.

Beka sent this command by one of the men guarding the Queen's apartments. The guard's eyes grew wide as he ran. No Great Wife in any memory had ever sent such an order.

Kamare was awakened in the barracks by the palace guard who spoke the order. "The supreme ruler of Egypt, Queen Hatshepsut, commands you to her now, this moment." It was, indeed, a portentous moment; Kamare must either obey the Queen, or inform the stewards and viziers of Pharaoh Thothmes of it and do nothing else. But he had been one of those who saw Thothmes bend knee and head to this Queen. The priests had paid homage to her first; and even before her birth, it had been said she was the holy and royal child of Isis and Horus. Kamare was a strong man of middle age, brave in battle and brilliant in strategy. He was aware that this was the time in his life when he must make a great decision, a firm commitment. And he made it.

Accompanied by the palace guard, Kamare, in full battle regalia, was on his way to the Queen's apartment within minutes. The wooden doors swung open for him, and he followed Beka into the innermost chamber and saw before him the vision that had so struck the old woman.

Hatshepsut had moved not a step, and the moonlight glowed brighter as the moon was low in the sky. Her head held no great crown; her hands were empty of flail and crook; but Kamare felt within himself the swallowing up of his soul. He prostrated himself before her and waited. He dared not speak first.

"Rise up, loyal Kamare," said Hatshepsut. "You are called by this name because it is the same as that of the great Bull of Maat. You will be my strength of peace also. Do you accept the charge I will give you?"

Kamare's face reflected his belief. "Yes, great Queen. I know you to be anointed by the gods. I am yours in all ways, for all the days of my life in the world of the living. Command me and your desire shall be done."

Hatshepsut's voice had betrayed no physical weakness, nor was there a quaver of doubt in her tone. Training had created a musical lilt to her pronunciation of words; but tonight, the voice she used was quiet, yet strong. "The moon is low and waning. Before Ra begins to light the sky in the east, you will choose the strongest troops and only those who swear loyalty to the cartouche I now give you. Beka, bring me the small cedar chest from beside my bed."

Beka handed it to Hatshepsut. She opened it and took out an oval of solid gold and a gold ring with a smaller crest. Both held the hieroglyphics of her cartouche, and both would allow the bearer to make orders of his own in her name. It was a gamble but a wise and ambitious one.

She handed both pieces of gold to Kamare and reached up and placed her hands upon his broad shoulders. "I will rest easily now, Kamare. I have the wisest general of all the armies of a new Egypt. Begin to build my strength within my empire. Take from the mines all the gold that is needed. My troops must be the finest. Their horses will be the fastest and their weapons the cruelest, if need be. Do not, in your haste for strength, neglect the families of those who are to serve me. For I would own the hearts of these soldiers as well as their arms. For now, I will need no additional palace protection from enemies within, but I will call upon you when that time arrives.

"You may appear to serve Pharaoh Thothmes as usual, but I must know all before it occurs. We must be wise, you and I, for through your help, I shall rule Egypt alone; and together we shall rebuild old monuments and raise great new ones. Your neglected armies will train once more, but they will train for Queen Hatshepsut alone. Are you one in thought with me, Kamare?"

"My heart is filled with strength, and you have my promise and word of truth that all shall be as you desire, and more. I have great knowledge of these things. You armies will be built and trained away from other eyes. I request only that I may choose new guards immediately for your halls, rooms, and garden," said Kamare.

Throughout the conversation Hatshepsut had looked intently into Kamare's eyes. Her gaze had not faltered. "You have my permission to do anything you feel necessary. There is no end to the gold you will need. Egypt has much of it, and it is mine. Take what you want, and do not account to me for it. I place my complete trust in you. My last order is that you build a great house for your family. A man who works as hard as you in the future shall have safety and comfort for his family. It is not natural to stay always in the barracks. Your rank now entitles you to a general's comforts. One will balance the other. Maat, peace, peace always with you, Kamare. One day we shall need remembrances of these days of peace. Go now, General Kamare."

Hatshepsut dropped her arms; and Kamare, newly made a general by his Queen, backed away and placed the tip of his sword upon the cartouche, then picked up both and left her apartments. In placing the ring upon his finger, he dedicated himself to the huge challenge before him.

Pharaoh had not sought Kamare's advice or his company for many months, and then only to hunt with him or have him as one of hundreds of guests at a great feast. Now, his talents would no longer be wasted. Queen Hatshepsut was right. The army lay in partial ruin through lack of discipline. There were still many good men to be found in the ranks and many strong, young men, often second sons of farmers, who would desire honor as a soldier of the Queen. So much to do and so little time in which to do it! As for Kamare's family, he had none except an aged mother who dwelt in Thebes. She had a small house there, and he sent her money upon which to live. Now, he could build a fine house on the riverbank, and she would live in luxury with a suitable staff of servants. He would have superior horses and, yes, he would have a young and beautiful wife. A man needed children.

A smile had appeared on his face as he thought of his great good fortune; but he stopped on the steps of the palace and shook his mind free. He had much to do in the name of Queen Hatshepsut before he could take time to think of himself.

As the eastern skies lightened and welcomed the sun god, a company of dauntless men stationed themselves at the entrance to Queen Hatshepsut's quarters. They had been hand picked for strength and experience and wore full battle gear. Each had sworn loyalty upon the golden cartouche, and, if need be, each would die in defense of it. The guards would change every six hours. Kamare had begun his work.

Hatshepsut awakened to the sounds of birds in the trees of her private garden. Although the singing made beautiful music, it did nothing to lighten her resolve. Her heart was cold in her young breast. She had truly intended to sacrifice all for the royal succession of her country, but the brutality forced upon her body caused devastation worse than pain. She was filled with disgust and hatred of Thothmes. How dare he use her thus! She was a goddess; and, now, due to the Pharaoh's public display of subjugation, she was more royal and godlike than he! No one as insensitive as Thothmes would touch her again. She would procreate with another Pharaoh, a man of her own choosing. *Thothmes would be replaced.*

Like an old and battle-wise general, she had called upon her mind as she feigned sleep for so many hours; thus her first move with Kamare. Only by holding a position of great strength would she be able to fulfill her visions. This she now had. Kamare, the strong bull of Maat and leader of victorious armies, was hers alone. What a relief it had been to have her first step executed so easily. After her morning bath, she dismissed her attendants, ordering them to the outermost room of the apartments, and asked Beka to fetch Euripides.

At the time Hatshepsut had sworn Kamare into loyal service, Euripides was snoring soundly in his lavish bed. He had watched the sleeping Queen for many hours from a hiding place in the walls. Yes, this Queen was impressive even as she slept. Finally, when the moon was high, he tired of his vigil and withdrew.

He knew nothing of the night's events when the guard summoned him, so he was unprepared for the man he found outside his chambers. What was this? This was no pale and painted palace guard. This man was darkened from sun and sand. Moreover, he wore full battle dress, and his limbs were firm and well muscled. Something must be afoot; and he, the great Euripides, was caught empty-headed. Nevertheless, he had been summoned. Obviously, the new Queen was in need of him. There were opportunities anew awaiting to be snatched from the great wealth of Hatshepsut. Euripides dressed quickly, taking time only to sweeten his breath and arrange his well-cared-for hair.

Carrying himself with a great sense of importance, Euripides followed the guard, soon having to skip a step or two to keep up. Had the guard been less fearsome, he would have upbraided the soldier for his undignified gait. However, he prudently discarded that idea and proceeded at a half run behind the monster to the hall outside the Queen's chamber, where he stumbled to a halt and gasped in astonishment. The apartments of the queen were protected by the fiercest of warriors, a full contingent of them.

Now, fully awake and aware, he saw that the thick leather breastplate of each man was burned with the cartouche of

Hatshepsut. Unheard of! What was this? Never had a Queen since Queen Titesheri dared such a statement—and Queen Titesheri had ruled alone. Slowly, Euripides began to understand the situation. Hatshepsut must be planning to set herself up as at least the equal of Pharaoh. Was there more? Well, he had not thrived for so long by missing opportunities. But what of Pharaoh? Unless the Great Royal Wife protected him, Euripides knew he could not serve her without great risk. All these thoughts raced through his mind as he was led into Queen Hatshepsut's receiving room. At sight of her, his decision was made.

Hatshepsut had been bathed, oiled, and dressed by her ladies. She wore a long garment of pleated linen and the single, white-coned crown with golden cobra rested on her brow. With sandaled feet braced upon an ebony footstool, she seemed to be at ease in her golden chair, even though her back and neck were rigid and unbending.

With graceful movement of arm and hand, she indicated that Euripides was to rise from his prostrated position and take a low seat by her feet. To show that she honored him, she sent a noble lady for an alabaster bowl of morning wine for "my loyal Euripides."

All was as planned. This evil but brilliant man at her feet must also be in her service, for she must deal in many dark things. He could be of use and then done away with. Dead men do not speak evil of anyone. Now to the task at hand. "Euripides, as Queen, I have need of your intelligence and loyalty. Do you give these freely?"

"Yes, my Queen. I shall endeavor to serve you in all ways. You need but ask and my unworthy services are yours. To show my sincerity, I would reveal to you the secrets of the inner walls of this great palace and all the means by which one may appear and disappear in many private rooms."

Hatshepsut was shocked. She, just a young princess a few days ago, had known nothing of these things. But she did not show surprise and simply nodded in agreement. "I shall value your loyalty; and as my confidant, you shall be rewarded." She knew well the necromancer's love of gold.

"As you have seen, Pharaoh has placed me above himself; and I have taken it upon myself to guard my godliness from further assault at this moment. The thing I need from you now is time. Pharaoh must not enter here, as I place my thoughts upon the welfare of Egypt. I need this time to formulate my plans. You were kind to me in my time of distress, and I do not forget. I give you now this ring in thanks and send you to perceive a manner in which Pharaoh can be rendered without desire. I do not wish him harmed. I wish him away from me. Go now, and serve me well. In two days time, you will be sent for, and we will explore the walls of my palace."

The necromancer left filled with glee, although he was careful to keep a solemn countenance. He, Euripides, would lead this one as he had led Queen Ahmose who now slept in the Necropolis. What great riches would be his! He went happily to his rooms, admiring the gold ring the queen had given him. Today, a ring; in months, chests of treasure.

As the necromancer went his way, Pharaoh awakened in his bed, sated with the pleasures he had enjoyed in his harem the day before. He called for food and wine. A healthy and robust man must feed the emptiness in his belly.

His thoughts turned to Hatshepsut. *My charming queen will be pleased to see me this morning. We shall talk; and if she wishes, I will sail with her on the Nile in my reed boat. She will take delight in watching her husband as he brings down the ducks upon which we shall later dine. First, however, she may desire to join me in a morning bath, and we shall breakfast together.* He called an attendant into his chamber and sent him to bid the Great Royal Wife a fine morning and to invite her to join her husband.

The noble retainer returned on halting feet, eyes wide in fear. Pharaoh had been known to deal harshly with messengers bearing bad news.

"Speak, Maspero, most favored of my friends. You appear to have seen the inhabitants of the Necropolis stalking your heels. What have you to say to me?"

"Great Thothmes, mighty Pharaoh, I would have you see for yourself. I dare not believe my own eyes."

Thothmes had entered his bath and would hear this thing from Maspero's lips. "Speak, Maspero," was the abrupt command.

And Maspero obeyed. "The quarters of the Great Royal Wife, Queen Hatshepsut, are guarded by many fierce-appearing men of war. They turned me away without a word. I have never seen these soldiers before, but they have the freshly burned cartouche of Queen Hatshepsut upon their chest leathers."

Pharaoh's expression changed from curiosity to a blank stare. He lay very still. As a royal man, he understood the meaning of this act; and as he was far from a fool, he would think about this carefully. To attempt to contradict Hatshepsut's actions as co-regent would be unwise. She was co-regent and more. Thothmes was now fully aware that his behavior at the time of the coronation had placed her in a very high position, indeed. If he were to retain his position and deal with Hatshepsut as a mere royal wife, he would need to use guile, not force. She was, after all, of a scant fourteen years. His confidence returned, and he beckoned to a slave to bring his linen and oils.

In her bedchamber, Hatshepsut sat still as her newly appointed cosmetologist, a young lad from the temple of Bek, applied her royal make-up for the first time. Before her coronation, she had been forbidden these attentions; and she watched with wonder in her tall mirror of electrum.

There was no need for heavy cosmetics to cover the perfect skin of her firm, young face. Her eyebrows were accented by a small brush that the boy dipped into a glass jar containing wax mixed with obsidian. He drew her plucked brows into a more upturned pattern. They had always had a winged look; but now they were darkened, and each hair was waxed so that it lay precisely where it was placed.

Her lips were patted with a rounded marble coated with thick glossy oil and wax. The tincture had been tinted by the juice of red berries. This same dye was rubbed lightly upon and below her cheekbones.

Next came the painting of her eyes. Kohl was drawn around each eye in thick lines. These lines joined at the outer edges of her eyes and extended and inch on either side, making her appear older.

A tray of eyelid colors was placed before her. There was bright blue from powdered turquoise, gold leaf, powdered gold, and many other colors from various materials. Hatshepsut pointed to a tiny box, filled with he carapaces of brilliant green beetles. The shells glistened an opaque blue-green. The priest put four into a mortar and, with a pestle, ground them into fine dust. He put an oil base on her lids from the inner corners near her nose to the tips of the black kohl lines. The dust was carefully laid upon the base, there to glisten a shimmering emerald green shot through with tiny hints of blue as she moved her head.

At this moment, the Great Royal Wife was indescribably lovely. Her near fifteen years were belied; her appearance and manner were those of a grown woman. The transformation was complete. The long-ago part of her childhood name, "more beautiful than anything," had proved to be true.

Hatshepsut did not call for her golden collar with its birds of blue turquoise, nor did she accept the heavy belt with swinging pearls that Beka proffered. The queen had studied long in the royal library. Not only had she learned the language of her Greek ancestors, she had absorbed the contents of their writings. To adorn herself with less would make her person appear to be more. She did, however, put on the large gold ring in the shape of a beetle. It carried two cartouches on its under side, hers and Pharaoh Thothmes'.

Hatshepsut stepped to the throne in her reception room and awaited his arrival. Although steeled to her purpose, she wore a soft smile.

"Beka, I would break my morning fast. I think a small fish and a shat cake. Send also a runner to Euripides. I am expecting a special wine for Pharaoh." Beka sent a slave for the food but went alone to seek out Euripides. She understood well. Sure enough, when she reached his apartment, he stood smiling in the doorway holding a fine jar of wine. Its seal did not appear to have been broken.

"Tell our Queen to partake of very little of this wine. It is for King Thothmes to enjoy. Be off with you now." Beka returned just as the Pharaoh was speaking to the captain of the guards at Hatshepsut's quarters. Oddly, he did not seem angry, but rather amused.

"Yes. Inform the Great Royal Wife that her husband would spend the morning with her." And he smiled. The guards had expected immense rage. It was with much relief that they led the amiable Pharaoh to the audience chamber of his Queen.

When Thothmes beheld the vision that Hatshepsut presented, he was rendered speechless. This was not the soft little girl he had taken to wife. Before him sat a regal woman of unsurpassed beauty, wearing cosmetics entirely new to her. Her gracious gesture invited him to share her large chair. The stars in her eyes glittered below her iridescent green eyelids as she smiled upon him with rosy lips.

Oh, lovely one, how warmly you receive me. How foolish I was to become alarmed because of new guards. We shall spend wondrous days in sport and love.

"My wife, I see that you have gone to much trouble to please me, and I am more than pleased. I am so happy with you. We will rule Egypt in Maat and in love. You are truly the finest treasure in Egypt."

Hatshepsut shyly lowered her gaze and patted the pillows at her side. Thothmes moved closer and placed his arm about her shoulders. His eyes devoured her loveliness, and his groin pulsed with desire. He would have her this morning—but this time he would be gentle.

"Pour the wine, Beka. My lord would share a bowl with me to celebrate the peace of the morning." With her own delicate hands, Hatshepsut raised the bowl to his lips, pretending to sip from the other side of the vessel. Thothmes drained the bowl and smacked his thick lips. The sight sent a shudder down the Queen's spine.

Thothmes motioned to Beka to refill the bowl. The wine was delicious; and while drinking, he nibbled at the charcoal-broiled fish. "Sweet Hati, you are so devoted. Shall we sail in my boat today? You shall see the gallant hunter bring down many ducks with his throwing stick and his arrows." Without his realization, all lustful thoughts had melted away. His strength remained, but his mind was far removed from lovemaking.

"Yes, my lord. Let us do as you suggest. It is a lovely morning and one that would be well spent upon the river." Thothmes and Hati walked to his apartments and out onto the balcony. A slim reed boat with folded sail was moored at the foot of the steps leading to the water. The smiling pair stepped into the boat, and an oarsman rowed them through the canal to the marshes of the Nile.

Thothmes was expert in the sport of hunting and soon had many ducks lying in the boat. He felt he had never been happier. Occasionally Hati handed him a clay bowl of the wine she had brought with her. A shade had been erected so that the sun would not darken her skin, and she glimmered in her loveliness as she sat smiling beneath it.

Hatshepsut was enjoying herself even though she had not expected to do so. The river was green and cool; the lotus blossoms and water lilies were sweet. Even the breeze held a caress. She forced herself to think of the coming evening. Could she continue to give Pharaoh this wine? Would he awaken in his bed and come upon her in her sleep? Could her guards keep him from her? Surely not—one invited punishment by death if he dared to oppose Pharaoh. She decided she must soon put an end to this miserable man.

Ambition burned in her, and Thothmes stood in her way. In the warm sun, the Nile-green eyes of the Great Royal Wife turned cold as stone.

The oarsman tied up the boat at the foot of the stairs and helped the royal couple ashore. They both seemed merry and tired. A favorite sport had left each yearning for a cool bath and rest.

Thothmes escorted Hatshepsut to the door of her apartments and promised that they would later feast upon a meal of roasted duck. She bowed slightly in recognition of his thoughtfulness and slipped away. He went to his chambers where he prepared for his bath. As he sank into the rose-colored pool, it flitted through his mind that he had planned lovemaking for the day, but that somehow, they had hunted instead. Well, no matter. After a refreshing sleep, they would have the cool night to themselves.

In her quarters, Hatshepsut bathed in the tubs below her bedchamber. Make-up removed, eyes opened wide in concentration, she seemed a child again. Inwardly, it was quite different. *Not again. No, not ever again! He shall not touch me!* "Beka! Send for Euripides at once!"

As the messenger turned to obey, the necromancer stepped from the shadows to the side of the pool. "No need to send for me, royal one. I am here, and I anticipate your thoughts. Dismiss all but Beka, and we will speak of this night."

Hatshepsut did as he bade, and then turned to the man who had come through the walls. "What of tonight, Euripides? Treasure is yours if you can hold Pharaoh at bay this night. I need but one more passing of sun and moon. What can you advise?"

"Great Queen, send word tonight that you are ill with your monthly flow, and you will have four or more days rather than one. In the meantime, I have in my employ a woman who dances as a sorceress does. She will inflame your husband and perform such acts upon him as to render him helpless under her spell for a day or two. The rest we can contemplate at the end of four days."

"You shall receive a cask of pearls this night, Euripides. You have earned them. When Pharaoh is safely occupied with your harlot, we will explore these walls. I would have all your knowledge of them."

Euripides thought, *And for this, a cask of pearls. Better and better.*

6

Hatshepsut sank gratefully into her cool bath. She did not need four days. She had decided that afternoon on the marshes what would befall Pharaoh. Her plan must not fail.

When Beka informed Pharaoh of her mistress's illness, he was disappointed but knew these complaints of women to be unchangeable. He put his best face upon the circumstances and sent the Queen the promised roasted ducks.

The evening gathering of nobles was already heavily into drink when Thothmes arrived at the great hall. He chewed dispiritedly upon his ducks and bread and washed the food down with jar after jar of wine.

Smoke from incense drifted through the room. The crowd fell silent noticing a voluptuous woman weaving through the haze as a snake might rise from beneath its rock. An oiled body was crowned with flowing black hair; dark and sultry eyes dominated a sensuous face. The gauze she wore concealed nothing, and her pelvis began to sway to the quickening beat of drums. Her own hands held up her breasts to point them at Thothmes, and her tongue flicked in and out as she licked and sucked her lower lip.

Pharaoh's eyes bulged, and he panted with animal lust. He strode to the stage, grabbed the woman by her arm, and pulled her after him to his bedchamber. His garments were on the floor in seconds, and he ripped the flimsy covering from her body with one swift tug. They tumbled into the bed, and she proceeded to tease and play with him. She would not let him mount her, but reached out and took his pulsating organ into her mouth only to let loose after a moment so that her tongue might lick elsewhere. She twisted and turned, slithering over Pharaoh from head to toe. Thothmes could no longer control his need. He grabbed the woman by her long hair, threw her on her back, and thrust himself deep inside her. Again and again, he plunged until orgasm released him from lust's grip. He fell into a deep sleep, the harlot close beside him.

Hatshepsut sent a trusted guard to summon Kamare. Euripides had promised four days, but she must prepare well, and now was the time to inform him of the part he would play in Pharaoh's fate. The guard returned to tell her that Kamare was out of the city recruiting men for her service. The guard further explained that he had taken it upon himself to send five riders in search of Kamare to tell him of her summons.

Kamare gone! But of course, he would lose no time in his work. Still, I need him here now. Will he return shortly? Bah. Be still, my mind. I can put these hours, perhaps days, to good use. "Beka, send for Euripides. After that, I want you to go in my boat to my floating pavilion. Swathe yourself in linens and stay there as if you were I until dawn is about to break or until I signal you with a moving light. You will do this each night until I direct you otherwise."

The moment Beka left for Euripide's rooms, the man emerged from behind the altar of Isis. *So, he can see all and hear all. He can spy at will upon the gods of Egypt. Oh, ambitious man, once I know all that you know, you will be a meal for the crocodiles.* For the first time, her composure slipped, and Euripides saw anger on that beautiful face.

"Beloved Queen, be not displeased. I seek only to serve you, and have I not done all that I said? Join me now, and I will reveal to your eyes the innermost parts of this palace."

While he was making the effort to appease Hatshepsut, she regained her composure and cast a benign and approving gaze upon the necromancer. It would do no good to alarm him. "Good Euripides, you please me well. When we have seen the secrets of the palace of one hundred rooms, I shall give you the chest of gold pieces I received the day Pharaoh made me his Great Royal Wife."

Greed is a wonderful deceiver. It can blot out all dangers and harden or soften any heart. Thinking all the while of his magnificent reward, he chose to reveal everything. *When she realizes how much I know of palace life and how I can serve her by my stealth access to private chambers, she will rely upon me even more.* Euripides pressed a recessed statue of Bek, the cat goddess, and, without a sound, the altar to Isis swung open. They stepped into a wide hallway of clay bricks, and he closed the altar behind them.

First, he took her into the underground chamber where he devised and mixed his cures, poisons, and other potions. He pointed with pride to the rolls of papyrus upon which were written ancient secrets of the occult world. Then they went up, pausing at the great hall, where he showed her how to turn a hollow pillar on the wall, to slip in and out. Up again, and across the roof of the great hall into another corridor above the quarters assigned honored guests. In the floor were many peep-holes that looked down into these rooms. Small tiles fashioned to slide aside when the holes were in use covered them.

Next, he led her to the eastern side of the palace through a honeycomb of arches and halls to stand at last in the cool space secreted behind one wall of Pharaoh's bedchamber. Euripides lifted a panel above the bed as Pharaoh and the woman were beginning their debauchery.

Hatshepsut watched in fascination as the experienced harlot worked her sinuous wiles upon Thothmes. *So this is how to please a man.* She watched as they fell apart at the end and slept. Strange—the woman seemed to have actually enjoyed the act. *Evidently I have much to learn about this world of love-making.*

Euripides showed her how to slip into Pharaoh's bedchamber and then took her back to her own. "Loyal servant, I am tired from our travels through the inner palace. I shall have the chest of gold delivered to you from my treasury in five days' time. Return to your quarters. I bid you goodnight."

He left by way of the altar, overjoyed with the anticipation of the treasure soon to be his. With this vast fortune, added to all that Ahmose had given him, he could return to his native Syria and live as a king himself. Just a few more days—that was all. Unless, of course, Pharaoh Thothmes would care to hear that Hatshepsut was building an army and had sent for Kamare.

Also, would Pharaoh be interested in knowing his finest leader of armies sworn allegiance to the Great Royal Wife and to her alone? Possibilities, possibilities. But first, to secure his gold.

It was two days' time, before Kamare's chariot wheeled to a stop at the palace steps in the late night hours. Kamare had not slept for a day and a night, so hard had he pushed his teams of horses. Throwing the reins to a guard, he leaped up the stairs and passed without challenge to Hatshepsut's doors. Wakened by his voice, Hatshepsut rose, wrapped her naked body in silks, and hurried to greet him.

"Kamare, there is little time, and we cannot speak here. Open those drapes a little and light this lantern and wave it back and forth in the opening." He did as commanded, all the while stealing glances at the Queen. The lids of her kohl-lined eyes were covered with crushed pearls, and gold dust burnished here scented body. She had changed so much since their last meeting; it seemed almost as though she were a different person.

Just as Hatshepsut threw a cloak over her silk wrappings, the gold boat touched the steps at the water's edge. Beka and the oarsman stepped out, and Kamare and Hatshepsut got in. "Row out to the floating pavilion, Kamare. We must not be overheard, and there, I know it will be secure."

Hatshepsut had slept little, and it was not by chance that she was so exquisitely made up at such an early hour. She had watched Thothmes and his wild harlot through the peephole in the walls; and the sight had roused an excitement in her, a churning of blood she had never felt before and did not fully understand. She sat facing her great general. The sight of the bulging muscles in his chest and the man-scent of him sent her heart racing.

Night-blooming flowers perfumed the mists rising from the water. Kamare nudged the little boat into its mooring and made it fast to a post. Hatshepsut said, "Help me, Kamare. I am small and bundled in my cloak. Should I attempt the step to the platform, it could prove disastrous. I do not care to fall headfirst into the lake and provide breakfast for the huge crocodile that is no doubt lying in wait for just such an opportunity." Kamare laughed and his strong arms lifted the slight girl as he would a child, and she laughed against his chest. Silver bells tinkled with the sway caused by his weight, and her scent made him light-headed.

"Draw the curtains facing the palace, Kamare. No one must suspect that we are here." She sat down upon a silken cushion and pulled him down beside her. Leaning close to him, she whispered, "I have been taken by Pharaoh Thothmes once, and I shall never be taken again. Your oath ties you to me. He will wait another day as I have arranged for a wanton woman to fulfill his appetites; but soon he will be upon me. I know that what I am about to ask of you is right for Egypt. You, yourself, have seen the fallen monuments, the undisciplined armies, and the fat, corrupt tax takers. My people grow discontented and have no pride in a pharaoh who would venture no further from his golden palace than the duck marshes." As she spoke, she had thrown aside her cloak, and her silk wrapping loosened more with each move and gesture she made.

Heat rose in Kamare, and he knew he would give her anything—anything. Bowing his head, he said, "Command me, Queen Hatshepsut. My heart, head, and body are here to do your bidding. Have I not ridden like the wind to answer your summons?"

"You have served me well thus far. What I am about to propose, however, will require your unswerving loyalty, possibly your life."

"A general could ask for no greater honor than to die in your service, my Queen. Only tell me what it is I can do for you, and your wishes will be met."

Hatshepsut felt great relief. If Kamare had not agreed so readily to do whatever was asked of him, she would not have dared continue with her scheme. "When my husband inquires about my health, I will say that I will be well in the evening. But I will also say to him that the joy of a lion skin, from a fresh kill, will make me laugh with him, as it will prove him to be the strongest of men. Then, Kamare, he will call for you. He no doubt does not know that you have been gone, so entertained has he been of late.

"In the desert, surrounded by soldiers loyal to me, you will find a lion; and you will arrange that his lion shall attack Pharaoh. His blood must flow unto death. I will leave the doing of it to you, my general. From this, I shall rise as sole ruler of Egypt. Queen Hatshepsut will be a great queen, a queen to make Egypt strong once again."

Her recent observations of Thothmes with the devil-woman had made Hatshepsut curious, and she longed to cry out in pleasure as they had. With breasts exposed, she put her lips close to his as she asked him again, "Are you mine, Kamare?"

There was no need for her to seduce the general. He was a strong, healthy man; and he beheld before his eyes and close to his body, a woman of great sensuality. She was innocent of the ways of men, he was sure. But there was no mistaking the invitation in her voice and in the pressure of her thighs against his. His arms enfolded her, and as they kissed, she felt as though all breath were drawn from her lungs. His erection pressed hard against her, and he moved slowly back and forth across her body. Oh! The sensations that swept over her. She burned; she pushed against him and brought his mouth down to her breasts. He sucked her breasts, first one and then the other, all the while continuing the movement against the cleft between her legs. Hatshepsut cried out softly, never knowing she had done so.

Kamare removed her silken wrap and she lay bare beside him. He kissed her, and his hands caressed her body in long, slow strokes. He was an experienced lover, and he could see that she could no longer wait. He held himself over her with one hand and used the other to lift her small round hips to him. Kamare covered the small, panting mouth with his and slowly entered her. He stayed buried in her tight passage, only moving gently from side to side.

She could smell him, taste him, and oh—the feel of him! It was an ecstasy such as she had never imagined. Then he began to push in more deeply and withdraw slowly. With each withdrawal, her hands grabbed at his thighs, straining to pull him in more deeply still. His movements became more and more rapid. Then, paralyzing pressure, wild, bucking joy. She called his name over and over. He whispered his love in the midst of his ardor. And then, peace.

They lay a little apart, she on his arm with hand upon his chest. Kamare could scarcely believe what had passed. *What have I let myself do? True, queens have taken lovers in the past—all know this to be so. But she is so young, and I am but a hardened soldier of nearly thirty-five years. And yet, I love her so.* His heart thumped in his great chest, and she felt it with delight.

Now she understood what lovemaking was. She felt the exquisite peace it brought to man and woman and realized that the act manifested and bound the love held only in minds. The flesh was a wonderful instrument.

"Kamare," she whispered. "Kamare, when we are thus and alone, you must call me by the names lovers call each other, for I feel a great love for you."

"Yes my lovely Queen, my Hati. I shall call you my love. But now, morning approaches, and my identity will be visible to all in an hour's time. I go willingly and with devotion to do as you have asked. If Pharaoh returns alive, I shall not. No, my love. Do not let tears fall. Know that I am Kamare, the invincible. You could not have chosen a man more capable of helping you create the world you wish. I must go now, love. Let me go."

Hatshepsut had held him close for one last kiss. She draped her long cloak over his shoulders and drew the hood forward to conceal his face. "Go then, my strong and handsome lover and send Beka to me. May your arms be as strong as your heart is true. My father, Horus, shall guard thee."

And so Kamare rowed back across the lake to make preparations and choose the most trustworthy soldiers of the few army units still stationed in Thebes. He assured himself that, among these remaining, there were many men who would follow the Queen without question.

The majority of the troops were in Karmak and the desert oases, breaking in new horses and forging new weapons. Kamare had shown his ring to the Master of the Treasuries, and he had used large quantities of gold to good purpose. The soldiers were well fed and well housed. The horses they bought, many from the wandering desert tribes, were the best to be had. The men in the service of Queen Hatshepsut had left homes well provisioned and families well cared for because they were being well paid for the first time in a decade. Without apprehension they had all sworn on the cartouche Kamare held before them. Only a just and divine Queen would be so generous. They wore her colors on their new uniforms with pride: green for the mother river, the Nile; and gold for the greatness of Egypt. Yes, long live Queen Hatshepsut. It was understood that no praise was to be given to Thothmes I. Let him raise an army of his own!

7

Thothmes had tired of the woman. She was as a snake, forever writhing. She had inspired him for two days, but he sent her away early in the morning of the third day wearing a gold necklace and carrying a small bag of silver pieces. He bathed and ordered breakfast brought to his rooms.

Rested and with appetite appeased, he gave considerable thought as to how he would pass the day. His first notion was to invite Hati to his chambers. *We could play some games perhaps "senet" or "jackal and hounds." Surely one of these would amuse her. No, I think better of that. It is a magnificent morning, and I would be away from the palace for a time. I will drive my chariot to the Valley of the Kings and see what progress is being made in the construction of my tomb. Too much time has passed since my last inspection.*

Thothmes halted the chariot and called to a workman, "Here, man. I need a message delivered. Find my royal architect, Ineni, and tell him that Pharaoh awaits without the tomb and wishes to consult with him immediately."

The trembling man backed humbly away, then turned and ran as though a pack of hyenas were at his heels. Thothmes descended from the chariot and studied his surroundings.

There was a village nearby which housed the workmen, but little else to show that an elaborate tomb for a mighty Pharaoh was anywhere in the vicinity. Slaves had been at work for tens of years upon the tombs of Thothmes I. It was cut into the cliffs across the river from Karnak, and he had named the site the Valley of the Kings. His tomb was the first to be placed at this site, and it was his aspiration that his tomb would not be robbed or his mummy desecrated by looters tearing at it for the gold it contained in its wrappings. The chief royal architect, Ineni, was gifted in these things. He had raised many monuments to

Thothmes I. One, a giant sphinx, had the body of a lion, which symbolized power to the Egyptian people. The stone face was that of Thothmes. It had the protruding teeth that were a family characteristic of the seventeenth and eighteenth dynasties. Hatshepsut was the first to be spared this deformity.

Ineni had constructed Thothmes' tomb in secrecy, using a downward tunnel much copied in later years. The top of the narrow steps in the main tunnel was to be sealed with a flat rock with nothing to show that a king rested there. The steps went deep into the earth and ended in a small room with a few articles of wood and a plain granite sarcophagus in which a mummy had already been placed. The sarcophagus bore the cartouche of Thothmes I. But, two-thirds of the way down the staircase a door was cunningly concealed in the wall so as to be invisible to any who did not know of its existence. Before it had been covered with plaster, it had swung easily on round balls of copper and marble. This door opened into a passage that led upward into a massive room in which was stored a great treasure. Space had been left for the final placement of gold and food and wine at the time of death. At the top of one wall was an opening through which a large coffin could be passed. This opening admitted to a deep hole, meant to kill any plunderers getting past the treasure room. Now wooden scaffolding, which would be removed after Pharaoh's mummy was interred, had been placed across the hole to allow access to a wide hallway with narrow steps on each side. In the middle of the hallway lay a huge ship covered in hammered gold. Pharaoh would sail this ship through the underground River Styx at night and ride his golden chariot across the sky with the sun god, Ra, during the day.

The hallway containing the ship opened into a room magnificent in its detail. Life-sized Nubian slaves, sculpted from ebony, ivory, and gold, held spears to guard the Pharaoh's solid gold chariot. Gold wings extended from each side. Horses carved from granite, with ivory eyes and electrum-covered hooves, stood in gold traces. The granite was filled with grace and movement, as was every carved being in this, the most important of rooms.

Great artists had labored day and night to carve and paint,

and the wall depicted scenes in vivid colors. The scenes showed how Thothmes had lived his days. The pictures told stories of love of family, duty to all the gods, and the heart of the Pharaoh being weighed on the scale of life by Anubis, the jackal-headed god of the underworld. Thothmes was depicted in a reed boat hunting ducks and catching fish in nets. He was shown judging his subjects with fairness and protecting them in war. Hieroglyphics sang his praises as a just king deserving of the leisures of the afterlife. And, lastly, a polished sarcophagus of rose quartz lay open. It was so huge and heavy that many hands would be needed to place the lid over the gold coffin of the king. Above all was the ceiling, dark blue with silver stars.

Ineni was the first architect to solve the problem of light by which to work. In the past, painters and workers used candles and torches when working underground. These left the ceilings covered with soot.

Ineni ordered huge disks of electrum, the metal that was a combination of gold and silver and the nearest thing Egyptians possessed to a mirror, to be made. Slaves stood outside the tomb and turned these disks with the movement of the sun so that large shafts of brilliant light were sent down the staircase. There, other slaves held a large disk to direct the light to bounce off even more disks until, finally, it reached the room where the artists, painters, carvers, and goldsmiths could enjoy the benefits of daylight while working far underground.

The tomb room containing the sarcophagus and the death pit with sharp spears at the bottom had been prepared first. They were then walled with stone and plastered over so as to appear like other walls.

It seemed a long time since the workman had disappeared, and Pharaoh was growing impatient. He was about to summon another messenger when Ineni stepped forth from what looked to be a shadow on the face of the cliff. He approached and bowed his head, waiting for permission to speak. "Well, royal architect, how goes the construction of my tomb? What progress have you to report?"

So great was Ineni's genius that he had become a revered

confidant of Pharaoh, one who held the safety of Thothmes' after-life in his mind and hands. "Mighty Pharaoh, great god Horus, may I give pleasure to your ears with my report. The work on your tomb is near completion. A few more weeks, and all will be done. Please reflect upon a suggestion I wish to make to insure that your resting place will not be plundered."

Thothmes nodded. "What is it you wish to say? Do not be afraid to speak. I trust your wisdom in these matters."

"Mighty Pharaoh, I suggest you have orders drawn to put to death all workers and artists in the village near the tomb once it is finished. No one must remain to tell of this secret place. Such an order has not been given in the past; and eventually, the guards left there for protection of the tombs have sometimes violated them. I will supervise the sealing of the secret rooms and then cause boulders to be thrown down the staircase upon those men. Priests will enter the lower chamber willingly, there to take poison and enjoy the afterlife with Pharaoh, but they will know nothing of the secret rooms. Then four others and I will place the final flat rock over the entrance and cover it with sand. I shall give these four opium-laced wine in celebration; and, as they ride back to the river Nile, across from Karnak, they will fall from their donkeys one by one. A loyal and trusted officer of your guard will slay them, and the jackals of the desert will erase all parts of them. May it be a final offering to the god Anubis."

As Thothmes drove back to the palace late in the day, he was pleased at the sights that greeted his eyes. The Nile was receding from the annual flood, leaving rich, black soil behind, and crops were about to be planted. This signaled, also, the time for him to visit Karnak. He looked forward to the sail on the river. *The priests must provide a smaller bull this year. The one I wrestled last year was far too strong. Yes, I will order a small bull, and it shall be given a mild potion that will render it less vigorous. Hati will think me as strong as in my youth. Not that I am old by any means! But my life these last ten years has been less active. There have been no campaigns, and I have grown soft. No matter; all will be well. I will do some planting of my own, and Hati will bear our son. She is the last young female wholly of the Thothmesid line and must be fruitful lest a half-royal child from the harem eventually follow me as Pharaoh.*

His thoughts awakened his impatience. *Hati has had time enough to recover! I will send word that she will dine with me tomorrow evening.*

When he arrive at the palace, he instructed his messenger to present his command in the form of a polite invitation.

At the hour Pharaoh was leaving to visit the site of his tomb, Beka was removing the oldest form of birth control in the world from Htashepsut. All the women of Egypt who lived near where the gray moss grew by water used it. No one knew why, but when a woven wad of this material was placed high in a woman's cervix, the seed implanted by man could not create a child. Hatshepsut would bear only a royal child; in the meantime, she could take pleasure as she would. And she was greatly pleased and happy this day.

Hatshepsut hummed a love song as Beka and four court ladies escorted her to her bathing pools. First, she would have a hot bath and have her hair washed. Then a cool dip before a soothing massage. Sleep would be almost impossible but she must try.

There were so many things to think about. Recollection of her newly discovered body and of her lover were hard to push from her mind, but other thoughts must replace them. She had to make certain of every move. Her astute mind came up with one plan and then another. Foremost, she must decide upon the way in which she would assume the role of sole ruler—the stage must be set, the second red crown, worn only by a Pharaoh, close at hand along with the crook and flail to hold crossed upon her breast. All must seem the most natural thing to do. There must be no opportunity for any priest to press forward with a half-royal son to sit upon her throne.

Of course! "Beka! Send word to Pharaoh's grand vizier that I will receive him when I am prepared for the day. Set forth sweet morning wine and bread fresh from the ovens." As the old woman scurried off to obey these orders, Hati motioned to one of the noble ladies permitted to be in her presence. The ladies holding these positions of honor were alternated often with others of equal station.

Nefertum, whose name meant "fragrant lotus," was the daughter of the vizier. It would do no harm to bestow honors upon her, for surely, she had ears in her head and spent much time with her father. Poor Nefertum. In spite of her lovely name, she was plain and overly plump. She was forever snacking on shat cakes and honey and would have difficulty in finding a handsome, highly placed husband. That was, of course, unless she became a favorite in the service of her Queen.

"Gentle Nefertum, most favored of your Queen, go now and by your own excellent endeavor prepare my bed for rest."

Nefertum was thunderstruck by this unexpected distinction. She could barely murmur her acquiescence before she turned from the chamber, leaving behind a smiling and peaceful Queen and three pairs of jealous eyes.

My Queen has chosen me first for honor; I cannot believe it! She has noticed and been pleased with the services I have performed for her in the past. I will not disappoint her now. She will continue to be pleased. I will prepare fresh bed linens with my own hands.

The grand vizier, Imhot, answered the summons of Hatshepsut with dispatch and presented himself at the doors to her rooms. The Queen, obviously just returned from her bath, was seated in the innermost chamber. She gave him leave to sit and courteously offered him wine and bread. Although Imhot was a vain man, he felt honored to be so treated. He was speechless when his daughter Nefertum appeared carrying the Queen's personal bed linens and walked with assurance into the bedchamber.

"Imhot, your Queen must beg a favor of you. Your sweet daughter pleases me so well that I must have her with me at all times. Do you then give her leave to stay by my side? I have heard that you love her dearly; therefore, this cannot be an easy thing for you. But please consider my wishes and allow your daughter to grace the company of your Queen."

Imhot was hard put to keep from responding with a shout of joy. Of course he would not miss her. He had four other daughters, each as ill favored as Nefertum. He was delighted to be well rid of one daughter, and at the same time, have such a wonderful opportunity. The girl would be a companion to the Great Royal Wife and could someday marry well. This Queen was kind and thoughtful and appeared to be such a wise young woman. He must pay more homage to her.

"Yes, of course, Queen Hatshepsut," he said. "You are a child of the gods, and I can deny you nothing, even if it should break my heart." He drank deeply of the wine and rose. "I ask your permission to retire. You seem weary, and I must not keep you from your bed."

"Thank you, Imhot. I shall show my gratitude to you in time. You may go," she added with a gracious smile.

Hatshepsut reclined upon her golden bed, her head held not by the usual wooden headrest but nestled in a down pillow, with wet hair spread to dry. Nefertum wrapped the queen in loose linen to allow her to rest more comfortably. Beka had drawn the drapes so that heat and light would not reflect from the lake into the room.

"Nefertum, you have done exceedingly well in preparing my bed. Leave me now so that I my take my rest." And, indeed, her tryst with her lover had made her drowsy at long last. As Nefertum proudly left the room, Hatshepsut had just the energy to give Beka one sly wink before she slept.

At the time the messenger was delivering the spoken invitation to a soldier at the door to Hatshepsut's apartments, the Queen was partaking of her evening meal. The soldier passed the invitation from Pharaoh to a lady of the court who delivered it to the Queen. *He sends for me, does he? Well, I shall send a messenger back with a flattering reply.* thus, Pharaoh learned of Hati's desire to have him hunt down a lion so that its pelt might adorn her bedchamber and always serve to remind her of his great prowess.

Thothmes was amused by the reply. *So, she will play games with me, will she? Very well. I shall call upon the great captain, or is it now "general" Kamare.* In the past, Kamare had made it easy for him to spear gazelles and lions. And if there were danger, he could count upon Kamare to slay the lion and let no one know that he, Pharaoh, had not made the kill. And that was as it should be. A messenger was dispatched to warn Kamare to be ready at break of day to accompany Pharaoh on a lion hunt to honor the Great Royal Wife.

Hatshepsut called Nefertum to her side as Beka was removing the remains of her dinner. "Tomorrow evening I will be dining with Pharaoh in the great hall. I ask you to choose the garments I will wear. I understand that he has directed General Kamare to arrange a lion hunt in my honor. Therefore, I would look most pleasing for him, and I trust you will choose wisely."

Nefertum bowed her head in compliance. As she backed from the room, she was certain of one thing overall. With one stroke, Queen Hatshepsut had made her the most important woman (after Beka, a mere nurse), among her ladies. She would reign as the most favored noblewoman in the palace. For this, Nefertum would serve her Queen with constant devotion. And her father would be even more proud of her.

She went to the outer chamber and lifted the lid off the chest of silk bolts given to the Queen as a coronation and wedding gift. With much anxiety, she finally chose one and returned with it to the bedchamber. In the hearing of the three ladies preparing to rest in the adjoining chamber, Hatshepsut said, "Let me see what you have selected for me to wear to the banquet. What color did you choose?" Nefertum tentatively held up a bolt of translucent peach-colored silk with gold threads woven through.

"How beautiful this is. You have chosen well, I shall surely please Pharaoh in this color of love. Before you take your rest, Nefertum, make certain to consult my cosmetician about the best shade for my eyes to complement these wrappings. You may go now. I feel sleep approaching."

8

Out near the rocky precipices, Thothmes rode in his chariot close behind Kamare. The soldier was looking below, pretending to search the desert floor for a favorable beast.

In reality, Kamare's men had netted a huge lioness just hours before and held her snarling and in pain not far ahead. Her swollen teats showed that she had young cubs, and the soldiers knew that the longer she was separated from them, the more ferocious she would become. As a signal, one of the men climbed an outcropping ahead and pointed down into the desert.

Kamare wheeled his horse about and stopped the chariot. He removed a long spear from its holder and handed it, along with the reins, to the eager Thothmes. "My lord, I stay to guard your rear. Many soldiers are ahead to help you spot your prey. Cause your horses to walk to the path below the ledge where the lone soldier stands. When he has shown you where the lion is, call to me, and we will go down together so that you may kill the beast and bring joy to your Queen."

Thothmes proceeded to do as Kamare suggested. His horses shied and reared as they reached a site below where the soldiers stood. They were high-spirited animals and such behavior was to be expected. The soldier smiled and bade Thothmes turn his back to the cliffs so that he might direct his gaze to search in the rocks below. Since lions were the same color as the desert floor, they were difficult to spot; and Thothmes was not disturbed when he saw nothing but brush and rock and sand.

He was still staring intently downward when his horses went berserk. Suddenly, every ounce of his concentration was bent upon controlling them. Just before the lioness landed upon him, he looked up into the face of death. The enraged animal sank her fangs into his neck and pulled at his belly with the long claws on her back feet. Thothmes was disemboweled and his neck broken before he could scream.

Soldiers had discovered the lioness's den and captured the cubs. As she completed her leap, they rolled the little ones down a sloping cliff over one hundred yards ahead. The lioness left the body of the dead king and rushed away to protect her squalling young. It was over in minutes, every detail reflecting the careful planning of the general.

The crazed horses turned, almost upsetting the chariot and lunged forward to go back the way they had come. Kamare's strong hands grabbed onto their harness, and he jumped into the chariot. As they ran, wide-eyed in fear, along the path, he slowly managed to bring them under control. Kamare raised a fist as he stopped the chariot, and ten of his men galloped to his side. Kamare spoke to the youngest.

"Kahar, ride quickly to the palace to tell the tale as I have told it to you. Tell, also, the grand vizier that I ride in deep sorrow at a slow pace. Very respectfully, suggest to him that the funeral tents be set up immediately as Thothmes I is badly mangled and will need priestly attention if all his organs are to be properly mummified. If anyone asks, tell the same tale. We came upon the lioness with cubs at an unusual place, and the mighty Pharaoh leapt out of the chariot in great bravery to face her. As fast as I followed, I could not prevent this horrible tragedy. Also, say to Imhot that he must give the poor Queen the terrible news, as I cannot. My sadness has a terrible grip upon me. I would have parted with my own life had it been possible. Go now!"

Kahar raced away on a fine Arabian mare. The others settled the body in the chariot as best they could, pushing his entrails back into his abdomen and binding all together with a banner bearing Thothmes' colors. Then they closed around the chariot. The tiny procession proceeding at a walk would reach Thebes well after dark. By then, all in the city would know of the brave death of their Pharaoh, and the wailing would reach far into the night sky.

The time for quick action had begun. Hatshepsut must move now. She must be absolutely invincible and undeniable. How

Kamare wished he could be by her side at this moment. And who was left to do battle with? The wine-soaked and flabby remnants of Thothmes' army? Kamare thought not. If his Queen was the brilliant strategist he sensed her to be, she would already have the vizier and the priests in hand.

Hatshepsut feigned sleep as the uproar began at the city gates and grew to great shouting and wailing within the palace compound. Imhot appeared at her outer doors, and an attendant was sent to the Queen's bedchamber to say that the grand vizier bore vital news and requested an immediate audience.

Nefertum was assisting her in rising to a sitting position when Imhot entered the room and knelt at the foot of her couch. At this action, she consciously caused her eyes to widen in alarm. But Imhot did not see this. He had seen the Queen cradled in the arms of his daughter. It was his future that he saw clearly.

Tasty dishes are made from cracked eggs. Hatshepsut has shown my family favor these last few days. Perhaps she will lean upon me as did Thothmes. I must make every effort to achieve this end.

He prostrated himself at her feet and repeated the tale told to him by the young soldier. "Life, health, prosperity, Queen of the Upper and Lower lands, supreme Ruler of Egypt, born of the gods Isis and Horus. I dare not look upon you as you listen to the terrible news I must impart. Our mighty Pharaoh and living god, your most beloved husband and ruler, Pharaoh Thothmes I, has been killed by a powerful lioness. He is, even now, being transported to the funeral tents by his great general, Kamare, who was unable to save Pharaoh's life. Pharaoh leaped with great courage to face the lioness but is dead. All honors to the Queen Hatshepsut who is now sole ruler of this land."

When Hatshepsut had heard the first shouts, and while the ladies of her court were still resting in the second chamber, she had called Beka to her side and had her apply white alum to her face. Now, as she bade Imhot rise, and he gazed upon her, he saw eyes distended in horror and an unearthly pallor of shock. *Poor young Queen. You will need all my wisdom. I shall truly dedicate myself to your service.*

"What shall I do, Imhot? I am beside myself with grief and do not wish to commit foolish acts during this time of anguish. My memories of Pharaoh are strong, and I cannot have a half-blooded boy brought to me to wed when Pharaoh sleeps and lives in his tomb. Shall I send much gold to the houses of the priests? Is that what you think?" asked Hatshepsut in her most innocent tone. And Imhot believed that that was what he had been thinking, so clever was she.

"Yes, royal one. I tell you that is what to do. I suggest you order it immediately."

"Nefertum," Hatshepsut called as she heard stirrings from the other room, "Come and comfort me in my sorrow. Imhot," she continued, "There is no pharaoh alive to place the red crown over my white crown or cross my arms over my breast with crook and flail. Who is the next most powerful man who is not a priest to do this for me?"

Imhot stood tall and grasped what he believed to be his great opportunity. "I will be most honored to perform this service for you, my Queen. Send much gold to the house of the gods at once, and this night you will be the lone ruler of Egypt. Yours is the only true blood, and it must not be tainted. Will you trust me and grant me this honor?"

As all was progressing exactly as she desired, she responded with warmth, "I, Queen Hatshepsut, do accept your stewardship, and you will guide me in all matters. I send a tablet to the treasury at once as you have directed. Go now and prepare for my coronation this night. We must be quick and keep our thoughts to ourselves until it is done. I am indebted to your wisdom, Imhot. I could ask for no better counsel."

The grand vizier backed away and left to inform the keeper of the royal vestments of the impending ceremony. Queen Hatshepsut had agreed with him that she must receive the full crown of Egypt and crook and flail without delay. Imhot was sure he had decided upon the best course for the future of his country. And, also, he had been able to place himself in an even more powerful position. This slip of a girl with her ashen, helpless face would follow his every directive. In fact, it would be he, Imhot the wise, who would be the guiding hand leading the royal ruler of Egypt. To a young servant, he called, "Go to the keeper of the royal vestments. Tell him that it is Imhot, grand vizier, who speaks in the name of the Great Royal Wife, Hatshepsut, who issue these orders. He must act in all haste. Run as quickly as you can, but answer no questions from any other. Also, tell the one I send you to, to be silent, upon pain of death, as to my commands."

The boy covered the distance to the lower rooms of the palace in minutes. The bronze doors were well guarded by soldiers, but these were soldiers from Thothmes' army and had a casual air about them.

"Ho, boy," said one. "What is the hurry? Mighty Pharaoh is dead and will need nothing from this vault tonight."

The servant replied, "I have been instructed by the grand vizier to speak to the master of the vestments at once. Please call to him. My message is urgent and must relayed immediately."

The soldier in charge of the sentries rapped upon the door. A peep-hole opened, and the keeper of the vestments spoke. "What is wanted of me in this time of sorrow? Who is this boy? Who sends him here?"

The lad was intimidated but dared not fail the grand vizier who intimidated him even more, and he replied, "Grand guardian of royal vestments, I come from two most important personages. I have been warned that no one must hear what I have to say other than you."

The guard recognized both urgency and fear in the spoken words. Since it was only a young stripling who stood there, he opened the doors at once. The keeper drew him into the small entryway, closed the doors, and bade him relate his message.

"The grand vizier has told me to say this in secrecy in the name of the Great Royal Wife, Hatshepsut; and you, also, are bound in secrecy. With your own hands, you are to place Pharaoh's red crown of holy office, his crook and flail, the ancient gold battle collar of our dead Pharaoh's father, and the cobra uraeus of all ancient pharaohs into a chest and transport it immediately under guard to the great hall. There you are to wait behind Pharaoh's throne in the vestment room. The vizier also warns that failure will insure your instant and unpleasant death. This message is also from Queen Hatshepsut. I was further instructed to add that you would receive no mercy from her if you fail. I leave you now to report that I have fulfilled my mission."

As the keeper of the royal vestments closed the bronze doors upon the boy's back, his hands were shaking. He was certain of two things—something of great importance was about to happen, and he was no match for the grand vizier and the Queen. Had head priests arrived here first to lay hands upon the royal symbols of power, he would have already given them without question to those fearsome men, in the name of religion and the fear of death. Thanks be to Ra the grand vizier's messenger had arrived before them.

Even as the vestments of power were on their way to the small room behind the Pharaoh's throne, all major priests in all the different houses of the various gods were receiving handsome gifts of gold and precious oils in the name of Queen Hatshepsut. These were accepted as an expression of her grief. Gifts to the all-powerful gods would warrant additional prayers for her dead husband and thus better prepare him for his long journey into the underworld. With the gifts went a request that the chief of priests of each god meet her at the break of dawn to celebrate the rise of Ra and to mourn with her.

The priests were flattered. Of course they would respect her request. What a generous Queen she was, and how thoughtful of her to ask them to join her in her sorrow. There would undoubtedly be tables of fine foods and wines; and in her innocence and youth, she would surely rely upon their guidance. Thothmes had paid little honor to the priests in years past. It seemed things would be different now. All the head priests prepared to bathe themselves and don their finest vestments. Oh, and Thothmes—may the gods receive him well.

It was not yet daylight. As the body of Thothmes I was receiving its first treatments in the mummification process, a long line of priests, richly clad and in high good humor, filed into the great hall with vaulted ceiling. Burning torches, held to the pillars with bronze wrappings so that they stood away from the stone at an angle, helped to illuminate the room. Lighted wicks flickered in large bowls of oil, and each low table and man-high urn held bunches of reeds and lotus buds and other flowers. Aromatic incense smoldered in handsome braziers.

As each priest came forward, his eyes were captured by the figure on the throne. Electrum mirrors placed behind torches on either side of the tall, gold chair shone brightly upon the still form of Queen Hatshepsut, shining as had no other queen before her.

Her dress fell in woven, golden folds that glittered as the torches wavered in the breeze. Her long hair was caught up in the white cone crown. She wore the gold collar, scarred in places by deep hack marks, that been worn by Thothmes I and his father before him, as they led armies into battle. Black kohl outlined her closed eyes and was drawn to her hairline. Her arms were crossed upon her breast, and she held the gold and lapis lazuli crook in one hand and the flail of authority in the other. She was both shepherd and ruler of her people.

Silence. All was silence.

Imhot stepped from behind the tall throne and stood facing the gathering of priests. In his hands he held the high-backed red crown and gold cobra uraeus of all the pharaohs. Imhot stood as though he were one of the great stone pillars of the hall. Well he knew that what was about to be attempted had no precedent. No queen before had been crowned as full Pharaoh—not even Tetisheri, of so many years ago, who had ruled long and well. Not even she had attempted to wear the Pharaoh's crown.

The priests who had gathered so eagerly, each lured by the idea of his own importance and by the opportunity to feast, stood immobile. A few worked their mouths like fish out of water, gasping for air.

Before any could protest, Imhot moved to the Queen and placed the red crown over the white one, with the large hooded snake resting upon the queen's brow. In a loud voice that boomed and echoed in the half-empty hall, he intoned, "All in this place prostrate yourselves before the new Pharaoh of Egypt. Life, Health, Prosperity to Queen Hatshepsut, she who alone rules Egypt; she who will bring Egypt, our Motherland, back to its former place in this world; she who will support and give great honor to all the gods of Egypt."

The deed was done. Hatshepsut was now Pharaoh in name and crown. All that remained to complete the transition was the obeisance of the priests, some of whom held enormous power.

None had anticipated what was to occur; yet, as one, they lay face down upon the stone floor and murmured over and over, "Life, Health, Prosperity to Pharaoh and Queen, Hatshepsut." These servants of the gods had received chests of treasure just hours before. And all believed that Hatshepsut was born the child of Isis and Horus.

It was a deed well done for all concerned—for the gods, for Pharaoh Hatshepsut, and for Egypt. When the priests rose to their feet, Hatshepsut opened her eyes wide. All could see the black stars in them. She spoke in a grave voice. "Go now and make sacrifice for my work to be well done. I must build again. Make sacrifice also for Pharaoh Thothmes I as he prepares to make his journey to the west. In sixty days, he will be buried in the new tomb site across the Nile. Each of you will assist Pharaoh Hatshepsut in her holy duties." When she had finished, the priests left quietly. As they went down the stairs and out of the palace, they saw company upon company of hardened soldiers lining the way. It was not lost upon them that the cartouche of Hatshepsut was burned into the breastplate of each soldier.

Done, well done. The time had passed so quickly that the Queen had been unaware of her exhaustion. Now tension left her, and she would rest. Hatshepsut lay in her bed and, for the first time since her marriage to Thothmes I, felt pleased and contented. Had it been but one week ago that she was the wise little princess, spending hours in the royal library? A princess then, Pharaoh-Queen now. At any point, she could have erred. But now, crowned Pharaoh, no one could oust her other than by death. She decided, as she lay there, that she would be known as Queen Hatshepsut. She would wear the crown of Pharaoh, but she would be a woman. There was time enough to think of the perpetuation of the dynasty; time enough to think of marriage. After all, she had love. Dear Kamare, giver of such pleasure. His strength had been instrumental in the success of her first important step. How pleasant it was to know that she could also have him in her bed. She would have him remain in the city. Soon she would send for him.

As Hatshepsut lay in the rooms of Pharaoh Thothmes, to which her possessions had been moved, the dead Pharaoh slept in the mortuary tents outside Thebes. The mummification process had reached the point where the body is covered with salt. His wounds were hideous. Even now his face bore an expression of shock and insupportable pain. But the muscles would relax and the expression would disappear as the juices dripped from him, and he was soaked in oil.

The embalming priests had worked hard trying to salvage the intestines mangled by the lioness. Had the loyal soldiers not shoved them back into the gaping hole and wrapped his wounds, the Pharaoh would not have had a complete body in the afterlife. The embalmers had been told that Queen Hatshepsut had been graced with the crown and uraeus and proclaimed Pharaoh. It was fact. They continued with their work on the corpse of the dead king.

Up and down the Nile, from Kush, Nubia, and Mitanni in the south and east, to the lands of the Hyksos, Hebrews, Abisinnes, and Elkiookions, to the major cities of lower Egypt—Karnak, Abydos, Luxor, Memphis—all would hear that Queen Hatshepsut had been crowned as Pharaoh in Thebes. The Greeks also would know of this event since Egypt controlled trade in the Aegean Sea.

Queen Hatshepsut now held the known world in her hands, the first woman to do so. Time alone would tell if she were worthy. Time would test her will and control. Such people are born as they are and cannot be formed or created.

Kamare was, at long last, soaking in his bath. He was amazed at the speed with which Hatshepsut had moved. His love was no longer a trembling princess. She was Pharaoh, and he but the general of her armies. Well, he was not a fool. The queen would bear children of a royal father to sustain the dynasty, and his, Kamare's, blood was that of a noble, no more. He felt his heart beat faster as he remembered their night of lovemaking. Although enslaved by his love for Hatshepsut, he could hope for little. He was certain he had been the first to give her pleasure in the act of love, but would she want him again? And even if she did, he knew he would not remain first with her. Egypt was her husband and her burden.

No, all he could hope for was to serve her in every way. With his love to bind him, he would make her kingdom militarily indestructible. As he was contemplating this future, a slave appeared at the side of the pool bearing a wax tablet sealed by the ring of Hatshepsut. Kamare took it from him and read the message and smiled in spite himself. *She will send for me. Oh, foolish man, must you grin like a desert hyena? But she needs me. Perhaps she wants me.* He would have his rugged body oiled and plucked clean of hair. Lying on the marble table as a slave anointed him, he seemed a part of the stone, so hard of muscle was he. Not an ounce of fat was to be seen. Kamare smiled in his sleep that day. This man would teach his Queen all manner of pleasures.

The night of the next day brought a summons for the general. The Queen would discuss her armies with him. Wearing the short, pleated skirt, leather belt, and sandals common to a soldier, he threw a thick cloak over his shoulders. The only indication setting him apart from the men under his command were his immense size and the ring his Queen had given him. This same ring made him second in command of all the territories of Egypt, on land and sea.

Ordinary people were deceived by the pleasant face and courteous manners of Kamare. Among his soldiers, he possessed the reputation of a fierce warrior. There were those in the armies who could speak of seeing a huge madman sweeping his sword in gigantic arcs and hurling lances at the foe as he stood in pools of blood that had streamed from the bodies of slain enemies. The madness stayed with him for hours after the battle, and none dared approach him.

Was it not a shame that such a man could not sire a Pharaoh? He would be a fine child who would grow into a respected ruler, well educated, yet with the temperament and ability to defend his land.

Queen Hatshepsut sat upon the throne in the full regalia of Pharaoh. She had held court for two days, dealing with many of the minor problems facing her people. She had dealt lastly with the harem, pretending to listen to the grand vizier, and then doing as she pleased. Of course, she had no need for a harem, but she was wise. She would leave no snakes in her garden.

The women who had borne sons to Thothmes I would remain there, living in luxury. The helpless elderly women would live out their lives there in comfort. The rest of the women, the young and the beautiful, she would have examined by Montu. He had been sent for and knelt before her, awaiting his instructions. "Montu, you served my father and husband well. I entrust the examination of the young women to you. Those whom you determine to be virginal will be selected as gifts for various kings in our allied countries. Of the rest, they may choose to return to their homes with honorable chests of gifts, or they may perform as palace dancers when I have need of them and live on wherever they choose. They alone are free to choose. As my loyal servant, Montu, your duties will continue, and your word is supreme in the harem. As each female leaves, you will be rewarded."

Montu was the last personage scheduled to appear before her, and her eyes were flickering toward the open doors. At last, the form she longed to see approached between the columns. Was he really so huge? His face shone happiness as she smiled at him.

Hatshepsut spoke to Imhot and asked that he clear the hall, as she would discuss military matters. All but her guards and General Kamare must leave. Imhot pounded his staff on the stone floor and announced her orders.

Kamare knelt at her feet and waited for her to speak. It was always thus with a pharaoh. "General Kamare, you are welcomed to this court by your Queen. We have items of vital importance to discuss. I invite you to share my evening meal. Since there will be no feasting until my husband is placed in his new home, we will go to my chambers and be served food as we talk. You may escort me."

Kamare rose and held out his hand. Hatshepsut placed hers over his, and they stepped to the vestment room behind the throne. The keeper of vestments removed her crown, and her luxuriant hair fell below her waist. The keeper took the crook and flail from her and placed them also in the chest.

Nefertum held out a thin circlet of gold and Hatshepsut put it upon her own head. The Queen had transposed herself, before their eyes, from the living god, Pharaoh, into a beautiful woman. There remained about her, however, that invisible cloak of royalty and immortality that she possessed naturally.

Reaching again to place her hand on that of Kamare, she smiled up at him in plain adoration. Those few who remained in attendance followed as they retired to the Pharaoh's chambers, now renamed the Queen's chambers. They thought her joy was born of gratitude. Only the lovers knew that their eyes kissed and their touching hands burned.

Hatshepsut had Kamare sit beside her on a painted bench with high-backed wings for support upon which to recline. They were served the evening meal, the largest of the day. There was a fine goose that had been filled with onions and salt and basted with honey and wine as it turned over a charcoal fire; a platter of tender vegetables; and loaves of warm breads. Hatshepsut poured the wine herself, and they raised their goblets in silent salute. Kamare had done all for her. Every scheme she had devised would have been for naught had Pharaoh Thothmes lived.

Uneasiness crept over Hatshepsut as they sat dining. She felt eyes upon her, as though her every move was being assessed. Could it be Euripides? This was intolerable; she would be spied upon no more! She leaned forward and whispered, "Dismiss them all for me. There is one last life to be taken or all may not be saved."

Kamare rose, displayed his ring, and said, "Leave us now. My Queen would speak alone to her general. Close the doors and interrupt us upon pain of death." His manner was so fierce that even Hatshepsut was alarmed. All the serving people and the noble ladies hastened from the room, shutting the wooden doors firmly behind them. Kamare stood still, hands flexing, every nerve alert.

"Come, Kamare, sit beside me, and I shall whisper my

thoughts to you," said the Queen. As he sat and turned toward her, fire danced in his eyes. He feared no one, but whomsoever caused fear in Hati would regret it and pay with his life.

"Kamare," she whispered, "there are walls within the walls of my palace. The evil Euripides was Ahmose's necromancer. He showed all to me, and I know he spies into all rooms. He possesses knowledge of many poisons. I have been to his vaults below and I have seen the papyri. They contain books of spells and recipes for desire or death. I feel that, even now, he is listening to us and watching us. He must be silenced. I believe Ahmose's death was not an accident. I fear him as no other, for he is a truly evil man."

Without revealing any emotion at all, Kamare posed one question: "Can you go through this secret wall and show him to me?" She nodded slightly, and her general stood and walked slowly to the closed doors of her chambers. It was forbidden to wear a sword in the Queen's rooms, and he had left his in its scabbard with the guards.

Kamare opened one of the doors and spoke quietly to a guard who retrieved the sword and handed it to him. The heavy sword was an old friend; its hilt rested comfortably in the general's calloused hands. Kamare returned to the Queen's side. She led him to the altar of Horus and turned the head of a small gold cat that rested at the feet of the idol, and the panel swung open.

Euripides had been casually observing Hatshesput and Kamare enjoying harmless chatter as they dined and was puzzled when the room was cleared. Then he saw the powerful soldier with sword in hand moving toward the wall behind which he stood watching and listening, and he knew! He knew but could not move. Even as his mind raced in terror, his body was frozen in fear.

Light fell upon Euripides as the panel to the inner wall opened. His eyes bulged in horror as Kamare's arm came up and then down on the side of his neck. This was the only blow that guaranteed no outcry. The necromancer fell instantly dead. There would be no chest of gold for him, nor would he do harm to another royal person.

Hati stepped through the opening to stand beside Kamare

and, touching a lever, closed them into the secret hall. A distant torch, lighted earlier by Euripides, illuminated the two standing together over the body of the dead man.

"You have struck another blow for me, Kamare. Together, we will be strong. This man was evil and his life is well ended. Come with me, and I will show you all."

"Hati, love, we must be practical before we can be sure of being secure. Does this secret place lead to Euripides's vaults as well?" She nodded, and she realized that the body could not be left there.

"Show me the way, and I shall carry this odorous thing with me." So saying, he wrapped the body in its heavy cloak and followed her. They went deep down under the palace where Hati stopped near the magician's room of magic. Another torch lighted this part of the passage, and a small door was visible in the wall, but there seemed to be no way of opening it. Hati felt all around the edge of the door until she came upon the lever. She pressed down upon it and a narrow opening appeared, one which barely allowed Kamare to squeeze through with his ungainly burden, the former master of this room.

Hati entered and after closing the panel behind her, looked about, remembering the first time she had been there. It had been just a few days ago; and imbedded in her memory were the musty-earth smell and odors of oils in labeled jars, mixed with those of papyrus and leather—at once mysterious and interesting. She could read the ingredients in the recipes found in the rolls of papyrus. She could mix and administer as well as had Euripides. She would keep this room for her own purposes.

"Now, Hati, I must open the door into his bedchamber. If any are alive there, they must be slain. Trust me in this. No tales must be told of how Euripides met his fate. I direct you back into the hallway while I do what must be done. When I asked for my sword at your doors, I sent some of my soldiers to clear and seal that room. But if it has not yet been done, you cannot be found here. Go now."

Hatshepsut returned to the dim passageway and watched Kamare through a peep-hole. He carried the body of the evil one over his left shoulder, leaving his good right arm free to wield his sword. He went through the doorway and she, at first, heard nothing. Then, distant sounds of male voices.

In minutes, Kamare returned to the room of potions and magic. Hatshepsut went in and clasped him to her. His face was easy to read. All was well.

"Hati, love, I have given orders that the body be thrown into the Nile; and, even now, workmen come to seal the wall in the bedchamber so that no door will lead from there into this room. The other luxurious rooms remain untouched, but the bedchamber will have one wall of thick, new bricks. This room will be yours to use as you please. There may be a time when you will wish to make use of the knowledge here. Is this to your liking?"

Her delicate face turned up to him in gratitude. He was so wise, so strong. And he was hers forever. "My beloved Kamare, this night's work completes all transitions. We can be at peace at last. But have you looked upon us, my love? We are both smeared with foul blood. Come with me to my bath. There are two of my handmaidens whose loyalty is total. And who dares deny Queen Hatshepsut what she desires?"

Her face was solemn, but her eyes danced when she said severely, "Do you deny me your company, General? I have other deeds I require you to perform this night, and you are mine to command. Is this not so?"

In answer, he grasped her and hungrily covered her mouth with his in a long, deep kiss. They had walked slowly down the dim hallway; now they ran back. They must cover their mouths so that the walls could not hear their laughter.

Hatshepsut called for Beka and Nefertum. Both women stood wide-eyed with mouths agape at the sight of the blood-spattered forms of their Queen and General Kamare. Neither dared speak; they simply waited meekly for their commands. In a voice filled with happiness, the Queen said, "You honored two will prepare the pool for General Kamare and me. It must be very hot. Tonight the water will be scented with oil of gardenia. And we both desire a good scrubbing."

The rooms that had been Thothmes' which were now occupied by Hatshepsut, were exquisite. All walls were mirror-like electrum, hung here and there with linens and silks, to be drawn closed for softness and warmth. The floor and large pool were of a softly polished rose quartz, fashioned in large slabs. Such a size was rarely seen.

Hatshepsut's furniture had been mixed with the pieces not taken to Thothmes' tomb. Beautifully carved woods of all kinds were inlaid with ivory and ebony. Some of it was covered with hammered gold leaf, and the chess-like game of jackals and hounds had playing pieces carved from different shades of jade. This material came from the east, beyond the land of Punt, from which came the most favored of all Egyptian fragrances, myrrh.

The balcony, open to the Nile, was redolent with plants and flowers; and steps led to Hati's little gold boat. She would keep the Great Royal Wife's lake and pavilion and would also use the giant royal barge for travel up and down the Nile. All in all, it was the most delightful and beautifully appointed palace in Egypt's world.

Hatshepsut and Kamare were lathered and shampooed as they sat upon gilded stools. Following this treatment, they descended hand-in-hand into the depths of the large pool, luxuriating in the warmth and the pleasant aromas.

Hatshepsut would be alone with him now; she dismissed the women for the night. Her happiness was infectious. Beka and Nefertum smiled at each other, happy for their Queen, and complacent in the knowledge that they alone were privileged to share the secret romance.

As she looked upon his arousal, Hatshepsut wondered how she had managed to accept such a huge organ into her small body. Kamare held her loosely, and they floated in the water, each rinsing the other. He ran his fingertips all over her, and she felt lubricating juices start up deep inside her body and flow outward. He sat upon a step just underneath the water and pulled her to sit facing him, upon his lap. They kissed more deeply. His hands made the pupils of her eyes dilate with desire; the irregular black stars became the whole of her face.

"Oh love, sweet love. Give me pleasure again. I would cry out in joy from the joining of our bodies." Kamare had wanted to bring her slowly and tenderly to the summit of desire, but now he could wait no longer. He was as eager as she. Big hands encircled her waist. He raised her up and brought her down upon him. His organ filled her completely, and he began to show her how to rock upon him. This time she would set the pace.

Small pink tongue licking his face, she moved back and forth and then in circles, rising up and almost off him before sliding down once more. Faster and faster, holding on tightly on each other, they reached ecstasy at the same time. Hearts beating hard against each other, they clung together until they could breathe without gasping.

Oh, to be so at ease as they, so devoid of trouble. They needed only sleep. Again hand-in-hand, as though it were the most natural thing in the world, they went to the big bed and fell wet and naked into its softness. There they slept, limbs entwined. Above their heads, the hooded gold cobra was arched upon the wall.

Outside the doors there was a change of guards; and below the balcony and in the marshes, the loyal soldiers watched over all. These two lovers, Queen and General, had accomplished much, yet much remained to be done. For when a great power becomes lax, the minions begin to stir, begin to believe they can throw off the yoke of the master. Kamare had made a good beginning, but much remained for him to do.

9

Kamare had been gone two weeks, and Queen Hatshepsut had realized the need for this long separation. She knew there would be many more, for his labor must be vigilant and continuous if he were to amass the armies as she directed. If she were to reign supreme, she must be able to send an armed force instantly to quell the smallest revolt. Her conquered lands were vast and supplied great tribute to her treasury—no uprising could be tolerated. *I am so fortunate to have a general wise in the ways of war. If only he could father a son for me.* It was an ever-returning thought; but because it was not the way of Egypt, she struggled to put the thought aside. In time, she would select a husband from among the half-royal sons of the harem brood.

As for the harem, one of her first priorities after Kamare's departure had been a visit to the place. While it was correct for her to do this as the Pharaoh, it was unusual for a Queen to do so. Nevertheless, on this day, word was sent that she would arrive in time to partake of her noon meal at the harem, and she set off with her personal guards. Hatshepsut drove her chariot as she had always done, rapidly and recklessly. She drove, as did most charioteers, with the reins wrapped around her wrist. This literally tied her to her horses; and in the event of an accident, she would go down with the animals. She had chosen two horses instead of one, two delicate mares. They were fine Arabians with small dancing feet, heads held proudly upon arched necks, and deep bay in color.

Hatshepsut wore the double red and white crown and the ancient, gold war collar of her grandfather. From behind, the guards could see her feet planted wide, her back straight, and her whip at the ready; truly a warrior queen.

She now drove Thothmes' chariot, and she briefly recalled her first ride in it with him on their wedding night. So much had passed, and it would soon be time to lead the procession for his burial across the Nile and deep into the Valley of the Kings. She had gone to the mortuary tents to personally deliver the small gold images of the gods that were to be tucked away in layers of his funeral wrappings. Yes, Thothmes was almost ready to live again in his new home. The grave robbers would not find him. Ineni had been very clever. Ineni, an unusual man, was always drawing temples not designed in the old way. He claimed that he could use shadow as part of his design; and indeed, it did look fascinating on papyrus.

She arrived at the harem and Montu attempted to take the reins of her mares. This had very nearly been the end of him. Kamare had left instructions that no one was to touch her or hand anything to her, and one of her personal guards leapt between Montu and the chariot with drawn sword pointed at the enunch's throat. "Hold back," cried Hatshepsut. "There is no harm in this person."

As the soldier grabbed the harness, Montu prostrated himself on the ground. His muffled voice could barely be heard. "Spare me. Oh, spare me, mighty Pharaoh. I mean no harm."

"Rise, Montu," said Hatshepsut as she tried to contain her laughter. "The soldier did not understand. You are perfectly safe."

All of this was so new to her. Everything must go through the hands of her guards. And then there was the food taster. A child had been chosen to taste everything before Hatshepsut ate it. After half an hour, she could accept what had been tasted; the theory being that a child would show symptoms more quickly than an adult. There were always children of the poor available to serve in this position. If a child were so close to Pharaoh or Queen, he or she would be greatly honored, and the family well paid. Besides, although it had happened occasionally in the past, tasters rarely died. The crafty Egyptians were much too sophisticated and clever to be so obvious in their attempts to assassinate a ruler. On this day, the child had been taken to the harem two hours before Hatshepsut was due to arrive so that there was ample time to test all the foods being prepared.

Hatshepsut entered the compound and was escorted into a large room where all the women were gathered. She was charming and kind to all. She reassured the old women and the young who had decided to stay. Sitting upon a raised dais, she called to the virgins to come forward. To these, she spoke glowingly of the opportunities that awaited them when she would send them to foreign kings as second wives.

Lastly, she called forth the women who had borne sons who were now living in the houses of the priests. These women were asked to stay and share food and wine with her. At no time during the meal did she behave as would an ordinary woman. She was kind but did not smile; carried herself regally, and the ladies were awed by the Pharaoh-Queen. Then each was asked to tell of her son or sons: his name, age, temperament, and the extent of his studies. Each mother was thrilled as she spoke of her offspring to Queen Hatshepsut.

For the first time since any in the harem could remember, a son could be chosen as co-regent, as Pharaoh! Many young men had been selected for various princesses or even as husbands for maidens of noble houses. They were, after all, of royal blood. But, a son as Pharaoh! This was the opportunity of a lifetime! Thothmes I had been virile. There were many male children of an appropriate age. One of these mothers might live in the palace as a revered Great Royal Mother.

All in all, Hatshepsut's visit to the harem was a huge success. Messages would be sent out to the many sons and to the priests with whom they were housed. Doubtless, all would contain praise of the Queen and her wisdom. Each priest knew that if the chosen son were a member of his household, his power would be increased many times over. And Hatshepsut knew that tribute alone would not keep the powerful priests in line. For control, the queen would hold out the opportunity for even greater power to these men. Power and greed: used wisely, there could be no more important tools than these.

As the time for Thothmes' funeral approached, Hatshepsut's

thoughts turned inwardly to think of her own tomb. Her great desire was to leave her mark upon this land. It must be more than an invisible tomb or even a large temple. It must be a monument so grand that all who passed would stand in wonder.

There were already two pyramids, the great Sphinx, and obelisks. There were many tall and awesome statues and temples. She would have something far different. Soon, she would find time to talk to Ineni about it; then, there would be a lifetime to build it.

Thothmes I had promoted Ineni to royal architect. It was he who had rescued and renovated the great temple at Karnak. He had had innumerable copper ingots brought from Asia; and from these he had forged great, gleaming gates for the temple. It was he, also, who had helped select the new site for royal burials and who had designed the invulnerable tomb.

Hatshepsut had sometimes amused herself during her studies by leaning over the architect's shoulder as he drew great and auspicious designs. Of these, Thothmes had accepted only two. Hatshepsut, however, was intrigued by his innovations and was certain he could design the sort of monument she envisioned in the many years that must be left to him.

And she would supervise the writings that were to be etched on the walls and pillars. There were six hundred phonetic sounds made by marks upon papyrus. She had learned them all from Ineni, and she read them in wonder as her fingers followed the forms of these symbols etched in the stone of temple walls, tombs, statues, and the sides of obelisks. She longed to be remembered equally well.

10

Egyptians began their days with long baths. The bathroom was the largest and most important room in the home. A toilet was in an adjoining room, and there was another room for the massage that was a part of the daily routine. The wealth of the home-owner dictated the kinds of oils and perfumes with varying aromas that were used. No other culture devoted so much time to cleanliness and scent.

Upon the morning of the funeral for Thothmes I, Hatshepsut spent hours being bathed and massaged. Her mind floated at peace as strong hands rubbed scent into her limbs. A musician sang and played his harp. All was in Maat; all was at peace. She was prepared to dutifully perform her role in the ritual ceremonies of the long day. Since there would be a lavish funeral feast, she had only fruit accompanied by a light wine for her breakfast.

Hatshepsut dressed all in white to show grief over the death of her husband, but she wore garlands of fresh flowers to celebrate his entering the underworld with Anubis. There he would be joined with his ka, or soul. After his heart was weighed against the weight of a feather and found pure, he would sail over the edge of the underground world as the sun set, to return again with the dawn and live again in his body.

Outside the palace, Pharaoh's giant barge was turned into a funeral barque. The coffin of painted wood was placed upon a catafalque in the center of the ship, and Hatshepsut sat behind it in a tall, gold chair. Below, many slaves rowed in unison as priests lit the braziers filled with incense.

Tall fans made of white feathers shaded the queen as the sun bore down on the procession. The funeral barque was followed by many smaller ships bearing priests, nobles, royal sons, and the honored priests who would remain in Pharaoh's tomb with him as it was sealed.

The priests had said farewell to their families and friends. Faces wreathed in smiles, they anticipated an eternity filled with luxury and pleasure in the company of Thothmes in the underworld. Anubis would most certainly accept them if they accompanied Pharaoh.

The funeral barque approached the opposite shore, and Hatshepsut could see at the landing site a familiar form astride a skittish stallion. Kamare had returned in the night and was there with his soldiers to see that no harm came to her. It was not unusual for accidents to befall a daughter of Egypt at such a time, as the ferment among half-royal sons was stirring.

Oh joyous day, sang Hatshepsut's heart. *I will have you for a time. Surely your work is nearly at an end. Your daily reports tell me that Egypt has never been so strong.*

The ship grounded and ropes were thrown ashore as the anchor dropped. The musicians and paid mourners disembarked and began the climb up the cliff. Nubians carrying the wooden coffin followed them. Then came the litter chair of the Queen, still shaded from the sun. Her General walked his horse beside her, and guards surrounded them. They did not look at one another; they could not do so. But later, later, all would be laughter and love.

Kamare's eyes looked straight ahead. Still, he caught glimpses of her when his horse pranced sideways. How beautiful and serene she was, with a slight smile lighting her face. Her slender body, draped in flowers, swayed with the motion of her chair.

There was a mesa at the cliff top, and here the procession halted. Only a few had seen this immense valley of stone and sand as entry to tomb sites was always denied. The valley was so barren, without shrub or any blade of green, that it appeared to be a huge open tomb in itself. Down into this valley they wailed and walked and rode until they reached a tent set up at the base of a cliff. The soldiers stationed themselves at strategic locations, and everyone else went into the shade of the tent.

Hatshepsut, joined by Ineni, the architect, and the priests

who would remain with Thothmes, entered the shaft cut downward under the cliff. They went down the long staircase, far below ground. The darkness was dispelled by light pouring from electrum mirrors. Halfway down, the secret door on the left was swung open, and the priests carried the wooden coffin through the secret passage into the treasure room. They gasped when they saw all it contained; gold in great quantity as well as magnificently carved cattle, sheep, and fowl. All would become real that night. Jars of wine that would never empty stood beside loaves of bread that would never grow stale. The room was furnished with every kind of luxury, and the priests would live as did Pharaoh. Here, too, were the linen beds where they would lie after drinking their poison.

With the use of ladders leaning against the wall, the priests raised the coffin and passed it through the opening high over their heads. A rope net had been strung across the deep pit containing the pointed stakes, and planks had been laid over all so that Thothmes' coffin could be carried to its final resting place. It was raised to slip over the golden boat in the hallway and into the final room of wonder. Once inside this last room with its ceiling of stars, the painted wood coffin was placed within the gold one waiting in the womb of stone. Six priests on each of six ropes lowered the lid to cover all. It fit perfectly—to Ineni's great satisfaction.

Hatshepsut was the last to enter the room. Only a few who entered the tomb would leave. None who could profit by speaking of the intricate steps taken to hide the mummy would live.

Carefully, and with much beseeching of the gods to accept her husband, Queen Hatshepsut removed her flowers and placed them atop the sarcophagus. She was deeply impressed by the final arrangements and the beauty amid which the dead Pharaoh lay. He would surely live again in great splendor.

All who were in this room returned the way they had come, down the hallway past the golden boat, across the pit, and through the high opening. The planks and rope net were removed from their fastenings and let fall into the deep pit so that no grave robber could ever make use of them.

Beside the ladders in the treasure room were plaster and

stacks of bricks. Hatshepsut watched as the priests sealed the opening. They had been practicing bricklaying for thirty days, and now they knew why. The task was completed in minutes and plastered over. As the plaster dried, it would seem to be an untouched part of the wall, as the lower portion of this room had been painted with scenes from everyday life. This, also, was deliberate.

The Queen bade the priests be kind to her husband when they all became alive together. And, once again, they blessed her in the name of many gods for allowing them an afterlife of such splendor. Then they lay down upon their linen beds and swallowed the poison. They dared not linger alive too long, or they would not be able to ride with Thothmes in the golden boat.

Only Ineni and Hatshepsut left the treasure room to stand upon the steep stairs as the secret door swung closed. Ineni called to the four workers in the false tomb below to come up and shove plaster in the cracks and seal it smoothly around the edges. The wall in which this door was concealed was painted blue to show the sea, and the plaster used by the workmen was of the same hue. Even while the plaster was still wet, the door seemingly disappeared. These walls had been deliberately left rough textured, with pieces of natural rock protruding in many places. Surely Pharaoh Thothmes and his priests would live here undisturbed forever.

Hatshepsut had been advised by Ineni's plan to dispose of the workmen, but she conceived a scheme she thought would be less likely to miscarry.

"After all," she had asked Ineni, "what will be done if the jackals do not scavenge the bodies of the workmen? Let me think on this."

Hatshepsut directed Ineni to give the workmen the jar of wine she had seemed to casually select from among those in the treasure room. In the wine was a sweet-tasting but slow-acting poison she had concocted from recipes found in the necromancer's papyrus. The men gleefully opened the jar, and each took a large swallow.

Hatshepsut, Ineni, and the laborers reached the sunlight.

Those waiting under the tent saw the happy workers return to the desert floor to feast with the slaves and serving girls. Turning in the light, the Queen accepted her crown and the gold jewelry with which Nefertum had been entrusted. The music began and food was served; a last meal was shared with a loved one.

Under Ineni's guidance and the watchful eyes of Kamare's most trusted soldiers, the workmen sealed the tomb. They placed the stone bearing the cartouche of Thothmes I above the steps and covered it with sand eight feet deep. They then rejoined the others for one more drink of wine before starting the trek back to the river.

And now the remainder of Hatshepsut's plan took hold. The four men fell, one by one, only to be picked up by soldiers and tied on the backs of donkeys. Since everyone had consumed much wine, there was no suspicion; and when the men died in a day or two, it would not be connected to the funeral. They would never be conscious again; therefore, they could tell no one the secrets of the interior of the tomb. It would be well done.

Ra was fast sinking in the west when the Queen's barge reached the palace at the end of this exhausting day. Hatshepsut longed for her bath and cool bed. When she arrived at her apartments, her pool was ready, but there was one last task to perform.

She called a guard into her room and directed him to oversee the transport of a chest she had before her. "Take this to the master architect Ineni. Tell him his Queen is well pleased with him, and restores his titles and estates as befits the builder of royal tombs. The gold goblets and ingots in the chest are additional reward in remembrance and honor of Pharaoh."

This was a necessary step. Most architects built for only one ruler as that ruler usually commanded that after his burial the architect be killed to ensure secrecy. Because Thothmes had not anticipated death, he had never issued this command. Hatshepsut wanted others to realize that she valued and trusted Ineni. By rewarding him so handsomely, she was letting the court know that he would soon be designing a tomb for her.

At last she was able to relax in her bath. Hatshepsut lingered there enjoying the warm, perfumed water laving her soft, rounded body and washing all tension away. Finally she emerged from the pool and went to a massage table. Slaves massaged her body until all weariness disappeared.

Her renewed energy turned her thoughts to Kamare. *I have been so long without my love, I will send for him now.* "Nefertum! Send for my great General. There are serious matters that need his attention, and they cannot wait. Quickly now!"

Nefertum hurried to send one of the guards in search of Kamare. He left immediately, giving no thought as to the reason his General was being summoned. After all, his duty was to obey—to obey without question.

Beka combed the Queen's long hair and helped her slide into bed ensconced in crisp linens. Hati lay there thinking of her love; and despite her intention to be awake when he appeared, she drifted into sleep.

Kamare arrived at the palace bathed and oiled. He went alone into her bedchamber; and as he closed the door behind him, he beheld his love. She was in a deep sleep with lush lips parted. Her sweet breath blew into his face with gentle warmth. Under the mild aroma remaining from the perfumes used by the slaves, her body had the smell of fresh, warm bread. The little amount of sun that had reached her had placed a blush upon her face.

Silently, Kamare shed his pleated garment and slid into the bed beside her. He bent over her body to devour her with his eyes and his senses. She was so lovely, so innocent, so trusting! *I will hold her tonight as a man holds his wife in sweet companionship. She will lie safely in my arms.* She curled against him with the small sounds of contentment.

It was enough to hold her in his strong arms, to know that he could protect her as well as love her. Kamare was soon asleep. If one were to look upon this scene, it would appear as though the bed had only one occupant. So great was he in size, the small woman pressed against his chest was hidden.

In the hour preceding dawn, the peacocks shrieked their morning calls. The pair in the great bed moved against each other. Half awake, lips found lips and hands pulled bodies close. Soon they rocked in passion so deep and intense that their love-making was quickly consummated. Back into slumber they drifted, content and satisfied.

Outside, lying on her mat by the door, Beka had also been awakened by the peacocks. Her ear was by the crack at the bottom of the door, and she had heard the small cries of love. Suddenly her eyes flew open in alarm. She had been exhausted, and her Queen had fallen asleep quickly; there had been no opportunity to insert the gray moss! Beka's mind frantically added and took away the days of the waning of the moon. The time was exactly right for conception, and the result could be disastrous. Queen Hatshepsut was unmarried. She had not yet selected a half-brother to share her throne. If she had conceived this night, she must make a difficult decision. Beka would not disturb her small Hati now with this problem; it was done. And, knowing how the mind of the Queen worked, Beka knew Hatshepsut would come to the same conclusion as she.

The old nurse rose and went to her morning bath. At her age, she must try hard to stay clean and sweet smelling.

Hatshepsut awakened in the arms of her lover and looked at his face in repose. He was deeply tanned from the desert sun. There was a line above his dark brows where his skin was pale; it was where the material for his kabah, a striped piece of cloth in her colors, was tied around his head to fall to shoulder length on each side. It resembled the shape of a fine lady's short wig and covered his hair with thin cloth.

Men also wore black kohl around their eyes, drawn to the hairline. For the fighting man, this was a necessity, not a decoration. The dark lines absorbed the glare of the sun so that vision was sharper. Whenever possible, armies traveled at dawn or twilight or under the light of the full moon and rested beneath shade in the heat of the day. They had learned to use the desert wisely, for the desert was relentless in its destruction of the reckless.

Kamare's mouth curved into a smile. He knew she watched him.

"Awaken, you great beast, and do not laugh at the Queen of Egypt!"

With this, the laughter rumbled from his chest, and he opened his eyes upon her. Laughing still, he grasped her tightly and would not let her move.

"If a small kitten in her bed does not give the great beast some food, he will eat her instead, piece by sweet piece. By all the gods of Ta-mare, you are most delicious. I tasted of you in the night, and I hunger for you again. With what will you buy your freedom?"

Hatshepsut kissed him over and over, saying between kisses that she would pay nothing. He must be forced to eat her once more. And so he did as she asked. He did it slowly and with deep satisfaction.

As they lay together in the bathing pool, there was ease between them. They could be friends as well as lovers and conspirators. The morning food was served as they dressed. Hatshepsut's handmaidens were trained to discharge their duties on an instant's notice; and many times trays of food became cold as they waited outside her doors, only to be replaced by others upon her command.

On this happy morning, Hatshepsut and Kamare enjoyed a new drink that her envoys had discovered in Asia. Fruit was plucked and then mashed to release the juices. There were pears, peaches, oranges, kumquats, and pomegranates. All were grown in the royal orchards and were usually eaten out-of-hand, or with honey. But today, these fruits were juiced. There were hard-boiled eggs with salt and hot brown bread to fill their stomachs. Kamare devoured a large fish also, his capacity was great and liked heavy foods at every meal.

Hatshepsut found a special pleasure in the day. For the first time, she knew for a certainty that she had complete control of the throne of Egypt. Pharaoh was living in his other world now, no doubt enjoying a large feast with his priestly friends.

"We shall ride in your chariot this night, Kamare. This morning, much must be done at court; but, after our afternoon sleep and the evening's feast, we will visit the moon and stars." She felt so happy and complete. She wanted her love to share in this happiness but realized that he had fallen silent and appeared to be lost in thought.

He reached over and took her hand in his. “Hati, my love, we have accomplished much, but there is much left to do. Your armies are almost ready. The new barracks enclosed in the high walls are ready to receive them, and the stables are filled with the finest horseflesh in your kingdom. We have the tips of your toes upon the line of preparedness. You will be the most powerful Queen in all history. But there are rumors that the Hyksos have raided across your borders and killed many of your people. They believe you to be weak. You must give me leave to amass the soldiers and march under your name. Queen Hatshepsut cannot allow the defacing of temples and the loss of life from these vicious hordes.

“If I fly as the sand does in the wind and see as does the hawk in the sky, all will be well. Your soft arms and sweet lips bind me, and I can deny you nothing. But, see these truths, and send me on my mission to punish your enemies. It does no good to have a bowstring pulled tight, if I cannot release the arrow.”

As he spoke, his eyes told her he would rather remain with her. But his rank as General of all the armies of Egypt was well deserved; he was a man who saw his duty clearly and would do it if she would but let him loose from her arms.

Hatshepsut smiled and kissed him even though the thought of his going so soon filled her with anguish. She spoke as a Queen must. “Go then, Kamare. You must remind me of our duties more often. I am but a love-besotted woman and think only of the pleasures of your company. If I am to be a mighty ruler and build great monuments, I must be strong. Now, I have something prepared for you. Beka, the chest for my General, please.”

She opened the chest and removed a wide, flat band of gold. It was made to be worn on Kamare’s head, and she placed it there. Instead of the hooded cobra, it bore her cartouche. It was not only a beautiful ornament; it bestowed more honor upon him and gave him even greater power. Kamare presented a most royal appearance as the band settled upon his brow.

All would know his power. All would know his value to the Queen.

"And finally," she said, "you must allow me to choose your house for you while you are gone. I would have a hand in choosing furnishings for your home as well. It will help to keep my mind at ease while you are defending my lands and my name."

"You have made me so happy, my love! Do as you will. And now I must be gone. I promise you that there will be long evenings together and many chariot rides when all is secure."

Hatshepsut watched from her balcony as his chariot disappeared through the palace gates.

11

During her morning bath, Hatshepsut had begun to think of the days of the passage of the moon, and she came to the same conclusion as Beka had earlier. Secretly, she desired the child of Kamare, this most handsome and wondrous of men. However, she accepted the realities concerning royalty. The Queens of Egypt were sacred vessels. Through them, through the giving of birth, passed the dynasty of the Thothmesid. If she did not bear fruit in the bed of the gold cobra, a half-royal son would take her place and would wed a half-royal female of the harem. His blood would be only half-pure and diluted—but the dynasty would continue.

What would she do if she were impregnated by Kamare? Could she bring herself to destroy the child at birth? Many queens had done this very thing. To attempt to cause a loss of the child in the early months could not be risked, for fear that the Queen might die or become barren. Thus, "accidental" children were thrown into the Nile immediately after birth.

The immortality of Queens and Pharaohs was never questioned. They were gods—children of Ra, Isis, and Horus—and would do as they would do. Nevertheless, it was understood in the palace that, if the queen or a princess had an "accident" while pleasuring the body, the child could not live. In the case whereupon a purely royal Pharaoh found a half-royal wife sleeping with someone other than himself, he had to choose between forgiving her and having her put to death (an accidental death, of course).

Hatshepsut, being fully royal, of almost pure Greek blood, was above reproach. She could choose lovers at will, and her half-royal mate, made Pharaoh by her choice alone, could do nothing openly. In fact, he had best watch himself, lest she have him fed to the crocodiles.

But to the dilemma at hand: Hatshepsut came in from the balcony and called Beka to her side. She dismissed the other ladies so that the two of them could be alone. They sat talking earnestly, heads close together.

"My lady, if you are with child, you will know in two weeks when your flow does not come. Also, your breasts will grow larger and most tender, and your nipples will expand and change their color from pink to brown. If all this comes to pass, what will the Queen of Egypt do?" Beka covered her head and moaned, and Hatshepsut shook her gently.

"Be quiet, dear nurse. I am not possessed of my good mind for no reason. There will be a way to save the child; for, in all truth, I long for the child of Kamare, even though it is misfortune. I shall go to the great temple of Isis. She will comfort me and grant me further wisdom. Tell the guard to have my chariot made ready with my white mare in the harness. Handling Lazuli will make me feel alive and sharp of wit. Also, send the ladies to dress me and advise the Vizier that I crave his company and counsel this day. Go now, and no more moaning."

The Grand Vizier bustled self-importantly through the halls of the palace, telling all along the way, "Queen Hatshepsut, Pharaoh of all Egypt, requires my company and good advice for the day. Do not attempt to delay me, as my lips are sealed as to the importance of this counsel." Of course, everyone knew his sealed lips were easily loosened by wine, and by nightfall everyone would know all.

He entered the Queen's audience chamber and found her dressed to drive her chariot. "Come, Imhot, you will accompany me to the house of the goddess Isis. In your wisdom, you shall help me to worship. The Hyksos are on rampage again; and as General Kamare goes to do battle with them, we must beg the gods, one each day, to make him strong and give him the foresight to lead our army to victory. You will ride at my side. I have arranged for your sweet daughter to follow in a chariot filled with lotus blossoms, the favorite flower of Isis. We shall honor her with this gift.

"Imhot, give close attention to the driver of your daughter's chariot. He is a handsome young officer whose family possess great parcels of land and who are also nobles of my court. He looks with favor upon your child; and if he proves worthy, I may make him the gift of the lovely Nefertum to take as wife. Loyalty must be rewarded."

At first, Imhot had been filled with fear. He knew that to ride with Queen Hatshepsut was to ride as fast as the horse could run, and he was an old man. But her following remarks regarding the future of Nefertum brought a smile to his wrinkled face and momentarily drove all fear from his mind. *A handsome and rich husband for my eldest daughter? If all goes well, who knows? It is possible the Queen will accept my second daughter into her service.*

Imhot had served as an able and intelligent vizier for many years and should have recognized some underlying purpose in what Hatshepsut said. However, there they were again: vanity and greed. How often the two block good reason . . .

As for Hatshepsut's reasoning, she was thinking months ahead of all the others. Nefertum knew of Kamare's time in the queen's bed. It was now up to Hatshepsut to arrange such a happy life for the girl, to bestow such honor upon her, that her loyalty would be complete. Some other could fill her place as a lady of the court.

Off they rode—Hatshepsut, with hair streaming from beneath the gold cobra crown, driving the spirited mare, her vizier crouching in terror at her feet. For one so slight, she drove with the skill and fearlessness of a warrior, thus endearing herself to the members of her guard. They admired courage and daring above all.

Nefertum and her driver rode at a more decorous pace. The captain's free arm was about his passenger's waist, and he turned occasionally to smile down at her and murmur some compliment. Captain Senu was not a simpleton. He had understood his Queen well. He had but to take this plump young woman to wife and much reward would be his. He was brave in battle; and she had hinted that one general might not be enough for Egypt.

Besides, there were always other women to be had, perhaps even a second, more beautiful wife. Yes, he would obey.

As for Nefertum, her bliss was boundless. That Senu wanted to marry her fulfilled her every dream. *Hatshepsut has been so good to me. I vow to Isis that if I am granted this great happiness, I will serve my Queen forever! I will give my life for her.* Nefertum decided she would never be able to do enough to repay the Queen's kindnesses.

Hatshepsut and her guards arrived in their chariots long before the others. The chief guard leapt to take the reins of the foam-covered mare. Another guard ran to the gates of the temple of Isis and pounded upon the door.

Startled priests rushed to greet the daughter of Isis as she walked in serene majesty into the open-air temple. It was generally unwise to favor one god above the others; however, since she was known to be the daughter of Isis and Horus, Hatshepsut had been exceedingly generous to both their temples.

This temple of worship for her mother, Isis, was open to the blue sky. Pools and fountains filled the courtyard. Trees shaded stone benches where worshipers waited their turns to pray and make sacrifices upon the altar in a small, roofed building. Behind that building were the houses and storerooms of the priests and priestesses. The person of highest rank was the chief priestess of Isis, an elderly woman haughty with self-importance. Dressed all in white and adorned with gold, she stood in the doorway leading to the altar as though she were guarding it. "Queen Hatshepsut may enter now," she said.

And Hatshepsut replied pleasantly but with force, "The Queen Hatshepsut goes wherever she pleases to go. The Queen Hatshepsut chooses to be alone with her mother, Isis. The priestess may wait in the courtyard."

The priestess hesitated an instant too long. Guards rushed forward, took her by the arms, and hurried her away. *This is not a good omen,* thought Hatshepsut. *If all does not go well, she might die.* Hatshepsut walked into the cool, mud-brick building and faced a simple gold altar draped in white linens. The disk of Ra stood behind a small gold statue of the goddess Isis.

The chariot containing the lotus blossoms arrived, and they

were carried in, a bundle at a time, and placed in the Queen's arms. In turn, she placed them upon the altar until it overflowed. She then threw powdered incense into the brazier and wispy smoke arose.

The Queen stood tall with eyes closed. The scent of lotus and the smoke from the incense swirled around her. She felt the spirit of Isis, her mother, enter her soul and mind. "Speak to me, oh Mother, Isis. I have need of your guidance. It may be that Egypt, Ta-Mare, will need many young princes and princesses as heirs to the throne. I depend upon you to guide me in all things, and I will obey."

She stood motionless, eyes still closed, in meditation. As the smoke of the incense increased, thoughts began to take shape in her mind. A plan took root there, a plan that could save the babe if she were, indeed, with child by the non-royal Kamare. Hati believed these thoughts to be the guiding voice of Isis. She must say aloud something to place her plan in motion, should she need it—a plan that would not necessarily be followed if she were not with child. In the meantime, however, she would give many of the priests and half-royal sons of Thothmes food for hope and thought.

And so, opening her eyes, she spoke in a voice that all in the courtyard could hear. "Oh Isis, I obey you. I shall seek friendship with the half-brothers, sons of Thothmes I. Perhaps it is time to give Egypt many heirs so that this most grand of all dynasties does not wither and die away. I will be fruitful as you direct. All who know me know that I am Isis and that I must serve Ta-Mare, my land."

Hatshepsut turned from the altar and walked to the doorway where she looked out upon the astonished faces in the courtyard. She smiled beautifully for Isis had spoken to her. Her happiness was infectious, and all there began to laugh and smile. The Queen had been instructed by mother Isis to take a husband so that she would bear royal fruit. Clearly, she was a goddess.

Hatshepsut radiated great joy; and as she drove her chariot back to the palace, the smile remained in place. Imhot was grateful for the much more leisurely ride and vowed that he, too, would be more generous to the temple of Isis if she brought about such wonders as these.

Thinking to herself, Hatshepsut decided that she would interview many of the half-royal princes serving as priests in the houses of the gods. One would be selected for marriage in case her flow did not arrive. Deep in her heart of hearts, Hati knew that Kamare had given her the gift of a child—but no one must know that the child was that of her favorite General.

Before Hatshepsut reached the palace, word had spread like chaff upon the wind, from temple to temple, from priest to priest: "Queen Hatshepsut will choose a Pharaoh!"

Half-brothers of marriageable age were struck with excitement. Each hoped to be the chosen one. In reality, the high priest of each god's house would select, from among the young men in his charge, the one he felt would be most attractive to Hatshepsut. She would doubtless meet with and talk to all the half-brothers, but each priest felt that he must try to sway her decision toward the young man of his choice. Certainly, the new Pharaoh would be most generous to the priests with whom he had spent most of his life.

The days passed for Hatshepsut, each bringing with it increasing anxiety about her condition. Were her breasts more tender? Or, was she overly concerned, to the point of exaggeration?

The days also brought news from Kamare. He had formed a huge army and organized a supply train. The time was one thousand five hundred twelve years before the birth of Jesus Christ; and the fighting machine that Kamare had put together was the finest that would be seen until the time of the Roman legions.

The General was as wise as he was strong. This army would have fresh bread and live animals to slaughter for fresh meat. They would have dates to eat to prevent the scaling disease; and in their saddlebags would be good wine and water, dried fish from the Nile, and dried millet cakes. The Queen's gold had provided well.

The fine horses and the chariots, the bows and arrows—all were embellished with the colors of Queen Hatshepsut. The sun-bronzed soldiers wore the green and gold with great pride for they were cosseted and nurtured, as had been no other Egyptian army.

Kamare had also spent time in restoring the Queen's sailing fleet. He had chosen a young admiral, Thutre, to oversee the rebuilding of the ships with lumber bought from traders. The ships were repaired as needed, stripped to bare bones if necessary. New sails and new rigging were installed and provisions were made to put the ships into instant service. Volunteers instead of slaves served on these ships as rowers, and they trained constantly, practicing coordinated maneuvers. Although subjugation of the Hyksos would not involve sea battles, Kamare was determined to be able to wage war on any front.

Even now, as the land army began to march upon the Hyksos, Thutre put to sea with half of his fleet. He sailed for Thrace in Greece. The holds of his ships contained chests of gold, set side-by-side with amphorae of oil, wine, dates, and wheat. His mission was to trade for more ingots of copper and for weapons of war—swords, bows and arrows, lances—any armament with which the Thracian king would part.

The quarters on the top decks of the two largest ships held the "cargo of persuasion." Thutre was charged with the delivery of six beautiful virgins from the royal harem, gifts for King Aristos of Thrace. They were a varying array of womanhood, each chosen for beauty in different skin shades, for musical prowess, and most importantly, for intelligence.

The Greeks were very knowledgeable and held philosophers and teachers in great esteem. They worshipped the gods of the mind. It would be pleasant for their king to receive exotic young women with outstanding musical talent who also could keep pace with lofty conversation. King Aristos would be pleased with them. Hatshepsut had selected them herself, and she knew well what she did. Her library was filled with the words of Greece, and she was directly related to the king of that country.

Out of this voyage would come alliance, full war chests, and strength, for Hatshepsut had written a message to the king in her own fine hand. Into the script of Thracian words, she had poured honey—King Aristos could depend upon the new Great

Queen-and-Pharaoh, Hatshepsut, to aid him in any way he desired at any time. She would welcome an invitation to sail to Greece in person; the ruler of Egypt would grace his palace in friendship.

Hatshepsut had no intention of ever leaving her beloved Egypt, but the gesture was a grand one. Her scheme would bring this fleet home in a year or less laden with the items necessary to remain strong.

In actuality, Egypt was the ruler of Greece at this time, but Hatshepsut chose to treat King Aristos as an equal, on papyri at least. She could have sent ships and soldiers to demand tribute and simply take the supplies she required. In doing as she did, however, her kingdom maintained the security of good will. No evil would come against her from that direction.

Another ten ships had set sail for the Red Sea. These men were bound for the land of Punt on the African coast. They would return with cargoes of myrrh and other perfumes, oils, and rare cloth made only in that land. Hatshepsut need send only a few expeditions a year to other lands to keep all the Egyptian nobility and lorded gentry in full supply of the luxurious scents used in their bathing and anointing. Every land welcomed the emissaries of Egypt, for they possessed gold in vast amounts. Gold bought everything and anyone, and Egypt had more of this precious metal than any other country.

Kamare drove his chariot at the head of his army. In developing his tactics, he had decided to array his war machines and vast hordes of soldiers in controlled units. He set a medium pace, never rushing, but moving steadfastly toward the border that lay between Egypt and the lands of the Hyksos. He wanted the spies that he knew were observing him to send swift messengers to King Obinninos in his walled city.

These messengers, with fear in their hearts, raced their horses to the waiting king. Fear showed upon their dirt-stained faces as they knelt before the cruel Obinninos to tell of what was to befall him.

The king had heard that a mere girl ruled Egypt. Queen Hatshepsut, he was told, ruled alone. His advisors had spoken of the weakness of the army of Thothmes I; it had not marched in ten years.

Taking advantage of this change in leadership, as had happened so often before when a new ruler came to power, the dominions under the thumb of Pharaoh stirred with ambition. And this new ruler was a very young woman. She possessed vast lands—lands ripe with wheat—huge gold mines, and countless other treasures.

The king of the Hyksos had led his warriors across the border to rob, rape, and kill. The Hyksos were monsters with no mercy, and Kamare intended to show them none.

As the reports continued to pour in, King Obinninos clutched his robes around him and ordered the defense of his walled city. The countryside was stripped of all that could be eaten or drunk, and it was gathered inside the walls. Many people, the elderly, the weak, and the children, were shoved outside the gates as they cried for mercy.

Only the royal family, which included the harem, the members of the court and their many slaves and servants remained, along with the soldiers and other able-bodied men who had been forcibly separated from their families so that they could defend the king. If there should be a siege, the city could sustain itself for two years or more inside the thick, tall walls.

To amuse himself and to ease his tension, the king occasionally had a woman from his harem thrown into his pit of wild dogs to be pulled apart before his eyes. Such a sight raised the lust in him, and he went to his women for hours on end. If any in the harem displeased him, she was remembered for the next drunken entertainment. And all the while, the Egyptians came on.

Two weeks after beginning its march, the army of the Queen passed the Hyksos' border unopposed early one morning. In another two weeks they were camped before the great city of Kadesh. Kamare had his own spies, and he knew all that had transpired. He decided to give the king the opportunity to become very nervous, perhaps afraid. The battle Kamare intended to fight was one that would result in as few Egyptian losses as possible; his friend and ally was *time.*

12

Hatshepsut sat at her dressing table, staring at the image reflected in the electrum mirror. She had missed her most recent monthly flow, and her breasts were swollen. Her nipples were wider and dark brown. There could be no doubt; Kamare's child was growing inside her. As daughter of Isis, and as Isis, herself, she had a solemn duty. She was the chalice of Egypt. Only she could bring forth the heir of truly royal blood.

It was no secret that all the inbreeding of the Thothmesid dynasty had generated faulty offspring, some little more than idiots. Mothers had married sons; fathers had wed sisters and their own daughters; and, in her case, she would marry a half-brother. In her studies in the great library, she had learned that royal lines benefited from an injection of strong, non-familial blood. Whose blood could be stronger than that of her dear, beloved Kamare? Would he accept what she must do? Yes, he must, for there was no other choice. It was marriage to a half-brother or death for the child.

To the task at hand, then.

The Queen sent Nefertum to bring her father to her. As she waited, her ladies dressed her and the cosmetician applied make-up. When Imhot entered the reception room, she was seated upon her winged chair, feet resting on an ebony stool. She held lotus blooms in her lap as a sign of fertility and smiled a little as she spoke to the vizier.

"Imhot, I charge you with a responsibility of great importance. I will, this very day, choose a husband. Isis had spoken to me, and I must be fruitful as is my duty. Assemble all of my half-brothers, from the eldest to the youngest, into the great hall this feast time. We shall dine together, and I shall choose. Go now."

Imhot had heard his Queen's words at the temple and was

expecting this command. He anticipated large bribes from priests and the half-royal brothers, who would vie for advantageous positions at the banquet. He sent out messengers with the summons and then informed the cooks and the provider of the wax cones to make preparations for an elaborate feast. Another messenger went to the harem to inform Montu that the most beautiful and talented dancing girls were to perform that evening for the Queen and her assemblage.

Imhot was unaware that Hatshepsut already knew the kind of husband she sought and had narrowed her choices to a few young men of appropriate age. Not for this Queen would there be a strong, power-usurping man. No; she would choose a boy who was easily manipulated. He might be crowned Pharaoh to rule as her equal, but he would be no threat. The co-ruler she envisioned was one who would be weak in mind and physical strength. She did not entertain thoughts of the physical side of marriage, but she knew she would do her duty. She was, after all, well trained in the performance of duty.

That evening, Queen Hatshepsut had her maidens dress her with great care. She adorned herself with all the accouterments of power. She would be overpowering in her person alone, assisted by the fearsome guards always by her side. She wore her coronation dress, set off by her necklace of wide gold with blue birds. With hair tucked up into her double crown, her face was painted in stark black and white.

When all one hundred twenty sons of Thothmes were seated with their guardian priests, she appeared beside the raised throne and sat, holding the flail and crook crossed upon her full breasts.

This beautiful, yet fearful, sight silenced the throng. Cymbals clashed three times, and the vizier rose to tell them what they already knew. Before he could speak, Hatshepsut's voice cut like a knife. "On your knees, under pain of death!" Upon hearing this command, the guards drew their swords. The sound of steel slipping against steel sent all falling to their knees. She let them remain there in silence a full five minutes before gesturing to Imhot to resume.

"Queen Hatshepsut, living forever, Pharaoh of Egypt, and

the upper and lower regions, will choose a co-ruler from among the children of her father. She has instructed me that each of you shall walk to the throne and speak for himself. All infants are to be removed from the room."

Fully forty children under the age of nine were removed, and the remainder stood in uncertainty. How should they approach? Would names be called? A few stood aloof with airs of quiet assurance. These were the more mature young men, well educated, strong, and handsome. They had no idea they would not do at all.

Imhot called them to the throne one by one, starting with the oldest. He introduced each to the Queen and also gave the name of his mother. Each young man spoke confidently, giving a glowing account of his prowess in battle, his knowledge of books, and by lowered eyelids and ardent glances, his loving nature.

The Queen's expression never wavered. She smiled benignly at each and seemed not to be impressed with any. But her mind was churning; she waited for the ones she had had investigated. Of the handful she was prepared to consider, it was the son of Mutnefret who seemed to fit her plans best.

She knew this boy only as the son of Mutnefret, but he was perfect. His hair fell in ringlets to his shoulders, however, the curls were not natural but had been formed by heated rods. His nails on both hands and toes were painted in bright colors. Obviously he loved the table, as his hips and stomach were far wider than his slim shoulders. He wore a friendly , rather whimsical smile, and he spoke well and with kindness. He would make a good companion and apparently would demand little of his wife in the bedchamber.

After some hours, the introductions were completed. Platters of food were served, and all turned to the feast and the excellent wine.

Hatshepsut allowed herself one goblet of wine before gesturing to the son of Mutnefret to come sit beside her. A low chair was brought, and he sat here chatting away as he pushed food into his mouth. His hands were slim and delicate, and his manners were not offensive despite his greed. His conversation was witty and free, and Hatshepsut trilled with laughter at the clever remarks he made.

Bit by bit, feasting in the hall slowed, and conversation finally ceased altogether. It had occurred to them all that possibly the Queen had already decided upon the silly boy at her side. This was impossible, of course. Obviously, he did not have the strength needed by a Pharaoh.

There were some who nodded in sudden understanding. They knew what she was about but were powerless to prevent it. As she had established, they were there "under pain of death."

The clash of cymbals called forth the dancing girls who would perform to please the young men. These lovely young women were among those who had chosen to remain in the harem, some the daughters of Pharaoh. Since they, too, were half-royal, they were excellent marriage material for the ambitious sons of Pharaoh, as each would have a large dowry plus the surname of "daughter to Thothmes I." Offspring of such marriages were often pushed forward as fully royal, especially if a dynasty ended without an heir.

The girls wore only waistbands of gold and the gifts of jewelry they had received from Thothmes. The perfumed cones of wax on their wigs began to melt as they writhed in feverish dances. The wax ran down their shoulders and breasts, and their oiled bodies steamed.

Many of the young men grasped at the girls to pull them down into waiting laps. The wine and the warm flesh mixed with the beat of drums to boil the blood of the lusty sons of Thothmes. Young half-royals would mate this night, and marriages would follow in the morning. It was the custom.

It was also the custom for the ruling Pharaoh to grant estates and slaves to these couples. The chest of gold each man and each girl possessed as a child of Pharaoh would allow the pair to live elegantly.

Egypt's wealth was so great that there was more than enough for all.

Hatshepsut leaned toward the young man beside her and spoke kindly to him. "Son of Mutnefret, it is my intent to choose a co-ruler. He will be crowned Pharaoh of Egypt and will have great power and riches. Do you think you could love me as your Great Royal Wife, to live in harmony and Maat? And within this peaceful love, could you give the chalice of Egypt many heirs so that our dynasty should survive?"

As she was speaking thus, her gaze had captured his attention because of the black stars in her eyes. Her loveliness and sincerity were enhanced by her seemingly endless power. Try as she might, the beautiful Queen could not mask the strength and wisdom she possessed. To many, she was unapproachable and frightening. But this hapless boy was not intimidated; he was merely startled. Of all in the great hall, he, alone, had been unaware of his position.

"Great Queen," he said haltingly, "I am without words. I am in total surprise." He sat with jaws agape, staring at Hatshepsut, as he would at a statue suddenly come to life. All at once, it struck him. He could be Pharaoh! He could have all sorts of beautiful possessions and eat whatever he liked. As for the giving of heirs, he knew next-to-nothing of such things; but was he not a man? Ah, what joy! What a blessing for his mother and for the kind priests of Amon with whom he had grown to manhood.

"Queen Hatshepsut, I am honored beyond any words. I cannot imagine why you have chosen me over the many handsome men here tonight. But you will find me to be a kind and grateful husband. I shall do all that is possible to please my lovely wife. I promise you that you will not be sorry for the choice you have made."

He offered her his hand with slender fingers and painted nails. She took it in both of hers and bowed slightly to him, and it was sealed.

She was content. The boy was not repulsive, and she could manage him with the crook of one of her little fingers. It seemed that the babe within her was content also; for, in the innermost recess of her mind she heard Isis's voice as clearly as her own: "Great Queen Hatshepsut, I, Isis your mother, Isis the Goddess of Life, give thanks for the child that comes into this world without danger awaiting him. But, heed this warning—if this boy is easily led by you, he will be just as easily led by others."

Hatshepsut did not doubt that the voice in her head was that of Isis. She would make certain only those under her influence approached he new Pharaoh. And she would begin with the mother of her husband-to-be.

Hatshepsut spoke softly and placed her hand gently upon his arm. "Sweet young Prince, your quarters have been prepared next to those of mine. I shall take you there now. Tomorrow morning, we shall ride side by side to the temple of Isis and also of Amon where you have lived. In both places we shall be married, and you shall be crowned Pharaoh by the high priest of Amon, who brought you here tonight. Come love, we shall go and none shall speak against us. You are very powerful now."

She called to the captain of her guards, and he came to her instantly. "Captain, assign a stalwart escort for the son of Mutnefret and treat him with all the honors bestowed upon me. As the sun rises, we shall set forth to the temples of Isis and Amon to be married. You are charged with the care of your new Pharaoh. Also, you will come to my rooms after the Prince is installed in his apartments. I would speak to you alone. We go now." the cymbals clashed and the queen and prince arose. Arm in arm, they walked to the hall leading to the royal apartments.

The carousing stopped just long enough for them to disappear; then once again young arms entwined, and lips that tasted of wine pressed together.

Several sober pairs of eyes were intent upon the proceedings. These eyes burned with disappointment and deep resentment. Try as she might, Hatshepsut would not be able to go through life without making enemies. She was a woman of action; fortunately, she was also a woman of fierce strength, and she would need all of it.

As they walked down the hallway with the mosaic floor that seemed to be a living pool of water, the fishes and birds in it charmed the young prince. His eyes glittered at the sights of the ever-increasing splendors of the inner palace—something few ever saw. When Hatshepsut threw open the doors to the rooms which had been hers as Great Royal Wife, he was charmed beyond words. The rich, feminine furnishings of silk, gold, and fine woods suited his tastes perfectly. How kind an thoughtful was his dear wife. He would please her in all ways if he could.

"I leave you now to your bath, husband-to-be. If you desire anything at all, you need only command it of the guards beyond your door. They are there to protect and serve you. You must understand that many are disappointed this night because I have chosen you. Therefore, you have also a food taster here, the child by your tables. Do not eat or drink until the child has done so. I bid you sleep well; we go forth before the sun rises." At the mention of a food taster, the eyes of the prince widened. It now occurred to him that this wonderful new life carried hazards of which he had not dreamed.

The queen closed the doors and was escorted to the rooms that had been Pharaoh's. She would keep them. She would keep Pharaoh's power as well. The captain of the guard followed her into the reception room where she sat and took a little wine, as the day had been long. The captain stood with head bowed, awaiting her words.

"Captain Senu, you cannot know my reasons for the choices I make, nor need you. But this much I tell you. The man whom I shall marry tomorrow is easily swayed in thought. No doubt many believe that they may make use of him to achieve their own desires. I charge you with the duty of seeing that only those loyal to me have access to him. Do I make myself totally clear?"

Senu bowed deeply and, thumping his fist upon his chest, gave a solemn oath that her command would be obeyed, as he thought, *Oh, that Nefertum could be as lovely as the Queen.* But he must allow no thoughts such as these. He knew he would be handsomely rewarded for his dutiful marriage, and a soldier could climb just so far. Still, he could silently adore Hatshepsut; after all, who could not?

She spoke again. "Captain Senu, I go now to bathe. Before I sleep, I would have the mother of our new Pharaoh brought from the harem in great ceremony and honor. After I have spoken with her, she will be installed in the many-roomed apartment that was used by the necromancer Euripides. On your way to fetch the mother, send Nefertum to me. You may go, and you have your Queen's favor."

He left and, shortly, a beaming Nefertum appeared. "Nefertum, you whom I have trusted with my own comforts are now charged with readying rooms for the mother of the new Pharaoh. Choose among my ladies and make ready the empty rooms of Euripides. Ask the storerooms for anything you need and find ladies to wait upon the grandmother of the new heirs of Egypt. Make this woman content, and I shall have your house selected by the river within the week. I would have you happily married to Captain Senu. He has told me he is eager for this marriage, and I would reward you both."

Nefertum was overjoyed with the trust the Queen placed in her and the news that Senu was eager for her. Lately she had begun to doubt his affection, but now she knew they would soon be together in their own beautiful house. She bowed and flew to the tasks before her. The rooms would be perfect in every way.

Senu arrived unannounced at the harem in the middle of the night. He pounded upon the doors until a sleepy Montu opened them. "Greetings, keeper of the harem. Queen Hatshepsut would have an audience with Mutnefret at once. See to it."

Mutnefret had been awake all night, along with the other mothers of the sons of Thothmes I. She had harbored no hope at all that her son would be chosen. The other mothers talked endlessly about the masculinity and handsome appearances of their offspring. How could her sweet boy compete with such as these? She smiled and smiled although her heart was breaking. Not only would she spend her whole life in the harem, she would probably never know the joy of grandchildren. She supposed his only hope was to rise through the priesthood, but even that was unlikely. Her affable son cared nothing for politics.

The bell sounded at the inner gate, and all the women fell silent. The moment was here. Each held her breath as Montu strode into the courtyard where they were gathered. He paused for effect; then walked slowly to Mutnefret, knelt down before her, and reached out and placed her hand upon his head.

Mutnefret could scarcely breathe. It was not possible—her son chosen to be the co-ruler of Egypt, consort of Hatshepsut? Surely, Montu would never dare to jest with her in this way.

Montu prostrated himself and said, "Mighty companion of Thothmes, Queen Hatshepsut has sent an escort for you. You shall be taken at once to the palace. Your son has been chosen and the Queen would speak with you this night. Please honor me by allowing me to conduct you to Captain Senu."

For a moment, Mutnefret dared not try to stand, so certain was she that she would fall into a heap. She did not believe it possible until she realized the other women were fawning upon her; great favors could come from the mother of Pharaoh. The bitterness of loss caught in the throats of many; but in a land of connivance, they knew a good face must be put upon such disaster.

Slowly Mutnefret rose and followed after Montu as if in a dream. It was easy to see the resemblance between mother and son. She was small of stature, and in her youth had been quite pretty. But she had succumbed to the lure of wine and sweets, and now she waddled rather than walked.

Mutnefret had entered the harem at the age of twelve and had remained enclosed in the gilded prison for thirty years. Even in the middle of the night, her first view of the outside world was breathtaking. She tried to take in everything during the chariot ride to the palace, but all sped by in a blur. The captain spun into the palace courtyard with a flourish. He descended from the chariot and turned to help her down as though she were a princess. She was mute with disbelief.

"Come, mother of tomorrow's Pharaoh. Your queen awaits you," Senu said, as he made a courtly bow.

Mutnefret was even more dazzled than her son by the wonders of the palace, for he at least had previously seen some small part of the world. "I feel as if I am in a lovely dream," she murmured to herself.

Hatshepsut sat as before upon the gold chair in her reception room. She had decided to bathe when this chore was over. The sight of her new husband's mother was most reassuring. This woman was exactly the kind who could be manipulated. She would be no arrogant, demanding mother-in-law. The trembling woman knelt at the feet of the Queen, and tears ran down plump cheeks.

In pity, Hatshepsut leaned down to help Mutnefret rise. She assisted her to a chair and called to Beka. "Some wine, please, for our new mother. She is overjoyed but weak. We must make her welcome."

After Mutnefret had been seated and had sipped from a goblet of wine, her fear abated somewhat; but as court etiquette demanded, she waited for her Queen to speak first. Seeing this, Hatshepsut became more pleased. *Yes, I can handle this one as easily as her son. I can afford to be kind and generous.*

"Dear Mutnefret, when we are alone after tomorrow's ceremony, you must call me Hati. I was born of the gods, but my mortal mother died at my birth so that I might live. I shall enjoy having a mother that I share with your son, soon to be Pharaoh."

Mutnefret could not believe her fortune; she replied simply that she would. The Queen spoke again. "I have sent my ladies to prepare rooms for you that are worthy of the mother of Pharaoh. You must leave all your possessions in the harem for I shall provide everything you could wish for; and among them will be garments for you to wear tomorrow when you accompany us on our journey of marriage. Also, outside your doors are guards and inside your chambers are ladies of service. You need only to verbalize a desire for something and your wish shall be done. Go now and rest well, as we rise before the sun. I say good night to you, dear Mother." Hatshepsut smiled warmly upon the heavy woman as she rose and walked dreamily to the door. Mutnefret stopped and turned to wave shyly before leaving.

Oh, but I am so tired, thought Hatshepsut. It seemed as if the child within her wanted her to sleep and sleep again.

There was but a day and a night to get through, and then she could rest. Her bath this night would be short, and sleep would come quickly. She congratulated herself for placing her new husband's mother in Euripides's old apartments. The room of magic had a spy hole into the bedchamber of those quarters. If she had misjudged Mutnefret, she would know soon enough. And, no doubt, if any plot were raised against her, it would in all likelihood begin either with her husband or his mother. She would watch them carefully and would deal swiftly with any would-be manipulators.

Before the sun was fully raised—while it was a glow just visible in the east—the royal procession began. Trumpeters blared their horns from the walls of the palace to awaken the city. The sounds of these trumpets informed the city's inhabitants that the living gods were about to appear to perform some important function. By the time the gates opened, crowds were gathering everywhere, drifting toward the main thoroughfare of Thebes.

First came a squadron of mounted guards who lined themselves up along the route to the temple of Isis. Next were musicians bedecked with flowers and dancing about, as they played their flutes and harps. The crowds realized that this must be a joyous occasion.

Hatshepsut's white mare pulled her chariot. She was alone and wearing the double crown of Pharaoh. A simple, pleated, white linen dress hung from her neck to her gold sandaled feet; and she smiled upon everyone, the picture of peace and Maat.

Behind her, Captain Senu drove the soon-to-be husband in a chariot pulled by a dark mare. The symbolism was direct and noticeable to even the most dull-witted in the crowd. There could be no mistake about the identity of the real ruler of this land.

The third one bore Mutnefret who was clinging to the side of her chariot in fear. Her driver was courteous and careful to make the trip as comfortable as possible, but the many upturned faces on all sides, cheering and laughing, terrified the woman. It was all so overwhelming. Never before had she seen so many people at such close range.

All sorts of vehicles followed the royal conveyances: chariots bearing important officials, bearer chairs, wagons filled with minor members of the court, and horsemen. All were bedecked with flowers, and many of the passengers carried blossoms to throw to the people.

The procession moved slowly through the city until it reached the temple of Isis where the doors were standing open. Hatshepsut stepped down from her chariot as Senu helped the Prince from his. The couple met at the open doors and clasped hands.

A roar came up from the crowd for they now realized, even before the proclamation was issued, that this was a royal wedding. They were happy because they loved their Queen and because a royal wedding meant an open feast for the citizens of Thebes. They would drop their work at any excuse to enjoy themselves, and this was a perfect reason for revelry. And when Imhot stood in the gateway and proclaimed that the new Pharaoh would bear the same name as the mighty Thothmes (now living in his tomb forever and ever), the news spread swiftly and was received with great shouts of approval from the multitude.

Hatshepsut had sent notice to the aged priestess of Isis along with a gift of a lambskin of gold. She wanted to make amends with this powerful woman if such was possible.

Slaves had spent the night preparing the temple for the ceremony. The altar enclosed in the small building was strewn with palm fronds, and upon cushions before it were two necklaces woven of lotus blossoms. These were the marriage wreaths, symbolizing the fertility of man joined to woman.

The priestess, dressed in gleaming white, awaited them with outstretched arms and with head shaven and oiled. She radiated great joy for she had never been so happy. Never in her time had a royal marriage taken place in the temple of Isis. It had been one hundred years since Queen Tetisheri has brought a chosen husband here to wed. Now, she and she alone, would be priestess above all others. Because of this, and the lambskin of gold, she chose to disregard her earlier humiliation. She felt it wise to remember only that the Queen was imparting great honor upon her.

The two young people, Queen and Prince, knelt before the priestess. The old woman bowed to Queen Hatshepsut and asked, "What name shall this new falcon in the nest be called?"

Hatshepsut replied, "My husband shall be called Thothmes II, in the hope that he will rule as wisely as my father-husband did during his lifetime. He will be bold in battle and fertile in seed so that Egypt's Queen shall bear many royal sons and daughters. Please give us both your blessing from Isis."

Upon hearing the words "brave in battle," the new husband found the smile slipping slightly from his face. He recovered somewhat as the wedding necklace of lotus flowers was hung around his neck. The priestess intoned at length that he was now Pharaoh Thothmes II, strong of arm, loving of heart, living forever and ever. *Peace and prosperity to Thothmes II, Pharaoh of all Egypt, the upper and lower lands, and all dominions!*

Turning to Queen Hatshepsut, she lowered the lotus wreath of marriage over her double crown and spoke again. "Great Royal Wife, Queen Hatshepsut, living forever and ever. Isis will give you fruit in your womb. You are her daughter, and Isis herself on earth." Her eyes narrowed a bit as she continued, "Pharaoh Thothmes II, ruler of all Egypt, upper and lower lands, and all dominions, will raise his strong arm to protect you."

The old woman had discerned at a glance what was truly happening. The queen would be Pharaoh still. This short, dissipated man-child would dance to the queen's desires. She realized she had underestimated the Queen, and she now admired her shrewd move. *No one will fault Queen Hatshepsut for failing to produce heirs as is her duty. The real problem will be to obtain a strong child from so weak a union. But no matter. The wedding ceremony has been completed. This consort might receive all the crowns he can carry in the temple of Amon; it will be Hatshepsut who rules Egypt.*

Thothmes II rose with difficulty—it appeared that he soon would be very fat—and offered his hand to his wife. The Queen was playing her part to perfection as she blushed and gathered lotus buds in her arms. The couple appeared at the gates of the temple to the deafening roar of the citizens of Thebes.

"Queen Hatshepsut! Pharaoh Thothmes II!" they cried, over and over.

Hatshepsut insisted that Thothmes II ride with her. As she wrapped the reins around her arm, the new Pharaoh braced his feet and grabbed onto the side of the chariot. It spun on one wheel, and they dashed for the temple of Amon with the others following as best they could. She was eager to have these ceremonies over with as the sun was merciless, and there was a hot of nausea roiling in her stomach.

A ceremony similar to the one performed at the temple of Isis followed at the temple of Amon—with but one exception. Here Thothmes II received the double crown of Egypt and was given the crook and flail of authority. He was of noble birth and well educated; therefore, he conducted himself honorably. Had anyone cared to note the fact, the double crown of Thothmes II was fully two inches shorter than that of his Great Royal Wife. Done and done again.

The news spread swiftly from city to village to farm, and all up and down the Nile, the cry went out: "There is a falcon in the nest." This was the phrase used to indicate the rise of a new Pharaoh by whatever means. In this case, the cry meant that Hatshepsut had married. The details would sift down eventually, but for now the phrase alone was enough to cause excessive feasting and celebration.

Pharaoh Thothmes II retired to his rooms after placing a chaste kiss upon Hatshepsut's brow. She continued down the corridor to her quarters. Had he known anything about the palace, he would have realized that he entered what had been the rooms of the Queen, as his wife went on to occupy the larger, more opulent ones of the Pharaoh.

In all likelihood, it would not have mattered to him at this moment had he known about the rooms. He was already ordering food, a great deal of food. While waiting for it to be brought from the kitchens, he directed his servants to help him disrobe and conduct him to his bath. The pools were beneath his bedroom; and as he descended the spiral stairs, he marveled at the luxury. Serving boys stood by with soft sheets with which to dry him. Others were prepared to perfume the water with fragrant oils of his choice. He relaxed in the pool and thought that no man had ever been so honored.

I am actually Pharaoh! I wonder if I will be expected to issue orders of some sort. Well, I shall ask Hati, who has been so good to me and so kind to Mother. Yes, I can depend upon Hati to tell me what to say. I think she really is quite fond of me and impatient for my embrace.

Tonight, I will be required to copulate with her in an effort to produce a child. May Horus attend me, for I am unfamiliar with the act. But does it not come naturally to all men? I will not think on it now. I will bathe, receive a massage, eat heartily, and rest. All will be well. I am actually Pharaoh!

In her pool, Hatshepsut rested, floating weakly on her back. She had been violently ill, attended only by Beka. This very night she must have the Pharaoh perform as best he could when the time came to fulfill the marriage vows. At that the child would be born some weeks early, but she knew this was not unusual. Nor did she fear childbirth; her hips were well spaced making them ideal for giving birth. She raised her head and thought defiantly. *The Queen of Egypt fears nothing!*

Early in the evening of her wedding day, before the time for the celebratory feast, Hatshepsut went through the hidden passageways to the secret room below. She pored over many recipes for potions, hoping to find relief from nausea. All potions made for this purpose contained notes to show the side effects of each ingredient. She feared to use any of them, for the child must be perfect. She would partake of nothing that might bring harm to an unborn babe.

At the feast later in the evening, it was difficult to appear well and harder still to eat her meal. She sat beside her new husband daintily picking at her food, as all in he great hall watched. They seemed such an unsuited couple, but most of the court assumed the Queen had chosen wisely. Surely this must be so, for she was known by all to be intelligent and not one to act impulsively. She was, after all, doing as she must do. The falcon would infuse the royal blood of Egypt with new vigor, and there would be many heirs.

Hatshepsut laid her crowned head upon his soft shoulder. With love in her eyes, she whispered, "Great falcon, I am longing for you. Your beautiful face and form make me bold in my love. Let us go to your bedchamber now, for indeed I would wait no longer. We can enjoy a feast later in privacy and contentment." Thothmes was drunk enough to believe it all. Even had he been sober, he would have believed it, for it was well known that Pharaoh was a god. And so, rising unsteadily, he was assisted by Hatshepsut to the hall that led to his chambers.

Upon seeing the two walk away, clasped in love and desire, the revelers shouted wedding night wishes for fertility and returned to their foods and wines. The dancing girls would come soon, and the festivities would not end until dawn.

The raucous noise from the Great Hall of Pillars fell away from the newlyweds as they took a slow and stumbling course toward Pharaoh's rooms. One harpist sat with the guards. He strummed his instrument and sang tender love songs as the pair entered the outer chamber.

Hatshepsut had not come away from the room of magic empty handed, however. In her readings, she had come across a reference to a powder stored in a sealed clay jar. This gray powder was made from mushrooms that grew in Asia. They dried during the long trip to Egypt and then were pulverized to produce a talcum-fine dust. The dust was placed in clay jars and sold to the physicians and necromancers who understood its use and value.

According to the papyrus roll she had read, this powder, when dropped into wine and given the space of twenty beats of the heart to achieve its effect, would place the drinker in a state of euphoria and an out-of-body trance. While in this state, the person could be told anything. Later, upon awakening, the imbiber of the potion would believe he or she had actually done the things or planned the actions that had been cunningly implanted in his mind.

Tonight, to guard against failure, the queen had with her this powder concealed inside a massive ring worn on her left hand. The blue stone, which held a star captive, could be slipped aside, exposing the pocket holding the powder. She was prepared to use it if need be.

Thothmes II had drunk three large goblets of wine and was intent on ordering more food and drink. This could not be allowed to happen. He had already drunk too much; and if he were to eat more, who knew if the beats of his heart would forward the altered wine to his blood.

Once inside, Thothmes began to complain of hunger, and his bride appeared willing to see his every wish fulfilled. "Come sweet husband and recline upon this couch. I will pour a bowl of new wine for you as I order your food. There will be wondrous fowls stuffed with small birds, fine breads, and many kinds of sweet cakes."

Hatshepsut realized he could perform no act of love that night as he had fallen victim to the goblets of strong wine. So thinking, she turned her back to him and poured wine into an alabaster bowl. The opened ring moved across the surface and spilled the gray powder which dissolved immediately. With the grace of a loving wife, she held the bowl to his lips. He drank it down greedily and, smacking his lips, began to tell her of the foods he would like.

In the midst of his speech, a silly grin spread across his face. His eyes glazed over and he fell back upon the cushions. As he lay there motionless, eyes open wide but unseeing, Hatshepsut knelt by his ear and spoke. "Oh, great king, you have thrown me upon your bed, and I am surrendering myself to you. You are huge, and you penetrate my body with tenderness. But passions burns within you, and our lovemaking goes on and on. At last, you spurt the seeds of your son into the Queen, and she cries out in joy. You are indeed a great king in the bedchamber. You are certain that you have made a son this night. Tomorrow you will tell all near you that you have given Egypt an heir."

Hatshepsut had poured all her memories of Kamare's lovemaking into these suggestions, and she felt a yearning for him. *Oh, Kamare, I must let you know why I have chosen a husband. You must hear it from me before you hear it elsewhere and turn your heart against me.*

She repeated the statements time and time again to insure that her consort would believe them to be truth when he awakened. She removed his garments and placed them in a jumbled pile beside the couch just as an ardent lover might have discarded them. Then she rumpled the bedclothes and pulled them aside, leaving the Pharaoh only partially covered with a linen sheet.

It would appear to all—servants and even Thothmes, himself—that much activity had taken place in that bed during the night.

After returning to her rooms, Hatshepsut sent for Captain Senu. She believed she could trust him to get a message through to Kamare and that the message would arrive in the General's tent intact. She knew that when heard by the wrong ears, messages could be cleverly manipulated.

Senu sent a reply that he would be with the Queen as soon as he could ready himself for the journey. She had indicated that he would be required to travel a long distance, and he wanted to be prepared to eat and drink in the saddle. He had sent a rider to a station a four-hour ride away with orders that fresh horses were to be waiting for him and the men who rode with him. Another rider would carry the command forward to the next outpost.

Along the route taken by the queen's army, there would be fresh horses for the men at every supply station. Senu and the three others would sleep but twice along the way. It had taken four weeks of tedious march for Kamare's huge army to travel in chariots and wagons to within sight of the walled city of the King of the Hyksos. Captain Senu and his three aides would be there in six days, barring accident or foul play.

A guard announced Captain Senu to a lady of the Queen's court who, in turn, informed the Queen. Hatshepsut appeared in her audience chamber freshly bathed and scented. Her pale skin glowed from the day's exposure to the sun and the oil just rubbed into her body. Her long hair was damp, and in her simple robes, she seemed delicate and vulnerable.

Senu, bronzed, muscular, and handsome in his youth, was touched deeply by the sight of the newly married Queen. He silently rededicated himself to her service. What she asked of him he would perform. She had been kind and generous to him and to General Kamare, a man he admired greatly.

Queen Hatshepsut carried a small, folded piece of doeskin in her hands. As Senu knelt in obeisance, she seated herself. Still holding the small item in her hands, she said, "Captain Senu, there is an urgent message that must reach General Kamare before any other person contacts him. I dare not write these words and depend upon your loyalty to speak them to one man only—or die with them unspoken."

The queen motioned for all the ladies to leave the room and motioned also for Senu to rise and come closer. When his face was near hers, she whispered, "Say to General Kamare these words: 'There is a falcon in the nest. The child born of the Queen is a gift from Isis, given weeks before her marriage. Make sacrifice to Isis in the name of Queen Hatshepsut.' "

Senu's expression did not change. He blinked not an eyelid, for he was dedicated to Hatshepsut in all ways. He was proud that she had chosen to entrust him with so delicate a mission. He knelt at her feet again and gave his earnest answer. "It shall be done, my Queen."

Perceiving his devotion, she smiled and unwrapped the leather in her hands to show a large gold emblem. It was round and carved upon it was a flail, or whip, with many lashes hanging from it. She rose and asked Senu to rise, saying, "You knelt as a captain; you arise as a General in the service of your Queen! You are General Senu, most trusted of men. When you return, we shall celebrate your marriage to Nefertum in the royal manner. Go now. Be swift but careful. You cannot serve me well if your head is severed from your body. I shall make sacrifice to Horus for your safety."

So saying, she pinned the heavy badge to his cloak and walked from the room. The new general stood frozen for a few moments. *A general! Most trusted of men! Oh how I will honor her and serve her. All glory to Queen Hatshepsut.*

General Senu's badge would not open the treasury as it lacked the queen's cartouche, but its power was enormous. He could command anyone, seize anything, and most important to Senu, he would command respect wherever he went. Now his prestige was just slightly less than that of General Kamare.

13

General Senu turned on his heel and strode from the Queen's rooms. When he reached the bottom of the palace stairs, he found three of his soldiers waiting for him. He told them what had transpired during his audience with Hatshepsut and showed them the prized badge. His men thumped him on the back, and Senu allowed himself a wide smile for a brief moment. Then, he repinned the badge so that it was fastened to the leather vest under his cloak. He would display it only when going to war or when necessity demanded.

A slave had held Senu's horse in check during his absence, and he now brought the animal forward so that the general could mount. Senu turned to the other three and said, "We ride as though all the gods of the underworld pursue us. We ride for the camp of General Kamare. Do not spare your horses, even though it seems as if they will die beneath you. I carry a spoken message from Queen Hatshepsut. Your mission is to see that I get there alive. If we are attacked, one of you will remain to fight and hold, as the rest of us ride on. Thus we will do until my safe arrival is assured. I anticipate no trouble; but if it finds us, this is to be our strategy. Now, let us be off; and we ride as the desert shamsen, when the winds howl from the farthest reaches of the earth. Food and drink are in our bags. We go!"

The four men, each mounted on a swift Arabian thoroughbred, thundered through the city gates of Thebes. These horses would not die under them. Senu had chosen stallions for their high endurance. They were more heavily muscled than the geldings and mares but equally fleet of foot. They could withstand the pull of deep sand when the group's journey took them over trails not trampled flat by caravan.

The sun beat upon the travelers by day, and the desert air chilled them by night. Every four hours found a sentinel waiting with fresh horses. They quickly changed from their fatigued animals to the new ones, scarcely touching the ground between mounts. The men ate as they rode, chewing on dried dates and millet cakes taken from their saddlebags. Senu had hoped to travel in this manner for three days before stopping to rest. But at the end of the second day, after forty-eight hours atop galloping horses, he looked at his companions and realized they must have sleep. In their current condition, they would not have the needed strength to fight if an enemy should attack.

At midnight on the second day, General Senu halted the riders and bade them dismount. He forced the men to stay awake until they had eaten bread and drunk wine. Then all slept like the dead for six hours before awakened by the guard at the provision post. There was no bath, no food other than what was carried with them. Once again mounted upon fresh stallions, they were away at dawn.

The wagons of the army supply train were proceeding across the desert at a slow but steady pace. They would be on hand to provide support to the army by the time General Kamare was ready to launch an offensive against the walled city of King Obinninos. In the afternoon of the third day, the four horsemen of the Queen went galloping by them at a furious pace. The riders leaned into the wind they created in passing with head scarves wrapped around mouths and nostrils to keep out the dust and sand rolled up by the wagon wheels. The riders were rested, and these young men now gave no thought to fatigue. They served the Queen of Egypt.

Had Senu been commanded to ride through flaming coals, he would have done so. The living goddess, Queen Hatshepsut, trusted him, as she did no other man. The secret message he carried in his mind must be delivered with all speed. And it was also true that he owed his good fortune in large part to General Kamare. Senu admired the older commander, and his loyalty to the man was unfaltering. Of course, Kamare knew well what he did when he chose Senu for promotion. Having been a commander for many years, he had easily spotted the honesty and courage of the young soldier.

As the men rode on, Senu silently repeated the message. He

wondered if the real message was cleverly couched within an ordinary one. *Did Isis really give the Queen a child before her marriage? Why must General Kamare hear of her marriage first from the Queen herself? Of course, Queen Hatshepsut is a living goddess; and with such, all things are possible.*

Having arrived at this conclusion, Senu decided he would deliver the message in a straightforward manner and leave this business to those it concerned. Matters of royal marriages were not within his realm. He would think no more upon the meaning of the message. The newly made General would be as always: obedient, loyal, and courageous. These qualities had brought him great good fortune so far, and he would continue to be guided by them.

Time wore on, and, again, it was Senu's judgment that rest was needed. Upon arriving at a support station, he was about to order a halt when a messenger appeared riding from the opposite direction. Senu learned that the siege of the Hyksos kingdom was about to begin. They could not stop. On the four rode, eating and drinking as best they could when the terrain was level.

On the evening of the fourth day, the trail took them through deep sand. The horses were fresh and strong, but it required extreme exertion for them to pull their hindquarters free. Soon the stallions were covered in foam, and heat rose from their bodies even though they rode at night.

When the sun was hot and high on the fifth day, Senu called a halt and led the party off the trail to a shaded area under some high rock cliffs. The men dismounted and poured water into their bowls so that the horses could drink. They removed the saddles and used their fingers to rake the hair of the horses away from their hides so that it stood up in wet ridges. Steam was released from the animals in clouds.

Only then did Senu and his men swallow food and water. Each man lay down in the shade with the reins of his horse wound around his wrist. All but Senu slept. He was not traveling as rapidly as he wanted, but he realized there was a fine line drawn between foolishness and wisdom. It would take him seven, perhaps even eight, days for this mission. However, he realized the value of both horses and men. They must not be wasted or overused. As it was, the horses that he ran for four hours at a time would need a quarter moon to recover. As Ra began to disappear in the west, and the sand reflected less heat, Senu roused the men. In moments they were up and off, much refreshed. On they galloped, stopping momentarily to change mounts and then pound away again. Time snapped at their heels.

When dawn broke on the sixth day, the outposts still had received no news from the battlefront. Of course, it is a wise general who does not claim victory before it is his, and Senu was aware that this could be a long siege.

The trail had been ascending slightly these last three hours. Ahead was a greening of low mountains, and the air they breathed no longer came from a furnace. Would these mountains slow them even more? Oxen pulling wagons appeared as tiny specks on the mountainside. To Senu, it seemed that they crept along at a snail's pace. It would be tricky passage to get around the wagons on the narrow trails had he not come prepared. He had expected just such a problem, and lashed to the front of his saddle was a horn.

From behind, he would blow the horn; and the wagons would pull aside as far as possible and stop. This was a standard maneuver in the army of Egypt. Military missions were all-important. Everything and everyone bent to the will of the army.

At the low hills, close by the base of the mountains, the guard post, complying with the instructions from the messengers of Senu, had prepared four stallions and fresh water and food bags. *Only one more change of horse and then we four will sleep until we are refreshed. Perhaps Kamare will need me in battle. After all, I am a general now, too.*

The riders began the ascent. The brush thickened and gave way to scrub trees and olive groves. Many sheep and cattle were pastured here, no doubt as meat supply for the army. Since few herdsmen dared to live close to the Hyksos, there were few homes to be seen. In reality, the citizens of Egypt preferred life on the lush banks of the Nile. True, there were the nomads of the desert—fierce people who moved from one oasis to another. It could not be said that they felt loyalty for anyone. They were not considered desirable co-habitants of Egyptians cities, nor did they wish to be, for they were of a barbaric nature and clung to their free and wandering lifestyle. Nevertheless, they were so skilled at breeding fine horses that Pharaoh after Pharaoh enforced the ban against selling or trading these horses to anyone but Egyptians.

The warriors of the Hyksos nation rode horses that were narrow of chest and bony in the rump. One of the reasons border raids were carried out was to acquire the splendid Arabian horses of the desert tribes. As always, however, the merciless enemy enjoyed the bloodletting the most.

When reasonable words fail, diplomacy becomes a lash; and the pain of an Egyptian lash was usually long remembered. Thus, General Kamare now had the task of bringing down the empire of King Obinninos of the Hyksos. Once the king had been put to the sword, an Egyptian regent would assume his throne, probably a strong half-brother of Hatshepsut. A sizeable contingent of Egyptian soldiers would remain behind as his personal bodyguard.

As in all times, once blood is shed, it is followed by innumerable deaths. All of the king's close family members would die; sons of dead kings are dangerous. All of the army officers would die; their organization could not be left in place.

Eventually, if all went well and the Hyksos truly learned their harsh lesson, the Egyptian king could abdicate in favor of an obscure relative of King Obinninos and return to his homeland. There he would advise Pharaoh on all things concerning the land he had ruled.

The heaving horses reached the top of the mountainous gorge and stood spread-legged, heads drooping in exhaustion. The four riders leaped upon the last four they would need and started the descent into the valley below.

It was the morning of the seventh day. No others could have made the journey as swiftly as they. Senu was confident that

General Kamare would have heard nothing of the royal wedding before his arrival. He ordered his companions to eat well and drink deeply in the coolness of the mountains' shadows. Their last dash to Kamare's tents outside the walled city would be in the searing heat of day through sand hot as fire.

When the sun was at its zenith, they reached the point where the ground cover turned to brush; then came sand with bare rocks protruding here and there, showing wagon wheel marks. Senu sounded the horn over and over against as he rode. They dashed unimpeded past heavily loaded wagons stopped by the wayside, wagons that were headed for the Egyptian camp. On the other side of the track, wagons moved swiftly on their way back to the halfway station where stores sent from Thebes and Karnak were stocked. Egyptians were well aware that an army travels and fights only as well as it is supplied.

The soldiers with Senu had remained strong through the torture of the past week. Now, with the camp only short hours away, they began to slump in their saddles. Ever mindful, Senu removed the last item from his saddlebag. It was a slim pole carrying the colors of Queen Hatshepsut emblazoned on silk. Placing the bottom end of the pole on his stirrup, he straightened his back and let the banner unfurl as he rode. Seeing this, the three riding with him felt their chests swell with pride; and they rode tall once again. They were the chosen messengers of the Goddess Queen. They would show the army what strength they had—how resilient they were to hardship.

Thus they galloped into the midst of Kamare's camp, their horses nearly dead beneath them. Their faces and the exposed parts of their bodies were burned dark by the sun. Gaunt cheeks spoke of physical sacrifice, yet they rode ramrod straight. They turned neither to one side nor the other and answered no man.

General Kamare's flag was visible on a rise of ground, and Senu whirled through the army toward it. Wide-mouthed guards gave way. It was as though ghosts of the desert had appeared carrying the banner of the Queen.

Hearing the commotion, General Kamare emerged from his tent, sword in hand, a stern and imposing figure. The breadth of his chest, the sturdiness of his arms and legs, his unwavering, piercing gaze—these identified him instantly as a man who eclipsed all others. Kamare immediately saw the banner of Queen Hatshepsut rising above the heads of his soldiers. As the four weary messengers drew near, he looked upon their haggard condition and realized that only a mission of vital importance could account for the ordeal to which they had been subjected.

"Dismount, Captain Senu, and come refresh yourself in my tent. You there, you soldiers standing by. Care for your comrades and for their horses. They have traveled far in the service of our Queen. Do all that can be done for them. And have a tub and clean water laced with soothing oils brought to my tent for Captain Senu. Bring meat and wine as well."

General Kamare turned and walked back into the tent, sheathing his sword. He would not offer to help Senu from his horse. The man must be allowed his dignity. As he seated himself to await Senu's appearance, his mind leaped from one thought to another; and he wondered what had been of such importance that his Hati had sent these men plummeting across the desert so quickly, so dangerously. No one observing the general would have been aware of his inner turmoil. With imperturbable demeanor, he waited.

Senu entered slowly, near collapse, and said in a hoarse, croaking voice, "Great General Kamare, Queen Hatshepsut has sent a message to you by my mouth. She would not write it, and I would have died with the words unspoken rather than repeat it to any other."

Upon hearing this, the General held up his hand to stop the flow of words. "You servants and soldiers. Leave now and do not return until you perceive my signal. And stand clear of this tent. The message from our Queen is meant for my ears alone."

Senu swayed on his feet, and Kamare asked him to sit and drink before giving the message, but Senu would not. "The great Queen Hatshepsut bids me give you this message. 'There is a falcon in the nest.' " At this, Kamare's heart sank. *My own love has taken a husband?*

Senu spoke again. "She also bids me tell you that the goddess Isis placed a child within her, a son, three quarters of the moon before her marriage. She bids you make sacrifice to Isis."

Having said this, Senu collapsed into a chair. Kamare rose and strode from the tent. He signaled to the nearest guard and had him order attendants to hasten with the tub and warm water for a bath. He sent another to see that the serving boys did not delay in bringing jars of wine and a joint of mutton.

Senu's mission was over. The Queen's message had reached the ears for which it was destined. He allowed himself to be undressed. With the last of his strength, he climbed into the tub and rested there immobile as the warm water was poured gently over his aching body. He ate a few bites of meat and swallowed a bit of the wine. He was asleep in the tub long before the attendants had finished washing the grime of a week's hard riding from his body. He would awaken a day later on a clean camp bed, fully recovered.

All this time, Kamare sat in stunned silence. A slight smile curled the corners of his mouth. *A son!* Hati, his precious love, carried his son in her warm belly. Of course she had had to marry. Otherwise the child would be killed. He, Kamare, was to be the father of the next Pharaoh of Egypt. His pride and happiness were boundless. Yet what of this new falcon in the nest? Whom had she chosen from among her half-brothers? When Captain Senu awakened, he would know all. Until that time—*At last I will have a son. He will be a great Pharaoh. He will be as strong as his father and as clever as his mother! Oh, my sweet Hati. How I long to be with you, to hold you and kiss your sweet face. But I cannot leave here until the battle is won.*

His newfound knowledge gave General Kamare reason to crush the Hyksos's city and its hated ruler with all possible haste. He wanted to be in Thebes when his son was born.

When the men were undressing Senu, Kamare had seen the badge of "General" fastened to his leather vest. So, there were now two generals in the army! It was of no matter, for there were numerous sites along the borders to be patrolled and defeated. And Hati had chosen well. Kamare was, nevertheless, gratified that the badge bore only a flail. The cartouche of Hatshepsut that embellished Kamare's badge made him supreme General of all the armies, cities, and gold treasuries. It provided certain privileges held only by the ruling Pharaoh and Queen—and by General Kamare.

While General Senu and his men slept, Kamare wrote upon a papyrus scroll. He wrote to the Queen of his undying loyalty. He wrote of his hopes for a happy and fruitful future. He wrote everything except what was deep in his heart; that he dared not. She surely would read and know what his heart would say had not great distance separated them. As a last attempt to convey his true feelings, he made an unusual promise: the battle would be won, and he would return to Thebes in seven-and-one-half passages of the moon. He sent the company carrying this message on its way, giving orders that they move with haste, but to rest each day when the sun was at its height. He had understood Hati's need to send her message as she did, but he knew his could travel more slowly.

The beat of horses' hooves still sounded in his ears as he sat down at his campaign table. Upon this table was a re-creation of the walled city. Over the last month, he had studied it, his sharp eyes missing nothing. There might be an elegant falcon in the nest; but in this commander's tent hovered the giant hawk of war, Kamare.

14

Thothmes II awakened the morning after his wedding and coronation to bright sunshine and a pounding head. By the beard of Ptah! Never had he drunk such powerful wine. Then the memories crept like smoke into his befuddled brain. Ah, but he had been an ardent lover to his bride. He remembered her cry of joy when he was within her. He was certain that he had given her a child. The time was propitious, had not Isis told her so? It was really somewhat of a relief to find that he had been able to perform as he should; he had never before felt desire to indulge in such behavior. He knew, from the talk of other men, that this act was forever on their idle minds. Thank goodness he need not repeat it soon. Besides, there were so many wonderful things to explore in this beautiful palace. He was now mighty Pharaoh Thothmes II, and he could command anything he desired!

First, of course, he would, as was the custom, have a lengthy bath. The room adjoining his bedchamber was unbelievably opulent. The new Pharaoh looked around in wonder, as he lay propped up by soft, feather pillows. There was so much gold! Oh, and there was a lovely table with a game set upon it.

Menservants came at his call and opened the linen drapes that ran across the eastern wall. He saw, sparkling before him, a man-made lake filled with lotus. He could see bright birds flitting among the bushes and foreign trees bordering the lake. Paradise to anyone, but especially to a young man from the harem who had lived with the priests and had slept two to a small room behind the temple of Horus.

"I will bathe and then eat," he informed the servants. As he was well educated with refined manners, he sent word to Queen Hatshepsut that he would visit her shortly.

While Thothmes II was being bathed, massaged with oils, and, most curiously, having his hair curled even though he would wear a wig, he received an answer from the Queen. Hatshepsut sent word that she had been so pleasured and used by her husband, that she could not leave her bed. She begged him to wait for a few days to see her so that she could appear before him at her loveliest.

Thothmes was greatly pleased. Obviously, the Queen thought much of him. Now, all in the palace would know of his prowess in the bedroom. His reputation as a man was made. He remembered again the events of their wedding night and shuddered. Thank goodness he need not to do that again soon. Besides, Isis had said he had placed a child within the Queen.

Servants dressed him in a short, pleated, white skirt and laced golden sandals tightly to his skinny legs. Hatshepsut had provided many belts, armlets, rings, and bracelets—all of glimmering gold. He adored each item but could not find a belt among them long enough to encircle his substantial girth. He sent for the palace goldsmith and gave instructions for two to be made into one.

To do justice to Thothmes II, it must be noted that he was a kind and considerate young man, full of pleasantries, although much given to self-indulgence. Even though formally educated by the priests, he was virtually innocent of the ways of the world and lacked any great personal ambition, therefore, making his selection as Pharaoh to co-rule with Hatshepsut, a foreseeable conclusion.

As he was dipping his shat cakes into honey and tearing apart a greasy, roast goose, he directed a noble of the bedchamber to ascertain the queen's favorite flower and arrange to have a bouquet sent to her.

The Queen was indeed in her bed. The bout of morning nausea had almost passed; each day it became less. She was one moon into her pregnancy. Soon, she would be over this. As she lay there, she thought of Kamare. How proud he would be; how strong would be his child.

Hatshepsut's thoughts turned to the eight moons left to her before she would be brought to the birthing chair. These months must be filled with activity, if only, at times, to draw her mind away from her love. She decided that she would soon send for the royal architect, Ineni. From the early years of her studies, as it became apparent she would be the heir to the throne of Thothmes I, she had turned over many possibilities in her mind.

The world must remember the Great Queen Hatshepsut. I will build the most beautiful temple in Egypt. My name will fall from lips for hundreds and hundreds of years. And I will know of it. I will, after all, be living forever and ever in my tomb, the beautiful and safe tomb that Ineni will design and build.

As she was about to rise, a bowl of gardenias, sent by her new husband, arrived. Dear, sweet boy. He would suit her purposes well. Did he remember the things she had told him while he was in a trance? She would know soon enough.

Queen Hatshepsut was weak from nausea, and maidservants helped her to her bath. Beka made certain that they handled her gently, as the Queen had informed them that Pharaoh had given her a child on their wedding night. Beka looked at her tenderly. *My Hati is a goddess, and she knows these things. I have always believed the words she speaks. But I have loved her long, since she was a newborn babe; and despite what she tells us. I know the father of this child is General Kamare. And a child of Kamare's seed will be strong and upright. This child will be what Egypt needs.*

Wrapped in fresh linens, the Queen reclined upon a half-raised lounge. Beka offered her bites of bread dipped in sweet wine, and Hatshepsut was able to eat a little. She heard from her noblewomen of the second chamber that Thothmes II was telling everyone within range of his voice that he had been a powerful lover on his wedding night and that he had placed an heir within the chalice of Egypt. He proclaimed that Horus had told him so, or was it Isis who had told the Queen? No matter. Even as he chose make-up and new, bright colors for his nails, both hands and feet, he continued to spread word that the great Pharaoh Thothmes II, falcon in the nest of Queen Hatshepsut, had produced a small falcon for Egypt.

Hatshepsut smiled upon hearing these things. Thothmes II had been such a good boy; she would reward him well. She would send musicians and magicians to amuse him. She would offer a gift of any horses he might choose, knowing full well his fear of riding in her chariot, much less riding astride a prancing stallion. Yes, she would keep him well amused, well occupied.

To ensure that he continued to gain in girth, she sent word to the master of kitchens that her beloved husband was fond of all things sweet. He must have honeyed cakes and dates at hand at all times. His meats and vegetables must be left in natural fats and not drained as were hers. Thus, she did display familial love; and thus, she would keep him fat.

Remembering that there was more in her garden to tend, she sent first the royal goldsmith and jewel maker. When she had finished with him, she would send for her mother-in-law. These waters must be tested and oil poured upon them to keep them calm, if necessary.

Khenem arrived and prostrated himself at the side of her lounge. "Please rise, loyal goldsmith. Seat yourself in my presence for I would ask your advice upon matters of importance."

Khenem was overly pleased with this. He was seldom consulted; only ordered to do this and make that. Never before had a royal one been so courteous. "Great Queen Hatshepsut, I am unworthy of your kindness; but all that I can do will be done."

"Khenem, I must honor the mother of my new husband. Have you anything in your workrooms that could please her?"

After giving lengthy thought to this question, Khenem finally replied, "Great Queen, I have many lovely things that I alone have made and many that my indentured helpers have made. All are exquisite, but the Lady Mutnefret is very short and very wide. In order for ornaments to balance her weight, I feel they should be large also. I have one necklace of round disks, each with amber set in the center of fiery opals. It is enormous. If you like, I can suspend from it a disk with the design of a falcon upon it to show all that she is Pharaoh's mother. I have long earrings of gold and opals also, but I do not have, ready made, armlets to fit such arms or circlets for her waist."

Hatshepsut smiled at him and complimented him for his knowledge of such matters. "Go now, Khenem; attach the falcon to the necklace with great speed and return within the hour. Bring the earrings as well. The Lady Mutnefret will be in my chambers, and I would present these lovely things to her at that time.

"Sometime tomorrow, I must speak to you of dishes and goblets. My good General Senu will take Imhot's daughter to wife. I would give Senu and Nefertum many beautiful objects for their new home. Also, when I gift General Senu with an estate, I shall present an even finer one to General Kamare. Even as we speak, he marches upon the Hyksos in defense of the pride and honor of Egypt. This brave man must also have beautiful items of gold and electrum to grace his home. I now place you in charge of choosing sites along the Nile where both estates shall be raised. My architect, Ineni, shall build for them, but you shall choose the furniture maker for the house of General Kamare. He has only an aged mother, and she knows nothing of these matters. When you have done all these things well, the reward for your family shall be great. One stipulation—all must be done in six moons. Go now and return with the gifts for Pharaoh's mother."

Nefertum was in the room and overheard the conversation. Her heart was full of love for her Queen. The other ladies looked upon her with envy, and she knew that they wondered how they, too, could attain royal favor.

Many times, in teaching a wayward horse to come readily to the rope, he is made to see other horses rewarded with grain as they submit to a halter. Soon, the wayward horse goes eagerly to the rope, associating it with grain. Much can be said about the comparison of training the horse and ensuring the devotion of the noble ladies who waited upon Hatshepsut. They would stumble over each other in their eagerness to serve.

A temple is only as strong as its foundation, and Queen Hatshepsut had gone a long way in creating a solid base for her reign.

Her beautiful apartment overwhelmed Mutnefret. Although the rooms could not be compared with those of the Queen and Pharaoh, to a woman who had lived much of her life in the confines of a crowded harem, this new world was heaven indeed. It was true that her bath was small, but it was all for her. And there were two serving girls and a cosmetologist of her very own. The wardrobes were filled with fine linens and silk; and, like her son, she had only to express a wish for food and sweets, and they were brought quickly.

Two of the Queen's ladies appeared in her sitting room and requested that the Lady Mutnefret accompany them to the Queen's chambers; their mistress desired to speak with the mother of the falcon.

"What great honor our Queen bestows upon me. Let me have but a moment to prepare myself, as I would not show disrespect by appearing before her in these simple garments."

Her handmaidens draped the bulbous body as best they could in the finest of the linens found in the wardrobe and placed the gold sandals from the coronation on her tiny feet. It was amazing that so fat a woman could be supported by such small feet and that she could move along as quickly as she did through all the halls, stairs, and halls again.

In passing through the Great Hall of Pillars, she was once more overwhelmed by the sudden, fabulous good fortune that had befallen her son and, through him, her. This very morning had brought the news that Pharaoh Thothmes II had given his Queen a child on their wedding night. Mutnefret was as surprised as any other in the palace of one hundred rooms. Since her son had been a small child, he had been, perhaps, not really unmanly, but certainly not overly masculine.

During the few times they had been allowed to visit together, always under the watchful eye of Montu, she had been dismayed to see his wide hips and large stomach, to say nothing of his curled hair and painted nails. Still, he was her only child, and she loved him as her whole world. And what blessings the gods had bestowed upon him—a child the very first night! But had it not been thus when, as a virgin, she had gone to the bed of Thothmes I? She had returned to her quarters bearing his seed from that single night. Even though he had never chosen her again, she had had the babe to love.

Arriving at the arched entrance to the Queen's rooms, Mutnefret was met by a smiling Nefertum, who put her at her ease, saying that the mother of the Pharaoh was welcome in the chambers of the Pharaoh's Great Royal Wife. She added that the Queen was resting upon a couch and eagerly looking forward to talking with her new mother.

Much reassured, Mutnefret entered the audience chamber and knelt before the Queen. Hatshepsut would not have her thus and so she said, "Come, Mother—your daughter, Hati, would sit with you as an equal, but cannot. Indeed, I am worn in body from my night with your powerful son. Please, call me Hati and kiss my lips, as we share a sweet, new gift."

Mutnefret rose, then bent and kissed the Queen saying, "Hati, my daughter, is what I hear of a child so?"

"Sit, Mother, and drink of this light wine, and I shall answer what you ask. Your son was as the Great Bull of Thebes. His manhood was so great that when his seed filled me, Isis spoke to me in the midst of my pleasure; and I did cry out. For she told me that I had been given a son. It was the hand of Horus that guided me when I chose your son. Surely I am the most fortunate of wives that I am favored by such virility. What say you, my mother, of all this?"

Lulled by wine and charmed by the familiarity with which she was received, Mutnefret answered freely, "Majesty, it is true that my father, the King of Assyria, fathered many strong children. He too was a great bull of the bedchamber. It is also true that your husband was born as the result of just one night with Pharaoh Thothmes I. It must be the strong blood of the two kings blended into the manhood of my son that has provided you with such a memorable wedding night. I am the happiest of mothers, and, truly, this child that is to be born shall be the most beloved of children."

Time passed pleasantly as the women engaged in idle conversation interspersed with scraps of humor. In scarce more than one hour, the royal goldsmith and jeweler was announced. Khenem carried a large, flat chest in his arms. It was obviously heavy for the small man. He knelt at the feet of the Queen and waited.

Hatshepsut turned to Mutnefret and said, "I have commanded that jewelry be made for you so that all will know the love the Queen of Egypt holds for her mother and so that all who look upon you will recognize you as mother of the falcon in the nest. I would have you receive honor and respect wherever you go. Open the box, Khenem."

When Mutnefret saw the necklace and earrings glittering with the lights held inside the fire opals, she was speechless. Then her gaze fell upon the medallion that hung from the necklace—the Royal Falcon. So! Wherever she went, all would know that she was mother to Pharaoh and grandmother to the new child and all other children to come. This was indeed a great honor. She wept with joy as Nefertum hung the ponderous necklace about her neck and pulled the semicircles of gold through her earlobes to hold the earrings.

"Mother, look in this mirror. Does this beautiful jewelry not become you?" Although Mutnefret could only nod, her unbounded pleasure was obvious.

"Now, dear Mother, I need to rest with your grandchild. I have ordered that a litter chair be always ready to carry you in safety wherever you care to go. You are free to visit anyone you choose and to make new friends. You can believe me when I tell you that your invitations will be many. After all, you are the mother of Pharaoh! Of course, your allowances for gold and stored goods will always be available to you. You must make known your every wish. Now I must sleep. Good-bye, dear Mother."

Mutnefret's words of thanks tumbled out, one over the other, and she left as though riding on clouds. Hatshepsut knew this woman well. She knew that she would go immediately, in all her finery and jewelry, to visit the place from whence she had come.

Mutnefret had been treated well in the harem for she was a kind and cheerful person. But, as is always the case, there was a pecking order among the women. Inevitably, there were those who thought overly much of themselves. Princesses who had come to the harem from faraway kingdoms, where they had lived in palaces, found life in the harem hard to accept. They often turned into petty tyrants, and each attracted her own following.

Now, Mutnefret would arrive at the harem in her own covered chair and would walk among the women in her fine garments, wearing the necklace showing all that she was the mother of Pharaoh. She would sit and eat with them and tell of the wonderful palace, of her own beautiful rooms, and of the gracious Queen who called her "Mother." And then the most wonderful wonder of all: she would call for her chair and would walk out through the doors of the harem, which she would have Montu hold open for her, to freedom.

Yes, thought Mutnefret. *I will do this many times. I will take nice, little gifts to those who have been my friends, and I will ignore those cruel creatures who thought themselves too fine for me. Ah, life is sweet. And will hear no word spoken against my new daughter.*

Hati had secured another loyal servant. If, in Mutnefret's visits to the harem and the homes of the noble families, she heard one word against her beloved daughter, well then, Hati would know of it at once. The source of Mutnefret's freedom and luxuries would be protected.

In the palace, Hatshepsut returned to her bed. She would be glad this illness was done with, for she had determined to call Ineni to her.

He had returned from his labors in Luxor to attend the royal wedding. He had been carving many red granite sphinxes there. At least the bodies of the crouched lions were sculpted; the faces were still large blocks of uniformed stone.

Before succumbing to sleep, the Queen sent a messenger to Ineni. She directed him to stay in Thebes for the time being; she would speak with him of her temple and her tomb.

15

Queen Hatshepsut remained in her bedchamber for fourteen days. For much of the time she was ill and without appetite, although there were some days when she was up and walking about with the vigor and well-being of youth. At last, however, the child was far enough along that the sickness eased and finally dissipated. She was now in her seventh week of child bearing.

Even though she was only weeks into her pregnancy, she was unusually round in her belly. But she was tiny, and the father was enormous. She would be fortunate to deliver this child without harm to either of them, even with hips set as wide apart as hers were. For now, she cast aside these thoughts and focused upon a more immediate concern—the design and construction of her tomb. A clever mind like hers needed to be exercised just as much as did her body. Hatshepsut called for the royal architect, Ineni, who had been patiently awaiting this summons.

While Ineni waited, he had drawn many sketches. One of them depicted a kind of temple never before attempted. It would be hewn from living rock. The face of a tall cliff would be worked upon. Pillars carved from the mountain itself. The tops and bottoms of the pillars would remain a part of the mountain and be as indestructible as the mountain. Such pillars would not topple with time. He would choose a site where the god Ra passed overhead from east to west. When seen at a distance—perhaps, say, from the Nile—the shadows would be long in the morning, would shorten to none at midday, and slowly lengthen again through the afternoon. The face of the temple would always be changing, never the same for a moment in daylight. Thus it would perfectly exemplify life itself. A deep bore into the mountain, behind the pillars, would be formed into a magnificent temple with side rooms for vestments and incense.

All of this temple that Ineni lovingly sketched would consist of living rock. Indestructibility was the dream of all builders. Those who had built in earlier times had done so by carving blocks of granite and limestone from mountains and quarries and moving them to the bank of the Nile by rolling them upon logs. There the blocks were placed upon barges and floated to points as close to their final destinations as possible. Many thousands of slaves were used to transport the enormous stone blocks over desert sands to the building sites where they were leveraged into place.

True, a slip of paper could not be inserted between the blocks of these great buildings and pyramids even now, centuries after their construction. These monuments were breathtaking, grand works indeed. However, the temple Ineni envisioned for Hatshepsut would be more grand and live as long as the mountain. It would exist forever.

Ineni did not possess an imposing appearance. He was careless of his attire and always had ink-stained fingers. Even so, there could be no doubt of his genius. The great temple at Karnak did him honor. His name was inscribed there; and in gratitude, Thothmes I had had a tomb prepared there for him. He would live his afterlife in the Pharaoh's company, perhaps continuing to build for him.

Hatshepsut had marveled at the new tomb in the Valley of the Kings and resolved that such a builder would fashion her temple and her tomb. She had no wish to be found and torn apart by thieves in her afterlife.

Ineni faced the guards at the doors of the Queen's rooms and presented his papyrus summons bearing the waxen imprint of her ring. The guards looked at him with suspicion. He was, as usual, somewhat of a mess. He had tried valiantly to scrub the tint from his hands and nose, and his linen was clean. He had bathed and even perfumed himself, which he hated doing. Still, he did not appear worthy; and, as the new guards were unfamiliar with the palace and those who frequented it, they did not know him as did the more seasoned ones. However, the Queen's seal was on the wax; and they reluctantly ushered him into the reception room where he waited upon fidgeting feet.

Queen Hatshepsut entered, and the architect found his fingers curling with the desire to carve and paint her likeness. She was enchanting. He felt himself to be in the presence of a living goddess; and he had heard that she was, indeed, the true daughter of Isis.

"Greetings to you, Ineni, master architect of Egypt. Your Queen has need of your legendary ability. We must sit and speak of the great things you will do for me. We will speak of all the ideas you have, for it is said that images of building forever consume your thoughts. Come, sit in this seat beside my chair, and we shall have wine."

Gratified by her charming manner and much pleased at the compliments she proffered, Ineni relaxed and sat down. He was not a young man; and if they were to talk at length, he preferred to sit.

Hatshepsut directed Beka to fill a golden goblet with the wine that had been placed on a nearby table. She handed it to Ineni and sat back to study him as he spoke his thanks.

Ineni had been dressed far more grandly for the funeral of Thothmes I, and she barely recognized him in these ordinary clothes. Surely, she thought, a man possessed of such exceeding talent, must work feverishly, as does an artist, who does not permit one painted area to dry before beginning another. Indeed, Ineni did work in this manner because he feared his life would come to a close long before his ideas were carried to completion.

The Queen spoke animatedly. "Ineni, I have seen the great works you have accomplished. I am eager to build a vast temple and tomb, but it must be more beautiful than anything before. It must make the beholders gasp in wonder at the power of Hatshepsut and then smile in pleasure at the beauty of Hatshepsut. And it must last until all time is ended. I ask you to do these things for me. I know I do not ask it of a man who is incapable of fulfilling my desires; but if you feel there is a reason you cannot do this great thing, you may say so."

Ineni clasped the goblet tightly as she spoke. He could not believe her words. *How can she know? She cannot, for no one has seen my drawings. Yet she asks for just the thing I am longing in attempt, the very type of structure I scarcely dare to propose. Will she be ready for such an unorthodox idea, or does she simply dream of a larger pyramid or greater alignment of pillars in a temple? Well, we shall see.*

"Great Queen, I believe that, in life as the daughter of Isis, you have looked into my mind; and there you have seen this temple for which you ask. Your wish is already a reality upon a roll of papyrus in my room of artisans. Give me leave to return to you tomorrow with these pictures and explain them to you."

The Queen nodded in assent and handed a small piece of papyrus to Ineni. Upon this papyrus was a likeness of Hatshepsut under a large falcon representing Thothmes II, her husband. Below her was the sun disk, laying claim to her divinity. Below that disk was a small falcon in an open egg.

"For this reason, good architect, what we do must be planned in haste. Should I not survive, I will have you build my temple for me. It will take many years; and I would live to see it; but should I not, you will have the gold to complete it. It is my right."

The Queen rose, turned, and walked away; and Ineni left with folded papyrus burning against his chest. He felt sure she would survive, but he understood her precaution. Many women died in childbirth. This one would not care to be tucked away in the Necropolis, not the daughter of Isis. He would not fail her. The plans, if she found them agreeable, would be ready before she sat in the birthing chair.

16

Kamare had studied the mock-up of the walled city of the Hyksos for days. At last, a glow began deep in his eyes, and he straightened his back to let out a roar of laughter. So, the pleasure-loving King Obinninos had arranged for an arm of the river to flow from the springs in the mountains to an inlet directly into the city and out again on the other side. It brought fresh water all year to the walls inside the walls, passed through one side of his wild dog pit, and then carried away all wastes at the southern end of the wall where it flowed once again into the main stream of water.

As a means of uninterrupted water supply, it was perfect. However, Kamare had recognized it as the weak spot in the underbelly of the beast; but, so far, he and his second-in-command, General Senu, had puzzled about how to divert this huge flow of water. And if they did manage to do that, there was undoubtedly enough water stored in cisterns under the city to last a year or more.

Clearly, if Kamare were to return to his love in six-and-one-half months, a different plan must be devised, one that could be accomplished in a much shorter time span. Besides, cutting off the water supply would not gain them entrance to the city. There would still be massive walls to climb and fierce warriors to face, resulting in great loss of life. Assuredly, the plan would result in certain victory, but the time was too long, and he was unwilling to sacrifice the lives of his handpicked and well-trained men.

Now at last! At last, the solution had burst open in a second in his mind. Again, he laughed uproariously. "Guard! Have hot water and a tub brought so that I may bathe and shave. Send a message to General Senu that I would have him come to my tent with dispatch. And order food—fresh meat and bread. At once!"

The guard ran to do his General's bidding as if hot coals were underfoot. He sensed that Kamare had reached a decision that pleased him. After sending servants to the tent with a tub and hot water, he delivered Kamare's message to Senu. Then he proceeded to the field kitchen for wine, meat, and bread—only the best meat and the freshest bread.

Upon entering Kamare's tent, Senu found the great man in high good humor. "Sit, General Senu. I have at last devised a simple, if devilish, means of subduing the Hyksos in little time and with the least possible loss of life for our side. Let me finish with my bath, and I will explain it to you."

Senu had pored over the model as eagerly as Kamare and had made numerous suggestions for assault. All were good, forthright versions of conventional battle; but as each proposal was made, Kamare said: "No, we shall use this only as a last resort. There is another, more subtle way. I know this, and I must wait for the plan to unfold in my mind. We wait yet a small time longer." And so all waited: soldiers, arms forgers, supply trains, servants, and slaves—all waited for the sound of Kamare's war trumpets.

Senu sat and observed General Kamare as his servants hastened to assist him with his clothes. The man's eyes were afire, and he soon paced the tent with panther-like moves. He needed only a long, black tail to twitch and fangs to bare to complete his look of blood lust. He held his clenched fist near Senu's face and growled, "We shall have them now, Senu. Come to the table with me again."

Senu followed him to the model. It looked as always; yet something was different. There! The waters that entered the city had been painted blue. They now were inked black, as was the center of each small well in the model.

The tiny, wooden dogs in the pit were knocked upon their sides, and Kamare had placed the head of the jackal on top of the king's palace. Of course! How clever! And it was only the Egyptians who were enlightened enough to possess the means to poison such an immense amount of water. The two men locked gazes, and Senu's eyes caught their gleam from the one in Kamare's eyes. They gripped each other's arms in commitment.

"Senu, call the master physician to me, and we shall see if

my plan is practical. If he agrees it is possible, a few men will go into the night to do this thing. We will light bonfires in our camp and sing great, loud songs. We shall send the scent of roasting meats wafting upon the air, and the camp women will dance wildly in front of the flames. I want all possible distractions to call attention to the south of their city. Death will slip into the north side by early light. The king and all his children must die. If there is one young nobleman left alive, he will be sent to Thebes to be taught loyalty to Egypt. If he is successful in his learning, then he can return here, a loyal ally to Egypt, to rule as king. If others who dwell there remain alive, they will be allowed to become slaves. Those who do not choose to do so will be slain. These terrible things we do are a necessary result of war. The Hyksos attacked an outpost of Egypt, killed all its inhabitants, and stole our fine horses. When others see their punishment, they will long hesitate to commit such crimes. Ah, our food is arriving, and we shall dine. First, however, send for the physician. There is no time to waste, and I would give Queen Hatshepsut the gift of this victory before she bears the heir of Egypt."

Kamare and Senu were eating heartily when the physician, Kadescher, a Syrian, entered and bowed low to both generals. Kamare greeted him with honor and bade him sit and take wine as they talked. Kadescher was asked directly if he possessed knowledge of a poison so strong, and available in such quantities, that it could be poured into the river that ran beneath the Hyksos city and remain strong enough to do its work even though much diluted.

"Great General, I know of no poison, however strong, that can withstand so much mixing with water. But there are two that can mix well with light oil and so float on top of these waters to do their work. Each is tasteless and fairly easily obtained. The first is belladonna. We can send for a great quantity of it. The other is the venom of the krait. There are many men among us who can search the desert for these snakes and milk their venom into vials. To do this will require six weeks of preparation; but, yes, it can be done."

Kamare frowned and his shoulders slumped. He banged the table with his fist. Having decided what course to take, he wanted to act now, tonight! Six weeks! Well, there was no help for it. He realized he must be patient.

"Go then, Syrian. Go quickly and begin immediately. You have my permission to order all that you need. I shall say to all that we have six weeks to prepare a giant feast. That will keep the men occupied and cheerful. But, a word of caution. No doubt there are spies among us. For now, speak only to those you know you can trust completely. Be warned that if these poisons fail or if the Hyksos learn of our plans, you are a dead physician."

The Syrian had not doubted that his last remark would be made, but he held no fear. The poisons would work. No, the most important thing was to choose good men he could trust. He went thoughtfully into the deepening night. Kadescher was a skilled physician. He had been chosen by Queen Hatshepsut to be the head physician of the army and had been instructed to utilize his time in the care of General Kamare. She had written to him in Thebes before he left his home and family to travel to the battle site and warned him that he must always be near the General. He was to see also to the General's diet and to the safety of his food. He was further instructed to delegate the care of all others to subordinate physicians.

Hatshepsut need not have worried about the General's food. He saw to it himself that his food was selected at random and guarded closely on the way to his table. He had done so always; he was not a careless man.

Kadescher's great concern was that Kamare would be wounded in battle. It was well known that the General rode at the head of his armies and led them into war. This brought him the love and admiration of his men but did nothing to ease Kadescher's mind concerning his welfare. The physician's ability was extensive, but no one could heal the fatal blow of an axe or of an arrow to the heart.

There was no time to think of ways to keep the General at the rear of the fighting force. Now, Kadescher must act quickly to gather a group of reliable riders to send to Thebes. They must return with the concentrated belladonna so that he would have time to prepare the poison before the six-week period was over. He had promised the "white blood of death" by then.

The soldiers that he chose to seek out the kraits, the most deadly of all vipers, were puzzled. He told them that they must keep the reptiles alive and bring them to him in sacks. If the men were careful, this held no great hazard, as Egyptians had always dealt with venomous snakes. Even so, the soldiers asked why this was demanded of them, and Kadescher explained that the Hyksos were to be put to death in the ancient manner.

The captives would be tied to stakes at the end of a narrow, "v-shaped" lane, and the sides of the alley would be lined with shallow pits full of hot coals. Since snakes could not live long in the intense heat, they would become angered and vicious soon after being released from the bags onto the pathway in the middle of the lines of fiery coals.

The hapless captives, tied to the stakes in the ground, could only watch in horror as the snakes coiled and writhed in agony toward them. Once there, the snakes would strike and strike again. Death came swiftly after that, but the horror leading to death was unspeakable.

Kadescher reminded them of the slaughtered families of their countrymen who had dwelled at the outpost the Hyksos had overrun. The people had been shown no mercy. Even the tiniest child had had his belly torn open and been left to die a horrible death. Some were still alive when the ravenous jackals came stealing in at night, he said. With his words, he painted a hideous picture of torture and suffering; and when he had finished, the grim-faced men went forth resolutely to collect the snakes for him.

After they left, he set others to digging a huge snake pit. It would be deep and wide at the bottom, narrow at the top, and covered with palm fronds for shade. Small game traps were set at all times to provide food for Kamare's sporting falcons. Now more traps would be built and set to provide food for the snakes. Once harvested, the venom from the kraits would become weaker with time. Therefore, he must see to it that the snakes were kept in good health until four weeks, one full moon, had passed.

Bow makers were also called into service. They were to fashion poles long enough to reach the bottom of the pit. At the end of each pole would be a loop of thin rope that extended back up the handle of the pole. The loop at the end would be lowered into the pit, the snakes would raise their evil heads, and the loop would be slipped over them. The man holding the pole would pull the rope as tight as he could and step back from the rim of the pit as he raised the snake. Another man would grasp the writhing snake behind its head and force its mouth open, which would cause the fangs to descend. The fangs would be hooked over the edge of a copper flask, and the venom milked in spurts until the sacs were empty. One by one, the snakes would release their poison for the physician's use.

The milked snakes were to be put into large clay jars that would be sealed when full. In this manner, each snake would be milked only once. In the day or so they coiled inside the jars, they would rebuild their venom and then could actually be used for execution, or left to die from the heat. It was a good plan all around, as the destruction of local kraits was desirable.

Kadescher wished he dared ask the men to bring back the asp snake, but he knew they would rebel, for it was far too deadly. If, by chance, a soldier was bitten by a krait, the physician might be able to save him, depending upon where he was bitten. Long ago, the physicians of Egypt had discovered that a horse that had survived a poisonous bite from cobra or krait possessed blood that, if immediately taken in powdered form, could save a human life. Rarely could a child survive, due to small body weight, but Kadescher had many pouches of anti-venom in his tents for any husky soldier who had the misfortune to be bitten.

The surgical tents of the Egyptian armies would have seemed a wonder to doctors in other countries. Fine instruments for every operation were available, as were opiates and mild belladonna for anesthesia. Clean linens and needles to stitch up wounds with catgut were there. The walls were lined with jars of oil and of wine mixed with vinegar, the first to soothe the patient and the second for sterilizing.

Clearly, there were many diseases that doctors could not treat; however, the doctors of Egypt were revered throughout the known world. They had even found a treatment for syphilis that could save almost half those infected. It was a painful course of alum and phosphorus, but it was all the hope there was. If it was discerned that a woman carried this disease, she would receive treatment only if she were high born and wealthy. The camp women who showed the ravages of the disease were killed out of hand, for they only spread the pestilence. This disease was a great argument for celibacy and faithfulness to one's mate. It was also the basis for the high price demanded for a virgin female.

Fearful of the disease, Senu had left instructions with his elderly manservant to find two lovely young virgins in Thebes and have them transported to the camp for his use. They had arrived only this morning, and he decided to share them with Kamare. He felt it was the least he could do to express his congratulations to his superior on the excellent plan he had devised.

The welcome coolness of the desert evening had developed into an unpleasant chill as night descended. All around the camp, men were wrapping themselves in woolen cloaks. The unexpected cold gave extra buoyancy to Senu's step, and he entered Kamare's tent in lively spirits, followed closely by two small, veiled women, so wrapped up that only their eyes were visible.

Since the men had become close friends, each admiring and respecting the other, Senu threw his arm over Kamare's shoulder and, with wine-tinged breath, offered him his choice of the girls. As the women removed their garments. Kamare saw that they were dark-skinned beauties, perhaps from Syria, for their hair was long and richly curled and oiled. They stood nude before him, and he saw that they were freshly bathed and perfumed. Their young bodies appeared as soft to the touch as fully ripened peaches.

Kamare gently removed Senu's arm from his shoulder, and Senu stared in disbelief as the General declined his offer with many polite thanks. Senu was certain Kamare had had no woman for these three months. He thought perhaps the leader had dedicated his body to battle, as was sometimes the custom.

Senu decided that his friend would enjoy at least the sights and sounds of lust, if nothing else. He drew the girls down, one on each side of him, as he sat upon a couch. He handed each a goblet of wine and sat there fondling their breasts. His arousal became so great that he shoved one girl on to her back, mounted her instantly, and thrust his throbbing organ deep into her body.

He cried aloud as he released himself into the screaming girl, who was overcome with pain. Senu believed she screamed in pleasure because of his size and turned with satisfaction to the other girl. She was more robust, yet barely developed. Despite what she had witnessed, she was determined to please Senu. When he moved his body so as to touch her, she smiled and pressed her tender body to him. He took pleasure in arousing this one; and when he finally began to pump his seed into her, both were lost to passion.

Thus was the custom with soldiers when among friends. Kamare sat throughout it all, drinking wine, and urging his friend onward with obscene shouts as was expected of him. Senu, however, knew not the pain he caused. The great heart of Kamare was about to break with desire and longing. His need for his love was intense. Desire rose up in him, but he put it away. He would drink himself into oblivion and feel no further pain.

Just before sleep, a beloved face floated above his. Her skin was pale; and in the green pools of here eyes floated black stars. "Hatshepsut, Hati, my love," he whispered before he slept.

Lying entwined with the naked bodies of the girls at the far end of the big tent, a sated and exhausted Senu heard the whispers. Slowly his eyes widened to stare upward in disbelief. *So, this is the way the moon rises in Egypt. The powerful Kamare holds his heart for his Queen. And what of her? Does she know? Is it possible she loves in return?* He thought back to the message he had brought so quickly to Kamare. After some reflection, Senu sat up and looked upon the broad body of the sleeping General. Unbelievable, but, yes, possible.

Senu might be a young and overly ambitious man, but he knew where his loyalties lay. He would serve Kamare in silence and with even more dedication. To hold the love of Queen Hatshepsut was no small thing. As he analyzed the sleeping form, he found he could easily understand how all women might desire Kamare. Truly, his torso rippled with muscular movement, even in sleep. He was perfectly formed and, when awake, darkly handsome in the most virile way. However, many other men had these attributes as well. What they had not was Kamare's ability to turn to hordes of men, raise his sword, and lead them into battle without fear. His magnetism could not be found so that one could place a hand on it, but it lived in him and in all that he did.

Senu collected his playthings and led them to his tent. Perhaps he would show the first recipient of his embraces what it was to feel pleasure, as had her companion. Yes, this he just might do before the sun rose and enveloped them in the heat of the desert.

17

The Queen's barge floated slowly down the Nile. The long, gold-leafed barque was designed for sea voyages; but since Hatshepsut and Ineni planned to spend a long time on the water, the many comforts afforded by the large sun boat were welcome. As the boat was rowed upstream, against the flow of the wide river, Ineni and Hatshepsut pored over the design she had selected.

On papyrus, the temple was overpowering even in scaled size and beautiful in the grace of its proportions. There were to be three terraces with a ramp in the center of each for the passage of her chariot. At the base of a granite cliff, two rows of pillars, one atop the other, would be carved out of the mountain. These would be the eleven-sided Doric pillars used centuries later in Greece. They would be formed for the first time now on the banks of the Nile from the hand of Queen Hatshepsut of Egypt.

Ineni had drawn two rows of sphinxes, ten per row, facing each other. These were on the lower terrace where all Egyptians would be permitted. The sphinxes would bear the Queen's face to establish her authority there and to show that it was her temple. Also, in this first terrace, would be lovely gardens and pools of water and palm trees. The Queen did not expect them to last forever, but she knew enough of Ineni's mind that she believed the temple would always exist.

Beyond the pillars, the inner temple in the depths of the mountains was to be filled with colored paintings, her cartouches, and all the words she would write down to be carved for eternity: *Queen Hatshepsut, life, health, prosperity, living forever.* Ineni would not put drawings of the innermost reaches of the temple, her tomb, on papyrus. He kept those plans in his head. He observed secrecy, above all!

For days, the barge floated slowly down the river, searching for exactly the right mountain or cliff. The sun must pass over this cliff from east to west, or the columns of stone would not cast an ever-moving shadow.

In the evening, Hatshepsut permitted the humble Ineni to share a meal with her. To the soft sounds of harps and water whispering against the hull, Ineni spoke of his plan for her tomb. Her eyes widened in wonder as he told her how she would live her afterlife in peace. The plan was brilliant and complex. It required the death of a member of the royal court and the subsequent burial of the mummy in this new temple very soon after its completion. That tomb would be on an upper level far above hers, which would be hidden hundreds of yards below. Although vandals might ravage the upper tomb, Hatshepsut's deep-in-the-granite base would never be discovered.

Ineni spoke also of his assistant, Sennumet, for whom he had great respect and hope. The boy was young, barely twenty, but his mind was as bright as his curly, golden locks of hair. He was pleasant to look upon, slender and graceful. Ineni told Hatshepsut that he had confided all his plans to Sennumet. The queen's architect was no longer young; and, as were many who spent long hours in the sun, he was withered and gaunt.

At night, when Hatshepsut struggled to find a comfortable position on her soft pillows, her heart flew over the desert to Kamare. His son moved restlessly in her womb, and she was hard put to balance the weight of her progressing pregnancy whenever she walked about. *Kamare's son, his beautiful, strong son!* She wrapped her slender arms around her belly, crooning to the unborn babe until he slept within her; and she fell asleep as well. As she slept, she dreamed that the black stars in her eyes looked down upon her love, sleeping far away in the desert.

The days passed. Each time a granite cliff was found that was set back far enough from the Nile to be above the spring flood, it was in the wrong juxtaposition with the sun and would not do. They floated on and on, endlessly it seemed. The boats tethered behind the barge that served as kitchens and also housed the servants, sent forward sweet delicacies to tempt her appetite. Ducks, freshly killed, were cleaned, stuffed with onions and spices, and covered in thick clay. This was artfully shaped in ways to amuse her, and the whole was baked, covered with coals.

When the clay creatures were smashed in front of the Queen, the duck within retained all its juices and the aromas of cloves, honey, and vegetables. Fresh bread, fruit, fishes grilled quickly with salt, and wine—these delights were all placed before her to tempt her appetite. And Hatshepsut ate well. She ate extremely well, and the fetus grew.

Upon passing Thebes from whence they sailed, Hatshepsut ordered that the banner of Thothmes II be hoisted to the mast in her husband's honor, and then lowered again once the city was behind them. Honor indeed! An appalling change had come over Thothmes II since their wedding night. Making use of her hiding places in the walls, the Queen had watched her husband take coarse advantage of the young serving boys she had sent him.

She watched as his plump body with all its curling hair and painted face and toes was splayed upon the bed. He gave explicit directions to the boys regarding the degrading acts they must perform. When his small man thing was aroused, he would choose one of the boys and bend him over the bed, using him to satisfy his lust, crowing as he finished his perverted pleasure.

The Queen watched with a mixture of revulsion and satisfaction and a trace of cruelty in her fleeting smile. She would continue to send beautiful boys to Thothmes. He believed he had honored her with a child on that first night and had made no further attempt to bed her. And that is how she would have it remain.

In their daily encounters, Thothmes retained his pleasant manner and continued to shower her with many expressions of thoughtfulness, but his growing mass of fat and his use of young boys made it difficult for Hatshepsut to return a kind word to him.

As her barque left Thebes behind, it occurred to the Queen that the tomb of Thothmes II would make an excellent cover for her own. Small sharp teeth bit her lower lip as she thought this pleasant thought. If such a happening could be arranged, then who better than a King to hide a Queen?

Two days after passing Thebes, Ineni called out to the oarsmen to row to the northern shore at a bend in the Nile. "Your majesty, please order the anchors to be dropped. I believe we have found your cliff."

Hatshepsut gave the orders, and the big sail came down, and the roped rocks were thrown over the side. "Ineni, I know this mountain well; it is called the mountain of Gurn, and the village is Deir el Bahri."

"Highness, imagine the village gone; then look at the sturdy granite of the mountain. And see, it is mid-afternoon and half the height of the houses lies in shadow on the western side."

With deep concentration that slowly turned to joy, she saw that all was as Ineni said. "Yes, Ineni, we have found our site, and it is Deir el Bahri."

The people of the village came in small groups to stare with big eyes at the golden boat from which wafted the aroma of perfume and incense of myrrh. The sides of the vessel were too tall for them to see who was aboard, but it could be none other. Why had Queen Hatshepsut had the anchor stones thrown onto their shore? Surely there was nothing of interest here for one so nighty: a few mud brick huts, some larger than others, but humble nonetheless. A few date palms gave scant relief from the sun, and the great cliffs of Gurn stood to the north. These offered protection from the winds. Goats mingled among the children in the crowd. All the people had been turned dark by exposure to the relentless sun. They existed upon the fishes and birds of the Nile and the crops planted after the spring inundation. Previous Pharaohs had barely bothered to stop here to collect wheat for taxes; it was too poor a place.

This Queen came for a different reason—one that would endure throughout time. A reason that would result in such a building that, centuries later, fascinated archaeologists would call the temple at Deir el Bahri the most wondrous monument in all of Egypt. The poor and simple people on the riverbank understood nothing of this; and even the Queen could but half envision what was to be. The site for the temple was selected, and the great, golden ship sailed back to Thebes.

As she had so often proven, Hatshepsut was wise far beyond her years. She would take pleasure in visiting the building site, and she would personally dedicate the first chalk lines, but all else would be left in the worn and capable hands of her architect, who now possessed the power to demand anything of the treasury and the people.

Hatshepsut quickly recovered from the rigors of the return voyage, which she had ordered be made as rapidly as possible. She then called Ineni to her chambers, and they set about making detailed plans for the construction of his masterpiece. Ineni brought Sennumet to meet with the Queen. As young as he was at twenty, he was four-and-one-half years older than Hatshepsut. The three of them talked long into many evenings, sharing a love for this project.

Sennumet was openly smitten by the beautiful Queen, even though she carried the child of another man. He dared not speak in tones of love, or stare overlong into her mysterious eyes. He knew he was not worthy, but he could fantasize and dream, and he could help build her temple.

Reclining on pillows, Hatshepsut spoke most frequently about the wall paintings and carved words. She gripped Sennumet's arm tightly one night and declared that there must never by any doubt that this work was hers and hers alone. Upon touching Sennumet, she was pleased to feel the firmness of his limb. He was an agreeable man, always so clean and well perfumed with oils. When her eyes gazed into his, she felt a remembered stirring in her body. Surely this could not be. It must be only because her love was so far away and did not share her bed. She would fight this feeling even if Sennumet was fair and handsome. Heart, mind, and body would obey her command and be loyal to the beloved General.

She decided to send Sennumet ahead with the workers who would destroy the old village and build another. The new one would house the artisans and master stone-carvers, along with the thousands needed for common labor.

"Sennumet, you will choose many soldiers, not only to keep the people working but to also see that all are well fed and content. They have no choice in this, but I would not spread misery. Ineni will join you when the village is razed and the ground leveled." At the stricken look on his face, she softened her tone. He was, indeed, an appealing young man.

"I will come to celebrate the dedication of the temple and shall myself snap the first rope of chalk. You will be at my side, Sennumet. All will be made aware of the Queen's love and respect for her architects. And you must come to Thebes often. It is not too far from the site. You and Ineni shall keep me apprised of all things." She smiled sweetly at him. He seemed to glow from the radiance of her smile, and her body began to burn. It was well that she was sending him away.

Later that night she had Beka rub her back. She was in her sixth month now and had grown quite large. Beka rubbed oil gently on her abdomen as well. She did this every day so that there would be no striation marks. The child was so large that Hatshepsut felt as if her tender skin would burst, and there were at least three more months to endure. She looked forward to the birth without fear, for she knew little of it.

The royal physician had explained what would happen, and she understood that there would be pain. He had told her he could give her opium at the end only if there was no problems. He proposed to cut her upon the edge of the birth canal to prevent a ragged tear. She had shuddered at this suggestion, and he had patted her hand gently.

"Look about you, my Queen," he said. "All those you see are born of woman. And are there not many of us? Some women have had many, many children. Only the birth of the first child will give you pain. And I promise you, in the years to follow, your joy in this child will be so great that you will remember nothing of the pain of giving birth."

And so she passed each day, enfolded in soft silks and fresh cottons. She continued to sit in the throne room for a few hours every morning, attending to affairs of state; and in the afternoons, she was often found making offerings upon the altars of the gods.

The Queen had given up driving her chariot, however. Nothing must happen to endanger the babe in her womb. She entertained herself in quieter ways by playing board games and reading in the great library. As ruler of many different peoples, she determined to be fluent in the language of each, and so she polished her understanding of the different tongues. She also pored over the papyrus rolls that contained the theories and inventories of the dead necromancer, Euripides. She was fascinated by his means of hypnotism without drugs, and she practiced upon her handmaidens and her mother-in-law, Mutnefret. The older woman was so grateful to the queen and so unaware of anything of the outside world that she was the perfect subject.

During the course of a conversation, Hatshepsut would dangle a crystal so that it caught the light. As she slowly swung the object back and forth, her voice dropped into a low monotone. Soon Mutnefret's eyes would glaze over, and she would answer any question the Queen asked. More importantly, Hatshepsut could implant any opinion or suggestion she wished; and upon coming out of the trance, Thothmes' mother would believe the thoughts had begun within her. Hatshepsut realized that this skill could prove most useful, but she decided it first must be tried upon other, more strong-willed persons.

She also discovered an ancient formula for an incense powder that flashed when thrown into fire and which gave off an aroma that caused mild hallucination. She was excited at the idea of using it and determined to try it out on a visit to the temple of the god Amon.

She arrived at the temple of Amon early one morning, wearing the full double crown of Pharaoh with its accompanying eureaus of hooded cobra. A heavy gold collar covered her neck and shoulders. She had chosen a robe that enhanced her pregnancy and also contained pockets inside the sleeves. These were full of the flashing powder.

The priests were waiting at the temple entrance when she arrived as she had sent servants ahead to announce her impending visit and to present to the temple a wagonload of gifts: rare spices, oils, perfumes, and alabaster bowls filled with lotus buds and blossoms. She was graciously received, and the head priests motioned the others to step aside so that Hati might enter without delay.

The Queen invited the two head priests of Amon to join her

in the inner sanctum of the temple. There, before the golden, man-like god, a fire was always glowing. Her hands passed over the fire many times as she prayed aloud. Each time her hands passed the fire, a flash hissed and became smoke, which the priests inhaled, and before their eyes, the Queen seemed to grow tall and change color many times. The stiff, gold god shimmered and "moved" in their sight.

The priests fell to the floor and shouted the praise of Hatshepsut. Never before had the god moved before a Pharaoh or a Queen. Surely, she was the daughter of Isis.

Word of this "miracle" would wend its way all over Thebes and up and down the Nile. Hatshepsut had caused Amon to move, perhaps even to talk! All praise to the Queen! *Life, health, prosperity to Pharaoh Hatshepsut.* This was the first time Hatshepsut had been recognized as and called by the title "Pharaoh." And she decided at that moment that she would cause the words "Pharaoh Hatshepsut" to be carved into the walls of her temple at Deir el Bahri.

The results of her experiment suited her purposes exactly. She planned to visit the temple or house of each god in Egypt. In time, all would be exposed to the flashing powder that caused her and the god she visited to appear supernatural.

Of course, Hatshepsut really believed in each god and also truly believed that she was the child of Isis and to be Isis herself. She also believed in living forever and ever in her hidden tomb at the conclusion of a long life with other, less royal humans. In the meantime, she would use these new tools as a means to an end and perhaps discover others in that small, hidden room beneath the palace.

Time passed slowly for her, but it passed inexorably, leading ever closer to the time for the birth.

18

The pit was filled with writhing snakes; it was time to harvest the venom. The riders returning from Thebes with bags of powdered poison would arrive within a week.

The soldiers had used the five weeks to exercise their horses and to hone their weapons of war. Meanwhile, the servants and slaves were making preparations for the huge feast to be given by Generals Kamare and Senu. Fat cattle, fresh vegetables, and flour for making bread and sweets had arrived, along with large jars of wine. More camp followers had joined the women already there, and a happy mood prevailed.

The Hyksos watched in bewilderment from their barricaded walls. The camp of the Egyptians was far beyond the reach of their arrows, but they could discern the shouts of laughter and smell the aroma of baking bread when the wind blew from that direction. This was all very strange for they had expected to be engaged in battle by this time. The prolonged waiting put a sharp edge to tempers. King Obinninos drowned his impatience in wine. Secretly, he regretted his decision to not only try to break the bonds of Egypt but to also attack its borders. His Queen, Thesula, had urged him on. Greed had glittered in her dark eyes as she maintained her harangue. Over and over she told him that a young Queen with no experience in ruling a nation would be defenseless and was no doubt ignorant of the art of warfare. And she reminded him that Egypt had sat astride her many dominions without any movement whatever for ten long years. Surely, so soon after ascending the throne, the young Queen would not dare venture against a fearsome enemy like the Hyksos.

Thesula was beautiful in a thick, sensual way. She had urged Obinninos on, thinking of the many jewels and bags of gold that would be hers if she could only prod him into action. That was months ago. Now she cowered in fear as he raged against her. The other wives of the King shrank from her, sensing her impending death as his tirades became longer and more violent.

In desperation, Thesula had her handmaidens anoint her with costly perfumes and clothe her in her most appealing garments. She then sought out the captain of the King's guards.

"Long have I looked upon you as my guardian and friend," she told Neblus. "Will you not help me plan an escape and come with me? I have secreted much gold in my chambers, and we will take it with us. Let us escape to the east and live together in a life of luxury. The king is sleeping with his other women now and ignoring me. That gives us time to get beyond his reach.

"Don't you realize the Egyptian armies camped outside the walls will conquer this city in the end?" she whispered pleadingly. "There are no foreign armies to the north of the palace, and there is a tunnel known only to the king, which he has shown to me. We can escape through it and live. You will surely be murdered, as shall I, if we stay. Would it not be better to lie in my arms far away than wait for death here?" As she spoke, the Queen pressed her body tightly against the soldier.

Captain Neblus looked down at her and admitted to himself that fear gnawed at his gut. He would live—he promised himself that—but not with this woman tied like a rock around his neck. He was a man of the military, and he believed himself to be a man of honor. But Obinninos did not inspire loyalty, only fear. Neblus decided that he would take his chances with the Egyptians. He knew well General Kamare's reputation as a fierce man, but also as a man with profound respect for human life, especially the life of a trained and loyal soldier. Arriving at this conclusion, he knew he could not join in the plan of the Queen. He had no doubt that Egyptian sentries were guarding all sides of the walled city; and he knew that, if he were caught attempting an escape, Kamare would regard him as a traitor and have him put to death. No, he must find a way to stay alive until the battle ended and then surrender to Kamare and no other.

Appearing to be receptive to her idea and to her suggestive movements, Neblus smiled at Thesula and asked her to tell him the location of the tunnel. She would not; she would tell him only that it was near the cisterns below the palace. He could detect the faint, metallic odor of fear being given off by Thesula and decided that he must distance himself from her without appearing to turn her down. He needed time to think and to explore the area around the cisterns. At this moment, they were full of good, clean water, saved against the time of siege and the possibility that an army could divert the stream that fed the city.

The captain urged the nervous Queen to begin her preparations for departure. He assured her that he would think hard to come up with a path of escape for both of them. She returned to her rooms, and he went to his post in the King's chambers to wait and to plan. He would not go with Thesula. She was doomed, he knew. All royal personages were killed in these assaults. He must avoid her so that he might manage to live. With luck, and by the grace of the gods, he would stay alive and serve Egypt in his city after it was conquered.

King Obinninos awakened amid a tangle of naked women. It was midday, and no breeze blew through the gardens. His mouth tasted of stale wine, and his head hammered fiercely. Away in the distance, he could hear whoops and yells from the Egyptian army. What held them? Why did they not come to battle? He felt assured that his soldiers could protect him; but as he silently asked himself these questions, cold fear gripped him. He shook with that fear. More wine? That would help. And someone would die today; someone would pay for his agony. The miserable Thesula! He had made her his Queen; he had even had her predecessor killed so that she might sit upon a throne and become the supreme love of his life. Yes, he had loved her once and look how she had repaid him!

He had no love left for any woman and Thesula least of all. He would have her killed today. Once they had shared a wild sensuous bed; now he would laugh aloud as the dogs in the pit ripped her apart. He hoped she would scream terribly, the slut.

"Neblus! Guards! I want you here at once."

From his stance beside the throne, Neblus heard the shouts from the bedchamber. He ran as quickly as possible, collecting soldiers as he went. A slave admitted them to a sight of debauchery. The king was pushing his naked body up from a pile of wide-eyed women. He wrapped himself in a cloak as he arose, smelling foully, his beard uncombed and hair on end.

"Neblus, go now to the rooms of Queen Thesula and make her captive. She feeds the dogs today. Have all the gold and jewels removed from her body and take her to the balcony over the pit. Tie her there to contemplate her death until I come. The bull of the Hyksos will see the temptress Thesula pay for causing her husband's unhappiness."

Neblus replied, "All shall be done as you command, oh mighty one." He turned on his heel and left. He was sickened by what he saw but not surprised by what he heard.

Neblus had managed to stay in the city when others raided the Egyptian border village. He had heard that the Hyksos king had led his soldiers in the commission of foul murders. Obinninos had returned with twenty-five Arabian horses and a little gold. The soldiers had boasted of the horrible acts perpetrated that day, and all seemed pleased with themselves. The Queen had been feted at a banquet in the evening, praised by the king as his divine inspiration. Well, the king's divine inspiration was about to meet a fate much like, or perhaps worse than, that of the Egyptian men, women, and children of that small town.

Neblus sent three soldiers to seize the Queen, and as they did so, terrified screams poured from her. These screams became more horrible as she was tied to a post above the dog pit. The dogs, recognizing this as a precursor to being fed, began to fight among themselves out of nervous anticipation.

Thesula begged to be spared when she saw her husband stride onto the platform. Tears ran down her contorted face, and she screamed even more loudly as he replied only with a cruel smile. Obinninos had covered himself with a loose cotton robe and combed his hair. He clutched a half-filled goblet of wine, which he drained in one enormous gulp. He pulled a pretty young girl to him and kissed her as his goblet was refilled. "Would you be Queen, little one?"

The child-woman, only recently brought to the harem, nodded happily in her stupidity.

"Well then, so you may. First, however, to prove your love for me, take this knife and cut off a portion of the old Queen to feed to my sweet pets; and we shall enjoy this all the more.

"Neblus, call all the people in the palace to watch this. We don't always have a royal meal for our pets."

As Neblus went to find a larger audience, the king took a large knife from his waist scabbard and handed it to the girl. Her eyes had widened in shock at his awful request. But even in her ignorance and fear, the young woman knew that to fail to obey would only bring about her own death; she would join the Queen with the dogs below—dogs that were now howling in anticipation.

The girl raised the knife and thrust it at the Queen. The knife penetrated the woman's shoulder; and as the girl pulled downward on it, she sliced a piece of flesh from Thesula's upper arm. The piece fell at the Queen's feet, and her screams of agony mixed with the frenzied howling of the dogs. Blood dripped from the balcony onto the heads and forepaws of the animals jumping at the sides of the pit.

At this moment, Neblus returned with a score more observers who were attempting to cover their fear with giggles and quivering smiles. Surely the king had gone mad. He was feeding a piece of the Queen to the dogs. Henceforth, no one would be safe. Obinninos motioned his captain forward. Neblus cut the bloodied ropes and threw Thesula into the pit.

Mercifully, she had fainted. The dogs leaped upon her still body and ripped out her throat. She did not feel it as the rest of her body was torn and crunched. In a half hour, little remained but her head, which was held in the forepaws of the largest beast. He alternately licked it and growled at the other animals; he alone would enjoy it.

In the Egyptian encampment, all paused when the sound of screams and the howling of dogs reached them from the city. The knew what was happening. What poor soul had been thrown into the evil pit today for the amusement of the barbarians?

In the well-guarded area by the snake pit, the men milking the venom paused in their work to exchange glances. Even poison was too kind an end for such people. All were veteran soldiers and knew that using this poison to contaminate an enemy's food or water supply would save the lives of many of their comrades. They were aware that even if the poison were too diluted to bring death to the enemy, it would still incapacitate them so that they would be too weak to fight. Their respect and love for Kamare grew. He would save the lives of as many of his men as possible. And at the end, he would be the first to fight in the city if it came to that.

The bags of poison arrived from Thebes five days after the last venom was harvested. As the physician hastened to mix jars of powdered belladonna and the venom with oil, the camp erupted in celebration. Many large fires were built, and sides of oxen turned above them.

At this last moment, each company of soldiers was informed of the plan Kamare had made. Orders were issued that no fighting man was to drink any more wine than was needed to wash down the meat, onions, and bread. The battle would commence at morning light, and they must be ready. As night fell, the woman of the camp oiled their naked bodies and danced to wild music in front of the fires.

The sight of such brazen behavior fascinated the army of King Obinninos, and the aromas of freshly baked bread and roasting meat were almost too much for them to endure. Their food allotment had been meager for many weeks, and there was only water to drink. The king had commanded this in anticipation of an Egyptian siege. He was certain that if he could hold off the Egyptians until they tired of waiting, he would retain his crown and his kingdom. If his orders were obeyed (and a dreadful death waited for any who dared to do otherwise), the city could survive for at least two years. The wines stored beneath the palace were for the royal family and the nobles of the court.

The revelry continued through the night, and the sentries stationed on the city's walls had eyes only for what was taking place in the Egyptian camp. Although morning approached, darkness still cloaked the surrounding countryside; and no one noticed four small donkeys to the north of the city. Ragged men led them. Had they been spotted, it is almost certain that the sentries would have assumed they were traders newly arrived from the desert, and unaware of the impending warfare.

The men and their animals reached the river and followed it until they were within thirty yards of the city. There, they trotted down to the river's edge. Just before dawn, as the fires of the feast died down, the traders emptied sixteen large jars into the water and rode back the way they had come. Once out of sight, they crouched behind a rock outcropping and threw off their ragged clothes. From there, they would leave, one by one, each to report on the progress of the poison. Although they were far from the city, they were well above it and could look down on the movement of those confined within its walls. Dawn had risen, and they could tell whether or not people dropped to the ground or continued to move about after drinking from the wells.

In the city, men were drawing water. It was the one thing they had much of. They could drink all they wanted and bathe without concern. The few women left in the city, other than those living in the palace, were prostitutes serving the soldiers. They were about to share the morning meal, a gruel made from millet boiled in water. As they ate—the soldiers, the women, the cooks who prepared the food—all keeled over. They did not rise up or cry out, nor did they complain of the oily taste of the morning cup of water. They simply died.

The first of the erstwhile traders crept away from behind the rocks and ran off to Kamare's camp to tell of the people lying in the streets around the wells. None had moved.

In the palace, King Obinninos and his new Queen arose and had their morning wine. He embraced the child-woman in a drunken fog and called for his bath. The two girls who slept at the foot of his bed ran to fill the small tub in the adjoining room with water. The Hyksos had none of the artistic nature of the Egyptian people, nor had they the wealth. As a result, the dwelling places of the people, even of the rulers, were comparatively crude.

The girls filled the stone tub with water that other servants had heated in large cauldrons in the kitchen and which had then been brought to the King's chambers in earthen jars. Before returning for the King, each girl poured a jar of water over herself and also drank from the jars of cool water placed on handy tables. In seconds, they dropped to the floor, as they gasped their final breaths.

Impatient for his first bath in several days, the king grabbed his child bride by the hand and, filling his goblet yet again, staggered to his bath chamber. He stood, blearily taking in the scene before him. The bath filled, but the girls were obviously dead. The longer he stood, the quieter the palace seemed. Befuddled as he was, he realized that something was clearly amiss.

All the while, Neblus was deep beneath the palace. After Thesula's death, he had gone directly to the carved-out pools of granite that formed the cisterns. The king was absolutely mad, and Neblus wanted to be alone to think and to look for the tunnel. After Thesula had told him of its existence, he was sure that he could find it. He was familiar with the manner in which the water was collected and stored. The stream flowed directly above the cistern ceiling. Water was let in by a trap door made from a tightly fitted, wedged stone from which only a minute amount of water dripped when it was closed.

He had come down the winding stone stairs and paused in the archway. Before him were four huge ponds of water. In the farthest of these, he discerned the dark arch of an opening a foot or two below the water line. If a man were to dive into this and swim hard, he would come up in the main river not too far away.

Neblus spread his cloak on the damp, stone floor and slept the night in the cool chamber. It was forbidden to bathe there, but he had drunk long and well and had eaten millet cakes before retiring.

When he awakened in the morning, he knew that he must report promptly to the King as always or face the possibility of royal outrage. If that happened, he, too, would be fed to the dogs. He ran up the stairs and through the opening into the palace garden. Faintly, he heard Egyptian war trumpets. *At last, the battle will come. I have only to stay alive until the palace surrenders and the Egyptian general offers amnesty. Unless they have taken a blood oath of vengeance. If that seems to be so, I will return here and dive into that tunnel. I will not die for this vile king.*

Swiftly, he climbed to the top of the wall surrounding the garden, which allowed him to see down into the streets of the city. He was surprised and angered to discover that there were no sentries in sight. The king would have them all slain if he learned of this blunder. When he looked toward the city, he saw bodies lying all about, but in greatest profusion near the wells. Like a lightning bolt, the realization of what had happened struck him. *The Egyptians had somehow managed to poison the water supply!* He thanked the gods that he had been in the cistern chamber the previous night; for he was an early riser and would certainly have drunk from a well and died as had the others.

In the palace, Obinninos was still frozen in his bath chamber, trying to think. He threw down the wine goblet as he shook himself and strode toward the palace balcony so he could overlook the city. All along the halls, there were dead and dying servants. A few soldiers who had not been relieved of guard duty, and therefore had not had anything to eat or drink, were alert and asking questions of the dying.

One ran to the King and said, "My lord, do not drink any water or touch food made with water. I and my comrades have deduced that the Egyptians have somehow managed to fill the stream with a terrible poison."

At this moment, Neblus appeared in the hallway. Upon seeing him, Obinninos reached out and clasped his arm in relief. Surely his brave captain could assess the situation and devise a scheme that would save the King's life.

"Brave Neblus, most trusted of my soldiers, go and see what our position is at this time. Hear the trumpets! They must be at our gates! Go! Go, for the sake of your King."

Neblus bowed his head, then turned and ran back as he had come. This time he climbed to the top of the tower walls. The sight he beheld was one to freeze the blood of any man.

Hordes of Egyptian warriors stretched for at least a mile. At the head of the vast army, the mighty Kamares was astride a rearing stallion that he held in check with one hand. Gold armor glittered over his shoulders, chest, and groin. On his head was a gold skullcap with a peak of ostrich plumes. He was as unmovable as a rock as the soldiers cried to be let loose upon the walls. Slowly he raised his sword. He was about to wave the army onward when he spotted a familiar form on the palace tower. The man raised his arm in recognition.

"Senu, to me. Can you make out the tall officer on the tower?" asked Kamare.

Senu replied, "That man is Captain Neblus. I have heard much of him and have met him once or twice. He is brave and honest even though he serves Obinninos. We shall talk with him. Perhaps we can resolve this battle with honor and very little fighting."

Kamare shouted out, "Captain Neblus, I give you safe conduct to come to speak to me. Perhaps there is something to be said."

Neblus lowered his arm but remained as he was for a few moments. He deliberately wanted to appear less than eager to grasp this opportunity. The more honorable he seemed, the better chance he had to live on in the service of Egypt.

Deciding that an appropriate time had elapsed, Neblus climbed down from the tower walls. He picked two soldiers to accompany him and noted that fewer than twenty living men were in sight. He was careful to see that they each rode a small, ugly Hyksos horse instead of the fine Arabians captured in the raid.

The three rode forth to speak with the Egyptian general. Kamare and Senu moved toward the city to meet them halfway, and a hush fell upon the armies of Egypt. Silence issued also from the city, for it was a city of the dead.

Neblus spoke first. "My friend, General Kamare, and honored general by your side, I came forth to hear what you have to say. I have no doubt that you know what has befallen my countrymen; but few as we are, we are prepared to defend our city as best we might."

Kamare and Senu conferred for a short time. Kamare had already decided what he would do, but he wished to give Senu the honor of appearing as a full participant in these decisions. At length, both Egyptians faced the Hyksos captain and Kamare spoke: "I respect your loyalty, captain. But as reasonable men, we choose to give all your comrades who wish, the opportunity to live. Those who choose to do so may join my army as soldiers of the lowest rank; and, always, they will be watched for any sign of traitorous conduct. Those who would resist will have to fight as best they can, for we will take no unwilling slaves. In the end, all gold and treasure will be removed to Thebes; and we will take back our horses, leaving yours behind. Go now, and place my offer before the remaining inhabitants of the city. As for your King, I believe you, too, know him to be evil. He, and all of his male children, will be put to the sword. I can do no better than this, and, indeed, will have difficulty in holding the blood lust of my soldiers in check."

Neblus turned to the two soldiers with him, and they nodded their heads to indicate that they accepted the terms Kamare was offering. The three rode back into the city where they found that the group of twenty had been increased by five. All crowded close to Neblus as he explained with a stony face what they had been offered. He told them they could live to be a part of the Egyptian army, or they could fight to the death. There would be no slaves and no captives.

Without hesitation, all lay down their swords. They had not expected to be spared and grasped this offer of life eagerly. And they would still be soldiers; they would not be slaves.

No one spoke the name of Obinninos. In all such wars, it was inevitable that Kings and royal children must die. It was the custom, and one that made good sense in those ancient times. It was not prudent to allow kings and their heirs to remain alive; for, always, they conspired to regain what had been lost.

On the field beyond the walls, Kamare and Senu called the captain of each unit to their sides. These officers were told to return and explain to their troops that almost all the fighting men in the city were dead and that few other inhabitants remained, as the King had long ago forced them from their homes into the surrounding countryside to fend for themselves as best they could.

Kamare also told the captains that two hundred Egyptian soldiers would remain to garrison the city under the command of an officer he selected to rule. Any who remained could send for their families if they chose. If they were unmarried, they could select one of the camp women to wed. It was an opportunity to rise in military rank. For the very young, it was an adventure, especially for those from large families with no hope of inheritance.

At first, there was grumbling and disappointment. It was hard to understand why they had come so far and waited so long, only to keep their swords in their scabbards. Slowly, however, the realization came that there simply was no one left alive to fight. Ultimately, it was accepted as a great victory, and many stepped forth to volunteer to be a part of the occupation army.

Inside the city walls, the few remaining Hyksos soldiers looked to Captain Neblus for orders. "Pick up your swords. We must deliver the King and all his male heirs to the Egyptian generals. If we fail, we are dead men. Remember, all of you, that Obinninos was evil and cruel and deserves whatever befalls him. As for the children, I believe he sent all but the babes away from this city. Harm not the little ones. We will leave that decision to the Egyptians, who will no doubt hunt down the older offspring of the King. Come with me. We will rid our city of evil and in so doing save ourselves."

King Obinninos had put on his royal robes and his crown and adorned himself with the jewelry remaining in his bedchamber. Some weeks prior, slaves had hidden mos of his treasure in the tunnel below the water against the time he might be forced to flee. They had been put to the sword after completing this chore—no point in chancing that one of the fools might whisper about the secret affairs of the King. Now, he stepped into the hallway, uncertain of what he would find. *Ah, here comes my noble captain with a guard of honor. Surely, they are here to escort their beloved ruler to safety. Neblus is smiling and appears to be at ease. It must be that the Egyptians were not so successful in their cowardly attack as we first thought.*

"Gracious King, I have come to escort you to General Kamare of Egypt. All here is lost, as these are all the soldiers I have left. I believe you will be treated justly; and, therefore, you have nothing to fear. Please, mighty one, follow me."

Obinninos was transfixed with horror. *This cannot be. This smiling captain has become a lying devil, for he knows no Egyptian will permit me to live. Thesula was the fortunate one—her death was quick. Still, I may have a chance. My hidden treasure is immense; the General may see it as a way to enrich himself if I offer it to him in exchange for my freedom. There's no other way. It is too late to escape through the tunnel; and if Neblus is joining the Egyptians, no one is left to rescue me.*

"As you wish, Captain. I will indeed meet with this General. I have a proposal that may save us all." Despite his imperious tone, the King trembled inwardly as he tried to walk regally with the soldiers to the gates of the city. He was desperate to demonstrate that a Hyksos King was made of iron.

The city gates had remained unbolted and opened wide after Neblus returned from his meeting with Kamare. King Obinninos stood in the opening, glittering in gold, holding his head high before his soldiers. He waited for Kamare and Senu to come forward.

Before Obinninos could speak, he was grabbed from behind and wrapped in ropes. As Neblus removed his crown and jewels, the king began to shout that if his life were spared, he would give great treasure to the Egyptian generals. In his fear, he lost control of his bowels, and he trembled as a stalk in the wind.

Ignoring the foul-smelling and babbling King, Kamare addressed Neblus and his men, "Swear loyalty to Egypt, and you live. Do otherwise, and you follow your King to the kraits."

All swore for Egypt, Neblus last of all and directly to Kamare. "Noble friend, I would bear arms for Egypt. I love my homeland but have served its King without love and through fear. I am yours to command."

Senu and Kamare exchanged glances. Was this man one they could trust? Perhaps he would be well liked enough by the people who would soon return to the city to assume temporary leadership of Hyskonia and Kadesh. He obviously could command the troops who would remain there. They would see in time.

"Neblus, where are this man's sons? It is a sad duty to slay them, but it must be done."

"General, the older ones were sent into hiding places in the countryside. All that are left are small babes in arms. See, they come now."And, indeed, a group of women came clutching small bundles. There were not many, as only a few had not partaken of the poison. Tears ran down hopeless faces as they kissed the little ones goodbye.

It tore at Kamare's heart, as he was reminded of how much he yearned to hold his son, though yet unborn. For this reason, he was unduly merciful. "Surely, Senu, there can be no evil in the hearts of these little ones. Shall we not have Captain Neblus choose one over which to watch so that he can grow to rule this land? We will send assassins to search out the older sons and destroy them; however, I am inclined to save the babes. What say you to this?"

Senu agreed immediately. He had no stomach for this result of warfare; and besides, it was the logical thing to do. Although he tried to control it, a small smile graced the corners of his lips. He well understood the emotions his friend was feeling.

All in all, Senu believed the undertaking had gone well—almost too well. Not one Egyptian had lost his life, although a few had come close to it as a result of snakebite. A dire situation had been solved by Kamare's indomitable patience and crafty mind. He had no doubt that the same man could have slaughtered scores of the enemy at will and without regret if that had been the need. But, as things were, the package was neatly tied. Senu's only reservation concerned Neblus. Kamare knew him from an earlier time and apparently trusted him entirely. To Senu, however, there was a faint something about the man that rang untrue. For now, he would say nothing. Senu simply bent his head in agreement.

"Very well. Captain Neblus, I appoint you viceroy to Egypt, Vizier of Kadesh and Hyskonia and guardian of the future king of these lands. You will choose, at your own discretion, which child shall rule. You may dispense of all the women as you choose and to whom you choose. Never forget, however, that your life and your very breath belong to Queen Hatshepsut of Egypt. You will keep her well advised at all times, and your country will send double the annual tribute to her."

Neblus was stunned. He had hoped for life; he had been handed honor. Yes, he would serve Egypt. As for a babe-in-arms to be trained to be ruler? He rather fancied that position for himself. Well, time was his to use. "Mighty General, I accept with gratitude and great humility. You may trust me in this."

It was said simply enough; but at the words, "you may trust me," Kamare winced. So many who said these words were untrustworthy. Those who could be trusted wholeheartedly usually felt no need to remind anyone of it. He looked to Senu to see if there was doubt showing upon his face; but he saw only an impassive countenance. Perhaps he was being overly wary. He turned his attention to the nearly crazed Obinninos.

The man was not a man at all; he cried and wailed, as would the most craven coward. The mothers of the children had behaved more nobly than did this miserable dealer of torture.

"Honored Vizier Neblus, your first duty to your Queen is to hand over this cringing creature to the Egyptian army. I believe they have something in mind for him."

As Neblus dragged the gibbering King away, Senu addressed the Hyksos soldiers who remained. "Before you join our forces, it will be your work to stack and burn the corpses of your countrymen. You have your own customs and gods. We leave you to this duty. At no time will the gates be closed. Our physicians inform us that the wells will be clear by nightfall. However, to be safe, I advise you to use only the cistern water for three days."

Both generals turned their backs to the Hyksos warriors and rode triumphantly back to their own army where great revelry was in progress. They sang war songs as they rode together to the camp where Egyptian captains had broached jars of wine for all. Meat was roasting, and baking in ovens was honey bread to which raisins had been added. Fruited bread was the custom for celebration.

In drunken good humor, the soldiers had laid four long lines of hot coals on the desert sands. At the end of these, a terrified Obinninos was tied upright. They all wanted him to see what part he was to play in their amusement.

The organizers of the sport had chosen a wide depression in the terrain, with mounds of sand on both sides. These low hills were covered with as many soldiers as they would hold. The men drank from their jars of wine as they yelled obscene remarks to the King and told him of the new friends he would soon be making.

Two large jars containing the snakes had been placed where Obinninos could see them. Now and then, a long krait was carefully removed from the jar and examined and then returned after being rejected from all sides with loud shouts that it was far too small.

Obinninos had soiled himself again and again and was fast sinking into insanity. How could he make them stop? The horrible, terrible snakes! They would come to him; bite him over and over! He begged for a dagger in the heart. No one listened.

Finally, when the crowd was roaring drunk, and the coals were very hot, a big krait was set in each of the three lanes. They coiled and struck at rocks, crazed with pain from the heat, and moved inexorably toward the transfixed man at the junction of the lanes. Since there was the chance that one might expend its venom upon the rocks, three more were released into the lanes after the first ones had passed the halfway mark. And then another three.

The doomed King screamed until he lost all voice; his neck bulged in fear as he watched the tortured snakes slithering ever closer. When they reached him, he watched still as they struck again and again, a living nightmare. He died in terror. Had he undergone this torture many scores of times, it would not have repaid his debt of evil and the horrors he had committed upon so many others.

19

The army of the Queen was marching slowly home. The soldiers brought with them the honor of victory over Egypt's enemy and a wagon full of treasure for Hatshepsut. The new vizier had exposed the tunnel in the cisterns. He had guessed correctly that the treasure would be there.

Inside Kamare's doeskin vest, under his armor and cloak, was nestled a pouch with one huge blood-red ruby. It was the most beautiful stone in all the treasury, and he meant to give it to his love personally. It had been eight months since the Queen had married. The father of her child calculated that he had but seven to ten days to reach her. The army had marched but halfway home; and it had taken three weeks to get this far. The oxen moved steadily at one pace, and the men who walked must be considered.

Finally, he could bear it no longer. Calling to Senu, Kamare said, "I have urgent business in Thebes. I entrust our soldiers to your capable hands. I am away."

Senu waved him off, surmising full well what the business was. It would take Kamare three days and three nights if he did not rest, and Senu was sure that he would not. What a mysterious happening this was. He knew that he must never reveal his knowledge, never expose his friend or the child of his friend. And the gods knew he idolized his Queen. She was so beautiful, so elegant; and more than that, she was the most powerful person in the known world.

How had Kamare managed this? It was unimportant of course, because he had managed it after all. When Senu thought of the unappetizing bride who eagerly awaited him, he felt envious of the love shared by the other two. But, on the bright side, his fortune was made; and he was entitled to as many women as he liked. Nefertum was a small inconvenience in return for the honors and wealth he would receive.

On and on Kamare rode, pausing only to change mounts and relieve himself. He ate and drank in the saddle. The desert had become a rolling blur that rushed beneath the hooves of his horses. Whenever he arrived unannounced at a station, his cartouche ring and his bearing as the great and widely feared General Kamare instantly brought him whatever supplies he wanted.

He was chased briefly on the third day by a band of nomads on swift horses. Without stopping, he shook his sword at them and bellowed forth a war cry as he thundered on. The band prudently halted to wait for easier prey. Word that the Egyptian army marched abroad had made them doubly cautious, and the huge madman in gold breastplate did not invite further chase. Who knows—if stopped from his headlong charge, he might turn on them and eat them, one by one.

The moon was almost above his head as Kamare flew into the city of Thebes. Watchmen had heard his trumpet from a distance and had the gates standing wide. He blew hard upon his war horn all the way to the palace. He wanted her to know that he was coming.

In her bed, Hatshepsut was propped up, half sitting and half lying, and sleeping but little. She could find no position in which she felt at ease and in which she could rest her huge belly. Her abdomen was greatly distended, and she saw fear in her physician's face. The poor man would never know that the child's father was not the painted toad who waddled about his rooms on tiny, mincing feet.

Her physician had measured her pelvic bones many times that day and had found that they were separating rapidly. The child had dropped so low that the queen could not stand because of the pressure. The fearsome birthing chair had been brought to her bedchamber, and she stared at it constantly. There was a mysterious mound of fine-grained salt in a tray by its side.

What was that she heard? The draperies had been pulled away from her balcony, and upon the cool breeze floated the faraway sound of a war trumpet. It came on and on, sounding as though the rider were trumpeting with every few leaps of his charging steed.

Soon, she heard it more loudly and clearly, and in the city. Closer it came, to the palace itself. It could be no other. She had known of his victory and the manner of it for days. She had waited so long, yet never doubting that he would arrive before the birth.

The doors flew open and then slammed closed, and she was in his arms. Never had arms been so welcomed around her. Never had lips been so eager to kiss—lips that did not part for many moments. As Kamare gently drew back, neither could speak but could only look deeply into the other's eyes. His rough hand tenderly smoothed the skin over her swollen body, and a tiny foot chose that moment to kick.

Kamare's laugh was the roar of happiness he had kept hidden these long months. He could speak at last. "Oh sweetest love, tormenter of my nights and dreams, tell me with your own lips what I long to hear of this babe!"

Hatshepsut felt comfort for the first time since his departure. Leaning against his chest, she answered lovingly, "This child is ours, yours and mine, and always Egypt's. This child is to be Pharaoh in time. Never again shall I let you leave me. Life is not life without you. Before tonight, I was afraid of dying at the child's birth. No longer. Let life do as it will; you are with me always."

As though the child also waited the arrival of his father, Hatshepsut gave her first, small cry of pain. The next Pharaoh would soon be born.

Kamare had locked everyone out of the Queen's chamber. After one more long kiss, he rose against her will and called in the physicians. "Your Queen is about to give birth. I swear to kill all of you if there is the smallest hair removed from the head of the child or any more grief than necessary comes to his mother."

As frightening as Kamare appeared, the head physician did not hesitate to speak. "You are covered in dirt and road stains. If you do not cleanse yourself, you will harm them both. You must leave at once!"

From the bed came the pain-pinched voice of the Queen. "General Kamare is here because I need him. He will stay with me at all times. Beka, put him in my pool quickly and bring him back as fast as you can. My son hurries to be born."

As Kamare ran to the pool, tossing clothes in every direction, he ordered Beka to bring him food. He could not help the Queen if he were weak from the saddle.

A normal man could not have made the ride. A heroic man would have collapsed at the gate. Kamare, on the other hand, asked only for food as he soaped himself vigorously, rinsed, dried, and threw on a pleated cotton skirt. He was gnawing the last of a lamb's leg as he rushed back to her.

Hatshepsut, even in her pain, gave forth a small laugh as she saw the big man ripping meat from the bone as a lion might and tossing the remains to a maid.

He was beside here at once, holding her gently, and rocking her in his arms and singing lilting lullabies to her when the pains bore down. When they became so strong that tears rolled down her cheeks, he begged the head physician to give her something to ease them. The doctor refused and told him why he could not and then told him that what he was doing was the best anyone could do. Since the child was so large, she would soon be put into the birthing chair; and, just before cutting her to release the child, she would be given opium.

In the ancient manner of assisting women to bear children, many versions of the birthing chair were devised. Some were simply chairs with the seat cut out to allow he child to drop. The Egyptian version at this time was one with a sturdy, upright back upon which to lean; strong, thick arms to grasp when the pain was insupportable; and tall, firm legs with a seat so high that a woman was almost standing. Her legs were bent just slightly at the knees and hips. She could raise her feet off the ground by supporting her torso with her grip on the arms. In the last stages, she would be encouraged to raise her knees high with the surge of pain and place her feet back on the ground when it eased. A physician knelt behind her and between her feet. In this position, he could massage the birth opening with oil so that the muscles relaxed and allowed the baby's exit. If a cut were needed, he could make it precisely, put away the sharp knife, and grasp the head of the child as it was born. He could also reach up to slant broad shoulders in the birth canal or dislodge a foot caught above a baby's head.

Kamare carried Hati to the birthing chair and stood facing her as she fought the pain. "Accept the pain, sweetest one; help the pain to come so that it will soon be over." He bathed her face and body with cool water and urged the physician to relax her muscles and enlarge the opening as much as possible.

The physician exclaimed that the Queen had opened unusually wide and that he could see the child. There would be no cut for this woman; she was born to bear sons.

As the physician eased the head and then the shoulders of the child into view, a lusty wail announced his birth to all of Egypt. Hatsheput heaved a sigh of relief as the body of her son fell from her.

And it was a son—perfect in all ways.

The afterbirth came next as women kneaded the Queen's stomach. The child's cord was tied and severed. Then the physician performed his last task: he lifted handfuls of salt and pressed them into and around he opening from whence the child had emerged. Over and over, he lifted salt to her. This old and wonderful remedy caused the flesh to shrink quickly. If there were small tears, they would be cauterized by the salt, which would not be removed for a day.

Hatshepsut stood with her arms around Kamare's neck while her women bound her hips tightly together. She had had comparatively easy delivery of her first child. Could one believe this child?

The baby was cleansed with water and oil, then wrapped tightly in swaddling cloth. He lay gazing up at everyone with big brown eyes. He had short, curly brown hair and seemed as broad as two babes. His fists and feet were wide and churning; his thighs and calves were muscular.

It is often said that the child, immediately following birth, is more true to his future self than later when he is covered with baby fat. If this is so, then there on the low table lay an exact copy of his father, and perhaps a bit more. His face bore a delicacy unseen in Kamare, and his eyebrows were winged as those of his mother. He was beautiful.

Kamare carried Hati to the bed that had been freshly made up and then asked the women for the child. He stood holding his son, and they looked one upon the other. The warrior felt as though his heart would surely burst from joy. Never had a man held so wondrous a son.

Aloud, for all to hear, he said, "I, Kamare, General of Queen Hatshepsut, do now dedicate my life to this child, the son of our Queen and of Pharaoh Thothmes II." It tore his heart to speak these words, to say the babe was the son of Thothmes, but it must be so.

Gently, with many kisses and soft words, he placed the boy in his mother's arms. Hatshepsut looked down at the little face, so earnest, quiet, and sweet. The feeling in her heart was beyond words, and the last thing she remembered before she slept was a big hand holding hers.

Thothmes was irritated that he had been kept waiting so long. Did these cows always take this long to bear children? He was eager for it all to be over so that he could return to the feast to relish his achievement as the father of a son. And it must be a son! May the gods grant a son! Otherwise, he should have to bed the Queen again quite soon. In light of the discoveries he had made with little boys, the task seemed more odious than ever.

However, he managed to keep up appearances and to pat his mother's hand occasionally. Fortunately, they both loved food; and to calm their nerves, they consumed many sweet cakes. Mutnefret was honestly concerned for the Queen. Thothmes' mother was good at heart and had grown to love Hatshepsut as a daughter. The birthing of her own son had been a terrible ordeal, or so she remembered it.

Some women bear the pain of childbirth with stoic bravery, knowing it must be so. Others wear themselves out with screams and thrashing about because they lack the character to face reality and pain. Little had been heard issuing from the Queen's chambers. Hatshepsut belonged to the former group, and she had had Kamare to help her withstand the pain.

Now the doors were thrown open, and the physician approached Pharaoh with these words. "Great Pharaoh Thothmes II, the gods Horus and Isis have granted the Great Royal Wife the safe birth of your son. May you live forever and ever."

In a rush of relief, and with the aromas of many perfumes swirling around his body. Thothmes II, followed by his mother, tottered into the Queen's rooms to see his son. In matter of fact, it was the first time he had ever been there. He was so overcome by the massive grandeur that it took a moment to remember the child. Then he relaxed himself and spoke to Hatsheput.

"Ah sweet wife, I see I have given Egypt a big, healthy heir, and it is all rightly so." But she could not hear him in her deep sleep. Thothmes ignored the huge man beside his wife's bed, believing him to be a guard of some sort. "Well then, all is as it should be. I go to tell Egypt of my new son. We shall talk tomorrow when you have rested." And away he flopped to drink and eat and boast of his prowess as Pharaoh. And who could deny it?

Mutnefret would have stayed with the Queen, but Kamare banished all save Beka, Nefertum, and the wet nurse for the child. The nurse and Beka bound the breasts of Hatsheput so the milk would not come, and Kamare lay beside his love and gave himself up to the sleep he had denied himself for three days.

It was a beautiful picture. The lovely Queen, asleep with the child in the crook of one arm; the great giant by her side, sleeping at last, with his sword on the floor by his hand.

The god Ra began to shine from the eastern sky as Beka and Nefertum pulled the drapes against his rays and fell asleep in chairs by the bed.

The child in his mother's arms was the last to close his eyes. There, with Hatshepsut, Queen of Egypt, and Kamare, General of all the armies, lay the future pharaoh. He would be named later as Thothmes III. History would prove him to be the most powerful Pharaoh of all the dynasties of Egypt. It was enough for this night, however, for there to be the peace of new life and the everlasting love his mother and father held for each other and for him.

20

The gilding on the hull of the long boat flashed back the rays of the sun, making them dance across the water. Green and gold silk sails filled with gusts of late afternoon winds as the boat worked its way up the Nile. Forward, a three-sided tent, hung with gauzes, swayed with the motion of the river. All commands were silent signals so that only the wind and the notes of a flute could be heard.

Queen Hatshepsut lazed upon cushions in the tent, holding her sleeping son, Thothmes III. Kamare returned from pacing the boat to drop down beside her, and they kissed. "Dearest love, Queen of my heart, call for the nurse to take our son below to sleep. I would drop the inner hangings of this enclosure and be alone with you."

Purring her pleasure, Hatshepsut called for the nurse, who came at once for the four-year-old prince. She could barely lift the forty-pound boy, and old Beka called for a young slave to help her.

The prince's brown ringlets were long. His lashes curled against cheeks tanned by the sun and brushed with roses of good health. His father had seen him rarely, but his "Uncle Kamare" had given him a pony to ride. At age four, he pounded the little animal to go faster than its short legs could trot. He had his own small, dull sword and fought every soldier he could attack. The halls of the palace rang with calls of "Spare me, Prince Thothmes!" Laughter and happiness made up his wonderful world. He loved his mother very much, and she spoiled him in every way possible to her. Were it not for his uncle, he would have had many sweets and cakes. Kamare had set strict rules regarding the child's diet and exercise. This regime would toughen as he grew, and he would eventually be well versed in all physical activities.

The Queen had begun to instill in him a sense of his importance, and he learned small bits of palace etiquette and the rudiments of good manners from her also. Tantrums were not tolerated, but on the other hand, emotions were encouraged. It was all right to show displeasure if one were a prince, but this emotion must be controlled. Many a vicious tyrant began as a four-year-old child left free to scream and strike out at anyone he pleased. Most of all, however, little Thothmes was loved. All Egypt adored him, and he waved happily at anyone and everyone.

As the child was carried away, Kamare dropped heavy cloths from gilded ropes around the boat's royal enclosure. Hati fell into his arms; their lovemaking was still sweet and exciting. It seemed that each year brought them ever more love than either had believed possible.

Later they lay entwined, rocked by the passage of the sailing ship. There was peace, happiness, and love. Were it not for the necessary public appearances with Thothmes II, life for Hati would be perfection.

"When we reach the site of Deir el Bahri, all will be ready to snap the chalk lines for my lovely temple. It is a day I have dreamed of for a long time. We have watched the terraces take form, and they are wonderful; but, my love, this temple will be the most beautiful and unusual in all the history of Egypt and, therefore, the world. Today, I will speak to Ineni and Sennumet of my desire that there be a sarcophagus for you beside me in my hidden tomb. We shall live our afterlives together as we are living this life—never apart, always sharing."

Kamare breathed a sigh of contentment. He was now forty-one years old, and the gray in his hair looked well upon him. Although his body was still firm and massive, life at the palace had softened him somewhat. General Senu had taken over the practical management of the armies; however, he still answered to Kamare. Kamare adored his son and his "wife." He thought of her as "his wife" always.

Since Thothmes II seldom put in an appearance, it was a nearly perfect life. Egypt had never been so strong or so prosperous. Taxation brought in bushels of wheat, casks of olives and dates, and all manner of domestic animals. The gold mines produced the precious metal in a never-ending stream, and a new pit near the Red Sea yielded amazing riches.

This pit had been dug deep into layers of black shale mixed with vanadium and iron sludge. The stones began as a common beryl stone, pale and translucent. The iron-based sludge "cooked" the natural crystals over decades to the beautiful, perfect dolor of precious emeralds. They stuck out of the shaft in whole jewels, covered with black crust. After chipping away the crust, the craftsmen cut and polished the emeralds to beautiful shades of green.

Hatshepsut had caused a map of the world to be created from rubies, pearls, lapis lazuli, and emeralds. The whole of the Nile was depicted in emeralds so full of light that the river seemed to flow between the less dazzling jewels.

The Queen had set her jeweler to the task of making a wide collar of solid emerald set in gold with matching teardrop earrings that swayed from her ears in many lengths. Her eyes appeared a deeper green each time she wore this priceless collar. Always, she wore the ruby Kamare had brought her on the night of their child's birth. She removed the chain bearing it only to sleep. Whatever garment she wore, it was always there under all else, warm against her skin.

Life for Hatshepsut and her family was happy and filled with love. And soon she would lay the chalk line for the column bases at Deir el Bahri. Tonight, the boat would moor at the new dock, and Ineni and Sennumet would eat their evening meal with the royal family. She would propose Kamare's sarcophagus at that time, and they would all talk of her wondrous temple and its two tombs, one obvious and one hidden.

For an Egyptian pharaoh or queen, the work of a lifetime was the building of his or her eternal resting place. Many years, many lives, and much fortune were expended upon these edifices. Old Khufu had built the giant pyramid before Hatshepsut's grandmother, Tetisheri, was born. It was said that the entombment was so cleverly done that the whole of the inside shaft of the pyramid was deliberately collapsed upon Khufu's sarcophagus. It would take the hand of a giant to pluck the stones of granite away from his treasure. Surely, Khufu lived on in happy comfort, undisturbed by thieves.

At sunset, the royal boat tied alongside the wharf. Ladders swung out from hinged sides, and messengers ran off to find Ineni and Sennumet. Although they expected the Queen, good manners bade them wait for an invitation before appearing on the dock to board the vessel.

Hatshepsut had come full blown into womanhood. What had been coltish lines were now voluptuous curves. Responsibility rested upon her well. Every move she made was regal; every thought was well considered. This evening she sat in a ram-headed chair, draped in white silk and emeralds, the gold cobra malevolent upon her brow. Pale, velvety skin, winged brows, and black stars set in emerald eyes gave background to her gentle smile of welcome.

At her side sat Kamare; as always, he wore only a simple, pleated cotton skirt. He gave in to his Queen's wishes by wearing two thick gold armbands. He also wore the golden ring bearing her cartouche. However, no amount of pleading could put gold in his earlobes or around his neck, as was the fashion of noblemen and women. He was what he was. Honor rested upon him, as would an invisible crown. His presence made his every word instantly obeyed. He could not have led so many armies into dangerous battles without his mysterious cloak of honor. Many would-be officers adorned themselves with all the important trappings of office, weighed down by gold. Most would be lucky to lead soldiers into a drinking house.

Thothmes III sat upon his "uncle's" lap, content to be near him. He held his favorite toy, a wooden crocodile carved in three pieces. It was pulled with a string; and as the wheels turned, its jaws opened wide and snapped shut. He had many wooden toys, but he loved the fence snap of the crocodile's jaws.

Ineni and Sennumet arrived, both burned dark by the sun, and grinning broadly. Their Queen would make the first movement tomorrow the building of the new temple. All the carvers of stone were here; all the tools were prepared. Soon, the assault upon the mountain of Gurn would begin.

Hatshepsut spoke. "Welcome, honored architects, old and revered friends, your Queen is honored to share her evening meal with such loyal and brilliant men. Please, sit and be comfortable. Since all here are united in one purpose, we shall be as equals tonight. You may speak anything you choose."

Ineni and Sennumet sat down on cushions and both began talking at the same time, each trying to drown out the other. They unfolded drawings of a more precise scale than before, spilling wine in their eagerness.

"I see you have no interest in what you do here," the Queen laughed. "Perhaps you would prefer to redesign Pharaoh's dancing rooms instead."

For a moment, the architects froze, until they saw that she teased them. So, they relaxed and folded their papyri and settled in to enjoy the company and the upcoming meal.

Little Thothmes jumped down from Kamare's lap and went to the guests, whom he knew quite well. He pulled at Ineni's ears and climbed all over him. Ineni always brought something he had made for the little prince, and the boy laughed aloud when he found a wooden ball in the folds of Ineni's cloak. Because it was cool on the river, all wore fine woolen cloaks for warmth.

Thothmes' new wooden ball was not as it seemed to be. Before the child's eyes, Ineni took it apart in many odd pieces. He slowly reassembled it and rolled it on the deck. He then took it apart once again and handed the pieces to the boy. Thothmes looked up at the older architect and smiled. What a wondrous trick. He sat down and tried to fit the pieces together, small brow creased in concentration.

Kamare smiled at Ineni saying, "Many thanks, old friend. Perhaps this ball of tricks will allow us some peace as we talk. My Queen, shall we have some more wine?" She nodded, and the ever-present Beka signaled to a waiting steward to bring jars of light wine.

Since putting away his drawings, Sennumet had done little but stare adoringly at Hatshepsut. Four years had matured the boy into a man. Hours of heavy work in the sun had made his body dark, lithe, and muscular. Doubtless, Kamare could break him in two as he would a stick, but he was a beautiful young man nonetheless. The sun had turned his curls almost white, instead of the bright gold color they had been when he started this project. Many a woman yearned for him, and he had enjoyed many, but it was obvious to all who held his heart. Kamare, secure in his "family" laughed it away; but Sennumet always caused heat to rise in Hatshepsut, however hard she fought it.

It was the season of the shamsen, or north wind, and the night turned colder. The desert was always cool at night; but when this wind blew, the temperature seemed very low; and the wool cloaks were drawn more tightly closed.

Beka announced that dinner was ready, and the group went below where charcoal braziers and oil lamps warmed the dining area. There, on a large table, a savory meal awaited them. It was Ineni's favorite and had been prepared especially for him. The cook had broiled whole piglets over flame, basting the meat with honey and orange pieces. The piglets lay in beds of wild rice, their skins crackling brown and juicy.

It was one of the child's favorite meals too, and Beka came to take away the pieces of his new toy and escort him into an adjoining room to eat. Children did not sit at the table with adults at any time and so were not forced to sit quietly while matters were discussed which were of no interest to the young ones. Children were allowed to be children in every way. The time to grow up came soon enough.

When all had eaten their fill, and the dishes were at last cleared away, Ineni spread his latest, most complete drawings upon the table for the Queen to see. These drawings showed the pillars in shadow at different times of the day. Ineni had retained his original plan. The pillars would be a part of the mountain—remaining connected to the solid rock. Surely mistakes would be made and no mistake could be removed. No new column could be hauled in to replace a damaged pillar. The undertaking seemed to be nearly impossible.

"And what of error, Ineni?" asked Hatshepsut.

"My Queen, please put your trust in me," replied the architect. "The master carvers will use heavy tools for only the largest excavations. Work upon these pillars will be done with small hand tools. The eleven sides of each column will ensure the least chance of fracture. A pillar of this style has never been attempted before, but I am convinced that its very complication will make it strong."

Sennumet spoke up. He had been impatient to show what he had created for Hatshepsut. "Royal Queen of Egypt, the inner temple, carved from living rock, will be deep into the mountain. I propose leaving each wall for the inscription of symbols that you will decide upon. Upon the far wall there will be a simple altar, but the whole of the wall and ceiling will be covered with electrum and gold. In this simplicity, the offerings and the presence of worshippers will be the most important things. Simplicity has always produced a noble atmosphere, and it will be indestructible. The gold layered into the electrum will bear your likeness and the names of the gods Isis and Horus. There will be no doubt in this temple. All who read the carvings in the granite and view your likeness in gold will know whom they visit.

"We have also made plans for two small rooms on either side of the altar, each for the storage of vestments and incense for the priests to use."

Hatshepsut was immensely pleased. This temple would be as no other. It would live forever and ever, as would she. She wanted details of the most important plan of all. First, though, she called Beka.

"Beka, send every living being to the sleeping boat for servants. Stand at the back and allow no one to board before I command you. Go now and call out if there is a problem." When all had gone and the boat was silent, she asked the question. "Ineni, Sennumet, will you tell me now of my tomb?"

Ineni leaned forward to whisper his daring proposal: "Great Queen, when the inner temple is but a rough shell, there must be a royal mummification. I leave it to you. At that time, and while work continues through the years upon the carvings and art, we will sink a shallow shaft from one of the side chambers to receive the royal one. This work will take an unusually long time to complete, for, beneath the shallow burial room, a shaft one hundred yards long will be carved straight down to a room that will extend under the mountain. This large room will be yours, Queen Hatshepsut. It will need no girders of stone for support, and it will be enormous. There will be room for everything. After your passage to the underworld, I will break, or Sennumet will break if I am gone, great jars of oil in the upper chamber. These jars will be connected to high shafts I will create to hold sand from the desert. As oil spills into the room containing the sarcophagus of the soon-to-die royal, large tunnels will pour sand down the shaft that leads to your sleeping place, blocking it for all time. Since your chamber will be sealed with a wall thick enough to resist the pressure of the sand, your living place will be preserved."

Hatshepsut's eyes gleamed with satisfaction. How right she had been about this man! She would be safe forever and ever, living under a temple that would exist forever and ever. "Ineni, you are all I believed you to be. Although you are a man of simple needs and ask nothing of me at any time, I will take steps immediately to provide handsomely for each of your children: estates for your sons and large casks of gold for your daughters so that they may marry well. And, Sennumet, what will my other valuable architect have as his reward?"

Sennumet rolled his eyes in mild exasperation. The Queen had already given both him and Ineni vast fortunes. Of a sudden, he laughed and replied, "I shall have Lazuli, your white mare. She has carried you well for six years, and I would have something that you hold dear."

Hatshepsut tried hard to put away an evil little grin but was unsuccessful. "Granted, and with great pleasure. I cannot wait to see your limbs bandaged and knots upon your head. Sweet Lazuli will surely take your thoughts away from your troubles and give you new ones. She is aboard my boat now, as I believed her purity of color appropriate for the ceremonies tomorrow. She is yours when I leave. I also leave to you her little black heart."

They all laughed uproariously. When silence fell, Hatshepsut spoke to the architects again. "I have but one more request of you. There must be two sarcophagi in my tomb. It is my wish that General Kamare live forever with me." This was an unusual request, as there was no royal blood in the veins of her

General. However, Hatshepsut was who she was; and they were hers to command.

"Great Queen of Egypt, it shall be as you request," replied Ineni with bowed head and a blank countenance. "However, should General Kamare meet Anubis before you do, he shall have to lie in wait for you. I shall not break the jars of oil until you are safely in your tomb."

"It is done, good friends. And now we sleep. Tomorrow will be a glorious day for us all. I bid you a pleasant rest. Sennumet, spend a great deal of time enjoying the manner in which your body moves, for Lazuli awaits you."

There was more laughter and many farewells as the architects left the boat. The retainers were allowed back on board from the trailing boat, and the walkways were pulled into the ship. Hatshepsut and Kamare said goodnight to their son and retired to the upper deck of their floating palace to sleep in the bracing cold, warm together under down-filled bedding.

Looking up into a dark, star-filled sky, Kamare contemplated his singular honor. He felt he would, indeed, await his love for many years in her tomb. For many weeks, he had been aware of the hard distention of his abdomen. Upon consulting a visiting physician, he had been told that, in spite of all the modern medicine of Egypt, every operation that had been performed in an attempt to cure this malady had ended in death. After dissecting the bearers of this disease, the physicians found that the bodies contained large white or gray masses that apparently grew without abatement.

The physician explained to the General that there would be no pain until the mass grew into his lungs or his bowel—or both. Then, he would need opium. Whatever transpired, there was no other outcome; it would grow steadily. And, in nearly all instances, it led to a horrible death.

Kamare had no desire to suffer, and he would not allow Hati to suffer with him. He made up his mind that he would die in battle, a good soldier's death and a merciful one. It would have to be soon, he knew, as he was already having some slight difficulty with his breath.

Still, this night was his. His love was warm and soft beside him, and their handsome son was sleeping below. How fortunate his life had been, he thought. He had found real love, and that was all there was to life after all. And, too, his son would someday be Pharaoh. He wished he could remain here to protect little Thothmes. There were always those with unbridled ambition who would plot and plan to bring about the young prince's death. It might be a half-royal son, or even a half-royal princess, who had raised an army with promises of power and wealth. Yet, his true love was tender only with him and their child. She was determined and feared, and rightly so, by all those with whom she came in contact. It would be only a twist of fate that defeated Queen Hatshepsut of Egypt.

Kamare held her close, savoring each hour, each minute. Yes, he would wait in her tomb for her as many years as need be. He would no more leave her in death than he would in life. The pain that plagued his chest had subsided, and he drifted into sleep.

Beka awakened Hatshepsut before the sky began to pale on the eastern horizon. The Queen and Kamare bathed in cold water brought up from the Nile. It was as clear as glass and refreshed them both. It would be a joyous day.

Hatshepsut put on her coronation dress of spun gold. She wore the double crown and heavy gold cobra. Her eyelids were brushed with emerald dust, and lines of black kohl outlined her eyes and were drawn to her hairline. The wings of her brows arched up and away from her lovely eyes. In honor of her secret dedication, she hung the ruby from Kamare outside her dress. It dangled over the top of her ceremonial, battle-scarred gold collar—the collar that always gave her strength.

Lazuli had been harnessed into the traces of the gold-winged chariot. She reared and sidestepped as she was held there, awaiting the arrival of the Queen. There were many chariots today, and Hatshepsut would drive alone at the head of he procession—white mare, gold chariot, and glittering Queen.

As Hatshepsut walked down the ramp from her boat, she was outraged to see the sail of Thothmes II's barge rounding the curve of the river. How dare he intrude upon the dedication of her temple and tomb! She was the Queen and the real Pharaoh of Egypt! Now, all must wait in the morning sun for the docking of his boat and the arrival of his chair.

Ostrich feather fans shaded her from the glare, but the others stood in the bright sunlight. Strange, she thought, to see Kamare perspire so profusely. He was usually indifferent to heat. Perhaps he was becoming too accustomed to life at the palace.

Finally, the Nubians carrying the chair of Thothmes II labored up the bank. Thothmes was grotesque. Rolls of avoirdupois layered below his chin, and even the flowing robes could not conceal the shifting of the slabs of fat that hung from his body. Daintily painted fingers fussed with enough gold and jewels to purchase a fleet of war vessels. Under the roof of his palanquin, his curls bobbed with every step of his bearers.

Queen Hatshepsut bowed to her husband, determined not to allow this intrusion to mar her ceremony. She would let him try to keep her pace. Away she rode in her chariot, golden dress whipping in the wind. The other chariots followed her, and Thothmes II was left to follow slowly. Up rode Hatshepsut, up the two long ramps of the first two terraces, to spin and drive her chariot south beside the level granite parapet that edged the terrace. She was overlooking the desert floor that approached the mountain of Gurn.

Reaching the farthest end of the leveled rock, she stopped and threw her reins to a soldier. Dismounting, she took great joy in the sight of the stake in the rock. To this stake was tied a taut string which had been coated in chalk. The other end stretched away to the far northern end of the rock, where it was tied to another stake. The other members of her party arrived while the slaves carrying the Pharaoh labored far below.

She stepped forward to the stake and in a ringing voice declared, "I, Hatshepsut, Queen of all the regions of Egypt, upper and lower, living forever, do now dedicate my temple of Deir el Bahri. As I snap this line, I take for myself the name 'Makere, Pharaoh of Egypt,' supreme over all."

So saying, she bent and pulled up the string, then let it go with a loud snap. A long line of chalk appeared upon the granite.

Her architects had calculated this line to the finest quarter inch. Stonemasons began to engrave the line into the rock immediately before the chalk vanished with the wind. Hatshepsut would not make an offering in the temple until it was completed; but on this day of dedication, she poured water from the Nile into the air that swept around the mountain. Looking up, she could see the area heavily chalked for the tops of the pillars. There would be three tiers in all, rising to an unbelievable height made possible only because they would remain part of the mountain.

Her heart filled with joy at the prospect of the completion of her dream. Smiling widely, she handed the reins of her chariot to Sennumet and rode down the ramps with General Kamare. She held him at the waist and laid her head on his shoulder as they returned to the golden boat moored below. Sounds of flutes and drums drifted to them from the cit of the workmen, who had been given cattle to roast and fruits and cheeses to eat.

The morning had been full, and Hatshepsut and Kamare were content to rest in the covered area on the top deck as the craft was sailed and towed upriver to Thebes. On this trip home to the palace, he held her close. He tried to memorize every line of the dear face and to fill himself with the scent of her.

21

General Senu was enjoying himself immensely. He had recently returned from a month-long inspection of Egypt's land-connected possessions. Upon his return, the Queen's admiral advised him of the many war machines brought home from Thracian Greece. King Aristos had relied upon Egypt's gold for so long that his compliance was habitual.

Senu reclined in the audience room of the house Hatshepsut had built for him when he took the distasteful daughter of the vizier to wife. That had been four-and-a-half years ago. Nefertum was content to be implanted with his seed once a year and to know she was first wife. She was big with their fourth child now and happy as a dung beetle.

The house stood on a large estate side-by-side with that of General Kamare. Both were beautiful homes with tile floors and thick walls. Water, brought from the Nile, entered pipes at the tops of the houses, then cascaded through many fountains before finding its way back to the river.

In Senu's house, there were art objects of alabaster, copper, and gold. Golden plates and goblets graced his table. It seemed as though the chests of gold were bottomless. As for prominence, Kamare had virtually turned over the armies to him. Senu was a loyal man; he never forgot the two people who had assured his fortune.

At this moment, he was enjoying the company and the body of a beautiful second wife, whom he thought he loved. Sounds from the nursery wing fell pleasantly upon his ear; he was proud of his three healthy sons. Flutes and harps played softly. The wine was delicious and the girl delightful. Life was, indeed, satisfying.

Of a sudden, he was startled by the sound of a trumpet. *That can be no other. Has Kamare decided to part from his Queen long enough to pay me a visit? This is most unusual—he seldom leaves her side.* Senu sent the girl away and went to his door to greet his old and dear friend.

General Kamare threw the reins to a slave and grasped his friend in a bear hug. Senu was speechless. He detected the odor of opium. Surely, this could not be.

"Senu, old friend, pour us jars of good wine, and do not parade your three boys for me. I have seen them often enough, and nothing sickens an older soldier as does domesticity!" He joked, of course, as Kamare doted upon the three children. Senu realized something was wrong. He knew Kamare well enough to know when he was troubled.

Senu pretended to adopt a carefree spirit. "Come, palace chamber maid. I will pour wine to strengthen your long unused legs. I will tell you how brave I have been, and you will listen in awe and agree with me."

Arms around each other's shoulders, the two men responsible for Egypt's safety and well-being walked into the cool interior of the house and fell into lounges covered with cushions. While the wine was being poured. Senu took stock of his friend. He seemed a little less of himself and short of breath. It was something that could be hidden with effort, but today he did not seem to make that effort.

"Old friend, great General Senu, conqueror of women and breeder of sons, I have come to you laughing, for were I to be as I feel, you would see the slayer of hundreds weep at your feet." And as he spoke, he emptied a vial into his goblet of wine and drank it down.

Senu sobered at once. Here was great trouble, and here also was great heartache. He had only to look into the depths of Kamare's eyes to see the pain and desperation the man felt.

"How can I help you, my friend? You have come to a true comrade in arms. Anything I possess is yours, be it my gold or my life. Tell me now, what is this great stone upon your heart?"

"Senu, I have led a mighty life. I have carried my sword for Pharaoh and Queen. I have borne hardship on the march and in battle, and I have been richly rewarded in worldly goods and much honor. Most precious to me of all, though, are the loved ones of whom we have never spoken. Into this life, blessed by all the gods, an illness has crept. I have consulted physicians, many of them. All say the same. They say to me: 'Great General, you will die soon.'

"Senu, I have always known I would meet Anubis in the underworld, and my heart is waiting to be weighed upon the scale of justice. Many times in battle, although I felt no fear, I felt the possibility of death was near. Now, I feel real fear. I feel it, not for myself, for we all ride the same chariot, but for the heartbreak of the ones I love. I cannot allow her to watch me sink into the terrible pain that lingers long. I would leave her with the memories of the love we have. I would carry with me the look in her eyes, shining as she watches me ride away to battle. This once, I shall wear all the gold she can hang upon my wasting body, so that, even at a great distance, she will see the sun reflect from me. She will see me thus when we meet in the underworld and live forever in our tomb. Even though it be dark, she will know me at once.

"What I ask of you is this. Find unrest or rebellion in Egypt or a foreign dominion. Then come to the palace and petition me to put down the insurrection. None other will do. It must be me. After my death in battle—and I will be killed by a blade—you must bring my body back to her so that she may prepare me for my long wait. The Queen will live long, and I must have all the rituals of mummification if I am to wait for her."

Senu sat silently through this sad revelation. How could it be that so strong a man, possessed of all that life offered, would go seeking death? Still, he had seen something of this wasting sickness, and he would not want to endure it himself. Some had been known to hang on for years, hoping it would go away, or, simply that it was not true. No—it was always true. Rousing himself, and with no heart for joking or laughing, he replied as Kamare had known he would.

"Good friend, I am filled with a sadness I cannot describe. It shall be as you request. I am aware of reports of three minor insurrections. Ineny, viceroy of Palestine, sends reports that the people there are refusing to pay a full tax due to drought. In the north, it is said that the Hykosos' guardian. Neblus, has murdered all royal sons and declared himself King of Kadesh and Giza. The Egyptian soldiers who were not murdered have been imprisoned as hostages.

"It is also said that as the Greek King ages, his sons are building a large army to unseat their father and break ties with Egypt. All are fools; all can be put into place at will. The choice is yours."

Senu continued, "I tell you this in deep regret, and do not doubt me. I am here for you. Whatever you decide, I shall be by your side. I also pledge to return your body to the Queen and to say nothing to her of anything you have told me. My deep regret is the loss of my closest friend. I am near tears, Kamare. This soldier has not cried since he was a child. Yet, now I feel the need to cry like the boy I once was."

The two friends sat in silence for some time, soothed by the peaceful sounds of the fountains in the house and the water birds on the Nile. It was fall and birds were restless. Soon, the geese would start their migration.

Evening threw shadows on the floor tiles as Kamare stood and gripped Senu at arm and elbow. "It will be Kadesh and Captain Neblus, or should I say King Neblus? It is the only case involving the murder of our soldiers, and it was I who placed him at the head of government there. You must say this when you come for me. I have never deliberately lied in my life. Now, I ask you to lie for me. Say that King Neblus has openly defied me and my Queen. Hatshepsut will understand my going if this is the case. In the end, it will make no difference to Neblus. After I allow him to give me a merciful death, you must kill him for me. And this time, the city must be razed to the ground. It seems that little good issues from the Hyksos capital city.

"We part for a short time, Senu. You must come to the palace soon, as it is increasingly more difficult to appear well. Goodbye, my friend."

Kamare turned abruptly and left the room. With a heavy heart, Senu watched the brave man walk away. He reassured himself that this was right—a fitting end for the greatness that was Kamare.

In her rooms at the palace, Queen Hatshepsut sat with sadness welling up inside her. She could keep up a pretense when her love was close, could pretend that she did not smell opium on his breath or notice that he extinguished all the lamps when he undressed.

In the night, as he lay deep in-a-drug-induced sleep, she had held the lamp over his body and gasped aloud at the slow wasting away. She resolved to never let him discern that she knew he was ill. A tear escaped her eyes as Hatshepsut realized what she must face. *I must ignore any indications of his illness. He is so proud and still so strong. He is the dearest love of my life, and I cannot bear to lose him. Who will I cling to in the night; who else can support me, as has Kamare? Enough of this! I hear his footsteps; he approaches, and I must smile.*

"Sweet love, the night is so beautiful. Let us take little Thothmes and ride along the road you have built toward Deir el Bahri. The palms are well grown now, and the breeze from the river will be refreshing."

"Kamare, our son is in his bed, and I would have you for myself alone. We will take wine and food in baskets. No guards, no soldiers for us. We will be just as other lovers for tonight. What a pleasant surprise this is for me. Was ever there a more beloved wife?

"No, love; no man has ever loved a woman as I love you."

And so, away they drove in their chariot. The stones that paved the road were newly set and perfectly flat. They rode but an hour, then spread a cloth under a palm tree to drink wine and eat cold, roasted birds before loving each other tenderly. Each deceived the other. Each pretended to play a part to spare the other pain. Never was there so gentle or so noble a deception.

Kamare drove slowly back to the palace. The knife in his chest made him hold her more closely than ever. He would remember this night at the end of his life.

Two days later, Senu appeared at the palace and asked for an audience with Queen Hatshepsut. She was holding court with the vizier, Imhot, and the treasurer, Nihisi, present. She dealt personally with all matters of importance concerning her empire and territorial possessions, and no major issue escaped her attention. Smaller problems were screened and decided upon by trustworthy advisors, including many of the priests. As Queen, she could not be expected to be bothered with the theft of a flock, a claim of inheritance, or other such trivial concerns. Unless, of course, it pleased her. One never knew when she would decide to place her finger upon the pulse of her people.

This day, the ambassador from Heliopolis in Thrace was at court to plead assistance for King Aristos against his traitorous sons and their troops. The Queen sat immobile, crowns upon her head, crook and flail crossed upon her breast. She was resplendent in a pleated linen dress and adorned by her fiery emerald collar and earpieces. Small gold sandals rested upon a pillowed footstool.

The Greek ambassador was new to the court at Thebes and was misled by her radiant appearance. He couched his pleas in complimentary terms. Surely, he thought, a learned philosopher such as himself could cause such a young and inexperienced Queen to accede to his requests. He smiled with self-confidence and oozed charm as he commented upon her beauty. He could have saved himself the trouble.

After listening to his unctuous statements for a few moments, Hatshepsut responded, not unkindly, but in a firm and formal tone. "The position of the Queen of Egypt is this: your country is an arm of Egypt, one of our possessions. All that is required of Greece is that the taxation be paid, however small. I value the armature we have purchased over many years, and that you have honored your agreement to be peaceable toward my land. Nothing more is required of Greece. It matters not who wears your Thracian crown, and surely precious Egyptian blood will not be poured upon the soil of your islands. As a courtesy extended to all ambassadors, you will be feted this night in the company of my Vizier. You are dismissed."

The bewildered man stood there with jaw agape. He had been turned down and dismissed in but a few moments. He began to babble about how Pharaoh Thothmes II had assured him of Egypt's help. He added that he would report this conversation to the Pharaoh.

Ordinarily, Hatshepsut would have toyed with him for the sake of amusement, but today her thoughts were elsewhere. She pointed her flail at the posturing man. Soldiers immediately grabbed his arms and quick-walked him toward the door of the throne room.

Thothmes II unfortunately chose this moment to make one of his rare appearances. He saw the man being hauled away and screeched in his high voice, "Stop! Bring that man back. I have made the decision in this matter. Pharaoh speaks! Pharaoh speaks!"

The soldiers ushering the ambassador from the room missed not a step, nor did they give any indication that they had heard the Pharaoh. Curls bobbing, Thothmes jumped up and down, still screaming. "You cannot do this to me! You are only the Great Royal Wife. You call yourself Pharaoh Makere, but it is I who am the ruler. Obey me, or I shall see that you suffer! I will replace you and send you away, and I will rule alone."

Succumbing to anger and frustration, he had failed to notice the narrowing of Queen Hatshepsut's eyes. This would be as good a time as any—one side room of her temple had been completed. Well, she would suffer this fool no longer. Out flashed the flail, and the guards were upon him. In a voice edged with cold fury, Hatshepsut said, "My husband has suffered from bad wine. For his own protection, return him to his apartments. He is to remain there alone."

Thothmes was carried away ignominiously as he yelled vehement curses from the gods. The guards were strong, and Thothmes was weak; but his wide girth and hanging fat made him difficult to handle. It could be said that he was rolled and jiggled to his apartments. As instructed, his rooms were cleared of all save the Pharaoh. He sat there alone, beside himself with fury, deprived even of his pretty boys who told him always what he wanted to hear.

In the hall of pillars, Queen Hatshepsut had risen to leave when the pole of electrum pounded the floor, and Senu was announced. For General Senu, her love's best friend, she would remain a while longer. Resuming her seat upon the winged throne, she motioned for the treasurer to take the crook and flail from her; and she gestured for Senu to sit in her presence.

Senu accepted wine and waited to be told to speak. He knew he was in good favor with the Queen, but Hatshepsut (newly called Pharaoh Makere), was a god, a living god. Every Egyptian looked upon her with reverence and awe, and he was no exception.

She spoke kindly to the waiting man. "Good friend of the gods, General Senu, I am pleased to see you. The ears of the palace hear that you are a fine soldier and a good husband. You have three healthy sons, do you not?"

"Yes, your highness, and I am indebted to your generosity. It is, therefore, with great reluctance that I come to you with a request that will not please you."

Hatshepsut nodded her permission but said nothing. All the while, she was thinking that Senu was Kamare's oldest and closest friend. Her smile remained fixed upon her face, but small fingerlets of cold crept into her breast.

"My Queen, we have many disturbing problems. The most serious is a new development in the Hyksos land that requires the eye and hand of General Kamare."

So, she thought, *he believes I do not know of my love's illness. How shall I proceed? This must be of Kamare's doing, for General Senu has the means and the ability to put out many fires at once. Ah, I see it now. I must bind my heart against this hurt and give my gift of love to him that holds my every thought. I cannot give him long life, but I will help him seek a death full of a soldier's honor.*

In all the time the Queen sat thinking, her smile did not waver; but if eyes could hold pain, then one glance into hers would reveal the anguish in her heart. At last she summoned a soldier and bade him seek out General Kamare and ask him to join her in the Hall of Pillars.

"General Senu, while we wait for General Kamare, I would offer you an invitation to share the evening meal with Kamare and me. I warn you, though, that little Thothmes will search you well for a gift. You may use this time to order one of my guards to the market to get something, if you wish."

As Senu gave bronze pieces to a guard, he heard the click of Kamare's sandals on the mosaic hallway. In a moment he was there, striding forward with a look of pleasant surprise on his face, still fit, but more lean than he had ever been. A yellow pallor lurked beneath his sun-tanned face.

"Senu, you rascal hound. I had not heard that you were returned. No doubt you have been busy making a gift of a round belly to every woman in your household. Welcome! Welcome!"

It was an indiscreet remark to make in the royal court and not at all in keeping with the good manners Kamare had possessed all his life. Grasping his hand, Senu looked into his eyes. Kamare's pupils were small pinpoints, and droplets of moisture lay on his upper lip and forehead. His hands were damp and cold; there was an acrid, sick smell about him that he had tried to cover with perfume of oranges.

Queen Hatshepsut spoke as though nothing was amiss. "Dear one, General Senu has finally been faced with something he says he cannot control. Considering his regard for himself, it must be serious indeed. Shall we take him to our balcony to share our evening meal? He apparently needs your help, and we can enjoy his company as he tells us why."

With a roar of laughter, the older man put his arm around Senu's shoulder and promised to show him his beautiful "nephew," Thothmes, before they ate. "Have you a toy upon you, Senu? Thothmes has been known to show little mercy to those who do not grace him with a gift." Just then, the guard returned with a small horse on wheels—the gift Senu had instructed him to obtain. His own eldest son adored one just like it.

The three strolled to the nursery. As Kamare entered the room, the little boy leaped into his arms. He held his son tightly to his chest and buried his face in the soft curls on the child's head. In spite of all resolve, a bright tear escaped from the corner of one eye.

Hatshepsut and Senu saw but did not see. Each was determined to maintain a mood of happiness. Smiles were too wide, eyes were too bright, and laughter came too quickly over too little.

Hatshepsut's gaiety was not a reflection of her thoughts. *Oh*

Isis, mother and goddess, strengthen my arm so that I my drive terror away. Horus, god and father, give me the courage this brave man needs. How will I live? How will I breathe? I will make sacrifice so that you will grant my loved one, my heart of hearts, a quick and easy death. I see the terrible illness strong upon him now. I smell it upon him. And I see him trying valiantly to hide his pain. As heinous as it is to me, I will help to guide the hand that ends his life. It is his wish, and I deny him nothing.

The child noted none of this. He was delighted with the gift of the wheeled horse, and his father placed a wooden sword in his hand to slash at his enemies as he pulled the toy around the room. "I am a brave soldier like 'Uncle'," he said over and over. Indeed, but for his beautiful face, he was a replica of his father in every way. His legs were sturdy, promising strong muscular development; and his shoulders were so broad that he seemed top-heavy. This must have been the boy that Kamare was so long ago.

"Senu," Kamare said, as they stood watching the child at his play, "you must help me teach him everything we both know about self-defense, combat, and schemes of war. He is too young as yet, and I will be very old when he is ready to understand such things." A look passed between the two men, and Senu accepted the responsibility his friend asked of him. Well he knew that he could never be the teacher the boy's father could be. Of course, Kamare had learned all these things on his own; and perhaps the boy would have his father's instinct.

Senu turned to smile at Hatshepsut and encountered a gaze that shook him. *She knows. Of course she knows. How foolish I was to think she could be with her lover day and night and never realize the truth. Kamare believes she has no knowledge of his illness; I am sure of that. How can a man's love so easily blind him from reality? It has to be a combination of wishful thinking, the potent opium, and above all, the cleverness of the Queen. She has made it seem that she thinks nothing is amiss. She must be suffering deeply. Will she allow him to go to battle, knowing that he surely seeks death? Well, I will soon have an answer.*

"Come, both of you, and leave my son to his play. I recall that you are over fond of royal pheasant and peafowl, Senu. You have been away a long time and have not had the opportunity to dine upon either. And all know it is treason to catch my pheasant to eat. I have tolerated your gaming of this bird in the past, and now you can eat it at your leisure in my sight."

The three laughed at this mild joke and walked to the terrace adjoining the Queen's rooms. The sun was setting on the other side of the palace, and her lake and gardens were deeply shaded. Gentle breezes carried fragrances from the many flowers. The sounds made by songbirds and waterfowl quieted, to be replaced by the music from a group of flutists and harpists who played softly in the shadows below.

It was the most pleasant of evenings and the saddest. Kamare tried to implant the sight of every bright color and the fragrance of every slight aroma in his memory to carry with him for the remainder of his life. The pain distracted him—it was coming back again, stronger than before. It seemed that the intervals between attacks were shorter and shorter. He must find some excuse to dose himself again. And his departure from the palace must be soon. Even in his medicated state, he was aware that he could not hide for much more time this affliction that was claiming his life.

"Sweet love, Senu must provide you with amusement for the next few moments. I see that my linen was soiled while I was playing with little Thothmes, and I will not dine with you thus. Do not wait upon my return to have the food served, for I shall rejoin you shortly."

With a nod and a smile, Kamare turned and walked into the inner chamber. In this room was a long rack that held his cloaks and battle gear. There were all his magnificent gold body garments and helmets, swords, nets, maces, javelins, and such. There was even his new leopard skins that the Queen had had made into a long cloak. When he was arrayed in all this finery, one would think he was Pharaoh, himself. No matter—-his son would be Pharaoh; of that he was certain.

Beside the rack stood a large wooden chest. Kamare opened it and took out a vial of opium. He drained the contents into the goblet of wine he had brought with him from the terrace. As he drank, his hand shook from pain; but relief came within minutes.

He thanked the gods for the miraculous drink. As the pain quickly subsided, he felt an overwhelming weakness that always accompanied the use of the drug. Still, he was able to dash watered oil from crushed citrus fruits upon his arms and neck. And his strength gradually returned.

Kamare went back to the terrace and sat in his low chair and looked without appetite at the food. Ordinarily he ate with relish; but of late, he had had to force food upon himself, as he did now.

"Is this not delicious, Senu? My love thinks of so many tempting dishes that I shall soon be very fat. Perhaps I shall resemble Pharaoh Thothmes." As he said this, he tossed his head as though he had long curls. They laughed genuinely at that. The comparison between the two men was ludicrous.

Hatshepsut poured more wine for Senu as he devoured a pheasant breast. Here was a man who had still the appetite of a lion. "Now that Senu is no longer fearful of starving, perhaps he will tell us why he needs General Kamare. What is this problem of which you speak?"

Suddenly serious, Senu replied, "Great Queen, some four-and-one-half years ago, before the birth of Thothmes III, General Kamare offered a certain Captain Neblus of Kadesh, a leader of the soldiers of King Obinninos, the opportunity to ally himself with Egypt. He was known to the General from an earlier time and was believed to be an honorable man. And he swore to perform his duties faithfully. We learn now that Captain Neblus has murdered the young sons of the former king. In itself, that would be acceptable if none proved to be of good material to rule the Hyksos and the land of Giza. From all reports, however, two of the boys showed much promise.

"In addition, Captain Neblus has declared himself King of these lands. He has sent but half of his taxation, and he plunders camel caravans from the east. Many fine items destined for your royal highness have fallen into his hands. Lastly, I was informed only this morning that a small caravan carrying gold from your own treasury in Thebes to purchase silk and spices from Mitanni, was ambushed, the soldiers murdered, and your gold hidden away by the so-called King Neblus."

When Senu finished his explanation, Kamare leapt to his feet. He was so fierce when his voice thundered that Hatshepsut could almost believe he was his old self once again. "I will settle this turner of souls! He gave me, General Kamare, guardian of Queen Hatshepsut of Egypt, living forever, his oath of allegiance. There can be but one end for such a man: death! And quickly!" His body shook with rage; the hair rose upon his arms and the back of his neck, as though he were letting an enemy's blood in battle. Hatshepsut was forced to employ all her persuasive wiles to coax him to sit down, and still he fumed.

"Senu, we ride at first light. See that we are provisioned and a rider sent well ahead to have food and horses ready and waiting for us at the rest stations along the way so that we may travel as quickly as an army can. Even so, hindered by an army, it will take us almost a changing of the moon to reach the city. Would that I had him here at once. He is a dog and shall feed dogs."

"Gently, my love, gently," murmured Hatshepsut. "Surely this punishment, however just, can await the consecration of our son in the temples of Horus and Isis. Even though Pharaoh will be present, I would want my son's father with him." It was the first time she had said in the presence of another what many in the palace already knew; and for a moment, Kamare softened.

My son; my wonderful, beautiful son. How proud I would be to see him formally proclaimed heir to the Thothmesid Dynasty! Prince Thothmes III, Pharaoh to be. However, he stiffened his resolve. He had never been one to allow himself a luxury before duty. He would not do so now, especially now.

"Love of all my life, I go tomorrow. Would I be your protector if I lingered here for a pretty ceremony? I shall congratulate Prince Thothmes when I return and place the treasure I recover in his treasury room. I ask only that the traditional shaving of his curls, save one lock, be done before I leave. It would mean much to me to have those baby curls close to my heart when I go."

Now Senu saw what sort of woman and Queen Hatshepsut was. Though she was cold as though gripped by the hand of death, she gave Kamare a brilliant smile and lifted her glass in a toast: "Go forth, General Kamare. See that justice is done for your Queen. It is with great pleasure that I shall happily await the day of your return."

The three emptied their goblets, and Senu left to make ready an army. He had only to go to the barracks Kamare had established. Thanks to the guidance of that seasoned warrior, Egyptian soldiers could march with only a few hours' notice.

Alone at last, Hatshepsut and Kamare went to their bathing pool. Hatshepsut melted into his arms, and he held her tightly, stroking her lovingly with one strong hand. One final night together, a night to last until they met again below Deir de Bahri. A night to remember into eternity. They went unclothed to bed, and the General loved his dearest one as only he could. Passionately, then tenderly, over and over, seeking to devour each other, they loved until early light.

One last embrace, and they rose. She helped him into his shirt of gold fish scale armor that covered his shoulders, arms, and torso, yet moved easily upon his body. She chose a gold skullcap with white plumes at the top peak; and with her own hands, she strapped gold shin guards and sandals upon his legs and feet. She chose many bracelets and rings, and he allowed her to bedeck him as never before. She would surely see him from a distance as he rode away. The sun would glitter and reflect from him in every direction.

Hatshepsut maintained a happy face. She glowed with the radiance of love as she walked with him to the palace steps. At the foot, the officers he would command the march had assembled; and there, also, waited the General's chariot.

Before he stepped into the chariot and took up the reins, Hatshepsut pulled him down to her. She had one final gift for him. In a whisper that only he heard, she said, "I have saved this for a special time. I tell you now that I am with child again. Our love has been rewarded once more. I, Queen of all Egypt, your son Thothmes III, and the little one that is within the chalice that is Egypt send you forth in love."

Kamare's gaze held hers in a last, lingering embrace. His heart was full, and he could not speak. He could only lift her hand and press his lips into its palm.

Oh, Isis, my heart is breaking. I smile and laugh with him; but I, too, am dying. It is the death of loss. Keep me strong for I have held this pretense too long to release it now. I shall have him carry in his mind a picture of me with a smile upon my lips.

She looked up at him a with a smile and said, "As you leave, my love, I go to my terrace to watch. I shall not move or take my eyes from you until I can no longer see Ra reflected upon your armor."

One last smile, and he was away. Senu paused beside her and inclined his head in reverence. She was indeed the bravest of them all.

Hours later, and far away, Kamare removed the golden trappings and placed them in his war chest. They held the sun's heat and weighed him down. He would wear them again on his last day.

In the palace at Thebes, a forlorn Queen sobbed in misery. She was alone, as she had forbidden any, even faithful Beka, to come near her. She would have no one see her thus. As the night wore on and she thought of her love, she once again questioned why the obnoxious Thothmes II thrived, when one so good must die in agony. Was this the will of the gods? Well, then, she decided, he will not thrive. She would ease some of her sorrow by destroying the hated Pharaoh. His passing would be slow and painful and above suspicion.

The moon was overhead when she appeared at the door of his quarters. The startled guard opened the door and quickly stepped aside as Hatshepsut swept into the sleeping chamber. The fat thing was sleeping, rivulets of kohl on his painted cheeks where he had shed tears.

Tears! No doubt he shed tears from some imagined lack of wine, food, or pretty boys! While one so noble has ridden away in pain to spare me grief. How I hate this mound of corruption, this wicked man! Well, I will rid Egypt of him, and things will then be somewhat more even.

"Awaken husband; it is I, your dutiful Great Royal Wife, come to bed you. Awaken!"

Thothmes roused himself and sat up in total confusion.

What had she said? Great Royal Wife? Bed me? This cannot be; I cannot do it. My pretty little boys fulfill my desires. Why would I want to bed this woman? Still, I did do it once, didn't I? Perhaps with a little wine and food I can manage to do so again. Then she will no longer have cause to humiliate my magnificent person. Yes, as much as I abhor coupling with her, I shall do so; and then she must recognize me as Pharaoh.

Hatshepsut sat quietly on a stool waiting for Thothmes to recover from his befuddled state of mind. While she was amused at his bewilderment, she was enjoying even more the thought of what she was about to do to him.

"Sweet husband, call for wine that we might refresh ourselves before we enjoy our bodies. May I call for you?"

"No, I shall do so," he said, tossing his long ringlets. "I prefer my own wine. No doubt mine own has not received a questionable additive."

"As you wish, Pharaoh Thothmes," came the reply in a mild, subservient tone. Hearing these words, Thothmes swaggered to the door to demand wines from his own cellars. The guard looked over his head at the Queen, who nodded slightly. He turned on his heel and went to fetch the heavy date wine Thothmes preferred.

A servant poured each a glass bowl of the dark, pungent wine; and Thothmes drank down three pourings before he relaxed upon his cushions. "Now, wife, order food. I have had nothing for hours. Ask for two of everything as I feel great hunger."

Hatshepsut nodded at the servant and added that they wished to be alone while the food was being prepared. Moving her small stool close to Thothmes, she pulled the ruby that she always wore from beneath her dress. Purring in an even, toneless voice, she asked Pharaoh to look at the beautiful, new present she had brought for him.

Thothmes had never seen such a rare and beautiful stone. By lamplight, a bright red glow shone from deep within the ruby. As Hatshepsut continued speaking in a droning tone, the glowing stone swung back and forth, back and forth endlessly, before his captivated eyes.

She spoke slowly, on and on. She told him he was sleepy, and his glazed eyes closed. She asked if he could hear her. He answered only, "Yes."

"Listen to this voice, Pharaoh Thothmes. It is the voice of the gods. Do you understand?"

"I understand," was the muffled reply.

"Thothmes, the gods have come to save you from destruction. Listen to what the voice tells you. Thothmes, all food, all water, and all wine are poison to you. If you eat or drink, you will die. You will die. If you eat or drink, you will die. Do you understand?"

Thothmes repeated, "All is poison. If I eat or drink, I will die."

The face of Hatshepsut was a study in contempt and cruelty. She repeated the ritual two more times before she felt secure enough to arouse him. "When I clap my hands, you will come awake. You will remember nothing, but you will never eat or drink again. Do you hear the voice of the gods?"

Again, there was a faint, "Yes."

Hatshepsut clapped her hands; Thothmes opened his eyes and began to talk about his meal that was coming. He remembered nothing.

In came the slaves with platters of delicious foods. Hatshepsut had not eaten all that day, and she knew she would enjoy this meal as she had no other.

When the food was placed before him. Thothmes put out a hand to grasp a joint of fowl and just as quickly pull it back in fear. "This is poisoned. I cannot eat it," he cried.

"Nonsense," replied Hatshepsut. "Here, I shall eat it. Mmm—so good, so juicy. And the onions and piglet with honey. You must have some."

"No, no. I cannot," he whimpered. He watched as she ate a huge meal, savoring every bite; but he could eat nothing himself. His distended stomach growled with hunger, but he could not eat.

"Pharaoh, if you will not eat, at least have some wine. It is your favorite. Let me pour it for you." And Hatshepsut filled his bowl with the date wine.

He reached over and picked up the bowl but threw the glass

to shatter on the marble floor. "It is poisoned! It will kill me." Filled with an acute desire to both eat and drink, Thothmes allowed himself to do neither, and in his state of near panic, he pulled at his long hair and made new rivulets in his makeup with more tears.

"Pharaoh, if you refuse to dine and drink with me, then I shall return to my own chambers." With teeth bared in a vicious grin, Hatshepsut left him. The laughter that echoed from the walls as she passed through the hallway was unholy. The skin crawled upon the bones of the royal guard as he averted his eyes and lowered his head. The goddess Isis was pleased in an unusual way. And he did not want her pleasure to extend to him.

Before retiring, the Queen bathed. As she was being oiled and massaged, she called for papyrus and a messenger. Once ready for the night, she sat down and wrote upon the reed paper:

Greetings, Sennumet

Prepare a sarcophagus in the side room of my temple. We will have a royal funeral.

Pharaoh Makere
Queen Hatshepsut
Living forever and ever

When she fell asleep, her soul flew across the desert, seeking her lover in her dreams.

Day followed day, and Pharaoh Thothmes II called for food and drink again and again. Each time, however, he refused the food and wine, telling everyone that it was poisoned. To prove her loyalty and express her love for the "father of her son," Hatshepsut often joined him and ate some of the food before his eyes. It was a torture that drove Thothmes almost into insanity. He could not force himself to eat; yet the Queen sat only inches away and ate her fill of the most delicious foods the kitchen could prepare. In order to entice him, she wafted the aromas of hot meats and delicate sweets into his nostrils. The Queen called upon the court physicians to treat him but stayed in his quarters at such times to ascertain that none of them tried trancing. None did, and she suspected it was a black art from a far place.

In private, the doctors told her that he could do without food for half a moon and more; but if he did not drink, he would die in seven suns. To these men, she confided that she carried another child by Pharaoh, and all treated her with kindness and sympathy.

She pretended grief but did not pretend too much. After all, Queen Hatshepsut, Pharaoh Makere, was not as soft as an ordinary mortal might be. She would bend only slightly, and she would never break. No mortal eye would ever look upon the part of her that had been torn asunder.

As Thothmes weakened and came ever closer to death, the Queen's mind and thoughts were far away with her love. He, too, must be expecting life to end. It occurred to her that she should send a funerary tent, priests, and materials for mummification to the battle site. The body of Kamare would spoil beyond salvation if it had to be brought back to Thebes untreated. For this reason she sent a funerary delegation to General Senu.

The priests were puzzled. This had never been done in their lifetime nor did written records tell of such a thing. With her apparent awareness of future events, Queen Hatshepsut appeared to be more supernatural to them then ever. She threw dust in flames before them. The burning powder of strange mushrooms entered their nostrils, and the Queen wavered taller and taller; the floor beneath their feet became water. They all hastened to obey her.

Queen Hatshepsut called for Puembre. He was the most talented of the carvers and came from his work at Deir el Bahri where Sennumet had assigned him the most intricate projects and placed him above all the other carvers. She ordered the man to make a wooden coffin in the shape and size of General Kamare. She directed it to be covered in hammered gold and inlaid with precious stones. She gave him two moons to complete this task. He, too, went away greatly puzzled.

At last, the tormented and truly cursed Pharaoh Thothmes II died with his mother Mutnefret clutching his painted hand and sobbing in deep grief. The Queen comforted her and chose this time to tell her of the expected child. The news helped to assuage the poor woman's sorrow. She was a kind and good grandmother and spent much of her time with little Thothmes. Now, there would be a new baby to hover over and play with.

"Great mother of Pharaoh, you will have another of your blood to wear the royal crown. Perhaps we shall have a little princess this birth. I will need you by my side, as I am now alone."

Hatshepsut had learned that when a woman hated you, she was the worst enemy you could have. Women were kept in a subservient life and held a secret, dark place in their hearts. No time limit was set upon revenge, and no consequences were too great to bear. Love and revenge. The gods alone could help the one who hurt a woman's child or humiliated her before her peers. The reverse of this was also true. The most loyal, life-giving ally to be had was a woman who had been befriended or received a kindness. Mutnefret believed that she owed all that was good in her life to Hatshepsut. She would be the eyes and ears of the Queen in the innermost reaches of the palace.

In contrast, the Queen had found that the ordinary man could be had for gold. An intelligent man could be had for the use of power and greed. An exceptional man could be had only for the love of the rightness and order of things. And all of these men might possibly be maneuvered by lust—bare, hot lust.

Queen Hatshepsut played an excellent game of jackals and hounds on her game board. She also played people well, while staying outside the circle of play. She was distant and manipulative, devoid of any reason other than that of the good of Egypt. She allowed herself small pleasures and physical love but remained unwavering in the protection of Egypt. Beautiful, intelligent, and always aware of her place in the dynasty, Queen Hatshepsut had all the components of greatness.

As Puembre carved Kamare's inner coffin, the Queen composed the first of the carvings to be placed upon her temple walls. The translation reads as follows:

Deir el Bahri
Makere, Pharaoh of all the lands and dominions of Egypt.
Queen Hatshepsut, Great Royal Wife, ruling alone, living forever and ever

He who shall do her homage shall live
He who shall speak evil blasphemy
of Her Majesty shall die.
My name is Pharaoh.

It is clear that she used the female "her" yet took the male position of Pharaoh Makere. And so she was—the sole, powerful ruler of the richest and strongest country in the world. No hand wielded so much power as did hers.

Pharaoh Thothmes II was in his funerary tent, and the long, involved mummification process had begun. Eventually, his body would be placed in the upper sarcophagus at Deir el Bahri.

22

Kamare and Senu halted the army and made camp in view of the city of Kadesh. The strenuous ride through the desert brought the once mighty Kamare to low ebb. He was wasted in all his limbs, and there was a larger swelling in his stomach. His breath came with great effort, and he was forced to take massive doses of opium. Soon nothing would dull the pain, and the time would be upon him when he would willingly race toward death.

After much discussion, the two generals settled upon a plan to achieve the goals of a swift end to Kamare's life and just punishment of Neblus. They would challenge him to battle; and when he came forth, Kamare would fall upon the disloyal Neblus and, in his weakness, be slain. Senu would then rush in and kill Neblus. The Egyptian army would surge forward to storm the gates. The inhabitants of Kadesh were a mixed breed of adventurers. Without leadership, it was possible that they would surrender. The Egyptian troops that Kamare had left in the Hyksos city at the end of the last campaign would be quick to side with their comrades and put down any resistance.

The evening before Kamare was to give himself to death, he talked at length to Senu. He said all the things he had kept hidden in his heart. He spoke of his love for Hatshepsut, his pride in his son, and his gratitude for a good life. He felt that no other man had shared a love such as his with his Hati, and Senu felt sure that this was true. Senu had never known such love, but he knew he had witnessed it. At long last, the two men slept.

At first light, Senu, himself, served his friend. He adorned Kamare with the gold armor, the plumed helmet, and sparkling jewels. He even bent low to fasten gold sandals to his feet. The armor hung upon Kamare's wasted body but effectively made him appear as his former self. The odor of the sick man was that of decay. All the orange oil in the camp could not disguise it.

Before he drank a final draft of opium, Kamare held the tied bunch of brown curls to his cheek. "Senu, tell me once more. Swear to me again that you will guard my son's life and destiny, my loyal friend."

"With my life, friend forever. If the gods are willing, we shall meet in the afterlife, and I shall tell you all that has happened. Go to this battle with an easy heart, Kamare. I, Senu, will be your son's shadow and protector as long as the gods give me breath."

Senu had not suggested an easy death by poison for Kamare. He knew the General desired the honorable death of a soldier waging battle for his country, and he must have it. Watching him drink the opium with hands shaking from pain, Senu prayed it would come this day. He saw that the pain was beyond control.

He had not told Kamare of the message from Hatshepsut that a mummification tent with all necessary attendants was on its way to their camp. He would let the hero die with the belief that he spared his love anguish. Senu marveled at the strength of the Queen and the determination of her resolve. He did not believe there had ever been another like her in the world, and she was still very young. What marvels would she accomplish in her lifetime? Other women had been famous for their beauty or as mothers or consorts of famous men, but this woman seemed destined to take her place in history based solely upon her own achievements. He had no doubt that she would reach great heights. Even as she accepted the loss of her first love and planned an honorable funeral for him, she planned also for the destruction of old enemies. The message had included the news that Thothmes II had unfortunately contracted a strange malady of which the physicians had no knowledge and died eight days after Kamare left Thebes. Thinking of this, Senu shuddered as he and Kamare walked from the tent, and he helped him mount his horse.

The big bay stallion carried a faceplate and chest shield of gold. White egret feathers swayed in the top of his jewel-encrusted bridle. General Kamare had ordered them placed there. All the gods were known to favor egret and their tail feathers. Funeral procession always included them, as it was believed they made passage to the underworld easier and more graceful.

Grace was the most important personal quality in Egypt. If one could be said to move in grace, or love in grace, perhaps speak with grace, he was noble. To fight and die with grace was much to be desired, as one's heart weighed on the scales of righteousness by Anubis, could be balanced by an egret feather. If the gods were willing, today would mark the beginning of Kamare's long journey into afterlife, and he wanted to appease the gods in every possible way.

Generals Kamare and Senu rode at the head of their army toward the Hyksos city. The soldiers, with their leather helmets and shields of raw cowhide, halted within arrow length of the walls; and all the captains blew war trumpets. It was an arrogant and traditional gesture made to show power and lack of fear.

Neblus was watching this display from high atop a palace tower, but the army he saw was only a part of the Egyptian force. Another wing hid behind cliffs to the north. This wing had no chariots, only the swiftest of horses; and they could join with Kamare's troops in less than ten minutes by galloping at breakneck pace.

Having little knowledge of Egyptian tactics, and receiving no word of warning from the captive Egyptian soldiers, Neblus believed that the force of fifty charioteers, bowmen, and spearmen that he looked down upon were all the men his army would face. At the head of the army, he recognized General Kamare sitting stoically astride his bay. Although Neblus did not see him, Senu was some yards behind, directly in front of the army. He lay there in wait for Neblus to take the bait.

As good a soldier as Neblus had been in Hyksos terms, he had allowed his new "royalty" to affect his judgment. If Queen Hatshepsut was a goddess, then he, King Neblus, was most certainly a god. As it is with other vain and ambitious men, he valued his own opinion more then the opinions of others; and he had come to believe himself to be invincible. He would give these weak-kneed soldiers of the Queen of Egypt a taste of royal Hyksos steel.

Neblus ordered the gates of the city thrown open and led his army of two hundred out to slay the enemy. Remaining behind, the hostage Egyptians looked sideways at each other in knowing certainty that they would soon be free.

So full of opium and desire for escape from life was Kamare that he lifted his sword and charged to meet Neblus, his executioner. They clashed, and Kamare reeled back as though he were about to fall from his horse. He lowered his sword arm and turned his head. Seeing this unbelievable opportunity, Neblus slashed downward with his sword and nearly severed Kamare's head from his body. As Neblus paused to admire his skill, Senu screamed out a battle cry in fury and despair at the sight of his mortally wounded friend. He dug his spurs into his horse's flanks and was upon Neblus before he had time to react. Senu drove his sword deep into the lungs of King Neblus who crumpled and fell from his horse

The hidden wing had began their gallop when they received the signal that the gates had swung open and were now more than halfway to the battle. All the Hyksos men—bakers, basket weavers, servants, and boys—made up the body of the army, leaving none but women to oversee the seemingly passive Egyptians. In the city, the Egyptian soldiers broke loose from the women, and these former soldiers of Kamare's army ran to the gates and slammed them shut.

Leaderless, the soft-bodied, untried army of Neblus faced an experienced army to the front, closed gates to the rear, and a horde of cavalry charging from the north. The conflict was over in an hour. No quarter was given; all Hyksos were slain.

When the sounds of battle had died away, the hitherto captive Egyptian soldiers opened the gates and received warm praise from Senu—now the only General of Egypt. He allowed his men to feast and enjoy the Hyksos women for two days before he gave orders to level the city.

The soldiers, some of whom had followed him for twenty-five years, and who loved him, tended the corpse of General Kamare with gentle hands. His armor and other precious accoutrements were removed. While being held for the mummification tent and attendant priests, the body was placed in a shallow stone tub and covered with salt and perfumes. The tub would retain all the fluids necessary for the Canopic jars, and the layer of salt would slow the decay which his body had suffered long before his death, the sight of the funeral train three days later was a welcome one.

General Senu and the army remained encamped near the city while the body of Kamare was prepared for its wrappings. As they waited, destruction of the city took place. Block by stone block, brick by mud brick, the heart of the walled city was destroyed. The rest of the city burned easily, as it was not made of stone but of wattle and straw.

At last, all was complete; and Senu led a triumphant army home to Egypt, beautiful mother Egypt.

The white-tented catafalque bearing the dried and mummified remains of the great General Kamare followed at the rear of the army. Great had he been in battle, and great had been the love he had for his Queen, but he was no longer among the living.

23

The body of Thothmes II had undergone a very long mummification process. After all, he had been Pharaoh. Queen Hatshepsut—or Pharaoh Makere as she was now called at all times—had ordered that great honor be paid to the dead King. He would occupy a special tomb in her new temple, and a great procession of ships would accompany the one bearing him to Deir el Bahri. She smiled in pleasure at the thought of the final duty Thothmes II would perform for his country.

The royal boat drifted down the Nile, draped in the white of mourning. The Queen sat on her throne at the bow of the boat; and for the first time, she appeared wearing a gold beard tied beneath her chin. She could not hide her womanly curves, but for all visible purposes, she displayed every device that all preceding Pharaohs had used: two crowns, the red within the white; the euraceus of the cobra on her brow; the crook and flail crossed upon her breasts.

Her reign was providing Egypt with the greatest prosperity the kingdom had ever known. There was no hunger, little illness, and great contentment among her countrymen. Her personal image was one of a goddess of great beauty, a goddess to whom Horus and Isis spoke. So said all the priests of all the houses of the gods she had visited, and Egyptians were very mindful of the gods. Queen Hatshepsut, Pharaoh Makere, had placed Maat, or great peace and happiness, in the hearts of her subjects. Now, she could do no wrong. Now she could be anyone she declared herself to be.

By her side, the small prince, Thothmes III, stood for long hours. He had been well trained by his mother and father; and when called upon, he could conduct himself in regal manner. The only movement the boy made was to wave at the people who crowded the shores to catch a glimpse of the royal ones. They loved the boy, and they cheered him when he waved. And who could not love him? He was a fine young prince, sturdy and broad of shoulder, with the kindest of smiles.

Hatshepsut's heart was comforted whenever she saw her son. Here was no inbred weakling. Here was a future warrior Pharaoh who would defend and strengthen Egypt. Always, he reminded her of Kamare, and then her thoughts would lead her to contemplate the life she and her beloved would share in eternity. For now, the wrapped body of the General lay in the gold covered coffin stored in a tunnel below the palace. It would be there under constant guard during the coming years.

She intended to live a long, full life; but in the end, she would meet Anubis, so did all mortals; and she would be with her love forever and ever. Death was to be accepted, even anticipated with joy, but there were many things she planned to accomplish. Queen Hatshepsut, Pharaoh Makere, wanted to be remembered forever after as a great woman.

Thus, the Queen sailed on the boat carrying the mummy of Pharaoh Thothmes II to his resting place in her temple. Her heart was light as she envisioned a bright future. She had a perfect son at her side and another life within. The child would be born in six months. Unlike her first child, this new babe seemed tiny; in no way did Hatshepsut appear to be carrying a child. The only thing perceived by other eyes was that she had become more voluptuous, more full in her breasts. She was at the height of her beauty and adored by all men. No doubt many nobles were, even now, planning to ingratiate themselves and gain her affection.

Waiting on the dock at Deir el Bahri was the man who had loved her since first sight four years earlier. Sennumet was handsome and fair of skin. At present, his tan was deep, but pale eyes and sun-bleached hair belied his color. When he had heard of Kamare's death, he was not saddened. He had sensed that Hatshepsut was attracted to him, but he had not dared hope for more than a kind word and a polite smile while the General lived. But now . . . ? His body ached at the thought of her. The passion glowing in his eyes would surely give him away.

The boat appeared at the river bend and sailed majestically to the dock. Looking upward beyond the two terraces, Hatshepsut could see the outlines of two rows of pillars, one above the other. Workers were there chipping away at the mountain between them. In the center was a dark square opening.

The temple would be massive and perfect in every way. Surely no other Pharaoh, with the possible exception of Khufu, had built on so grand a scale. And the pyramid, in spite of its size and grandeur, did not possess the grace and moving shadows of the pillars at Deir el Bahri.

Hatshepsut was roused from her reverie by the crash of cymbals and the mournful wail of oboes. Pharaoh Thothmes was carried in his coffin down the ramp and placed on a catafalque borne by priests. None would remain to serve the Pharaoh in his afterlife, as was the custom. Since the tomb was not to be sealed at this time, not one had elected to stay. Until the Queen ordered the tomb sealed, he would be enshrined in the small cave beside the altar that was being hewn from within the mountain. He would be guarded from looters until he was walled in, and perhaps long after, perhaps until the Queen was laid to rest to live again. After that, she would not care if his body were robbed and torn apart, so long as she and the one other were safely hidden far below.

Ineni and Sennumet waited for her at the bottom of the ramp. Under lids coated with emerald dust, her star eyes glittered, as she looked downward to the upraised ones of Sennumet. The shock between them was electric. Hatshepsut had been without physical love for almost three months, and all parts of her body were throbbing for want of such love. Her sensitive nipples stood out in hard points. *I will have this man,* she thought. *His body will be hard pressed against mine, and we will enjoy each other greatly.* The Queen was transfixed with these thoughts for an endless moment and stood very still as she was caressed by the gaze of the young architect.

Her beautiful eyes enraptured Sennumet. Their black stars set in green had always fascinated him. Now they devoured him. He read her thoughts exactly, and a thrill coursed through his body. *Tonight my sweet one! Tonight!*

With her gold-brushed skin, green-tinged eyelids, and long hair tucked up into her crowns, she was a vision of beauty as she seemingly floated down the ramp. A pleated gown of white linen covered her lush body and brushed the sand. As though breaking from a trance, she went through the appropriate greetings for the occasion. Ineni and Sennumet placed wreaths of flowers around her neck, and she was handed the reins of the lead chariot.

"Everything is prepared, your highness," said Ineni. "After we have placed your husband in his sarcophagus, we will clear the chamber, and I will show you why so little appears to have been done in these years."

She had wondered at the slow progress but had withheld her questions. Now, she guessed correctly that hundreds of laborers had been working deep under the mountain.

The Queen led the procession of priests, mourners, and family members up the ramps, past the palms, ponds of water lilies, and lines of sphinx figures. All the faces of the sphinxes, twenty to a side, resembled hers. A beard representing the one she wore strapped to her own chin was carved below the chin of each lion's face. She would be glad to unstrap the heavy gold beard, but for now the image was important.

As they reached the square carved entrance to the mountain, workers came forward with huge plates of electrum. At once the light was bounced from the sun into the depths of the chamber. It was very deep. The procession walked along behind the coffin bearers. The walls were rough-hewn, and the future altar at the end was an untouched mass of granite. The tunnel turned at a right angle to the left and more workmen with plates and shields caught the light from the discs at the entrance. Except for the long shadows, the inside of the mountain of Gurn was as bright as the day outside. However, as the day outside darkened, the light inside would wane as the sun progressed to the west.

At the end of the side tunnel was a small chamber that contained a sarcophagus of black onyx, a very rare stone brought many miles overland to this site. The king was placed inside his new dwelling place, and Hatshepsut was handed a curved knife. She bent over the mummy and performed the final ritual. She cut the wrappings where the mouth should be so that Thothmes II could breathe again. Immediately, the lid was fitted into place, and the Queen removed the wreaths from around her neck and put them on the black lid. She turned to the attending priests and asked them to leave the chamber and return to the landing area to oversee the preparation of the feast to take place under the tents on the shore. She explained nothing. She was Pharaoh, to be obeyed always.

When all but Hatshepsut, Ineni, and Sennumet had gone, Ineni took down a lamp from a shelf and asked the Queen to look at the unusual design upon the floor. The floor was water smooth and polished. The sarcophagus rested inside a circle of copper, the dais of Ra. Reaching down, Sennumet removed two upright clogs at the ends of the onyx sarcophagus. He pushed against it with one hand, and the sarcophagus containing the mummy of Thothmes II slid around easily on the copper circle. As Hatshepsut watched in amazement, a wide stairwell appeared before her feet; and the sounds made by much chipping and talking reached her ears.

"This is wherein most of our efforts have been placed. It will need but a few more years to complete, as we work on the outer temple as well," explained Ineni. The trio descended the stairs leading ever deeper into the rock, their way lit by a lamp held high by Ineni. On three occasions, he paused to show Hatshepsut the wide openings of shafts in the ceiling that would pour tons of sand into this staircase when triggered from above.

"It will not matter if the workers who labor here live on," he said. "No one will ever be able to clear away the many tons of sand that will seal this pleasant place."

Although she was long inured to the eventual end she faced, Hatshepsut felt a chill course through her body; and she shuddered involuntarily. She reached behind to grasp Sennumet's hand. How willingly he held her hand, as he pressed his warm and firm body close to her. Both were instantly filled with longing. Here, far below the earth's surface, throbbing desire swelled.

The noises from below became louder and louder as they descended. It seemed they had walked down one hundred steps when the stairwell finally opened onto a room so huge that two rooms from the palace could have been placed inside it. As promised, no pillars were needed for support. The men were using oil lamps as in previous times. The little group had come so silently that it was only when Sennumet called out that the workmen turned to see the Great Royal Queen and fell prostrate before her.

In the hush of stilled lips and silent tools, the Queen moved to the center of her chamber and gazed in awe at the progress made. The men had been hard at work with adzes and chisels, smoothing out the walls in preparation for the paintings she would choose. Upon the floor were platforms for two sarcophagi, and resting upon these were massive blocks of rose quartz that would be carved into the matching sarcophagi. It had taken days to edge them down the stairs. The ceiling was polished to a smooth luster, and outlines of black stars were drawn upon it, to be painted later in a sky of blue. The ceiling would be painted last to cover the soot.

Overall, it was a gargantuan task. When finished and filled with her gold boat and many precious possessions, it would glitter for all time. And there would be enough food, wine, and servants sealed into the chamber to serve Hatshepsut through eternity.

An Egyptian never discarded anything. Every lock of hair, childhood toys and crib, small things of early youth—all were kept and added to the beautiful items gathered in later years. It was believed that, after each man's heart was weighed and found to be pure and good, and after the contents of the Canopic jars were returned to the body, life would return to the deceased; and he would rise to sail in the underworld river at night and ride the sky with the sun during the day. When such a one awakened, he would need the things of childhood in case his memory needed refreshing. Also, all those who entered with him would share the goods he held in his tomb. They would feast endlessly and play at many games. There would be music from instruments, and slaves and priests would be there to serve them. If the deceased were royal, he or she could converse with others of royal families as they rode the underground river at night and raced chariots across the sky in daylight. No one would be old or sick, and no one would bear the problems associated with the lives of those living above ground. However, all would be lost if a rich tomb were broken into and robbed of its treasures. For this reason, the Queen was greatly pleased with the plans of Ineni and Sennumet. She had seen many desecrated tombs with the mummies torn in pieces by the looters. This could not happen to her nor would Kamare be harmed.

It was time to return above ground as the sun would soon fade, and traversing the long tunnel through the mountain would be difficult when the light had vanished. Before turning away, Hatshepsut spoke to the still prostrate forms. "Good workers, loyal to Pharaoh Makere, I offer you a feast this night. Do you continue your happy work, for you give your Queen great honor."

She allowed Sennumet to lead her up the long, steep passageway. Their bodies brushed on the narrow stairs, and each touch left a searing scar of awareness. After they exited the passageway, the sarcophagus of Thothmes II was rolled silently back into place. The laborers would come up after the Queen had gone.

The funeral party emerged from the crude opening in the mountain as the terraces and river below fell into shadow. The deep throb of drums rolled up to them from the tents in which the feast was being held. Jars of wine had been broached, and the celebration had begun.

"Sweet Queen, ride with me. Lazuli will take us gently downward." Sennumet's eyes were but inches from hers, as were his lips.

She pretended lighthearted gaiety and replied, "If Lazuli is sweet and gentle, I shall reward you with a special prize, for you must surely be a magician."

It seemed that "sweet" Lazuli had changed not a hair. She reared, and then charged her way down the terraces, barely remaining on the ramp. Sennumet spoke to the mare in great praise and pride, for he admired her spirit. Hatshepsut laughed aloud and pounded small fists against Sennumet's back. She loved a spirited horse as well as he.

The Queen was in disarray when Sennumet drew up the chariot near the feasting tent. With eyes more alive than they had been in months, she turned to the handsome man at her side. "Sennumet, you have tamed the evil Lazuli; and I shall justly reward you. Come aboard my boat so that I may repair my appearance before you receive what you most desire." Her meaning was evident, and his heart thumped in his chest as he followed her up the ramp.

"Beka! Beka, come to me at once." The old woman appeared from below and saw happiness once more on the face of her beloved Hati. "Ask General Senu to take Thothmes III to the feast honoring his father. He may sit on my throne until I arrive. I shall require absolute privacy for a while. Please see to it."

Bowing low, the woman trotted away to clear the boat of all save herself. She then sat on the ramp with her own jar of wine and allowed her mind to be at peace.

Below, Hatshepsut pulled the silken hangings away from her soft bed. Turning to Sennumet, she removed her crowns. Long hair fell in thick waves to her hips. With eyes glazed with desire, she held out her arms to Sennumet. At once he enclosed her and covered her panting mouth with his open lips. Breath passed between them. Bodies hot with desire pressed hard together, and neither wanted to end the kiss. Even so, a kiss such as this brought about but one ending, and they parted. She unhooked the clasp that held his tunic on one shoulder so that it dropped to the deck. Ah, what muscles rippled on his lean body! At the sight of his arousal, she bade him remove the brooch that held her linen dress. The garment joined his clothing on the deck.

With trembling hands, Sennumet caressed Hatshepsut's body, rolling her painted nipples between his fingers. Soft, mewing sounds slipped from her lips as he lovingly covered her body with feather touches. When she placed her hands on his chest and allowed them to fall and clutch his manhood, he could bear it no longer. He pushed her upon the bed and began to suck her breasts while his hands caressed the soft inner skin of her thighs. Hatshepsut's back arched high in pleasure. She pulled him into her, and he began long, slow thrusts. It seemed she could not contain all of him, and yet each thrust went in deeper and deeper. Their intense passion reached a climax quickly, and they lay still, panting from exertion. As they lay entwined, he was still large within her, and he began to move again. Her breasts were tender and so aroused that his tongue on them brought desire as hot as before. This time, they spoke the words that make their coupling an act of love and not simply slaking of lust.

Said Sennumet, "I have hungered for you for so long. My love for you is forever."

And she replied, "I have always known."

Many more loving words passed between them as his thrusts came more quickly. They shared a great shuddering release and lay in swirls of drenched sheets.

The evening breeze blew through the passageway and roused them. They must appear at the feast, which was becoming noisier by the minute. Sennumet pulled her to him before they rose and asked if he would see her soon.

"Having tasted of the most delicious of all fruit, I am filled again with hunger. Will you allow me to be near you? When will I see you? How will I draw breath unless I am by your side, my sweet love?"

The Queen turned to him. Even in disarray, with curling tendrils of hair lying all about her, her beauty was ethereal. Dew points of perspiration lay upon her body, making it gleam. Winged brows shadowed her Nile-green eyes. The black stars of her irises were mesmerizing. She lay as a devil woman might, full lips holding a gentle smile.

"Beloved, I must tell you now that I am carrying a child to be born in six full moons. We two, you and I, shall be together when possible. But as Pharaoh and Queen, I cannot offer more. As a woman, I cannot give my heart again so soon. We shall be lovers for as long as we desire it and for as long as Egypt allows it. As surely as I am master of Egypt, Egypt is master of Hatshepsut. Let us capture all the happiness we can and keep it close. The gods alone know our fates." She kissed the smile back upon his face, and they then cleansed themselves so that they could join in the feasting on shore.

By the very nature of their positions, Egyptian queens were murderous, but they were not wanton. However, this Queen, was not to be compared with those who lived before her. Hatshepsut was fully aware of the many means of committing murder, aided by all she had learned from the long-dead necromancer. She possessed also the mind of a strong king, encapsulated in the loveliest of bodies. She understood well her duty to Egypt—to cherish her subjects and to perpetuate her dynasty. She held absolute, unopposed power in the richest land on earth. In a year of poor harvests, she could sell enough surplus wheat to other countries to secure necessities for her own nation for four months. Rain only fell regularly on the Nile delta, perhaps six inches a year; ninety percent of her kingdom was desert and shamsen wind. However, even the desert yielded its riches to her in the form of gold and gems. And she lusted in a manner unusual for one so lovely. The Queen lusted for conquest, for giant monuments, and above all, to be remembered for all time.

None of this was apparent as she and the adoring Sennumet walked to the festive tent where they would share a last meal with her late, unlamented husband. Little Thothmes was asleep on her throne, watched over by Senu, when the Queen joined the feasting and free-drinking nobles. At a gesture from the mother, Senu picked up the child to carry him to the nurses waiting aboard the two-hundred-foot-long ship. The sober General was not a man to set aside a vow. He would protect and instruct the boy. If duty forced him to leave for a time, he would see that the child was circled with men of unquestionable loyalty. At this moment, though, Senu's thoughts were elsewhere. He was far from being a fool and could see the sexual glow upon the Queen and Sennumet. All well and good, for the architect was harmless. He must be certain that all companions of the Queen were as harmless.

Sennumet and Hatshepsut sailed back to Thebes in the gilded boat. She delighted in his adoration and experienced lovemaking and had him dressed in robes of finest linen and cotton and placed gold bands and collars upon him. He was new; he was young and handsome.

Together, they composed the sayings for the walls of her temple. She decided that she would keep him by her side for two months and then send him back to Deir el Bahri. The new babe must not be risked, for she needed at least two heirs—more if possible.

It was a singular situation. A king must cause his queen to bear many children because of the low survival rate of that era. On the other hand, the royal princess must marry a brother or father and plan the murder of all surviving sisters and brothers in order to rule unopposed. It had always been thus. One wonders at a queen's emotions as she gave birth to many children, knowing that some would die in childhood from incurable maladies and the others, all but one or two, would be murdered by a sibling.

In Hatshepsut's heart of hearts, she knew Thothmes III would be a mighty ruler, strong of body and quick of mind if merely left to grow. She vowed to make him better. He would speak Greek, Egyptian, Hebrew, Syriac, Median, and Parthian as she did. His studies in geography, mathematics, astronomy, and philosophy would be continuous and in depth. As for the instruction in all things physical and pertaining to battle, she abided by Kamare's wish to have Senu oversee this aspect of the child's education. There was none better alive in Egypt at this time or, therefore, the world.

Each time Hatshepsut spoke with Senu or shared food and wine with him, she was aware of his great physical attraction. More importantly though, she enjoyed the games they played. He was a worthy adversary, and he was not afraid of her. He won often at many of the games and roared in laughter when she threw her wine goblet at him.

For now, the gentle Sennumet was the comfort she needed. This was not the time for deep attachment, only amusement. The Queen chose much as a man might. For now, she wanted no binding love, just love for the sake of pleasure.

At the beginning of her sixth month, Hatshepsut sent

Sennumet back to Deir el Bahri. He begged to stay with her, and she could see the hurt in his every glance, but it was time to be alone with the coming child.

To make his leaving less painful, she had a new boat made for him alone. On the bow was painted the inscription "Light of the Queen's Eye," and it was filled with luxuries. One of these was a lovely virgin from the harem. The Queen had realized for years Sennumet's love for her, and she had enjoyed him greatly, but she had known he was not her match. As brilliant an architect as he was, there was little else. His knowledge did not extend much beyond his profession, and his humor lay in the enjoyment of others' tales; he told none himself.

Sennumet set sail upon his lovely boat with his face turned toward Thebes until the city was hidden from view. The girl at his side set sail with her gaze locked upon Sennumet. Time would be the ally of the Queen; it would be impossible for him to resist so lovely a girl for months on end.

In what might have been seen as a symbolic gesture. Hatshepsut declared that she would have a leisurely bath at once. As she soaked away her tensions, hair floating around her, she unconsciously washed Sennumet from her and was at peace. Her child was moving in her; her kingdom prospered; and the wonder of her handsome son filled her with contentment and pride.

24

Hatshepsut felt the beginning of labor and sent for three physicians, two witnesses, and Mutnefret, her mother-in-law. There would be no strong man to help her this time, but she felt no fear. The child was small, and she had trod this path before.

The doctors hastened to her chamber with Mutnefret close upon their heels. After a complete examination, the head physician assured her that her period of labor would be brief, for birth was imminent. As the labor pains intensified, Mutnefret held out her hands for Hatshepsut to grasp and urged her to squeeze as tightly as she could. Soon after this, the Queen was placed in the birthing chair and quickly delivered a small princess.

Later, she lay bound tightly upon her bed, the babe in the fold of her arm. How strange was the little one. She was perfect in all ways but tiny, and wonder of wonders, the fuzz on her head was the color of bright gold.

Queen Tetishari, dead long before the birth of Hatshepsut, had been the daughter of Ptolemy II Philadephus, also called Soter. Pharaoh Soter had had hair the color of the sun. This child must hold his genes . . .

When the babe opened her eyes, Hatshepsut saw that they were light hazel and knew that eventually they would probably become dark brown. And there were no stars. No matter, love poured from mother to child, and the Queen held her close. Her name had been chosen months ago. Merit-re-Hatshepsut lay safely in her mother's arms as both fell into gentle sleep. Mutnefret tiptoed quietly from the room, all the while thanking the gods for her beautiful new granddaughter.

Senu was in his house by the Nile when he was informed of the birth of a royal princess. He and his family would celebrate the joyous news, as would the entire nation. While waiting for news of the birth, Senu had been devoting his attention to a message he had received a few weeks ago that a force was gathering on Egypt's eastern frontier.

It was told that this force included Asian, Syrian, and Arabian troops under a Greco-Iranian commander, Mithridates of Perganum. Most ominous of all, a contingent of Jewish troops from Judaeca had joined with them. One called Antipater led these Jews. By all reports, Antipater was a leader much to be respected. Since fully one-fourth of the capital city of Thebes was made up of Jews, who could be expected to turn against Egypt from within in order to assist Antipater, Egypt needed a healthy and physically fit Queen. Furthermore, it seemed that all the dominions of Egypt, with the exception of Greece and the Gabinians, had decided that the time was ripe to break the yoke of Egypt. If they were successful in doing so, they would capture all the lands and wealth of Egypt as had the Hyksos, over two hundred fifty years before.

Senu had not informed Hatshepsut of these dangers in her last month of pregnancy, as he knew it would take the gathering forces of the enemy a year to organize themselves. For, by their very different natures and customs, there would be much arguing and debating of rank and command. Yes, there would be time to defend Egypt, but just barely.

Senu had already sent ships to Greece to demand, and pay for, Greek mercenaries. He had also been hard at work conscripting an even larger army from all parts of upper and lower Egypt. This was not too difficult, as the populace of Egypt was a proud one. Men could always be found who were willing to fight and fight hard.

The nucleus of the powerful army General Kamare had formed six years earlier was intact. From this unit of thousands, commanders had been appointed to oversee and train the new Egyptian soldiers. Horses had been bred continuously over the years, and there were fine animals aplenty.

Many years of trade with Greece found warehouses fully stocked. And, if the ships returned from Greece with the warlike tribes of Spartans, Egypt would be nearly invincible. It was said that the mothers of Sparta stood by the gates of their city as their sons marched off to battle. As the men passed, each mother called out to her sons: "Come home to Sparta victorious—or die in battle." The mere whisper in an enemy camp that they were to face Spartans was enough to bring on a wave of fear.

Senu had seen to it that everything that could be done was being done. Only one thing remained: this army to defend Egypt needed more than a general to lead it. If Egypt were to survive and retain her lands, a king must lead.

Thus, Queen Hatshepsut, Pharaoh Makere, must put on the armor of war and lead her countrymen into battle. Egyptians would follow her to the end, and Senu had no doubt at all that she could lead them. When the time was appropriate, he would seek an audience with her. Plans must be made for her to sail the entire length of the Nile. She must show herself in full battle dress in all the cities and temples.

Senu was a young general, but the Queen's faith in him was justified. His knowledge was great, and he was insurmountable in battle. Convinced that all was proceeding as it should, he smiled again at the thought of the new babe and, resting his handsome head upon his pillows and thinking of Hatshepsut, finally fell into a deep sleep.

Outside his house, the guards were alert, as were the newly doubled guards at the palace. It was common to send spies and assassins ahead of an attacking force. Anyone caught trying to slip through would be questioned brutally and then put to the sword.

Weeks passed. The little princess grew strong and healthy. The Queen had placed herself in the care of her physicians who prescribed the leanest of foods and an ever-increasing regimen of exercise. She fairly glowed with good health and well-being.

She drove her horses to the limit, careening across the desert roads, arms locked in the reins, body strong and erect. Her escorting force followed closely, and more than one strong soldier found himself with a smile of admiration upon his face. Queen Hatshepsut was a tigress indeed. She had begun the habit of wearing Kamare's leopard skin cloak. It rippled behind her, as she lashed the bay stallions ever faster.

She decided she would have a lion, one she would kill herself. No matter how Senu argued the danger, she looked sternly down at him and demanded one be found.

"Senu, do not make the mistake of thinking you will kill it for me, nor will you follow closely behind. I am Pharaoh Makere; there is no danger. Even better—find a lioness for me. It is well known that females of all species are more dangerous." So saying, she looked down from her chariot and defyingly rattled her spears in their holders. She dared him by her look to oppose her. He did not, for this was what he had sought. This was the leader Egypt must have.

Riders rode ahead at once to search for a lioness while Hatshepsut rested in a tent. Late in the evening, as the moon rose, the Queen put on a short kilt of pleated linen like the ones worn by her soldiers, threw a cloak over her shoulders, and walked in the sands. Her body and her soul thrived with the power and fitness of youth.

Far away, she could see two pyramids clearly in the moonlight. Of a sudden, she recalled her decision that afternoon so many years ago in the temple of her grandmother. She would have an obelisk, not hewn from red granite as she had dreamed that day, but carved from stone and covered in electrum. It would be the tallest yet erected in Egypt, and her mind raced to think of the perfect inscription. There would be all the usual carvings of course; there always was. There would be her name, her ancestral line, a dedication to the gods; but an obelisk always carried one message from its royal builder. She must think about it.

As she walked back to her tent to rest before the hunt, it came to her. It was the thought she had molded into her life and, therefore, fitting for her obelisk. She entered the tent, lit a candle, and hastily proceeded to compose her inscription. Before resting, she called to two horsemen and handed them a roll of papyrus.

"This message must reach Sennumet and Ineni, master architects now building my temple at Deir el Bahri. I am giving each of you a pouch of gold to ensure that you will successfully complete this mission."

Each swore to the Pharaoh Queen that her command would be obeyed, and they rode off into the night. Upon the papyrus tucked into the leather dispatch pouch that was borne away were written these words:

> "Greetings, loyal Ineni and Sennumet. Your Queen greets you in love and respect. As you work upon my temple, I would have you set carvers to work upon a massive obelisk from living rock. It must rise taller than any other and be covered with electrum to catch the first and last rays of the sun. Aside from the carvings that must be placed upon this edifice, this saying will be foremost. They are my own words. Hatshepsut speaks them:
>
> 'Fill not thy heart with a brother.
> Nor know a friend.
> Guard thy heart against Thyself.'
> Place this obelisk at Karnak."

Having put this task in motion, the warrior Queen lay upon her cot to sleep, dreaming of the lioness she would face. She smiled as she slept.

The words Queen Hatshepsut had written were her own. It cannot be known whether she hardened her heart as she wrote them, but, surely, they were the words of one who steeled herself for battle.

For the Queen's sources were as fine and as competent as those of Senu. It had amused her to know he thought her too weak to be aware of all that was occurring. And it was not by whim or accident that she dressed as Pharaoh and went in search of a lion to slay. In believing that she was indeed a god, she took upon herself a fearlessness and disregard of danger that gave her a true belief of invincibility. Such confidence frequently leads to success in all undertakings.

Senu came to her tent at dawn, apprehension evident in his every move. His men had found a lioness with cubs in a cave not too far away. She had fed the night before on a goat they had staked out in the desert. From a safe distance, soldiers watched as she devoured half of it and then carried the remainder of the carcass to her cave in the cliffs. Obviously, her cubs were some months old if they could eat the meat she brought.

"Ah, Senu, if she defends her cubs, she will be fierce indeed. It is perfect."

As she rose and bound her hair in bright braid wrappings, Senu did his best to dissuade her. "Please, Great One, do not risk the chalice of Egypt in this manner. It is not necessary. Even the greatest of pharaohs has allowed others to make the first wounds and truly the first kill. Why must you risk this terrible death? There is no need."

Imperiously, the Queen turned to him, eyes aflame, gripping the hilt of the sword strapped to her hip. "Think you I know nothing of the battle Egypt must fight? Think you that what I do today has no bearing upon my right—nay, my necessity, to lead my armies as Pharaoh, not as Queen?"

In the short silence that fell between them, all became clear to Senu. Of course she was right. Who would not follow such a ruler? He bent his knee to her and said nothing.

"Come, General Senu. We go to fight a tiny battle so that the victory of the great battle is assured."

Hatshepsut emerged from her tent followed by Senu. Smiling gaily, she spoke to one of the guards. "Bring a large jar of wine from our supply tent. We will open it and drink to the success of our hunt." She held out a large goblet but took only one sip when it had been filled. Looking about her, she said, "Come, comrades—in-arms; we shall share the same cup today in our sport, for we are all one in Egypt." The cup was passed to all, and each wet his lips from the royal goblet.

A great cheer went up from the soldiers, some twenty of them. They adored her. Her chariot was brought forward, stallions rearing and wild, just as she liked them. Leaping up, she wrapped the reins around her arm and rattled her sharp spears. She carried only four spears, as it was unlikely that she would have time to use more than two. The first must hit home; the second would finish the big cat. If not, there were the two spares and her sword. In her mind, she gave thanks to Kamare for the many hours spent teaching her to be expert in the use of weapons. In the distance, a soldier waved to her; and she was off. She drove as would a madwoman, and her throaty laugh drifted back on the wind.

Not one who followed her doubted her; even Senu now feared nothing. The small, muscular figure of Pharaoh Makere leaned into the wind, as she shouted at the stallions. She would be upon the lioness before the troops caught up with her.

The soldiers whipped their horses as they were caught up in the spirit of the chase. They whooped and sang. They would follow this Queen wherever she led. Had they not shared wine from the same goblet? How proud they were to be a part of this fine hunt and to serve a valiant leader.

In her den, far back in the cool cave, the lioness shook loose from her cubs and rumbled in her chest. She was a full three years old, and a beautiful specimen. Muscles rippled under her tawny skin. She would have run from the pounding she felt in the earth but for the two furry cubs at her feet. Her ears went flat against her head, and lips drew back from long fangs. With these teeth, she could rip a leg from a cow or throw the body over her back and carry it for many miles. Claws extended from her paws and then drew back again. She felt danger for her young but no fear for herself. She growled low to the cubs, and they tumbled to the back of the cave to hide. They would not come out until she called them. The cat crept low on her belly to the entrance of the cave, still in shadow, every hair on end.

As the Queen neared the cliffs, the soldier who had waved to her pointed to the opening in the hillside. Up the incline drove Hatshepsut, only to wheel in front of the cave and then dart away. She did this twice. The horses were becoming harder to control, and her spear throw would be inaccurate if she could not calm them.

Cat smell was strong in the morning heat. The "cat" in the chariot flared her nostrils and bared her teeth also. Hatshepsut's blood was up. She needed the death of the lioness to prove her own life. Loudly, she called to the lioness to come forward to do fair battle, as had many Pharaohs before her. She lifted the war trumpet that hung over her shoulder and blew a loud blast toward the cave.

The lioness roared and thrust her head and shoulders through the cave opening. Hatshepsut saw that the animal was of good size and spitting mad.

Upon seeing the lioness, Hatshepsut's horses went wild with fear. The Queen plucked two spears from the holder and leaped to the ground. Pulled by the crazed horses, the chariot careened down the hillside just as the rest of the party caught up with her.

As they were about to rush to her assistance, she put up an arm with a closed fist; and they fell back into a semi-circle. All was quiet but for the roaring of the lioness. She would charge now. There was a small man-thing in front of her cave. She gathered her feet under her, tail twitching, and head low to the ground.

Hatshepsut calmly reviewed all of Kamare's instructions. She had killed lions before, but only with her first love and always in secret. How wise he had been! Knowing what to expect, she was alert to the moves of the cat. Lions were predictable. One who knew their habits and knew no fear could kill them easily.

She shouted once more to the lioness to come forward. She called to her to taste the blood of Egypt's Queen if she could. With her left hand, she held the trumpet to her lips and blew it again, right arm bent back by the weight of the thinnest spear. This spear had a long, narrow, and very sharp blade; the second was thick and strong with a wide blade. Each had a specific purpose.

Suddenly, the lioness charged. As she lifted her body in its last leap, ten feet from the Queen, Hatshepsut thrust the first spear at the exposed belly of the cat. The blade went completely into her. Now bending her knee, Hatshepsut held the thick spear up toward the oncoming chest of the cat. She kept it rock steady on the ground as the lioness' heart was impaled upon the broad blade. In a dying movement, the lioness reached down and clawed the shoulder of the Queen. Her gold collar bore most of the attack, but her upper arm was gouged by three claws that left deep lacerations and caused searing pain.

Hatshepsut did not move an inch. When the cat twitched its last and died, she stood and raised her arms high and shouted the battle cry of the Pharaohs. The soldiers repeated the cry, and the cliffs resounded with the calls of victory. Hatshepsut had killed the lioness in the most dangerous manner possible. There were other, safer ways, but hers was hands-to-claw, and her soldiers knew it.

The Queen called for wine, drank some, and poured the rest over her wounds. Since rotted flesh was usually caught in a lion's claws, there was great danger of infection. More than wine must be done for this wound.

Pretending to have no pain, Hatshepsut called her fellow hunters forward to examine her magnificent kill. The men set to work to skin the lion at once. They were close to Thebes, and the cat's skin could be tanned and softened there.

Blood still dripped from her arm as Hatshepsut called Senu forward. She spoke so that all the soldiers could hear. "General Senu, it is well known that you have a way with female cats, and so I charge you with the capture of the cubs." (This remark brought uproarious laughter from the soldiers.) "When they are netted, bring them to the palace. They will be trained to live there with me. It has been said that a Pharaoh of the early days trained young lions to hunt with him, and I shall have a pair, also."

These were the kinds of things a great man and king would say and do. These were the words that planted the seeds of legends. Senu smiled and said she was most kind to offer him such entertainment; but even as he laughed, his gaze took in the ripped flesh of her upper arm.

"Pharaoh Makere, Queen Hatshepsut, do you not think it wise to go at once to the palace so that physicians can treat and stitch your arm and give you opium for your pain?"

"No, General Senu. While you catch my cubs, I shall be treated by your captain in the way a soldier is treated in battle. It is fitting."

Upon hearing this, Senu drew in his breath, for he knew what she intended; and he could not believe it of a woman. However, he said no more and went in search of nets.

"Captain Axares, come forward."

The young captain knew also how such wounds were treated, and he fell on his knees before her. "Great Queen, I do not wish to cause you pain, but I will do anything you ask of me."

"Then you shall build a fire and put three spears into it, as there are three tears in my arm. And come, all of you; we will drink wine as comrades in battle while the fire heats the spears. We will sing old battle songs, for I know them all."

The singing began slowly and then grew in volume as the soldiers took up the chants and shouts, and the songs of old victo-ries. The wine jars passed freely, and they were comrades to-gether. These men had been selected from among the commanders the Queen intended to use in the larger battle ahead. What passed here now would be known in all parts of her land within days.

During the singing, Hatshepsut took out her ruby and did what she had practiced in private many times. She hypnotized herself. It was easily done; and as she felt herself going under, she told herself when to awaken and that she would feel no pain. Those who were watching thought she simply amused herself to turn her mind from what was soon to occur.

When the blades were red hot, Captain Araxes bade another captain hold out the Queen's arm at length. She seemed com-pletely at ease, with eyes focused on a cliff far in the distance.

"I must begin, Your Majesty," he said, hoping she would stop him; but she said nothing. Araxes pressed the first spear on the first tear, and the smell of burning flesh passed among them. He did this two times more. The burned flesh began just below her shoulder and ran down to an inch above her elbow.

During the whole time, the face of the Queen did not quiver. A quiet fell among her group of commanders. Surely this queen was the bravest Pharaoh of all!

When the last spear was lifted, Hatshepsut's eyes blinked once, and she looked about her and down at her arm. It was hid-eous, and it had been unnecessary, as she was close enough to Thebes to be treated there. She knew well, however, the value of this stoic bravery and disfigurement. When men heard this tale and saw these scars, they would follow her to the house of Anubis if she called them to do so.

Senu had returned with the nets and watched it all, unbe-lieving and in awe. Egypt would defeat her enemies. He gathered up the nets and took two men with him into the cave for the cubs.

25

After a week of rest and application of unguents, the wounds healed into scars of long ridges of burned skin. Hatshepsut wore them as badges of honor and made no effort to cover them at any time.

The story of the hunt and the Queen's killing of the lioness and her bravery in enduring the cure by fire had spread everywhere. Egyptian men and boys begged to be admitted into her armies. If she were invincible, so would they be. And if they died in support of her, it would be a death of great honor.

This story about the Queen of Egypt was carried even to its borders, where it was told to Mithridates, Antipater, and the other rulers. As each heard the tale, he fell silent. All bickering among them ceased, as they came to realize that Queen Hatshepsut was unlike any other woman. She must, in all truth, be a leader to be much feared, for they did not understand her and could not reason among themselves the causes of her actions. If a man cannot understand someone or something, then he often must hate it and fear it deeply.

At first these confident leaders believed the story to be a lie. However, too many told the same tale. In addition, spies reported that Queen Hatshepsut's ships had returned from Greece with three of those ships filled with Spartan troops.

In the camps of the enemies of Egypt, eyes could not meet eyes. There was a goddess who killed lions afoot and did not cry out when her wounds were closed with hot steel. The armies of Egypt had grown enormous. And now they would also face the sons of Sparta.

Nevertheless, as is the nature of men, the ones who had set themselves up to be seen as great leaders of a just and holy cause could not back down without destroying themselves. They had placed their futures and their very lives upon a roll of gaming stones when they believed Egypt to be weak and vulnerable. Now that they had learned otherwise, they could not turn back. Thus, their own pride would destroy them.

As the fears of Mithridates mounted, he dressed more grandly in armor of gold and silver. He gave great feasts for his followers and borrowed yet more bronze pieces to pay his army and buy the food and wine they required.

Mithridates called upon Antipater of the Jews to accept co-leadership with him, promising him half the kingdom of Egypt. The wise Antipater, however, declined to accept half of nothing and secretly sent a message to Hatshepsut, in which he promised to control the large population of Jews in Thebes if she would accept him in her service as a spy. In return, he asked for the lands of Syria as reward.

Queen Hatshepsut was preparing to set sail in her boat to travel the length of the Nile. She would show herself at the bow of her ship all along the way, dressed for battle. There would be no harps or sweet perfumes, only the slow beat of war drums and the blast of war trumpets as she passed each city. She would anchor only once, in Memphis.

Memphis was the site of the earliest Jewish temple in Egypt. Next to its undisturbed ruins was the new temple of Ra and Osiris. To visit here was to honor the main gods of all Egypt and, at the same time, to acknowledge the previous right of the Jews to worship freely in their way. Politically, it was an excellent choice.

As the one hundred thousand inhabitants of Memphis watched her golden boat tie up at the wharf, Hatshepsut, Queen of Egypt and Pharaoh over all, was seated at the bow. Upon a raised dais, the gold throne supported a figure in full battle dress. Her simple linen shift fell from one shoulder to a waist cinched with a sword belt and sword. She wore a small gold cone that fit upon her head and about her lower neck.

The ancient, scarred gold collar protected her shoulders and chest. Both forearms and calves were covered in gold sheaths. Around her shoulders was a leopard cape, thrown back from her right arm to reveal the three scars from the lioness. Chained to posts beside her were the half-grown lion cubs to which she tossed chunks of raw meat.

The soldiers based in Memphis had remained here for this ceremony. Others from her kingdom were staged along the eastern borders, with the largest contingent in tents at Thebes. Twenty thousand young soldiers roared the battle cry of Egypt as Hatshepsut walked down the plank from the ship. Her face was serene but severe. She carried herself with honor and showed no emotion.

Even Thothmes I had not enjoyed such total devotion. Here was a ruler who had been generous to her people in peace. Here, also, was a Queen who captured the hearts of her people with her astonishing display of bravery. And with all of this, there was also her divine parentage—mother, Isis and father, Horus.

Queen Hatshepsut did not walk meekly forward with lotus offerings for the gods. Rather, she strode through the city to the temple with a sword in each hand, head high, and steady of pace with stars visible to all.

Drums beat a slow, deep rhythm; and every man, woman, and child followed the beat with the repetition of her name: *Hat-shep-sut; Hat-shep-sut.* Over and over, until she reached the newly repaired temple of Ra and Osiris.

The Queen faced the crowds, and they were silent. She spoke, and her words were whispered back to those not close enough to hear.

"I, Pharaoh Makere, Queen Hatshepsut of Egypt, will not enter the peace of this temple, for my heart swells in lust for the blood of our enemies. In the lands we hold in conquest, new leaders have arisen. They believe us to be weak and would come here to make slaves of the sons and daughters of Egypt. I swear by all the gods that this shall not be so. I will protect you all from slavery. Some of you know that loved ones may die so that Egypt will be free. Such is the way of war, and it is not my choosing. Hear now, from my own lips, that Egyptian blood will not flow easily. I will use every means, every scheme, to preserve peace with as small a loss of life as possible. A man need not die to please his Queen. But fight we will, and win we shall."

As she finished, she laid one sword on the steps of Ra's temple and then walked across to the ruins of the Jewish temple. She placed the second sword upon the steps of those ruins.

Wild pandemonium exploded within the crowds. They roared their approval and threw flowers to show their love. The soldiers stood with arms locked together to keep open the path for her return to the wharf.

Hatshepsut resumed her seat on the bow of her ship as her soldiers distributed small cotton bags to every man, woman, and child. There were only three small gold pieces in each bag, but the deliberate evenhandedness of the Queen carried a message. The least fortunate of her subjects were in the eyes of their Queen equal with the rich and fat merchants and the landed noblemen.

She could not have acted more royally, nor could she have devised a more equitable way of uniting her people. The scribes present that day wrote down her words exactly as she had spoken them, and copies of her speech would fly over the land as leaves in the shamsen.

The Queen knew she had done well, very well indeed. The skin of her body prickled in excitement; and, truly, she longed for battle. First, however, she must show herself up and down the Nile to those countrymen who lined the banks of the river to catch a glimpse of their savior Queen. None were disappointed in what they saw. Hatshepsut made sure that all hearts were stirred and resolutions stiffened. For, if the battle could not be carried to the attackers, it would have to be fought within the borders of Egypt. She was determined to have solid resolve from even the most insignificant peasant.

By the time her voyage ended and she disembarked at Thebes, the Queen had united her nation behind her. Indeed, hearts were aflame throughout the country. She was ready. Egypt was ready.

26

Hatshepsut and Senu sat on her terrace sharing wine before a noon meal, when word came that a messenger wearing Jewish medallions had arrived. Hatshepsut knew that this messenger would report what he had seen, as well as what was said to him, back to his commander. Therefore, the Queen ordered that he be detained until she ordered that he be conducted to the Hall of Pillars. She directed Senu to have the lion handlers bring the cats to her there. Then she dressed as she had for the voyage and went to sit upon her throne.

The messenger from Antipater of Judaea was shown to a tall double door that opened to a huge, high-ceilinged hall filled with giant pillars. He saw a warrior Queen seated on a gold throne, atop alabaster steps. As he grew closer, escorted by Egyptian soldiers, he saw that Queen Hatshepsut caressed two half-grown lions, one on either side of her throne. The young lions had been in training for months; and although they could not be completely trusted, they were sufficiently trained so that Hatshepsut could have them beside her when she desired to impress a foreign emissary.

The messenger, a young man named Sharom, who was a prince of Judaea, knelt at the foot of the steps and looked up into the face of the most beautiful woman he had ever seen. The gold helmet that was her war crown hid her hair, but her face and body were exquisite. Her green eyes seemed to want to fly away under black wings of brows. Her eyes were so strange, unlike any he had seen before. And then his glance fell upon her right arm, and he flinched at the cruel sight of the claw marks. *Yet, she strokes the necks of those beasts with unconcern. What sort of woman is this?* He was familiar with court protocol and waited to be asked to speak.

Hatshepsut spoke in a Judaean tongue. "I see by your amulets that you are from Judaea. You have said you have a message for me. Who is your master?"

The young prince replied, "I have a written message, Your Majesty, as my master, Antipater, desires that its contents be kept secret. Even I do not know what it says." He removed a scroll from his waistband, and Senu stepped down to take it from him.

Since other leaders knew her linguistic prowess, Antipater had written the message in Hebrew. As she read, the Queen's expression did not change. At last she looked up and called for papyrus. The letter, offering to control the Jewish population in Egypt in return for the gift of Syria, had infuriated her. Only Senu, who knew her well, noticed the color rise to her cheeks.

Her message in return revealed her feelings.

> Hail Antipater, ruler of Judaea. Know you that I do not make a gift of land I possess to one who has planned to usurp my own. Know you also that I do not believe Syria would welcome a Jewish king any more than would the people of Egypt. This I will pledge to you. If you will withdraw the troops of Judaea from the camp of Mithridates and return to your own lands, I will allow you to live. You will send tribute and taxes to Egypt as has been done for many years. Consider yourself fortunate in this, as the armies of Egypt will have the heads of all rulers of countries who ally themselves with the unfortunate Mithridates.
>
> Queen Hatshepsut, Pharaoh Makere
> Living forever and ever.

The scroll was rolled and sealed with wax imprinted with the Queen's cartouche. "Give this messenger food, wine, and rest. He will leave tomorrow morning. See to it that he is treated well but is also guarded. The tempers of our people are high."

Days later, this same messenger rode into the plain that contained the armies united under Mithridates. As a prince, the messenger also understood many languages; and he slowed his horse to a walk so that he might listen.

As he wound his way through the countless tents, he found the grumbling to be the same: food was scarce; wine was sour. And there was the almost palpable feel of fear. No, this was not an army prepared to march to victory. It seemed more to be groupings of tribes, all ready to scatter. Here and there were seen a few stoic, professional soldiers. It was hard to read these battered faces; but to lead soldiers in battle, one must surely have an army, not just a handful of hardened veterans. And if that army were to be victorious, it must surely be confident and united.

King Antipater of the Jews reclined in his tent. He was a large, handsome man with a cruel, hooked nose over wide, sensuous lips. He wore a band of gold and the six-pointed Judaean star on his black curls. He was not a soft king, for Judaea was not a soft country. Its men and women reflected the harsh and barren landscape in which they lived. However, he was an intelligent man. He would grasp any advantage open to him and salvage the best from any situation. His was a proud heritage, based upon patience, hard work, and hard-cut negotiation. The young messenger was related to the king and well regarded by his family.

Antipater opened the missive and read quickly. His features fell in disappointment, and he threw the papyrus into the charcoal brazier and watched it burn. It would never do to allow others to know of his approach to the Egyptian Queen. Although he had heard the story of the lion hunt, he had not thought she would be so unbending and arrogant.

"Tell me of this Queen," he said after some time.

The boy answered, "She is most beautiful, my King. Yet her beauty is clothed in the armor of a warrior. She keeps half-grown lion cubs by her throne. She speaks our language as though it were her own. I cannot clearly describe the woman, as she bedazzled me. Truly, I do not believe there has ever been such a woman in all the history of all our nations. I can, however, tell you of Thebes and the palace.

"The city is enormous. Outside its gates are camped many thousands of soldiers, all disciplined and involved in constant training and exercise. The horses are large and strong. There are tents that appear to hold many weapons, and they are guarded well.

"Once into the city, I was overwhelmed by the apparent wealth of so many who live there. The markets hold bountiful stores, and the streets are laid out in a perfect wheel. All the spokes of the wheel are paved streets that lead to the palace in the center. I passed many large homes and buildings shaded by palms and fruit trees watered by sluices from the river. I am young, but I know prosperity when I see it. I was allowed to see only a small part of the palace by the Nile, but it was enough to make me remind myself to close my mouth. These Egyptians build for all time and for great beauty."

He described the giant pillars in the throne room and the many hangings of transparent cloth embroidered with gold and colored threads. "Most of all, Uncle, I saw gold. Gold must be so common to these people that they do not fully realize its value. All people wear it around their necks and arms. In the great chambers of the palace, I saw goblets and plates of gold. The Queen's throne is encased in large swept-back wings of gold, and the throne of the Pharaoh appears to be of solid gold, as is the round disc behind it. Never have my eyes beheld such wealth or such great armies of strong men."

The boy fell silent and seemed hesitant to speak further. It was obvious to Antipater that he withheld the worst news until last. "What is it you fear to speak, nephew? Your dismay is written upon your face."

"My King, when I was escorted from the city, I was compelled to ride along a path lined on each side by Spartans from the islands of Thrace. As I passed, each man made a slice in his chest with a sharp knife and bled for my eyes to see. As they bled, they laughed at me. Their eyes are clear and blue; heavily muscled and scarred in many places. Surely nothing that lives in this world can stop such men. And behind these stand the Egyptians, strong and determined."

The young man continued, his voice dropping to a whisper. "It is in my mind that the warrior Queen Hatshepsut is capable of leading this war machine herself. It is in my mind that something must be done to save the soldiers of Judaea from certain death."

King Antipater had listened attentively to the messenger's report. Evidently, the boy spoke with great accuracy; and the fear he felt was transferred to his uncle. *What is there to be done? How am I to save my men and prevent the other tribes from falling upon them? Mithridates is no fool, but I doubt I can make him see things as they are. Yet, I, the Judaean King, cannot seem cowardly. The revolt must come from within that greedy man's own companies.*

"Nephew, after you rest, I want you to go to a place where many drink wine, perhaps to the tents of the camp women. There you are to pretend drunkenness and reveal all you have said to me, leaving out only your audience with Queen Hatshepsut. Say that you were sent to spy upon the enemy. You have spoken to me, and I am not afraid. I desire to be the first to challenge the Egyptian hordes. However, you must confide in all that you have no desire to die and let them think you are going to slip away. Let us see what happens then. You may go, and you have served me well."

That night, the young man followed the sounds of drums and bells and flutes to an outside fire. Women with oiled bodies glistening in the firelight, twisted and bumped to the music, enticing the soldiers to part with a few pieces of bronze to share their beds for the night. Outside the circle of drinking men, where the shadows of night were deep, he stumbled across pairs of naked bodies joined in carnal writhing, accompanied by moans and shrieks. He felt a tightening in his loins at the sight and sound of such wild and abandoned lust, for he, too, was young and as strong as any.

As the light of the fire fell upon his cloak, he affected a drunken stagger and hailed some acquaintances who handed him a goatskin filled with wine. "Come, Sharom, drink with us. Drink to victory, and the Egyptian women we will have," they invited.

The boy, Sharom, fell down with them and pulled long at the skin of wine. "I need as much of this wine as I can drink, for I have seen things that chill my blood. Here! Give me more! I would sleep tonight; and if I cannot rid myself of these hellish visions, I will weep in terror."

Although his friends had drunk much wine, they still were sober enough to be aware that something was sorely amiss. One by one, they put aside their drinks and looked at each other in confusion. All knew Sharom to be brave and fearless and much favored by his uncle, the King. "Tell us, Sharom," said one. "You must tell us what you have seen and heard."

Sharom pleaded with them to leave him alone. He said he dared not burden any other with the knowledge of what he knew. All the while, the group of men grew larger, and now all were demanding to hear the story.

So, he told them. As his tale progressed, silence among the men grew deeper. More and more soldiers crowded in to listen, to listen and to draw back breath between their teeth as they heard of the Spartans laughing as they cut their chests. The flickering firelight caused strange shadows that had men peering over their shoulders in fright as though the Spartans might even then be among them. Word sped swiftly, on wings of fear, throughout the camp that night. There was not a tent upon the plain that did not hear the story Sharom had told. It would have grown worse in the telling and repetition if that were possible, but the truth was so horrible that it stood as it was.

King Mithridates sat in his many-chambered tent upon an intricately woven rug from Persia. If an olive complexion could have paled to white, so his would have done. His ministers sat around him waiting to hear words of hope; for if failure threatened his life, the onus fell upon them as well.

"You are certain of these reports, are you not?" They all replied that yes, they were, as at this very moment, Sharom was being held under guard just outside the tent. And he had told them the story himself.

"Bring the nephew of the Judaean King to me now."

Sharom was propelled into the tent by his guards. He was, at last, frightened. He had had no idea that the story would be traced back to him so quickly. The ruthless Mithridates had killed many for speaking a truth he did not wish to hear.

"I have heard what you said to many last night. It is the truth?"

Swallowing hard, Sharom replied, "Yes, King Mithridates, it is the same truth I told my uncle, King Antipater of Judaea."

Mithridates leaned forward with narrowed eyes. "And what said my loyal ally when you told him the results of your spying?"

"King Antipater laughed at it and said he wanted to be the first to face the Egyptians."

Mithridates leaned back upon his chair. This was not what he had expected. Why, when so many were in fear, did Antipater desire to do battle immediately?

As he sat with furrowed brow, pondering this riddle, a soldier announced the arrival of King Antipater of Judaea. The King bowed to the leader of all the armies and placed his arm around the shoulders of Sharom.

"Mighty King, I beg you to excuse my young nephew. His great fear is born of youth and inexperience. You and I feel no such fear, as we are set upon a holy war of vengeance. Our gods are with us, and we cannot fail. It is true that I wish to prepare for immediate attack against Egypt. Even now, as we speak, many men are slipping away from our armies. We must move soon, or we may lose them all.

"I propose to return to Ascalon to collect my second army which is now ready to fight. I then will march to Elephantine Island, called Abu, opposite Aswan in Egypt. There is found the largest Jewish community in Egypt other than Thebes. You will gather all the other loyal kings and princes and their troops of soldiers and march to Aswan, where I shall join you with a grand army of fifty thousand good fighting men collected from Ascalon in Judaea and the Jews in Abu. Abu is rich in grain and dates and oil. We need new sources of food, King Mithridates. I fear we must march toward that source, for we cannot remain as we are.

"As you travel to our meeting place, you can glean from the land to feed your horde. The city of Ascalon will provision me well, and we will be strong."

In the silence following this speech, King Mithridates mentally searched the plan of King Antipater for flaws and found none. In fact, it was an exceedingly good plan, and he decided Antipater was as brilliant as he was brave.

"Excellent, my fellow King. I hereby repeat my promise that you shall have half of the kingdom of Egypt. When can you set out for Ascalon?"

"We are already striking camp and shall be away by the height of the sun. Come, Sharom, I need your help in formulating our battle plans."

Before he left the tent, Antipater looked over his shoulder at Mithridates and made the soldier's barter: "We shall roll the stones for the enjoyment of the beautiful Queen Hatshepsut," he called, laughing loudly. He was rewarded with the sight of a much-restored, self-confident Mithridates.

Antipater said not a word to Sharom until they gained the seclusion of his tent. Turning to the boy, he confided, "All those who follow Mithridates will die. We, together, we'll save our army and our nation. I trust you with this knowledge."

27

Senu presented himself to Hatshepsut in her quarters. She was in her bath, sheltered behind a large screen. Acknowledging his presence, Hatshepsut said, "Be but a little patient, General. This may be my last luxurious bath in some time, as I intend to live the life of a soldier with you and my armies. So, I shall enjoy my perfumes. Please seat yourself and pour wine."

The heady scent of gardenia wafted into his nostrils, along with the more elusive smell of woman. More and more, Senu had realized that being her friend and General was becoming enmeshed with passion and love. He had wanted her for so long, for so many years.

She came into the antechamber wrapped in linens that clung to her damp body. She was so beautiful that he was without voice. Only his eyes spoke.

Hatshepsut understood the heat in his eyes. She had recognized it before, and her own body betrayed her now. When had friendship turned into longing? She could not remember. All she knew was that this handsome and virile man stirred her blood.

Senu was thirty years of age, his hair dark and short, eyes deep brown, and his body built for battle. It was his mouth that most entranced her. It was wide and always smiling. Usually, one side curled up as he pricked her with some piece of wit that made her laugh. And then there was the smell of him. He was always clean, but the male musk odor of his body was pleasing.

She knew he had had many women. His reputation as a rake and lover was wide and well deserved. When prodded gently about his conquests, he shrugged it off with a laugh. He always replied, "Women were made to be loved. I would be a poor man indeed if I turned away from such riches."

Once, not so long ago, he had told her he had never known

true love. As he spoke these words, his eyes, even his very soul, were full of love for her.

Queen Hatshepsut picked up a goblet and drank deeply. She then went to her bedchamber to be dressed. “While I am being clothed in warrior’s garb, tell me the last report of the enemy.”

In a deep voice, full of confidence, Senu responded, “King Mithridates has camped at Abu, opposite Aswan. He seems to be waiting for something. But he cannot wait much longer. I cannot understand why he has not forcefully entered Elephantine to gain food, as his army must surely need it. I fear he waits for another army.”

Hatshepsut returned, wearing a simple white tunic and the wide gold collar of her grandfather. Her arms and legs were encased in gold sheaths. Her hair had been wound tightly into her golden war bonnet shaped like a cone and covering the back of her neck. She held out her belt and sword to Senu.

“General Senu, we go forth together to save Egypt and kill our enemies. You will gird me for battle with my sword, as we are to be as one in this war.”

He asked her to reach across her body as though to grasp her sword. At the spot where her hand rested, he placed the handle of her sword where it hung in its sheath. Reaching around her hips with the belt, he drew her closer and then hesitated briefly, looking down into her eyes.

As Hatshepsut looked up at him, she let her feelings show. They stood thus for what seemed endless moments, each heart pounding swiftly.

Hatshepsut drew back. “This is not the time. Not yet. If we are victorious, you will find me in your arms. I shall seek your lips, all of you. But now, Senu, we must go. And I will tell you as we walk why Mithridates waits.”

She paused to choose a long whip from her rack and to throw her leopard skin cloak over her left shoulder. As they strode down the corridor leading to the palace steps, she told Senu of her message from Antipater and of her reply.

“Mithridates awaits the King of Judaea, who will not come. He does not raid the city of Elephantine because he believes the

King of Judaea can take all he wants from the city without doing battle and at his leisure.

"We have the combined armies of our enemies, with their leaders, in the claws of the crab. It is clear the victory will be easy. However, we must make the most of these auspicious events to make the Queen of Egypt and her General appear divine, chosen of the gods, and brave beyond belief."

Hatshepsut paused and placed her hand on Senu's arm. Softly, she said, "I will appear fearless to all. Yet, I tell you now that I am not a great conqueror, but a woman who needs your protection. Do not leave my side, Senu. I will feel safer with your strong body beside me."

In answer, Senu placed his hand over hers. Much remained to be said, but the bond was sealed.

28

Countless Egyptian soldiers were formed in regiments outside the gates of Thebes. Charioteers, lancemen, bowmen, and one contingent of Spartans mixed with the horse soldiers. The Spartans had been given beautiful and powerful Arabian stallions, promised a reward of gold, and most importantly to them, had been guaranteed many enemies to slay. They were supremely happy. All waited behind the chariot of General Senu. All waited for Queen Hatshepsut, lion killer, the bravest of the brave.

Hatshepsut drove her chariot from the palace grounds, as would an unconquerable warrior. She spun onto the plain, and her bay stallions thundered to the north end of the army. Knowing that all could not possibly hear her at once, she paused in her speech to allow the words to be repeated down the length of the army.

"I, Queen Hatshepsut, Pharaoh Makere, daughter of Isis and Horus, speak to you. One day's march from here stands the army of our enemies. They come to make slaves of good Egyptians. We will fight unto death to protect our families, homes, and lands. I have with me a whip much like the ones they save for our backs. I will show you what we will do to them. By Isis, I swear it."

The Queen paused so that every word could be passed through the ranks, then raised her war trumpet to her lips and blew the battle cry. Gathering up the reins with her left hand, she took the long whip in the other.

Queen Hatshepsut galloped down the line of soldiers and horsemen a full mile's length. The whip cracked out to snap in front of her many times. The arm that held the whip also carried her long scars. Because the battle would be fought in the desert in the full glare of the sun, heavy black outlines had been drawn with kohl around her eyes and back into her hairline below her gold helmet. She was the very breath of valor. Every man in her army drew upon this vision for his own resolve.

The drums began to beat, and wild cheering rose from the throats of the soldiers. As she trotted by Senu's chariot, they exchanged side glances. General Senu raised his fist and thrust it forward in the direction of Abu and Aswan.

Queen Hatshepsut led her army. There was no guard around her as yet. Senu drove behind and a little to the left of her to protect the arm wrapped in reins.

As they marched south along the Nile, the land rose; and every man could see the glittering body of the Queen, legs braced apart, leaning into the reins as she spoke to her horses. The whip was dangling from the shaft holder for her spears.

Her army followed quickstep and in perfect order. The Egyptian soldiers had trained long and well. Food and water were passed among the men as they marched and rode, and they ate and drank without pausing. Supply wagons far to the rear sent up anything needed. They also hauled the campaign tent of the Queen, along with the medical tents and the physicians.

The horsemen slowly moved up until they were directly behind Senu, and the Spartan commander asked the Egyptian General for his orders. Senu answered, "The body of our Queen is sacred, and she must not be harmed. Once the battle is joined, I cannot keep her from the midst of it. Your men must guard her well. It is no secret that Mithridates will order his best troops to kill the Queen, hoping to throw our army into disorder. If your troops surround her, you will find there the hardest fighting of all."

The Spartan captain smiled in pleasure and then asked, "Do we send troops to kill Mithridates?"

Senu replied, "Our Queen has sent a large segment of the army to circle behind Abu and Aswan. When the claw comes together, we will kill them all. All soldiers and kings will be slain even though they throw down their arms and beg for mercy. In this way, Egypt will have at least ten years of peace. As for women, the soldiers of Egypt and Sparta will have them. But warn your men that we do not tolerate atrocities. No children are to be harmed; no women butchered after use. We are not vile animals of the desert."

Senu marveled at the erect body of Hatshepsut. She had spent many hours driving her chariot, but this was a full day's march, and she wore heavy gold. The Queen turned her head to neither the left nor the right, pausing only to drop back to Senu's chariot to share water and bread.

Days before, Hatshepsut had gone into the passages secreted within the walls of her palace and down far below to the hidden room where Euripides has perfected his magic arts. She had spent hours reading in the books of potions until she found what she needed. It was a powder from the gum of a tree in Punt. Mixed with water and taken in small quantities, it made the user feel strong. The side effect was sleeplessness. She had made the potion and tested it upon an unknowing maidservant. The woman had half-run and half-trotted all day, lifting large cases for Hatshepsut as though they were feather beds. At night, however, she had tossed around until ordered to walk the halls of the palace. After a day and a half, she had fallen into a deep sleep for a long time. Upon awakening, she was as normal as she ever was.

Hatshepsut carried two vials of this potion with her. Senu did not see her as she sipped from one, thus he marveled at her vitality. Her eyes were wide with excitement. Never had the black stars in them seemed so large. She laughed with abandon, tearing at a piece of bread with her teeth. The two stallions seemed as easy to control as a pair of kittens, and she held them in check with one hand. As always, the reins were wrapped around her arm. If ever the chariot were separated from the horses, she would be dragged headlong across the sands.

Senu placed his chariot alongside hers and looked into the face of the ultimate warrior. She was at the head of the column, calm but apparently invincible. She seemed impatient for the fight and repeatedly drew her sword to slash at the air.

"Come, Senu, my comrade-in-arms! Start a marching song for my army to sing. We shall soon be upon our enemies, and I would lift the spirits of our troops. Also, it will do no harm for the enemy to hear our brave voices."

As she pulled ahead of him once more, he turned so that his voice would carry and began to sing a rollicking and bawdy song of a soldier's triumph. Soon the valley echoed with the singing from thousands of throats.

Less than ten miles away, the army of Mithridates, the Persian, was mounted and milling about. A forward observer had brought word of the gigantic army marching toward them, a glittering goddess at its head.

The clothes of King Mithridates were soaked through. Sweat poured from him as he rode hither and yon trying to bring order among the tribes. At the outer edges of the encampment, men were seen galloping away in an effort to save themselves. And the King of Judaea was nowhere in sight. It suddenly dawned upon the King of Persia that no one was coming to aid him.

The other kings and princes, mostly from Syria, shared his predicament. They could not go home in defeat, for they faced assassination because of their failure to end Egyptian domination. And clearly, death approached from Thebes, and it came singing fearless war chants.

Mithridates had managed to rally his own forces and had ordered them to start a retreat, but it was taking too much time. He gathered his personal guard, and they moved out toward the first cataract of the Nile. There, they could cross the river and then the desert, and leave the land of Egypt. Better to chance that he was strong enough to command loyalty at home and live, than face the certainty of death when the Egyptian army fell upon them.

Away they raced amidst the mounting confusion. The sounds of drums and war trumpets coming far from the rear fell upon their ears. Suddenly, there were the sounds of trumpets ahead of them. It could not be. Surely the valleys and the water created an echo. No, here came the deserters galloping back, calling out that they were encircled.

Baal had deserted them. Their calf god would let them die. What had once been a large, well-provisioned army marching against a helpless and weak Queen, had become a milling, shouting bunch of fifty thousand underfed troops.

There! In the distance, King Mithridates saw the chariot of the Queen of Egypt, shining in the late afternoon sun. Behind her, an immense army gradually came into view. All singing stopped. The Queen put her battle horn to her lips and blew a single, piercing note. All behind her who possessed these horns of honor blew them also, and the drumbeats came ever faster.

Hatshepsut put a vial to her lips and drained it. Taking her sword from its scabbard, she waved it in the air. Charioteers and horsemen galloped to follow her.

The Queen drove as she always had—furiously. Since her horses were the elite, she easily outdistanced all but Senu, the Spartans, and some favored charioteers who had received gifts of special horses from the Queen.

In her lust for blood, Hatshepsut shouted, "Death to them all!" The Spartans flourished their swords in her direction and returned her shouts. Senu pulled abreast and leaped into her chariot, slowing it by his weight.

Hatshepsut screamed furiously at him and would have slashed him with her sword had he not wrested it from her. He stood behind her, pressing his body to hers. If any threw a lance or shot an arrow at her back, it would find him instead.

As the main army closed in, the other wing swept down from the hills toward Abu and Aswan. Now, all three armies could see each other.

It was but a short time, although it seemed like hours, until the Egyptians smashed the army of King Mithridates between them. The scores of men in the center of the clash fought furiously for their lives, determined that if they were to die on Egyptian sands, then Egyptian bodies would also litter the desert. The armies surrounding them fought with the viciousness that comes of protecting a homeland against evil beings who came with the intent to pillage and enslave. The Spartans took pleasure in slowly maiming a man before he was killed. Hatshepsut could be seen by all, Senu at her back, laying about her with her whip and throwing spears into the chests of her enemies.

As in all great battles, there comes a time when no enemies

are left standing; and an unnatural stillness fills the battlefield, broken only by the piteous cries of dying men. Wild with the smell of death around her, Queen Hatshepsut cried out into the void the ancient battle cry of Egypt. The drums began to beat, and voices followed them as before: *Hat-shep-sut; Hat-shep-sut;* over and over, until she turned her chariot and rode back through her soldiers, fist upraised in praise of them. How they loved her.

Slowly, Senu unwrapped the reins from her arm where they had left deep welts. He pulled her back against him and could feel the wild beating of her heart.

"Great Queen, you must calm yourself. I shall take you now to your war tent so that you may rest. What our soldiers do now with the women and the dead is not for your eyes to gaze upon. You have done as you desired this day. Never will Egypt forget your name. Were there no temple at Deir el Bahri, were there no obelisks that carry your cartouche, the legend you have made this day will live always."

She looked up at him as he held her tightly while he drove the chariot toward the white tent a few miles to the rear. With eyes still wide, their black stars holding his gaze, she spoke, "Senu, my brave one, can it be that you have found love at last?"

In answer, he bent his head and covered her mouth with a deep kiss.

The Thothmesid dynasty was to be at peace for some years before it faced the turmoil of another fight for the throne. Queen Hatshepsut, Pharaoh Makere, living forever and ever, had found peace and great love for a time.